WAR OF OMISSION

WAR OF OMISSION

KEVIN O'DONNELL, JR.

WFP
WORDFIRE PRESS

WAR OF OMISSION
Copyright © 2021 Kim Tchang
Previously published by Bantam Books, 1982

EBook ISBN: 978-1-68057-243-8
Trade Paperback ISBN: 978-1-68057-240-7

Cover design by Janet McDonald
Cover artwork images by Adobe Stock
Kevin J. Anderson, Art Director
Published by
WordFire Press, LLC
PO Box 1840
Monument CO 80132

Kevin J. Anderson & Rebecca Moesta, Publishers
WordFire Press eBook Edition 2021
WordFire Press Trade Paperback Edition 2021
WordFire Press Hardcover Edition 2021
Printed in the USA

Join our WordFire Press Readers Group for
sneak previews, updates, new projects, and giveaways.
Sign up at wordfirepress.com

DEDICATION

To Robert J. White, who had a vision of a parking space that wasn't there, and to Ellen Couch, who found the first vision incomplete, I dedicate this book with many, many thanks.

ACKNOWLEDGMENTS

To thank everyone who offered critical advice and encourage-
ment while I wrote this would run to more pages than Bantam
would allow. I'd like to single out for especial gratitude the entire
New Haven Science Fiction Writers' Workshop, the 21st Milford
(at Telluride) Writers' Conference, Mark J. McGarry, and, more
than anyone else, my wife Kim Tchang, who really had to put up
with a lot.

1. St. Raphael's Hospital
2. Yale-New Haven Hospital
3. Peabody Museum
4. K. of C. Building
5. R.R. Station
6. Yale Old Campus
7. New Haven Green
8. Oil Storage Tanks

[1]

TEARS FOR EMILY

JULY 1994

The lookout at the monitors said, "Cops!" That froze the dissident leaders in Emily Kenyer's apartment. Outside, brakes screeched. Silence: then a shotgun roared. Big Dan Higgins took charge. "Stay put. It's not for us; it's across the street."

He's got good instincts, Kenyer thought. Cool-headed and sensible. I like that. I wonder how it jibes with his "modified anarchy," though?

"Emily, get the lamp by the window. Harry and Chelle, fade, now; I'll meet you at the van later. Out the back, soft but righteous, you know?"

She moved across the living room while his two assistants slipped through the kitchen. His gaze tracked her like radar; she felt it even with her back turned. Maybe you'll get your chance, Em, she thought. Make the most of it; convince him before he leaves town. She pushed the button of the Kmart lamp, and darkness swallowed them all.

Red shimmers streaked the ceiling. She glanced outside. Below, sheriff's men crouched behind open cruiser doors; a spotlight whitewashed the house across the street. "Dan, it's a foreclosure eviction."

"Doug, stash the monitors. Emily, is there a crowd yet?"

"Small—the cops are trying to break it up." Yet even as she spoke, T-shirted figures mushroomed around the fire hydrant. "Getting bigger."

"Folks," said Higgins, "I'd hoped we could get to know each other tonight, but let's be elsewhere when they come collecting statements. Anybody but me have outstanding wants or warrants? No? Good ... Win and Martha, out the front, pretend you live here and want to see what's happening—then slip away." He shook hands with the middle-aged couple, patting each on the shoulder, then turned to Doug and the other Yale student. "Out the back, around to the right, come up between the two houses and make like nosy next-door neighbors. Gape, mingle, vanish. Got it?" At their nods, he shook their hands, too. "See you soon, okay?"

When the metal-sheathed door latched behind them, he faced Kenyer and Sheila McDermot. "Let's get the extra glasses out of here, and we'll be set. I carry, Sheila washes and rinses, Emily dries and puts away."

Kenyer looked into his dark brown eyes. Bold and commanding, they irked her by taking for granted the obedience she granted only to those who shared her goals. She wasn't yet sure about Dan Higgins; he'd used the bystanders too glibly and gave a lot of orders for one who claimed to be a quasi-anarchist. "You're staying?"

Higgins ran a hand through his sandy hair. "I have to talk to you. Tonight." He scooped up the empties. "Come on."

Shrugging, she followed him into the kitchen, wondering not why he had singled her out—every dissident passing through New Haven got in touch with her, sooner or later—but what he wanted from her. Money? Refuge? Trustworthy assistants? He wanted something. Everybody did. Even she.

She was willing to trade. She'd give what she could; she'd yield the present to ensure the future (unless asked, "Who do we put on trial afterwards?" She'd never answer that one). But she had to know, first, that whoever she aided was marching in the right direction.

In the sink, the water ran brown. McDermot took the remaining glasses from Higgins. "Em's right, Dan. You ought to split."

"You armchair types get nervous easy, don't you?"

"Hey—"

"A joke, all right?"

Outside, a bullhorned voice ordered Irvine Gregory to throw down his weapon and surrender. The shotgun spat Gregory's reply; glass tinkles broke the night.

Higgins clapped his hands. "That's telling them, Irvine!" His bulk filled the kitchen. He pressed against the formica-topped counter to get out of the way. "Do New Haven cops foreclose at night for a reason, or just for kicks?"

"Both," Kenyer said. McDermot passed her a slippery crystal tumbler. She dried it carefully; it was part of a set. "The bastards time it for impact. You see your neighbor out on the streets at two AM, it hits home."

"God, if I could just glitch some computers so it would happen to them—" He leaned towards the doorway like a compass needle drawn to a magnet. "Maybe I'll put Harry on it."

"Who is Harry, anyway, your man for all seasons? Last week he was doing a report for you on our Olin campaign; interviewed me for hours." She still thought the time spent recapping the activities of the Checkbook Coalition was wasted and didn't keep her opinion out of her voice.

He chuckled; his sympathy ran warm and rich. "That's Harry, all right. He's a 20th Century Renaissance man—except that he has no aptitude for politics, of course. You have to let him do things his own way, but give him a problem, any problem, he'll bring you a solution you can 99.9% trust. We'd be nowhere without him."

Someone screamed high and sharp, and all three tensed. The shriek cut off. Far away, somebody else coughed.

"Damn!" said Higgins, lips tightening. "I wish we were ready now."

"In the Olin campaign," Kenyer said, closing the cupboard, "we—"

"Your Checkbook Coalition?" He cocked his head and regarded her with interest.

"Uh-huh. We set up a phone chain. When they tried to foreclose on a member's place, we'd pull the chain. Two, three hundred people'd race over to occupy the house and stay until the cops gave up."

"Yeah, Harry said that; I thought it was great! But look, I have to be honest," he said, touching her shoulder lightly, "I didn't have time to read the whole report. Harry's nuts about detail, which is crucial when he's breaking me out of Leavenworth—"

An insight delighted her. "That's why you sent him away first."

Bewilderment showed on his face, but only for a moment. "Oh, yeah. I get caught, the movement gets a martyr; he gets caught, we lose our best tactician." He studied her so closely that she had to step aside and hang up the dish towel, just to break his gaze. "Although, with people like you waiting in the wings, maybe now we could survive Harry's arrest."

"Thank you." She tried not to show how much that pleased her. "But is this what you risked hanging around to talk to me about?"

An explosion rocked the room; McDermot ran to the front windows to investigate. "A cop car's burning!" she called.

Higgins glanced at his watch. "Maybe fifteen minutes till those bozos get organized enough to shoo people away; we'll skip then. But first—" His eyes narrowed. "According to Harry, you say we should promise not to punish any of the crats." He jabbed a finger in the direction of the street. "Not even the bastards out there murdering Irvine Gregory. Why?"

"Because," she said, finally free to deliver the lines she'd been rehearsing, "a system born in vendetta dies of vendetta. Look at China, Iran—even Italy. It's reprehensible to punish people for being cogs in the machine you've supplanted. And by now, the technique of establishing a revolution's legitimacy by savaging the old order is so trite that it won't work in America. It will only deepen resistance. That's why."

Into the room seeped the stink of burned rubber. Higgins sniffed at it and made a face. "Dammit, those are arguments! Why do you feel that way?"

She took a deep breath and prayed that the explanation would make sense to him. "Because of my mother."

He frowned. "But she's not a crat. I know your father—"

"She's a victim."

His raised eyebrows told her to go on.

"My father travels a lot for the Defense Department," she began.

"I said, I know. That's something else we have to talk about."

"I thought it might be," she said, disappointed. A woman of talent and character, she knew she was more than a doorway to David Kenyer's attention, but it was difficult to convince strangers of that. Though she loved her father—even, at times, still visualized him as the looming giant who would tickle her toes, envelop her in huge, furry arms, and answer any question at all—she hated him, too. She could not stop being his child, and she wanted to be herself. It was one reason she'd moved out. "What about in particular?"

"It can wait. You haven't told me how your mother got victimized."

He seemed sincere; she awarded him a mental point. "Well, he was out of town so often that she decided to start an ad agency. She made a name for herself in a couple of years. Then—"

A siren whooped once, then moaned down into silence. "Go ahead," he said.

"Well, a Federal Trade Commission inspector stopped in for

the quarterly truth-in-advertising audit, and propositioned Mom. When Mom turned her down, she wouldn't issue the permit to place the next quarter's ads. Mom complained up and down the line; the inspector sued for 'defamation of a public servant.' Mom lost. The inspector owns the agency now. And Mom still owes half a million in damages. If she ever gets a job again—but no agency anywhere will touch an FTC enemy—the court's going to garnish 75% of her take-home. So she gave up. She became a housewife. She hasn't allowed herself to have an intelligent idea for four years."

"You sound bitter," said Higgins softly.

"Wouldn't you be? They ruined her!"

"At your mother, I meant."

She bit her lip. "Maybe I am. I know how badly she got hurt —some of the inspectors perjured themselves just to destroy her credibility—but I think she gave up too easily. That was her life. She should have fought harder."

"Not everyone has your intensity," he said.

"But it's symptomatic!" She clenched her hands. "There's two hundred fifty million people just like her, letting themselves get raped because, in the short run, it's safer than fighting back. That's why I started the Coalition, to teach people how to fight back. To get them to take that first step."

"I admire your passion," he said, his eyes fixed on hers. "But you still haven't explained—none of all that explains—why we shouldn't punish the crats."

"Because, damn it anyway, the ads were dishonest. By FTC standards, at least."

"What?" He blinked and stepped back.

"Don't you see? The system pukes up regulations it'd take a Talmudic scholar to decipher, and gives enormous powers to millions of petty bureaucrats, and—listen. Turn it around. By the book, my mother's ads were illegal, even though the inspector knew they wouldn't deceive anything smarter than a frog. The lie, though, is in the pictures—reshoot them, they cost forty or fifty thousand. Common sense says issue the permit anyway, but if the inspector does, she's risking her career, and why should she do that for nothing?"

He folded his arms. "You're justifying corruption?"

"No, damn it, I am not!" She wanted to shake him. "I'm saying our system puts normal, weak human beings in positions of terrible temptation—and for God's sakes, we shouldn't devote the new system's energies to punishing people for being human! We should concentrate on designing something that won't create the same goddamned situations."

"But you said this inspector perjured herself."

Exasperated, Kenyer said, "She had to! If she'd told the truth, she'd have lost her job—and the way Mom was filing complaints, not taking Mom to court would have been the same as signing a confession. It's my whole point: the system is totally screwed up, we have to replace it, but we cannot punish the people who didn't have the guts to do anything but go along with it!"

"Replace—not reform?" The question rang cool and aloof.

"Listen." She wondered if she were about to insult him but decided to risk it. "You claim your income tax strike is intended to choke the government into submission, force it to reform itself—and I don't buy it. I don't think you do, either. Get ten million regulators to stop bleeding us by making it harder for them to pick our pockets? Uh-uh. Look across the street, damn it; it just makes them desperate!"

He nodded. A very slow smile stretched the corners of his mouth. "Harry said you were more a revolutionary than a reformer."

"Well, he's right about that," she said hotly. "But I'm not an ayatollah; I say, pardon them all and start over fresh, *tabula rasa*. It's the only way."

"In that case, you might be able to help us a lot." He reached for her hand; the gesture was surprisingly innocent. "Come on, let's get Sheila and split, I have a favor to ask you two."

"All right." But she quickly slipped free of his fingers. She had yet to decide if he were serious, or if his talk were only an excuse to get close. Too many revolutionaries spent more time seducing than subverting; they were in the movement to stoke their self-esteem, not to cause change. She hated that type. Not that she objected to pleasure, but she had to be more than a body. She had a brain, and a heart as well.

Higgins pulled on his mask, a lifelike plastic sleeve that flattened his nose and rounded his jawline. He'd barely tucked it under his shirt collar when the doorbell rang twice, three times, insistently.

"Stay in the shadows," said Kenyer, crossing the living room. She swung open the door and caught her breath: two policemen stood there. "Y-yes?"

"Sorry to bother you, lady," said the one holding the rifle with the telescopic sight, "but we need your front window. The angle's better'n I can get from the ground." He pushed his way past her. His companion hurried to open the window.

Raising a hand, she spun on her heel, wanting to shout "No—get out!" but she thought better of it when she caught the worry on McDermot's face. "You mind if I leave?" she said instead. "I don't want to be here when they start shooting back."

"No," said the sniper's companion, "go ahead—we'll close the door on our way out."

"Thanks." She kept her body between the cops and Higgins as the anarchist, face averted, walked into the hall. He's so tall I'm probably not shielding him much, but what the hell. Can't hurt.

Before she closed the door, she heard the sharpshooter say, "Bill, see is there any beer in the fridge." She gritted her teeth. And left.

McDermot had parked her car around the corner; the two women flanked Higgins and chattered as they walked, giving him reason to watch the sidewalk. The police and firemen stationed up and down the block barely glanced at them. Yet Kenyer's stomach stayed knotted till they were in the car, anyway.

"God," she said, sinking into the '92 Datsun's back seat, "let's not do that again any time soon ... Dan, what's this favor you want to ask us?" As they pulled out into traffic, she realized she had been shivering.

"It's like you figured, Emily—I don't believe the tax strike alone is going to be enough to bring down the government. But what it will do is cause a cashflow crisis come November, and right about then the government will be very vulnerable. That's when we attack."

"With what?" she said. "Where are our armies?"

"I figure for this area, you two will do just fine." He smiled broadly. "What we've got is better than a suitcase nuke."

Appalled, she stared at him. The car pancaked through a pothole and threw her against the seatbelts. Oncoming headlights lanced into the Datsun. For an instant she imagined smoking rubble and wanted to puke. "No—all those people—no!"

He recoiled, blinking, like he'd expected applause, not a slap. "What?"

Her hands trembled; so did her voice. "How could you—I never met you before tonight, but from your books, your speeches, I thought I knew you and now—my God, nukes? No! You can't save the people by destroying them."

His jaw dropped. "No, wait, I'm not talking—" He reached inside his suit jacket and pulled out what seemed to be a microputer. "This is what we use. A T-SS unit—a Tisser—and it doesn't kill anybody."

Confused now, she shook her head. The vision of mass death persisted, but Higgins had just said that it was all wrong. There'd be no death, no destruction ... which made no sense: how could anything harmless coerce a government? But if, oh, what if, a magic wand to wave, no, that's silly, there are no magic wands ...

Deliberately, she flattened the hope peeking out of the trough of horror. "Dan, you're talking gibberish."

"Uh-uh." He smiled again. "I'm talking genius—E. David Kenyer's."

"Dad?" She wanted to put disbelief into her tone, but couldn't quite manage it. Her father had created too many implausible artifacts for her truly to be surprised. "Somehow, it figures." Fitting, though, that his brilliance would help her abolish his world. "May I see it?"

He passed it over. "It's off."

She took it gingerly anyway, wary of placing her fingers near a button. "You called it a T-SS unit?"

"A Time-Space Separation Unit. Nicknamed the Tisser."

"He never mentioned it, so it must be Defense Department. How did you—"

"You read about the terrorist attack at Fort Benning last year?"

She nodded and nibbled on her lip, suspecting what was to come.

He sighed. "It cost a million dollars and seventy-nine lives to take one breadboarded prototype away from the crats field-testing it, but last month it paid off. Two of our guys finally made some sense of its programming. That's production model number one, there."

She blinked. "That raid cost three hundred lives."

"The rest were crats."

"Scientists, a technician, a photographer—people!" She thought him wrong not to show more compassion. "Listen, we count their dead like they were our dead. We have to. Otherwise ... otherwise we lose our souls. We make an Iran, a Reign of Terror—"

"Nobody wants that—and that's where the Tisser comes in." Though the three were alone in the moving car, he lowered his voice—then chuckled at his instinctive precaution.

The rueful laugh restored some of her faith in him. Most

rebels took themselves far too seriously. If Higgins didn't, he might be able to give more rein to the compassion she was sure he had—and would need.

"Look, your father designed the T-SS unit so it wouldn't hurt anybody, but we've got to find out exactly how."

Now he had her off balance. She shook her head. "You lost me."

"We know how to assemble it; we think we know what it does—but we don't know any of the theory. See, it eliminates things. I don't mean destroys. I mean eliminates: sic the Tisser on something and whoosh! the target's gone, completely, no sign of it left." He paused ostentatiously.

Amused, she took the cue. "Where does it go?"

"The name suggests another dimension, maybe. But we don't know that, or what side-effects it has, or anything else. It makes things disappear and re-appear, too, later on. That's all we know. Are you close to your father?"

"He thinks so." She extended her hand for the weapon again. "But ... there are tensions." It was very light, very plasticky. It looked cheap. Yet it awed her with its potential to equalize—and sickened her, too. "How does it work?"

"The GI model is more sophisticated. With this bootleg one, though, you use a first-corner indicator—" He pulled from the case what looked like a telescoping antenna; unfolded, it opened into the corner of a cube. "—and punch in how many meters it should zap from each tip: width, depth, and height, in that order."

"And then?"

"Then you press the 'subtract' button, and that—that volume you described is gone. Along with everything in it." He spread his hands, splayed his fingers. "Now what we—"

"Does it come back alive?"

His eyes wavered for a second. "Yes, but ..."

"It dies quick?"

"No." He seemed surprised. "Paralyzed, yes, but only for an

hour or two. Nothing more, but ..." Looking retrospectively baffled, he puffed his cheeks, and blew air through his pursed lips. "There's something ... you forget what you Tissed out; you even forget that you did Tiss something ... when we tested it, we thought we'd failed, because we couldn't see that anything had disappeared. One of our techs wondered if maybe the memories hadn't started off full—to work right, it has to store a huge string of spatial coordinates—so he cleared all the memories ... and things came back."

Night wind whipped through the open window; she shivered. "What do you mean, 'came back'?"

"Well, actually, we had zapped things—but once they were gone, we couldn't remember that they'd ever existed. It wasn't till we brought them back that we recalled they'd been gone. Before, it was like they were not missing—it was like they'd never been. As a final test, we took out the mayor of San Francisco. Nobody noticed—no, that's not right; after a day or two, people started saying, 'Why don't we have a mayor?' Not 'Where's the mayor?' but 'Why don't we have one?' Honest to God, even when they looked it up, they couldn't remember the poor guy. Until he came back, and then everybody said, 'Where were you?'"

"Why does it work that way?"

"God, Emily, if only we knew ..." He slumped in his seat and suddenly looked like what he was: a thirty-five-year-old professor, and an Oregon homeowner so fed up with taxes and bureaucracy that he'd risked everything to force a change. "That's why we're trying to figure out some way to get answers from your father without tipping off the crats."

"He'd call them himself if you approached him ..." She stared hard at Higgins, trying to decide if he was, indeed, the kind of person who should run things afterwards. *I wish the deaths of those crats bothered him more* ... but he had that sense of humor, and she was sure she could make him see that there were already too many victims. "Would you like to get into my father's desk?"

His eyes widened. "Damn straight, I would. Can you set it up?"

"Right now, in fact. Sheila—let's go to my folks'."

"On our way," McDermot said, and turned onto the Boulevard.

At Edgewood Avenue, Kenyer checked her watch, then tapped McDermot on the shoulder. "It's three AM. Better drop us off here; we'll walk the rest of the way."

McDermot pushed a loop of blonde hair back over her ear and looked at them curiously. "I can take you right to their door, you know."

"And Dad will hear your car, and lumber down, and ..." She dug a cigarette out of the crumpled pack in her windbreaker pocket. "Can you see the introductions? 'Dad, this is Dan Higgins, Number One on the FBI's Hit List. Maybe you recognize him from tonight's facspaper?'"

"With my mask on you can introduce me as anybody," said Higgins.

"Dan, that plastic face looks real good from five meters, but at handshaking range it wouldn't fool a baby. Take it off as soon as we get there." Aware that nervousness was making her chatter, she snapped on the lighter. The butane flame danced blue and yellow as it warmed the palm of her hand; the smoke felt good, so she held it in. "No, we can't drive up; Dad keeps his window open, and some sounds wake him all the time: firecrackers, breaking glass, cars coming up the gravel ... Once we're inside, we're okay, though. The house is almost soundproof, and Dad's a heavy sleeper."

"How about your mother?" McDermot asked, looking meaningfully from her twenty-year-old friend to Dan Higgins. "Won't she wonder?"

"She's not home."

"I could have sworn I saw her at the store tonight."

"She's in Chicago, visiting Aunt Mae."

"Are you sure?"

"Listen, even if I'm wrong, even if she is home, you know her. She'll be vague and hospitable and a little relieved when I say, 'Nope, just popped in for a sweater 'cause the walk was getting chilly and your place was closer than mine.' Then tomorrow I'll get a phone call about dating older men who are probably married." She started, lips tightened, at the windshield's reflection of the cigarette ember. "That's your role, Dan—older man on the make for younger woman."

Higgins squeezed her shoulder lightly. "No trouble."

But McDermot seemed unwilling to be reassured. "What if she's home and if she recognizes him? What then?"

Kenyer dismissed the idea with a sniff. "If she got back early, there's about one chance in ten she even glanced at tonight's facs. Maybe one in a hundred that Dan's face'll ring a bell. Then she'll shake her head and accuse herself of being silly, because the man her foolish daughter brought home is wearing a suit, and everybody knows rebels are wild-eyed and smelly and carry machine guns under their T-shirts." Higgins snorted; she elbowed him. "Listen, you have to play it straight. She's living in a fantasy world, but she's not dumb. If you act like anything but a late date with sex on your mind, she'll get suspicious."

"Of what?" he said.

"She won't make the rebel connection, but she'll think you're, oh ... you're casing the place. You sweet-talked me into inviting you in so you could look around. Don't let her get going in that direction. The house is all she's got, and if she thinks you're threatening it—"

"I understand," he said. "I promise I won't ask where you keep your silverware, or if it's really a Ming vase on the mantel piece."

She chuckled, confident that things would go right. "Come on, let's go. Sheila, thanks for everything—let you know how it turns out."

"You do that," she said, releasing the brake. "'Night."

Companionably silent, they watched the taillights jiggle

through a stretch of potholes, then disappear around the corner. The night was still and clear; a sprinkling of stars glimmered through New Haven's haze. The moon filled in for the burnt-out streetlights. Somewhere birds called, and lovelorn fireflies signaled their needs. "Nice lady," said Higgins at last.

"She didn't like your crack about her being an armchair type."

"Isn't she?"

"She didn't grow up a barefoot farm kid like you, if that's what you mean. But her family has been political for three generations—her grandparents with the unions, her folks for civil rights in the sixties and the environment in the seventies—"

"Ironic, huh?" he said.

"What?"

"That she's fighting to undo what her parents wanted to achieve."

"Not really ... they honestly wanted to make America better. They told me once, when they saw the government bloating like a leech, they turned and aimed at it. They even worked for Reagan in '80. And when the crats came back in '84—with all those new programs and that huge deficit?—they led a march on Hartford. Sheila spent 1985 in a foster home because both her folks were in prison ... so don't call her an armchair type. She's paid."

"I guess I should have read Harry's report more carefully."

"Uh-huh."

"I'll apologize next time I see her."

"Good. Come on, it's this way." Exhilaration put bounce in her step. It wasn't that this man could trigger bloody riots just by twitching his finger. That, if anything, depressed her. She couldn't respect power when it created victims, but his notoriety thrilled her: proximity to it would make her important.

Dan Higgins scared the police, so his companions did, too. To the cops, whoever associated with the rebel had to be dangerous; housecats don't walk with tigers. At any moment, a cruiser could wail up. If that wasn't being taken seriously, nothing was.

"Dan. After the revolution, how are we going to shut up the people who want to restore the bureaucracy?"

"Shut them up?" He stopped and looked down at her. "We're not. That's what modified anarchy is all about—nobody shuts anybody up."

"Good." Reassured on that, she said, "What do you want Sheila and me to do? You never told us."

He looked into the night. Very quietly, he said, "While I'm in town, I'll be picking out targets for you two to zap at H-Hour. When the time comes—"

"What do you figure we'll take out first? With the Tisser, I mean."

"Police departments." Quiet, now, his low voice rumbled like gravel being stirred. A working streetlight tested the verisimilitude of his false face; orange brilliance bounced oddly off the dyes in the vinyl. He started walking again. "Without obedient local police, the government's helpless. See, we pay taxes, ultimately, because cops have guns. But if there are no cops, no guns, then the crats can't force the money out of us, and they can't pay each other. And you know that those parasites won't work for nothing. The whole structure will disintegrate. Then— then, we will be free!" The shadow of his clenched fist beat on the pavement. "Free!"

She frowned. It seemed simplistic. "What about the Army, the National Guard?"

"If they come, we'll do the same to them—but remember, they'll have to donate their services, too—and somehow, I don't think they will."

Emily's instincts said it wouldn't happen that way. It never went as quickly, as cleanly, as the visionaries promised. Like rowers on a muddy pond, they thought thirty strokes and you're across, that's all there is to it, but she knew there was more. Beneath the surface, the blades had to slash, scattering fish, cutting weeds, stirring up muck. The leaders saw the hull skim the ripples; she saw the turbulence. She vowed, once again, to devote herself to saving the fish. "We're here."

He turned and looked. "Nice place."

Behind the sloping-front lawn, the garage clung to the two-story, twelve-room house. In the half-acre backyard towered a climbable pine, in whose resiny branches Kenyer had used to lose herself for hours at a time. The house had been her home for nineteen years. She loved it. Quietly, she said, "They raised the mil rate again last year. Dad said taxes were so high he had to unload it, but the best offer he got was only twice the tax bill."

"Is it in bad shape?" They walked up the drive, careful not to crunch gravel.

"No," she whispered, "it's in beautiful condition—but who can afford a big mortgage on top of $1200 a month property tax? It's not like you get any services—usage charge for everything, garbage, sewers, streets ... The city has programs for everybody but the people who pay for the programs." She held a finger to her lips. "Ssh."

The thumbblock remembered her touch and let the door swing back into the dark entryway. A loose board creaked. Without switching a light, she led him into the long, high-ceilinged living room, and closed its door. Grateful for the orange shag rug that absorbed their footsteps, she seated him at a rolltop desk. She flicked on its lamp.

He skinned off the false face and wiped his cheeks—then stared at the desk in bewilderment. "Doesn't he use a computer?"

"Of course he does." She rested her hand on his right shoulder. "But it's voice-keyed, and you couldn't get into it. Besides, he sketches most of his ideas on file cards before he feeds them into the machine—says he can't think at a screen—and he keeps the cards in one of these drawers. Or in most of them; I mean, he has a ton of cards."

"Well—" Dubiously, he pulled on a handle.

"Good morning," said a mellow but sarcastic voice from the door.

"Mother!" Emily gasped. Spinning, she shielded Higgins with her body. "Did we wake you? I didn't realize you'd come home."

Sandra Kenyer's green eyes left Emily to touch on Higgins, then returned. Her hair was brown, long, and streaked with gray. The streak was chance; its retention, deliberate. She held herself with dignity, even when wearing the pink nylon gown whose ruffles brushed the floor. Crinkles around her mouth and eyes spoke of easy laughter. Tonight, her lips were compressed. "It's almost three-thirty, and yes, you did wake me. I flew in this morning. I thought you were burglars." She brought her right hand from behind her back. It clutched a small automatic. She looked at it, mouth puckering into a wry moue. "I was afraid I'd have to—"

"You can put it away, Mother," said Emily. She disguised her upwelling of relief. A shot would have sunk them. The police would have come, recognized Dan ... "We're harmless. But why didn't you wake Dad?"

"I didn't think the burglars would wait that long." Her relief resonated in her voice. "So. How nice of you to drop by."

Emily restaged mentally the scenario she'd outlined in the car. "We were walking; I got chilly." She dropped her eyes and pretended to fidget.

"I see," said Sandra Kenyer knowingly. Her tone was either condescending or embarrassedly casual. Clearing her throat, and glancing away, she said, "You know your father doesn't like you in his desk."

Before Emily could react, Higgins said, "Emily told me that, Mrs. Kenyer, but I had to have a sheet of paper. A line just came to me, and I have to get it down before I lose it. They come so laboriously, you know, like children."

Though she found his fluency in falsehood disturbing, Emily kept her face blank, and watched her mother's sense of hospitality struggle with her protectiveness. Confusion won. "A line?"

"A line. Poetry. I'm doing a—" Appearing to rein in artistic enthusiasm by brute force, he said, "Anyway, I needed some paper, and didn't think Mr. Kenyer would mind."

"Dr. Kenyer," said the scientist's wife, but she seemed reassured. "Well, if you're trying to compose, would you like a cup of coffee, maybe some cake or cookies?"

Emily said, "Mother—"

"That would be very nice," said Higgins. "I'd like to polish this line before I leave, which may take an hour or more. Coffee would be perfect."

"It'll only be a minute."

"I'll help." Emily realized at last that Higgins wanted privacy and time to search the desk. She hurried to the door, uncomfortably aware of the oblong bump in her coat pocket. She couldn't take it off because her good-housekeeper mother would hang it up, and maybe find the Tisser. She'd have to wear it a little longer.

Her heels tapped on the vinyl tiles in the corridor, finding and forming a syncopation with the swishes of her mother's slippers. After a moment she said, awkwardly, "Hey, Mom, I'm sorry we woke you—" She pushed open the swinging door and held it.

Sandra Kenyer grabbed Emily's arm and almost threw her into the kitchen. Sandra's teeth grated; her jaw muscles bulged. Her eyes had narrowed to slits of hostile emerald. While her hand plucked the phone off the wall and her fingers began to tap numbers, she hissed, "What the hell do you mean bringing a rebel into my home?"

"What do you m-m-mean?"

"I mean your 'date.' Dan Higgins a poet, pfah! His picture's all over tonight's paper; what did you think I was, blind? And letting him ransack your father's desk, I am so—hello, police? ... Yes, I'll hold."

Emily saw what she had to do, but rebelled. *Why do I have to make her a victim? Dan—* She moved towards the door, hand in her pocket.

"And don't try to warn him, either, because I will shoot him. You could have cost your father his job, his reputation—hello? Yes, dammit, but hurry!"

While Sandra Kenyer glared at the phone, Emily took out the Tisser. *I'm sorry, Mom, I'll bring you back.* Her fingers shook with fear, urgency, and—already—self-loathing. But I have to. She pulled out the first-corner indicator and began prodding the keys. On; 1 for width—

"What's that?"

—1 for depth—

Still jamming the phone to her ear, Sandra Kenyer thrust her hand into her gown, grabbing for the automatic. The billowy nylon thwarted her grasp.

—2 for height—

"Emily, what are you—"

She pressed the indicator against her mother's suddenly struggling body—and '—' to eliminate!

For a time, measurable only in microseconds, she knew horror. Her memory was a rope of many strands, and, in the instant, half their fibers faded away. Half her life disappeared. Half of herself died. She felt the loss and regretted her impetuousness. It was too much to throw away; she had to have it back, she had to have—she had to—she had—she—She gnawed on a knuckle and wondered what she'd lost. A victim, she thought faintly, or something to do with love ...

She was alone in the kitchen, staring at the wall phone that had never had a receiver. A T-SS unit quivered in her cold white hand. She couldn't understand why she was holding it. It was Dan's, and it belonged with him. Shrugging, she tiptoed back to the living room.

He was still at the desk, rifling through its thousands of file cards without disturbing their precise alignment. Somewhere he had found surgeon's gloves, thin and green. His back stiffened as she entered; his head turreted. He exhaled his fright at sight of her. "Geez, I thought it was your father."

"Dad? No. Once he's asleep, you could stage a rock concert down here and not wake him. Talk about heavy sleepers." She bent across him to set the Tisser on the desk. Deliberately, she pressed her breasts against his shoulder blades. "Did you find what you wanted?"

"No." He turned to take her hand, then winked. "Not in the desk, anyway."

Let him be grateful, she thought. It'll give me leverage to help save the victims. Because, of course, that was what she wanted more than anything. To protect the innocent. She smiled, slowly and sweetly. Avid for affection, for closeness and security, she lifted his insulated fingers to her cheek. "Like I said, once he's asleep he's dead to the world."

"Sounds good." As he stood, his gaze slipped away to the framed photograph on the mantle. "Who's that?"

She twisted around in his arms and leaned back against him. A woman with green eyes stared at her. "I don't know."

"Oh." Clearly, he'd asked only out of politeness. "I thought it might be your mother."

"My mother?" She probed that notion, but it was like looking for a thirty-third tooth. "No, it's not. I thought you knew. I never had a mother."

For no reason at all, she began to cry.

[2]

BANKED COALS

AUGUST 1994

The two revolutionaries stopped beneath the awning of the corner bar. The faded canvas flapped listlessly, blocking the sun but not the dirty steam that New Haven breathed in the summer. Dan Higgins regretted returning. Thick air put him on edge; it made the world feel like a trap whose jaws were closing. "This place is air-conditioned, isn't it?"

Harry Pisca nodded down at his friend and leader. "Rheanna figures you at least ought to plan a revolution in comfort."

"Did your homework again, huh?" Higgins stepped aside for a squad of lawyers and hid his distaste for them. They looked good, with their yachting tans and thousand-dollar suits, but vultures after a battle look sated, too. By Christmas you'll be out of carrion, he thought. We'll have beaten the system and the Sixty-Year War will be over. You'll have to find something else to feed on. "Funny she sets a meet so close to the courthouse."

"Her group hangs out here; it's convenient." He pointed across the New Haven green to a shopping mall entrance. "All the buses stop over there."

"Makes me paranoid." Higgins lowered his voice. "Lawyers look too much like FBI agents." Sweat trickled from under his mask and down his neck.

Pisca rocked back on his heels and grinned. "Hey, last time in, you wrote a best seller."

Even so light a reminder of his eighteen months in Leavenworth turned Higgins's stomach. "I'm not getting taken again, Harry—I've got to be loose on T-Day."

"You will be, Dan—amo see to that."

Higgins relaxed. "If anybody can, it's you." His own 190 centimeters barely came to Pisca's shoulder, which seemed bulkier by itself than Higgins's entire 90 kilos. *Thank God I've got one friend the size of my enemies.* It was a good feeling. Trying to overthrow the government might be quixotic, but having a Sancho Panza as huge and savvy as Harry Pisca shortened the odds.

"You looking worried," said Pisca. "Something feel wrong?"

He shook his head, thinking, *Yes, but not here on this pigeon-splattered sidewalk.* It was, instead, that he, Dan Higgins, home-owner and professor of American History at the University of Oregon, was mounting the strongest threat to the Constitution since 1861. That concentration of wild power appalled him. *It's too much for one man; it's wrong that I should have it ...* yet he couldn't share or even diffuse it, not until victory, for there was no one he truly trusted with it ... but each passing moment increased the likelihood that it would consume him. He'd lit a grass fire to burn out weeds, and now had to sprint to stay ahead of the flames. Then he yawned. He hadn't slept well in weeks. "Emily Kenyer says these people are worth talking to. Your report, though, said they were borderline berserk. Are you slipping, or does she have rotten judgment?"

"Ahwno." The ex-Marine shrugged. His eyes worked the crowd, looking for a threat amid the business suits. "They're small, but real well-disciplined, and they keep their word. Makes 'em useful allies of convenience—if you keep your back to the wall."

"Look, if they're crazy, I don't want them." A bus sprayed them with diesel exhaust. He coughed and, for a moment, wanted to flee. Then he cleared his throat. "Don't say it, Harry. We've got three and a half months to T-Day, and we need all the help we can get."

The big man nodded.

"But Jesus God, Harry, if we let fanatics into the leadership —" That thought made him shiver, even in the August heat.

"Don't you worry, Dan. Amo see to that, too." Deftly he stepped towards the street, then pivoted to interpose his broad back between Higgins and a police cruiser. "Even with that mask on, you taking too big a chance out here."

"Damn, it's supposed to look real!" *Nothing's going right today …*

"Yeah, if you don't look too close. Come on." His hand enveloped Higgins's upper arm, and gently urged him towards the door.

"Tell me first," said Higgins, "are they useful-crazy or just-plain-crazy?"

"Dan," said Pisca, half-closing his eyes as cool air rolled out to greet them, "amo let you make up your own mind on that one."

George Hardle raised his head as graying Oscar Thorn entered the cubicle. He nodded: a sufficient greeting for a Bureau supervisor with whom one had soldiered thirty years earlier. "What's movin', George?"

Thorn threw a facspaper down on the desk. Off a New Haven net, it was counter-folded so the last page of the first section lay on top. "I thought you said he was in San Francisco." His nicotine-stained finger stabbed a three-column photograph.

The headline read, IS THIS MAN IN TOWN?

"Dan Higgins?" His pulse raced, but he kept his voice light and even. Once he wouldn't have; once he would have given cry and chase as single-mindedly as a hungry lion. He'd been young, then—shallow. He'd put eighty hours a week into the Patty Hearst investigation because he enjoyed the procedures and believed he defended the Union. Now ... now the hunt itself still thrilled him, at least an unpredictable one, like this, but the belief had slipped away. Maybe he'd been in the capitol too long; maybe he'd gotten too close a look at what he was really defending. He would almost regret arresting Dan Higgins. It seemed a poor way to thank someone for a good game. "Shit, I never said he was in San Francisco—"

"Yes, you—"

"No, Oscar, I said that was the last city we could prove he'd been in." He skimmed the article, a rehash of other stories on the shaggy-haired orator who'd make a lot more sense if he'd stop lumping the good federal officials with the bad. Hardle frowned; the first column alone had six errors. For one thing, no more than thirty million people had stopped paying taxes. "We went to the same law school; I shouldn't have to spell out the difference for you."

"The memo you sent me—"

"Was a list, Oscar, was about six pages of place names that the word said he'd been in, you know?" He pushed the paper away. "Hell, take last Thursday, this phone call, somebody won't give a name, talks through a handkerchief, too, wants us to know Higgins is in Paris. Okay, so maybe he is, Christ knows I'm not his travel agent, but just then line two blinks, so I put guy one on hold, which really turns him on, you know, he figures I'm tracing him and is already waiting for a knock on his door, but I'm not, it's just this second guy whispering, 'Dan Higgins is in Rio.' He hangs up, guy one's hung up, but before I can hang up, this little old lady from Milwaukee calls and says she was just on an elevator with Higgins who, according to this lady who I know wears glasses on account I asked, Higgins unzips, hauls out his dong, and shakes it at her. On her, I hang up." He patted the briefcase computer on the corner of his desk. "Bubblehead here's keeping track of the rumors, 'cause God knows there're too many for me to keep straight, so any time you want to ask for our best guess as to where this joker is—" He flicked the hidden "on" switch of the briefcomp. "Where's Higgins, Bubblehead?"

"New Haven," it said in a toneless voice.

"Embarrass me in front of the boss, huh?" Excited yet depressed, he rose, and forestalled Thorn with a quick, "Book me a ticket on the next plane, Bubbly; call Jeff Novoski and tell him to coach tomorrow's game; and, oh yeah, let the Big Brother office know I'm out of town, they shouldn't call me, Pam doesn't like it."

"Hold it." Thorn's voice rasped unpleasantly: he smoked too much and slept too little. "Remember that goddam secret weapon the rads stole from the Army last year?"

"The one they didn't want to tell us about?" When Thorn's lined face showed uneasiness, Hardle dropped back into his chair. He'd heard rumors about that weapon—ugly rumors. The game's stakes had just doubled; two equally possible futures flashed. In one, he caught Higgins, reclaimed the weapon, and spared the government the bother of reform; in the other ... he didn't want to think about it. He'd never live to see it play out, anyway. For the last twenty years, revolutionaries around the world had agreed on the cure for unemployment among the law enforcement agents of failed regimes ... which of itself did not upset Hardle, who would rather die in action than in a senility ward, but which would leave Pamela and his three kids vulnerable as all hell. That worried him more than he could say. "Oscar?"

"Yes?"

"Oscar, you and me've known each other twenty-five, thirty years now, right? Now, you give a man, you give him twenty-five years, he develops an instinct." He laid his palm on the place just below his breastbone, the place where pain twisted like a white-hot knife. Radicals did not frighten George Hardle, but secret DoD weapons did. Not all of the Pentagon's toys killed ... "Oscar, I'd take it as a deep, personal favor if you told me my instinct was wrong, or that I hit retirement age this morning, or that you're yanking me to go look into a Congressman on the take instead, you know?"

Thorn shook his head. "Higgins has been on the goddam suspect list since the rip-off went down, George."

"Along with eight thousand other rads."

"Seven thousand eight hundred thirty-one. Only two hundred seventeen of whom were in San Francisco at the end of June. And the Army says their weapon was used there, then. Now, Higgins wasn't the only one in town—the big computer downstairs has all those positive ID's—but his probability rate's up to 12%."

Hardle winced, spun halfway around in his swivel chair, and took a half liter of milk out of the small refrigerator on the shelf behind his desk. He swallowed it in three gulps. "For my instinct," he said. "I knew last Friday this week'd crack my nuts. Always happens, however a weekend starts, the next week's going to be worse. I have a bad Friday night, I don't even go to the track, I know that's how bad I'm going to lose."

Thorn lit a cigarette and coughed. "What happened?"

Crumping the waxed paper milk carton, he tossed it at the wastebasket. "I pull into the garage, there's this guy there, guy with a clipboard, you know? Always a bad sign, that clipboard. And he says, he shows me his ID and says he's from the city, and the garage don't meet the new code. I got to tear it down, and rebuild it, and I got ninety days." He scowled. "That was the down payment on our Florida condo, too ... so what should I know about this damn secret weapon?"

"The prototype's all breadboarded circuitry—"

"In a brown vinyl case, two-suiter size, yeah, Oscar, I know what it looks like, but what I want to know is, I want to know what it does." The cold milk finally eased his ulcer; he belched. "Those shits at DIA never told us that, I mean, a half-decent person, now, he'd say it's a death ray, or a gas to turn you into a carrot, or a sonic thing that'll pucker you right up, so watch your ass going in, you know?"

"They still don't want to talk about it." Thorn spilled ashes on the desk, then brushed them to the floor. "All they'll say is that it makes things disappear."

Hardle looked up with rekindled interest. "You mean like invisible?"

"No, I mean like 'not there.' Not a disintegrator either, just ... 'not there.'" He looked unhappy. "I don't know anything more, George; I'm sorry. Approach with discretion. You know the routine."

"Yeah." Interest had already turned to anticipation—disappearing beat vegetating all hollow. "Yeah, I know the routine all right, twenty, twenty-five years you pick up things like that ..." He pushed himself to his feet and hefted the briefcomp. "Bubbly, am I booked through to New Haven?"

"Yes," it said.

"Okay, Oscar, I'm on my way, 'neither rain nor—' no, that's for mailmen, but what the hell, anything beats shit outta the old folks' home, at least it would if my insurance'd take care of Pam —" Hand on the doorknob, he hesitated. "Hey, Oscar, you want me to bring him back alive, or what?"

"Not 'or what,'" snapped Thorn.

"You got it; I'm on my way. Keep it movin' while I'm gone."

———

A bar backed the small cafe, and tables huddled by the windows. Four shadowed booths waited by the right wall, their air of secrecy resisting the scattered fluorescents. The air conditioners blew stale, chill smoke. Peanut shells crackled underfoot. The bartender wore a suede vest and stood at the cash register, where he made Tinkertoys out of toothpicks and olives.

Closing his burning eyes, Higgins took a deep, slow breath. The room felt good after the street. The sun was too strong out there, he needed a cool, dark place to hole up in. He just wished he weren't meeting Rheanna and company—if he decided not to tell them about T-Day, and not to enlist them, he'd have to slip out quickly, gracefully.

"Dan." Pisca shifted his weight and wouldn't meet Higgins's gaze. "These people, ah ... they're real guzzlers. You let them, they try to drink you under the table. With what you got in your pocket, you might want to watch out for that."

Touchier than usual because of his fatigue, Higgins flared up. "I can hold my liquor!"

"Right," said his friend resignedly. "Here they are."

Four people slid out of a large booth: a short-haired, broad-faced woman ("Rheanna Huo," said Pisca), a gangling man who nursed swollen knuckles ("Two-meter Irving"), a hand-crushing thirty-year-old with empty blue eyes ("Lou Fiammeggiare"), and a morose, bald, fat man ("Manny Delfuego"). Then they worked their way back into the booth. Pisca and Higgins took one side, Higgins to the wall. Huo sat across from him, with Fiammeggiare and the bald man at her right. Irving pulled over a chair and straddled it.

Higgins sighed with relief as they settled down and wished he could relax further. After the interview, he thought. And let's make that quick. With deliberate coldness, he said, "Two things I want to clear up, Rheanna. First, I hear your money comes straight from Hanoi."

Her dark eyes slitted and her nostrils flared. "I pee on Ho's grave," she said. "I was born in Saigon, yes, but I am ethnic Chinese. They put us in small, leaky boats and sent us to be raped by pirates. Would I take their money? Yes. But I would spend it to buy their humiliation."

"All right." He nodded, impressed despite himself by her fire. "The other thing I hear is, you have some kind of grudge against a UCLA sorority and want to take it out on every organization and association in the country."

"Another lie!" She thumped her mug on the knife-scarred

table, then pushed a napkin into the puddle. "Those crats work so well to smear me."

Higgins smiled ruefully. "Yeah, I've been there, too ... but you do want to disband all organizations, right?"

"Wrong. Only some. Three kinds in particular must be encouraged." She ticked them off on her fingers. "Familial, geographic, and economic. Perhaps I am too Confucian, but I feel people should be loyal to, united with, their families, their neighborhoods, their employers—or employees. That is good; it is what we need."

He sensed she'd like to let it lie there, so he said, "What don't we need?"

"Special interest groups! National labor unions, alumni associations, professional groups—they foster 98% of the elitism in this country, which fathers 72% of the discrimination. Yet at the same time, they not only divert people's attention from their primary responsibilities, they also prevent the unbiased from barring the rise of the incompetents!" She brought her fist down for emphasis.

He pulled a napkin from the dispenser and handed it to her. "What about, say, schools?"

"Thank you." She dried the crevices of an incised set of initials. "Schools? Public, yes; private, no."

"More elitism?"

"Exactly."

"But the people don't want more restrictions, they want less."

"A government," she said heatedly, "must give the people only what they need, not what they think they want."

Scratch her, he thought. Rheanna Huo depressed him. His mouth was dry, his throat sore, the afternoon wasted. The Revolution needed good, stable leaders, but he couldn't find them. Or not enough, anyway, though he had recruited Emily Kenyer and Sheila McDermot during his stay. But Huo ... He touched his pocket, shook his head, and hoped they hadn't noticed either. People like them had to be kept as far from power as possible. He looked up to meet the woman's curious stare.

"Please," she said, "join us in a drink."

"Ah—" He knew he shouldn't start so early. He had work to do; he couldn't afford to get blurred. Rheanna, who lived with three cats and a sixteen-year-old boy, was not his idea of a drinking buddy. When he swallowed, it felt like sand. "Sure."

Sitting up, she waved the bartender over. "Bring another round of Bud, Charlie. And I insist, bring them cold."

"Basil," mumbled the bartender, tapping the tag on his suede vest.

To the man in the end chair, Huo said, "Stand up."

Two-meter Irving stood. It took a while.

"Now ask Charlie, what is his name?"

"Charlie—" His voice was high and nasal. "What's your name?"

Basil raised his eyes, raised them some more, then surrendered. "Charlie." He gulped. "And you want six cold Buds, right?"

"Right." Irving patted him on the head. "Quickly."

"Sure thing, Irving." After sliding the empties onto a tray, he hurried off.

Higgins looked from Basil's back to Huo's smirk. What is it with this lady? It wasn't the kind of behavior he'd expected from a UCLA honors grad, even one who had been fired from three facspapers for distorting statistics. "Do you realize what you just did?"

"Of course," she said, surprised. "We amused ourselves."

He forced himself to stay silent. It was important that they part friends. Though he would never accept her as an ally, he didn't need another enemy. Enemies snitch. "Say, maybe you could help me—is there anybody in town I should touch base with?"

"I'll list all seventeen for you before you leave. But first—" She braced her elbows on the table and rested her chin on her hands. Her smile came tight and humorless. "Let us talk about the future. The *Times* has quoted you as saying the government will fall by Thanksgiving, unless it cleans up its act before then."

"Simple mathematics." Now that he had decided against her, it frustrated him to have to stick around and politick. There were a lot of people he'd rather drink with. Like Emily ... He wished the bartender would hurry, but the guy was still wiping glasses. He looked back to Huo and gave her the canned answer. "See, since the tax strike, the government's been so deep in debt that nobody will lend it money, The cupboard should run bare about November 1. No paychecks for the crats. I figure it'll take a couple of weeks for them to catch on, but by the end of the month, the whole machine will have ground to a halt."

"Crap," she said quietly.

He blinked. "Pardon?"

"Dan." Her smile broadened, baring her teeth. They looked sharp. "Last year you liberated a prototype from Fort Benning."

Inside he went cold. Outside, he managed to feign puzzlement, first, then evolve it into comprehension. "You mean that terrorist raid? No, I was in Leavenworth, waiting for Harry here to get me out."

Pisca grunted confirmation.

"It is not too smart to lie to me, Dan Higgins! I was a journalist too long; I know too much." She slapped the table. "You arranged it, you analyzed the device, and now you make more for T-Day."

He slipped bewilderment on, and some of it was genuine. Who's been talking? And who else's listened? "Look, if you've read my stuff, you know I don't believe in vio—"

"On the surface. This morning our DC branch, ah, visited your factory. They left with a small souvenir. In—" she glanced at her wristwatch "ten minutes, they use it on FBI Headquarters. Now. What results will they get?"

Stunned, he raised a hand and massaged the side of his head. Pisca stiffened, inhaling sharply. At the end of the table, Two-meter Irving sat up straight. Higgins said, "They've—well, if they don't know—"

"They know how to operate it, and have a vague idea of the end result, but they do not know how it will be accomplished. So tell me, quick—loud noise? Blinding light? Tell!"

He spread his hands. "Jesus, God, woman, call it off! You'll ruin everything."

She leaned forward. Her face seemed to broaden as her eyes narrowed into slits. "Why? What will happen?"

He tried to sort out his panicked thoughts. "Look, the T-SS unit's a great weapon; it disorganizes things, and just decimates the enemy. But when the enemy knows you'll use it, he can prepare for it. We'd planned to hold off till Thanksgiving Day, then strike across the country simultaneously. If you use a Tisser now, though, you'll tip off the crats, and they'll come down on us before we're ready. God's sakes, call it off!"

"I cannot." She shrugged, and again dropped her eyes to her watch. "It has already started."

"Damn!" He punched his right fist into his left palm. It stung.

"Now tell me," she said, "they press the button—what happens?"

Defeated, he sagged back. His head touched the booth's wood. "The target volume disappears." His hand brushed his pocket, traced the rectangular shape of his own Tisser, then lay still. He wondered if he would have to use the device on Huo ... and hoped not. "Disappears completely. Everything around it fills in, so there's not even a hole left. And nobody notices, see, because ... ah, hell, we don't know the because. You forget that the target existed."

She nibbled a thumbnail. "Why?"

"I don't know. You just do. Everybody does. One of our science guys has a theory—everything vibrates, he says. On a sub-atomic level, it emits a distinctive ... I don't know, radiation? But you can 'feel' it anywhere in the universe, even though you're not aware you do. According to him, when you look at something, you identify it by, ah ... oh, yeah—'letting the signature vibes give form and pattern to the light waves.' He says memory's a tuning process: selecting the right vibrations awakens the appropriate recollection. His analogy is brain cells are to memory what film is to holography. To make a hologram perceptible, you have to have a laser, even though all the data's there on the film. It has to be brought to life. By the same token, for a memory, you have to have the signature vibes to make it, ah, memorable. So by his theory, when the Tisser removes something, the thing stops emitting. You can't remember your target because the standing vibe pattern is gone. The cells won't come to life."

She looked confused. "Then what could possibly be wrong with using it?"

"Because after a while people begin to notice that things aren't right." He dropped his face into his hands while he tried to phrase it properly. "Look, Tissing something doesn't eliminate electronic memories of it, or photographs, or printed words—just organic memories. There are tourists in Washington ... And guidebooks by the millions. All of which list the FBI Building. People will be saying, 'Where the hell is this damn place?' And the army will make the connection that the Tisser we stole is right there in town. The next thing you know, everybody with even mild anti-crat views is being rounded up for interrogation." Despairing, he looked up. "That's why simultaneity is so important—if we strike everywhere at exactly the same moment, the whole government will be gone before any one part of it has time to react. But you, Jesus God! You've just told the crats it's open season on rads."

"You wait one minute, Dan Higgins!" Her cheeks flushed, dull red against old ivory. "You have this Tisser thing for a year, now—and they knew someone had it—but none of your police state fantasies happened."

"First," he said, as calmly as he could, "they didn't know

where it was; you, however, have just told them it's in Washington. Second, they didn't know if it was still in working condition. You just told them it is. Third—"

Irving stood up. "Rheanna, I'm going to call the DC branch, get them to move that Tisser out of town right away."

"Good thinking," she said. She turned back to Higgins. "Now, Dan—"

"Look," he said, nudging Pisca in the ribs so the big man would slide out of the booth. "I got some people down there to call myself; I don't want them caught in the roundup. So if you'll excuse me—"

"No."

"No?" he said incredulously. "What do you mean, no?"

Metal clicked. Delfuego said, "Dan, the lady said 'no.'" He gestured with his automatic.

"Manny," said Pisca, in a tone of reproach. His own gun materialized.

Empty-eyed Fiammeggiare said, "My .45's aimed at your crotch, Harry. Lay it down, nudge it over, then keep your hands flat on the table."

Pisca obeyed. He hung his head.

"Now, Dan," said Huo, "tell us more about this Tisser of yours."

Six miles high, George Hardle sighed. For a year Higgins had eluded him, had published manifestos and broadcast without a license and infected computer networks, and in that year Hardle had come to admire his skill. But it was time to force the mate. If Higgins had that damn Army weapon, he had to be taken, and fast, before the underground made full use of it. Otherwise ... otherwise the game would end soon, anyway; and because of Hardle's employer, that could be disastrous for Pam and the kids.

That's what it's all about, he thought, guarding the people

who wear your name; you never say it to them, almost never think about it, but it's what it comes down to ... I could, I'd like to meet this Higgins somewhere, neutral territory, do a deal if I could, I don't hassle yours, you don't hassle mine ...

There was more, of course, and he knew it. His professional pride was on the line. Maybe even his career, if he didn't make the arrest soon. Bubblehead was proof that while Oscar Thorn still had some faith in him, he had also grown tired of waiting. The Bureau wanted results, now. If he didn't provide them, quiet-voiced review boards would begin to question his competence—or worse, his loyalty.

He laid the briefcomp on his lap and stroked its simuleather. This would get him his man ... and his protection. "How did you decide he was there?" The stewardess shot him a wary look. He pulled the comset out of its socket, plugged the speaker into his ear, and pasted the disc mike to his throat. "Testing," he subvocalized, "one, two, three—"

"Four, five, six," hissed the mechanical voice. "Two-meter Irving Flackern, bodyguard to Rheanna Huo yet actually Special Agent-in-place—"

"Quit backplaying the files, I know'm personally, remember?" The old lady across the aisle glared at him: he was moving his lips again. With another sigh, he took out his rosary and pretended to recite it. Satisfied, she settled back in her seat. "Has he seen Higgins?"

"No. He phoned in at 7:00 AM. Huo is meeting Higgins now, and—"

"Where?"

"McClintock's. A cafe in downtown New Haven, near the Green. Huo intends to supplant Higgins as leader of the underground today—by killing him, if necessary."

A strangeness passed through Hardle then, like a cold wind on the outskirts of his soul. A part of him numbed, but when he tested his limbs, they all worked. Yet he felt diminished, as though the wind had blown that part of him away. He closed his eyes and rubbed his temples.

"George," said Bubblehead.

"What is it?"

"I have lost contact with Washington."

"Washington?"

"The headquarters building at 9th and Pennsylvania NW. Where your desk is."

"Never heard of it. Bubblehead, have you slipped a chip?"

"No. All subroutines normal. And you?"

"Then why are you talking about headquarters? The FBI doesn't have a central office, just field offices around the country. You should know that."

"George, something is wrong. I do not know what. My memory records one fact, yours another. By all available modes of measurement, mine is more reliable. But you are the Agent-in-Charge."

Plastic beads rattled on Bubblehead's case. The old lady stabbed him with her scowl, and he realized he had twisted the rosary to the breaking point. He rolled his eyes upward. She nodded approval.

Irving came back to the table looking puzzled. "They say they tried it and it doesn't work."

"Where'd they test it?" asked Huo. "Dan, what went wrong?"

"Um ..." He suspected what had happened, but they didn't, and in that instant of perception he formed a plan. It was risky: he could get shot. His pulse raced. Adrenalin quickened his breath, dried his mouth. "A few minutes ago we were talking about the place that your DC branch would zap—everybody remember the conversation?"

They all nodded.

"Anybody remember the name of the place itself?"

Five heads shook.

"Anybody write it down?"

Everybody looked around to see if anyone else had.

He turned to Huo. "The unit worked perfectly."

"Sure, Dan," she said with heavy sarcasm. "Nothing happened, so it worked."

"No, I told you, it affects the memory." He reached into his pocket. "Look, let me—easy, Manny, I'm moving slow—let me demonstrate." The weapon's plastic case cooled his palm; he kept his eyes on Delfuego's gun hand and held his breath. If this doesn't work—

"Give it here," said Huo, snapping her fingers.

"It's booby-trapped," he said easily. "First I teach, then you touch. All right?" He laid it on the table. "We used a pocket computer shell because it's a cheap, effective disguise. We added an antenna—" He tugged it out, and spread its tripodal tip wide, so that its three metal needles formed the corner of a cube "—because it's quicker than punching in coordinates. It's not quite as inconspicuous, maybe, but it's quicker. You also know that the volume of space you Tiss out is anchored at this corner—" He fingered the antenna. "—and defined in size by the three numbers you fed it: width, depth, and height, in that order."

"I can't concentrate when I'm thirsty," said Huo. She raised her head high. "Charlie, six more!"

"Coming up," said Basil, looking even more dour. He popped another kebabed olive into his RNA model, then set the tooth-picks aside.

Higgins almost hollered, "None for me," but his stein was as empty as Huo's, and his thirst ... "Okay, Rheanna, we'll skip the technical details, go straight to the practical applications. See, when you say the DC one failed because it didn't zap the target —but nobody knows what the target was—you're really saying the target is gone so thoroughly that you can't even recall it. It's when you remember the identity of the target that you know it didn't work."

"Dan," she said wearily, "that's gibberish."

"Just watch." He picked up the weapon. Careful not to alarm Delfuego, he aimed its antenna at the table behind Two-meter Irving, and a little to the left of Lou Fiammeggiare. "Lean forward, Rheanna. See that table with three chairs?"

"Yes."

He swiveled the antenna 180° so the field it would generate would propagate downwards and outwards, swallowing all of Two-meter Irving and Fiammeggiare, but not the table. "Now, this unit has some bugs in it; doesn't always work, but let's try, the table's pretty close." He tapped 1. "That's width, now for depth." He pressed 1 again. "And height." He pushed 2, and once more made sure the field would envelop Huo's two men. "Now, we take the table out—" He touched the subtraction key.

For the briefest of moments his vision blurred—he heard the silencing of a very small, very distinct hum—but a blink put everything right.

"Damn," he said.

"The table's still there, Dan." Contempt and, perhaps, a kind of boredom filled Huo's voice.

"Told you it still had a few bugs." I know I used it, wasn't aiming at the table, something else, closer, the numbers were 1,1,2 and I held it right in front of Harry, so ... but the far end of the table looked just as it had when he'd sat down ... Or does it? I don't know, I can't remember ... He looked around, trying to decide. Each of the other three booths projected half a meter further into the room. I musta cut off the end, he thought, desperate to deduce his actions before Huo caught on, if she ever did. But why? Unless ... maybe there were two more people there? Jesus, that's it, I just zapped two of Huo's goons ... Controlling his elation—keeping his face still and even a bit mournful—he said, "These are temperamental, Rheanna, and it's hard to make them do exactly what you want them to."

She checked her watch. "Okay, so that one didn't work

because I do remember the target—but the Washington one did work because I can't remember the target?"

"Exactly." The smile of pleasure came easily to his face. He hoped she would misinterpret it.

"Here you go," said Basil, sliding a damp tray onto the table.

Everybody reached for a stein.

Two remained on the tray.

Higgins froze. *Omigod, I forgot this'd happen!*

Huo, however, just looked disgusted. "Charlie, whyfor you bring us six?"

"You asked for six, didn't you?"

She frowned, then touched her forehead gingerly, as if something throbbed within. "Even if you count on your fingers, Charlie, you can see there're only four of us. Unless somebody here wanted two?"

It was too late for Higgins to say *yes, Harry and me wanted two each*. He had to grit his teeth and shake his head. Pisca looked bewildered, and Manny shrugged morosely.

"Take it away, Charlie—and don't even think of putting it on our bill."

Mumbling under his breath, Basil obliged.

Higgins lowered his face so Huo wouldn't see the fire of triumph in his eyes.

"McClintock's," Hardle told the taxi driver at the airport.

"The place by the Green?"

"That's the one."

"Ho-kay, we'll roll in a minute." He picked up a clipboard and began to fill in a form of many boxes. "Can I have an ID, please?"

Hardle passed it over, then passed over the driver's low whistle at his occupation. He leaned back against the seat cushion, hummed a small tune, and twiddled his thumbs. That helped him plan. He was going to ... dum-dum-de-deum ... no

John Waynes, too old, get my ass shot off without getting my man, not good, so no wild rushes, not today. Reconnoiter first, yeah, skulk around outside wishing I was invisible till I spot the dude, then alert the local field office and the New Haven police. Hold the fort till they show up, get in position, we all move in ... hoping that sucker hasn't been listening to the police band and slipped out the back door.

Who else would be there? There'd be Higgins, maybe a body-guard, Huo, a couple of her people, and ... he ticked them off in his head. Then inserted a finger between his neck and his collar and ran it around the front of his shirt. Hot day. Sweaty. Be a lot of guns going off. Wouldn't be surprised, day like this, tempers hot, a certain rabble-rousing pyromaniac dies resisting arrest ... It made him nervous to think how many people would hate him for busting Higgins, even if he were about the only cop in the country who'd take the rebel alive. But the hollow ache in the pit of his stomach didn't come from that, or from the weather. It came from the growing realization that he had no idea why he was so sure Higgins was at McClintock's.

He woke the briefcomp, attached the mike and earplug, and asked, "Bubblehead, how do we know Higgins is there?"

"We do not know that he is there—"

A chill sped through him.

"—but we do know that he is expected to attend a meeting there."

He sighed and went as limp as his collar. "That's good. How do we know?"

"Two-meter Irving told us this morning."

"Two-meter Irving?"

"Special Agent-in-place IJ Flackern?"

"I don't remember him."

"George, he's your oldest daughter's boyfriend."

"Dori wouldn't hang around with that kind."

"Dori does. With Two-meter Irving. Whom you have known for twelve years."

"Bubblehead, this is over, I'm alive, and you're not a pile of junk, we troubleshoot you, you know? Something's wrong with your memories. I mean, twice in one day, I could see it if you were a microwave oven or something, but—" A thought struck him like a lightning bolt and he stiffened, straightening his spine, bumping his head on the ceiling. "Ow!"

"Whatsa matter, Mac?" asked the driver over his shoulder.

"Ah—ah—nothing, nothing, just a cramp, trying to stretch it away, you know? That's all, lousy cramp, God, I hate flying."

"Tuckers your arms right out, don't it?" said the driver. He laughed snortingly, like a noisy sleeper.

Groaning, Hardle subvocalized, "Bubblehead, have any unauthorized personnel been tapping into the system, tampering with your files or something?"

"No. I'd like to ask you the same question, though."

He shut the briefcomp off and removed the earplug.

The cabbie, catching the movement in the mirror, shouted, "You know, they do make smaller hearing aids, Mac."

He wished he could shut the driver off.

"There." Higgins could smell his own sweat and wondered what they thought of it. "Soon as I pop the battery back in, it should be okay."

"I didn't see what you did in there," said Huo, leaning forward.

"Not a whole lot." Actually he hadn't done a thing. "Just improved a connection, cleaned a contact, you know." He snapped the battery into place, slid the panel back in, and flipped it over. "Now I have to bring it online, wake it up, so to speak." She and Delfuego were rubbing shoulders; he could take both of them out without adjusting the antenna. He turned the system on and touched a succession of inoperable buttons, hoping she wouldn't penetrate the mumbo-jumbo. Almost casually, he punched in the dimensions, then raised his eyes for one last aim, and touched the '-' button—

—just as Huo, reacting, slapped a saltshaker into the Tisser's side—

so the antenna jerked to face:

a bald man with arching eyebrows

a sudden cube that shimmered, then blackened

the linoleum floor and the louver at the bottom of the men's room door.

"Don't ever point that at me again!" Huo had her .38 automatic unsafetied, and drew a straight, unwavering bead on Higgins's chest. "Demonstrate it all you like, but the next time you point it at me, I shoot."

"Rheanna," said Pisca quietly, "this here tiny little table ain't even bolted to the floor. I got my foot up against it. The second your gun goes off, you get the table in your face. And me right behind it."

While Pisca talked, Higgins punched in the numbers that would eliminate Huo entirely. All he had to do was aim and 'subtract'—and she would be gone.

"Give me the Tisser, Dan," she said.

"No."

"I'll shoot."

"And die," said Pisca.

The gun unnerved Higgins, but he wouldn't surrender the T-SS unit. His gut tightened; he clenched his sphincters as tight as they could go. Jesus, God, do I die now? Here? He wrenched his gaze up and focused on Huo's brown eyes. They were large, stubbily eyelashed, and streaked with red in the corners. They panned slowly, keeping him on their periphery. Then they narrowed slightly.

Huo spoke, more to herself than to them. "What the hell am I doing here alone? I never travel a—" Her cold dark pupils swung back to Higgins like artillery locking in. "You took out my bodyguards," she hissed. "Back! I want them back!"

He guessed that even looming Harry couldn't restrain her now.

Hardle ambled past the plate glass window of McClintock's, glancing inconspicuously inside as he did. X-ray eyes, that's what I need, see through that shit you got to be Superman or somebody, got to be at least a health code violation, wonder should I ... Three people sat in a triangular booth halfway down the right wall. Odd-shaped place, too; much smaller inside than it looked from the street. He walked on, resisting the impulse to linger. Has to be Higgins, has to, can't miss that face, but he might know mine, not that the facspapers've hyped me any, they had I'd be Special-Agent-in-Charge somewhere, not just "Agent," but rads collect photos, survival instinct, and ...

Rounding the corner, he hesitated. Christ knows, it looked like Higgins, the hair and the build and all, but days like today, days nothing goes right, gotta doubt the ol' instincts, wind up busting the President's son and find myself monitoring whale harvests in Alaska ... he had to be more positive.

Sighing, he turned around, went back, and marched inside. A weird construction of olives on toothpicks rose next to the register. "Give me a beer," he said to the bartender. "Lowenbrau."

"Only one?" asked Basil.

"Do I look like a rummy, or what?"

The bartender held up his hands. "Just making sure, man—I been having problems this afternoon. One Lowenbrau, coming up. One."

Higgins risked a glance at the newcomer. He looked like a lawyer. Or an FBI agent, God knows I can't tell 'em apart anymore, so damn paranoid ... "Rheanna," he whispered, "any minute that guy'll see your gun. He'll tell Basil. And one of them will call the police. Then we both get put away."

She drew back her lips in a toothy grimace. "Not me, Dan, not me. You give me my bodyguards back, or when the cops come, I'm making a citizen's arrest on a notorious radical and his bodyguard."

Pisca moved nothing but his mouth. "Dan's got friends."

"Sure, but if you both try to run when the cops show up—" She shrugged; the gun barrel never twitched. "Give 'em back, Dan, now! Or I call the cops."

Nursing his Lowenbrau and staring obliquely into the bulging, clouded mirror behind the bar, Hardle tried to match a name from his memory to the face across from Higgins. It was no go. He decided it had to be Rheanna Huo, but he'd only seen one picture of her, and that from a bad angle. It made for a sticky situation: if it were Huo, he could take the whole table at once; but if it weren't, if she were just a female to whom Higgins happened to be talking, she could wind up a hostage and he'd be in trouble for not calling in the cavalry.

But it would guarantee Higgins's survival if Hardle took the rebel alone.

The thing was, he knew the dossier on Huo, knew it cold because knowing the files could maybe save his life again, and the file on her said in about half a dozen places, it said she never went anywhere without two, maybe three knuckle-walkers in tow, but this female didn't have any guards in sight except—

She had a gun in her hand. Shit. It's got to be Huo. Wonder there's any way to have Bubblehead see her ... 'scuze me, lady, like to introduce you to my briefcase,' little ratfink hasn't shorted out completely, it'll know, always does ... did, not does, did ...

He took another sip of his beer. Trying to decide whether to risk his life or Higgins's was not the way he liked to spend an afternoon ...

———

Higgins was stiffening from enforced immobility. The index finger of his right hand trembled on the subtract button. A little wrist flick and a jab, she's gone ... but she'd catch the motion and pull the trigger and that damn gun had a barrel bigger than a sewer pipe and the bullet would burst through his chest and ...

He drew a slow, deep breath. He searched Huo's rigid face. A trickle of sweat slipped past her right eye and inched down her cheek. Her nostrils flared wide. Her eyes flickered from him, to Pisca, to the two men at the bar.

The barrel of the gun quivered minutely.

The next time she looks at Basil, he thought. Do something, Basil. Drop a glass, something. Anything!

———

With a sigh he released so slowly that even he couldn't hear it, Hardle decided better safe than sorry. He fumbled a coin for the phone out of his pocket, then pushed off his stool. "I'll be back," he told the bartender.

"Pay now," said Basil. "Just in case."

He surrendered a bill. "Where's your telephone?"

"Over there, by the door."

"Thanks." He checked the radical tableau as he turned—still frozen, still ostentatiously ignoring him. His instinct flamed up again, and he massaged his upper belly as he walked. The Bureau Special filled his armpit like a crutch. He had to fight down the impulse to draw.

But, by God, if they moved an inch—

———

To Higgins's left, a bar stool scraped. The newcomer asked for the phone. He tensed. Look, Rheanna, look!

She did. Her eyes widened as the phone clattered off its hook. For one half instant, she seemed off guard.

He flicked his wrist and jabbed the button.

The other side of the booth kaleidoscoped but straightened out again instantly. He wondered what he'd zapped—and why he'd attacked ahead, instead of to the left, where the FBI man stood. Maybe there was another coming outta the men's room?

That seemed more than possible—probable, in fact. There was, in all likelihood, an entire flying squad of FBI agents scattered throughout neighborhood. Jesus God, I'm trapped. "Harry, is there a back way out?"

"Just a little crawl-through behind the cash register."

"Christ." Any minute they'd move, and he doubted if he'd survive the arrest. They'd douse his torch before he'd led his people to freedom. No!

The bartender was coming over—was he one of them? The towel, the smile, no, that was true paranoia, the guy wasn't bright enough to—quickly, Higgins set the Tisser. "Basil."

"Yeah?"

"Gimme your bill pad." The walls were closing in, threatening to smother him.

Pisca said, "Yeah, good thinking—Amo cover the guy at the phone."

Higgins could barely breathe. "Come on, gimme your bill pad."

"Whatever you say, man." He set it down.

Higgins tore off the top sheet, turned it over, and scribbled on its back. It was his only hope. Handing it to Basil, he added a twenty-dollar bill—and the Tisser. "Hold onto this note, okay?"

"Sure, but—"

"Just hold that right here—" He positioned the Tisser at the proper height and angle. "—and press the minus button, okay?"

"Is this some kind of joke?"

"No, it's not, will you please just do it? Now?"

"Okay, man, whatever you say."

If Basil said more, Higgins didn't hear it, because he was staring at the Tisser, holding his breath, wondering if his destination would be as cold and as dark as he feared ... and watching that finger come down in slow, slow motion.

Hardle glanced over his shoulder. The two men at the small table were talking to the bartender. He realized then that all he had to do was:

ssh the receiver onto its hook,

open the jacket with the left while the right slides deftly, surely up to the reassuring grip of the Special,

and the feet make the army about-face

then spread apart

as the heavy right hand lunges out, elbow locking, wrist braced with the left,

squint down the barrel, suck air and bark:

"FBI! FREEZE!"

The ulcer went off like a flashbulb. He could almost see its bright malevolence as he doubled over, grunting from the pain, and wobbly from the shock of drawing down on a terrified bartender. He blinked and straightened up. Shit, why'm I doing this, what's going on?

"God, man, I'm froze! Don't shoot! I'm froze, and the register's open, and just help yourself. Please, man."

He shuddered, squeezed his eyes shut then open again, and reholstered the Special. Unsteadily, he made his way to the bar and remounted his stool. "Shit, I'm sorry about that. I don't know what came over me, all of a sudden, a reflex? I just—"

"Jeez, man, you scared hell out of me!" Basil looked pale. He leaned on the far end of the bar and the pocket computer dropped out of his hand. It thunked on the varnished wood. "I'll bet I broke it."

Nothing made sense, so he manufactured some. "A calculator."

"The note says it's a computer."

"I thought it, I got these instincts, you know? Twenty, twenty-five years on the job, you get instincts, and I thought when I saw this thing in your hand, I thought, Christ, it's a gun, he's gonna blow me away." He rubbed his stomach and clenched his teeth against the agony. "Shit, I'm sorry, really sorry, shouldn't have thought it, I know, but—can I buy you a drink?"

"I think I need one." Basil walked over to Hardle, balancing himself on the inner lip of the bar. "Mind if I have a double?"

"You deserve it."

Basil set a twenty, a scrap of paper, and the computer down on the bar. "How about you?"

"All—" He was reading the note upside down, and it said: "Basil, before you close up tonight, please, turn on the computer, press 'M,' press '7,' and press ' + .' Please don't forget. It's very important." He looked up. "Ah, milk, please. If you've got it. My ulcer just—"

"Milk, yeah, I got it." He poured a large bourbon for himself, then set a glass of milk in front of Hardle. "Hey, lemme add that up on the computer." He turned it around, fed the numbers into it, then pressed the equal key. The screen stayed dark. "Damn, I knew I broke it. Always happens. Think it's worth repairing?"

Hardle looked at the cheap plastic shell. "Nah," he said. "Get yourself another, thirty, forty bucks, but this one, you want to fix this one, it'll cost you more."

"That's what I thought." He pitched it into the trashcan. "Damn, I always wanted a computer."

"Yeah?" Hardle lifted Bubblehead onto the bar. "You wanna

see a computer, this is a computer. Voice-activated and every-thing. Hey, Bubbly."

"Is Higgins in custody?"

"Who?" He passed his glass back for a refill.

"Dan Higgins. Is he in custody?"

"Never heard of him, Bubbly—you sure you're not broken?"

"All subroutines normal. Have you been drinking?"

"The man's just pouring me another glass of milk now."

"Are you near McClintock's?"

"I'm in it." Hardle accepted the glass with a grateful nod.

"Is it not dangerous to speak so openly to me in the presence of six dangerous radicals?"

"Six dangerous radicals?" He lifted his eyebrows and looked into the bartender's curiosity. "Bubbly, it's just me and Basil here —nobody else."

"Sounds like yours is broken, too," said Basil.

"George," said the briefcomp, "something is seriously wrong—"

He flicked the off switch, and it fell silent. "Shit," he said softly, "and we were working together so good up until this morning ..." He felt vaguely frustrated, like he did sometimes at night, when he'd awaken because he'd dreamed he smelled smoke. He'd sit up in bed, sniffing frantically, until he realized the air blew fresh, and the fire was but a fading nightmare. He hadn't done a thing, but the danger had passed. At times it made him feel superfluous. "Working so good ..."

"Everything was," said Basil. He finished his bourbon and leaned on the bar. The notes caught his attention. He picked them up, looked at both of them carefully—then pocketed the green one, and threw the other away. "It's a crazy damn world, man. And it gets crazier every day."

Hardle said, "I knew last Friday this was going to be a rotten week." He belched.

[3]

THE EDGE OF EMPTINESS
AUGUST 1994

Doug Singleton was three thrusts from orgasm when the bedroom door banged open. Feds! he thought. Fearing shots, he covered his lover with his body and yelped, "Hey!" Not that the gesture would save her, if death prowled that night, but he wanted to be holding her at the end. Soundless, she hugged him tight.

His sweat reeked of terror. Braced against pain, he turned his head slowly—then flailed for the sheets when the gunless hand at the wall switch doused them with cold fluorescence. "What the hell are you doing?" Shock had wilted him; he eased off Sheila McDermot and fumbled by the bedside for his pants. "Get outta here."

Short-sleeved and pasty, the crewcut intruder smiled mechanically and offered his ID like it was a certificate of legal blindness. "Connecticut Commission on Fireproofing, got to see if your house is up to code." A ring of master keys jangled at his belt.

McDermot exhaled with a shudder. She was scared, too, Singleton realized, and felt better for knowing he hadn't plunged into panic alone. "Chrissakes," he said, "it's seven PM."

"I know, I'm running late. Had to take my daughter to the

dentist." Clipboard in hand, he squatted to examine the floor-boards. "Varnish." He shook his head and made a note.

McDermot laughed shakily.

"What's so funny?" hissed Singleton, wishing for the self-assurance to rise naked and ease into his clothes.

"Your shoulder blades are blushing," she said. "Don't they teach you savoir faire at Yale? My tomcat's cooler."

The inspector went to the far wall; Singleton hopped out of bed and yanked his pants on. "I haven't taken Advanced Bedroom Farce yet," he muttered, though it enchanted him that her sense of humor could surface even at moments like that. If she can be cool, I can. With a scowl for the bureaucrat, he tugged a fuzzy blue sweater over his head. Absurd that someone as intelligent as he couldn't cope with the situation. His square-shouldered father, the colonel, would have had no problem—he would have frog-marched the intruder down the hall and booted him into the gutter. But then, his father stood firmly in the government camp, and could afford to burn a lowly inspector. Young Singleton's position was more ambiguous, not to say vulnerable. Further, he lacked the physical presence. An unlikely crusader, he was tall and skinny; his features and ideals were still resolving out of adolescent confusion. "Are you finished yet?"

"As a matter of fact," said crewcut, loosening his tie, "I am." He consulted his clipboard. "You're going to have to strip the varnish off the floor and wainscoting, and the paint off every-thing else. Put three coats of fireproof finish on all the surfaces; any paint store has a list of approved brands. The curtains have to go; so do all these posters. May as well soak the place in gaso-line as have them on your walls. Install a smoke detector with a heat sensor, and a good escape window. You're on the second floor here?"

McDermot said, "Yeah," and propped herself up on an elbow. Her blonde hair pooled atop the pillow.

"Oh, it's your house?" At her nod, he said, "I'll need your name and Social Security Number."

"Sheila McDermot, 872-29-4786."

"Right." He tore off the top copy and handed it to her. "I left one of these in every room. You have four weeks till re-inspection, that's September 15th. If it's not done by then, we'll bring in a crew and bill you for it. Keep your receipts—you may qualify for a tax credit. That's Form 11982 for the state tax, 23982 for the Federal, and 9982 for New Haven. Sorry to interrupt, and have a good evening." With a dismissive wave of his clipboard, he was out the door and down the stairs to the vestibule.

As Singleton shut and eyehooked the door, McDermot ripped the fireproofing order into eight flimsy pieces. "Fuck 'im," she said succinctly. "And, Doug—for what you were ready to do —thanks, huh?" Her blue eyes said far more, as they always did. Eloquent on politics, she turned tongue-tied when she had to speak of love. Her knack for harder, harsher words made her clumsy with the phrases of the heart.

Singleton knew that. It bothered him sometimes, but then she'd smile, or trace a finger down his nose, and he'd understand again that he didn't need to be told what she showed so clearly whenever they were together.

He crossed to the bed and sat on its edge. From the night table, he took the holo-cube he'd given her in the spring. His father stood in it with him, all starched and creased, but she hadn't minded. "How'd you stay so cool?"

"If I hadn't hidden my gun elsewhere, I wouldn't have." She threw back the sheets and swung her feet to the floor, unconscious of her nakedness. "What a bastard. He loved busting in on us. Willie's right. The only way to make those pricks treat us right is to kill a few of them."

"Hey, that's—"

"Doug, I know that mindset. My mother's like that—it's why I moved out—always barging in, hoping to catch us at something ..." She couldn't sustain that anger, either. An impish grin spread across her face. "She only caught us once, though, and that was because we'd staged it. Remind me to tell you about it some time. Think the inspector was a fed?"

"Uh-uh. A fed'd sense your place; you wouldn't see him until he had enough on tape to drop you." He looked at the door and wondered why he hadn't hooked it earlier. "Also, feds knock. Usually."

Smiling, she stroked the nape of his neck. "It's good to have my very own in-house Big Gov expert, you know?"

He seized the hand before it could withdraw and pressed his cheek against her palm. "Is that all I'm good for?"

The teasing faded out of her smile. "No," she said softly, catching hold of his hair like a lifeline, "you know better than that. You keep me ... sane. For the first time in my life, I'm not lonely or—or afraid. Because of you."

He basked in the warmth of her gaze. "I love you," he said simply.

"Which makes it very mutual, so just lean back—" she pushed against his shoulders "—and let me at your zipper ..."

The sick dizziness of fear and self-hate swirled later, in the shower, as he soaped away her scent. The blue fiberglass tub seemed to sag; its DoHHSoft surface, to swallow his ankles. He had to clutch at the stainless steel railings for support, and even then, he couldn't tell where he stood.

Ah, Jesus, he thought wildly. If she finds out I'm a fed—if they find out I'm a reb—instinctively, his own penchant for the light touch saved him—maybe one of them'll tell me what I really am. God, I love her.

Twelve months earlier, the picture had been clearer. Torpid in the Washington summer, waiting for Labor Day to summon him to New England and his junior year, he'd had his poolside reveries disturbed by an old family friend.

The toe had nudged him in the ribs. "About time you put some meat on them, isn't it?"

"Mr. Thorn!" Rolling and sitting, he'd shaded his eyes from the sun. "Long time no see—have a seat."

"Thanks." The graying, lantern-jawed FBI man dropped onto the chaise longue. "Your dad says you're up at Yale—lots of rads there, aren't there?"

He wrinkled his nose. "Symps is more like it, at least among the student body. The hangers-on ... I dunno, I don't have time for them."

"Doug—" His tone acknowledged Singleton as an equal. "—the government would like you to make time. Some of those people worry us: rumors of an underground armory, this damn tax strike, even a few bombs in government offices. The country needs to know what they're up to. It's coming down to survival time, and America might go under if we're ignorant. Will you help us?"

Little kids' laughter in his ears, he'd thought a while—a good, long while—then: "Sure," he'd said, and repeated the word a few months later, when a blonde with an intelligent face and an electrifying platform presence approached him after a rally and began, "Sheila McDermot. I've seen you at all these things this term, and heard you talk like one of us. The report is that you've got a lot of contacts in Big Gov. Would you be willing to tell us what you know?"

"About what?" Night had cloaked her eyes. He couldn't read them, but her nearness excited him.

"Anything that'll help."

The departing crowd swirled around him while he pretended to ponder. "Sure," he said at last. "Sure." Though it was what Thorn had told him to say, it was also what he wanted to say. He hadn't fallen in love, not yet—that would grow slowly, in the springtime planting of the garden that soothed her frets—but since his meeting with Thorn he'd begun to listen. What he'd heard had dismayed him. Government news release or underground party line, it didn't matter. Both camps scared him because each elite had ordained itself America's guide into the 21st century. Each was wrong. He knew that, even if he couldn't pick the right road himself.

In ways too visceral for his Ivy League articulacy to express, he loved the country. An Army brat, he'd lived all over: Seoul, Austin, Fort Dix, Singapore, St. Louis, Bonn, and L.A. He'd seen people and lands and systems and had learned not truly enough about any of them—but he had absorbed a lot. Among other things, he'd sensed their varying potentials for evolving into societies that would treasure the individual and offer the individual as much opportunity and respect as possible. Of all he'd encountered, America's potential was the highest.

But he knew America's elites, so he feared for the future should either hold power unchallenged and unchanged. Each, in its own way, was ruthless. Each could oppress. Each would destroy.

Co-existing, though, they moderated each other's excesses. They circled like binary suns, each disdainful of the quality of the other's light, yet envious of its energy. The gravity of animosity drew them together; fear's centrifugal force whirled them apart. They dreaded the final confrontation, but ached for it, too: until one swallowed the other, the lights would blend, and the gravities would cancel, and neither could shine in the solitary splendor it desired.

What Singleton sensed, but knew both Big Gov and the underground would reject, was that the tension which throbbed between them was essential. Mounting here and dropping there, it forbade equilibrium, and ripped open stations of inflexible ideology. It kept society from solidifying; it excited it like a magnetic field does a plasma. The raised energy levels spat photon-artists into greatness ... and drove house-spouses into fits of anxiety soothable only by basements filled with canned goods.

So he'd decided, months before sick dizziness threatened him in the shower, months even before he and an intellectual blonde radical had begun to shape a private Utopia, that he would keep the two elites apart. That he would be a triple agent, reporting to both, but loyal only to his ideals. That he would lessen their mutual hatred and encourage each to respect the other. Jesus, he thought, as he shut off the water with a shaky hand and sat on the tub edge, head between knees, and in my spare time, why don't I whip up a cancer cure?

The terror factor was that if either elite knew the truth, it would kill him.

Downstairs an hour later, he leaned against the peeling wallpaper of the living room. Nobody objected to his presence. He'd been active for ten months and trusted for three. They expected him to attend the nightly meetings of the Committee on Revolutionary Tactics.

Twenty-some people sat or sprawled on the floor, nodding, smoking, and contemplating. Time and friction had worn the Oriental carpet down to its backing. The two couches served as adornment: by common consent, no one used them during policy discussions.

As usual, the hotheads wanted an armed assault on the nearest IRS office. "Now listen up," said Willie Willams, a thirtyish black in a T-shirt and gym shorts, "'cause we done our homework. Won't take but twelve bombs to rubble that place, computers and all. We go in at eight AM, chase those mothafuckas out of there, set the bombs on real short fuses, then we gone. In and out, fifteen minutes, and what we leave behind is gravel. Now you tell me the people won't love that."

"Willie," said the elegantly tailored observer representing the twenty or thirty rad groups in the greater Boston area, "I feel the people would appreciate it rather more if we ensured that the taxmen were inside."

"Backlash," muttered somebody from the shadows, but his

was a solitary voice. The others rumbled approval, and three people jumped up to volunteer for the mission. Even Sheila McDermot nodded enthusiastically.

That bothered Singleton. When he'd gotten involved, McDermot had been the local underground's most reliable violence-stopper. But she'd changed, perhaps because so many of the people she spent time with wanted the roar and the flame of an armed revolution. He'd done what he could, but to little effect. It had been like telling a moth to stay in the dark.

He felt as helpless and as appalled as a witness to suicide. The assault would give the government an excuse to savage the underground. The tax strike might have won widespread support, but bombs in a business district would lose friends. He sighed. Even if they became suspicious, he had to talk them out of that plan ... maybe, he thought, I can come up with something that'll get those crazies isolated and exposed, so the government can clean them out without going after the rest of the underground ... anybody provokes the final confrontation, it'll be the crazies, and I can't let that happen. Dammit, I can't.

"Wait a minute," he said. A few heads turned in his direction, but the rest of the group chattered to itself. He raised his voice. "Wait a minute!" As the room fell silent, he took a deep breath, and held it until their curiosity crystallized in the air.

"Willie—" He pointed over the upturned faces. "—that idea will get you glory, not gain. It's a headline grab."

"Hey, we need some good press, man."

"Fat lot of good it'll do you in Danbury Pen! You'd need fifteen or twenty people to make the raid work—like half the activist list of this group—you know how quick Big Gov'd drop you? You go through that IRS door, the sensors pick you up, and they photograph, measure, and weigh you. They memorize your walk and your talk, and they zip all that information to a Maryland computer two milliseconds later. When the building blows, Big Gov pulls that tape, they say, 'Well now, we got us a black man, 185 centimeters, 85 kilos, x-rays show a four-year-old collarbone fracture, accent says he's born in South Carolina and raised in Harlem, and the walk with the talk with the bones say he's thirty-one years old. Now we just ask all our good ol' ID computers can they tell us the names of all known radicals who fit this description.' And you know something, Willie? They can." He let that echo off the cracked walls. "They can. They'll list all suspects who match the descriptions of each individual raider, and the odds are nine-to-one that any list will include the guilty party. Ten or fifteen of you? It's a mathematical certainty that some of you will be suspected, interviewed, then sensed and interrogated—and it's damn near as certain that one of you will confess and finger the rest. Is that what you want, Willie? The New Haven underground destroyed?" He caught his breath and waited.

"No, man," said the other, "you know I don't want none of that shit. But we just be sitting here talking and talking and never doing nothing! We got to act. We got to show Big Gov he can't just go walking all over us. We got to show the people that we are on their side. That's what I meant."

"You want to show the people you're on their side?"

"That's what I said, man."

"Then why—" Pausing, he tapped his finger into his left palm, and let the others wonder on their own for a moment. "Then why do you want to hit a place that exists for the people's convenience? They don't collect taxes there, or process returns— some auditing, yeah—but mostly it's an information center, a place where people can pick up forms and get some free advice. Take that out, you hurt the people, not Big Gov."

Frustrated, Willams kicked a bottle cap across the thin carpet. The light of blood lust had left his dark eyes, but his tone was stubborn. "We don't go in somewhere guns blazing, how we going to hurt the government?"

The crowd, siding with him, murmured "Aahh." They looked at Singleton with almost contemptuous inquiry, as if confident he couldn't parry Willams's thrust.

He returned their gazes, meeting all the eyes he could. Then he asked, "How many guns can we field?"

"Fifty easy," said Willams, and swept the room for confirming nods. "Maybe sixty."

"Uh-huh." He bobbed his head, held a beat, and asked, "How many guns can the New Haven police alone field?"

"That's not the point!" protested the other. "We never going up against all of them. What I mean to say is, you ever heard of guerrilla warfare?"

"Have you ever heard of POWs?"

"Say what?"

He leveled a finger at the Bostonian. "Let's say you're on a raid, and you get captured. What's the first thing that happens to you?"

"I hear my rights read out loud." To general laughter, she shrugged. "To be serious, though, I'd be interrogated."

"Could you hold out on them?"

She hesitated.

"Against drugs? Hypnosis? Torture?"

Biting her lip, she shook her head. "No," she said in a low voice, "I'd name names. Anybody would."

Pivoting back to Willams, he demanded, "How big is the government? How many people does it have?"

"Shit ... six, seven million?"

"On the federal level alone. And the underground?"

"About the same size."

"Not counting symps," snapped Singleton.

"Oh ... now, nationwide, maybe ... fifty, sixty thousand?"

He let those numbers sink in for a while. Then, more gently, he asked, "How many rads do you know by name?"

Willams scratched his jaw. "Hey, man, I—"

"How many are going to get busted forty-eight hours after you're caught?"

An uneasy ripple spread through the committee, and Singleton knew he had them. "So they nab one of us, in the act or afterwards, and we lose a bigger proportion of our forces than they do of theirs. Who survives? They do. Is that what you want, Willie?"

"Shit, no! But you got any better ideas?"

"Yes." He felt them rise to the promise of security like a bass to a worm. "Use Tissers, instead."

McDermot's head jerked up. "They're too iffy," she said flatly.

"They work just fine."

"But we've already tried to get some, and—" She frowned, then scratched her head. "I can't remember the details, but we didn't get them. We couldn't."

He waved the argument away. "We know there're some rads outside Washington bootlegging these. We get in touch with them—"

"Even if you talk them out of some units, you can't just ship a crate of Tissers up here—it won't pass an electronic security check."

"We'll use a van," he said.

"And cross state lines? Not without an Interstate Commerce Commission permit you don't. And that takes like a year."

He smiled. "Uh-uh. The Director of Applications Processing served under my father in Southeast Asia; he's been a family friend ever since. He's told me, any emergency, he can get me a permit in forty-eight hours. No charge."

A reflective silence filled the room. McDermot finally broke it. "We'll need a totally different strategy if we get the units, but it might be worth it. At least it's worth trying. Willie, do you think you can find that bootleg factory and do a deal with them?"

He made a face, but said, "Yeah, you just leave it to ol' Willie."

The Bostonian looked confused. Knocking her cigarette ash into a grubby jelly jar, she asked, "Tisser? Can't say I recall the term."

At McDermot's nod, Singleton explained. "'Tisser' is short

for T-SS unit, which we believe is short for Time-Space Separation unit. It looks like a pocket computer but fights like an army. What it does is, it removes its target from the time-space continuum. Completely."

She blinked and stroked her Thai silk scarf. "A disintegrator?"

"No." Nibbling on his lip, he arranged his thoughts.

"The theory is abstruse, and the mathematics are—" Theatrically, he rolled his eyes and waved his hand. It drew a chuckle. "Let me put it this way. Matter, energy, and the dimensions of space exist only because of time. If you prevent time from flowing through a given volume of space, then that volume and all it contains cease to exist. Got that?"

"Not a bit of it," she said. "Where do they go?"

"They don't go anywhere. They don't exist anymore."

She jabbed out her cigarette. "I see."

He relaxed, then, and shifted position. "There's one side-effect to this, and it's a kicker. At the moment you erase something, you also erase all organic memories of it. This is confusing, so let's do a simple example: we zap Willie."

"Hey!" protested Willams. "Tiss off, jack."

"The instant he's gone, we all forget we ever knew him. More: we forget he existed. His own mother won't remember him. Now understand, this doesn't mean he never lived. His birth certificate will be on file, the high school yearbook'll still have his picture, and the computers will keep on telling him that he owes them money—but no organic memory will recall him. A stranger to your own dog, Willie," he teased. "This holds true for everything—people, places, things—everything. Remember it, 'cause it's important."

"Doug," called McDermot, "have they figured out why it happens like that?"

"Not that I know of. My guess is that it's got something to do with the natures of reality and perception—people have suggested that what we call reality exists only when it's being perceived; others have argued that 'reality' is a construct erected by a consensus of the perceiving minds. My guess is, either Tissing something out sets up a feedback effect that then erases the memory from the minds that created the reality in the first place, or—and this is even odder—it attacks the perceiving minds first, directly, and by eliminating their memories, eliminates the object from 'reality.' But that's only a bullshit guess, and I'm probably wrong. Anything else?"

"Yes," said the rebel from Beacon Hill, "is this elimination irrevocable?"

"No, that's the nice part," he answered. "You can bring anything back—I'll show you how when we get the units—but when you bring back living beings, they're paralyzed for an hour or so. That's why the Army likes it: you can disarm an enemy without killing the civilians around him, and without damaging any property."

"How do we use them?" asked Willams.

"I'll show you when they come."

"No, man—I don't mean mechanically—I mean tactically."

"Oh." He gulped. "I guess that's up to the group."

On that same hot August night, he made a phone call. It was part of his plan. Burning off the lunatic fringe would lower the animosity levels of both camps—would lessen the gravitational forces of the binary suns and let their orbital speeds pull them back from a collision.

Midnight had passed; trash blew down the heat-softened street. Six houses up, college kids drank beer on a porch and slung raucous laughter at the tired dark eyes of the other buildings. A car sped by, its windows closed and doors locked. Its suburbanite driver had confused the dying with the dead.

Singleton punched the plastic buttons on the pole-mounted corner phone. The streetlamp shone coldly. Brilliance frosted the pavement around his feet. He turned through a casual circle, looking not for observers but eavesdroppers. "Hello, Mr. Thorn?"

"Doug," crackled the receiver, "good to hear your voice. Everything okay?"

"Not really. Listen." He took a breath, and another nonchalant turn. Half a block away stumbled a drunk. No one else. He dropped his voice and set his plan in motion. "I told you before, there's a couple thousand rebs and symps here in town. Most are good, honest people who sincerely believe the government's gotten too big, too invasive, and they turned to the underground 'cause there's no place else for them to turn, you know?"

"Uh-huh," said Thorn absently. He rattled a sheet of paper—probably to doodle on.

"The thing is, any movement draws crazies—and when one gets this big, it draws a shitload. We got a lot here, and it's like they've reached a critical mass—they're talking about taking independent action. In fact, they had a mission all planned. I managed to convince them to drop it, but they were going to launch a guns-and-bombs assault on the local IRS building. Murder all the clerks and blow up the place. They were really hot for it, so to get them to give it up, I had to turn them on to something better."

"Doug, if they had the weapons, we could have moved in."

"No, each person hides his own, and I've got no idea where the hideyholes are. What I told them was—" His heart hammered wildly; would Thorn sense the trap? "—fact, I've already sold them on their end of it; they think it's great stuff—what it is, see, is the T-SS unit."

"You told them about that?" Thorn demanded, in a harsher, colder voice.

"No," he said, surprised. "They already knew about it."

He inhaled sharply. "How? I only found out yesterday."

"Boy, I'll be damned if I know." He paused to scan the street again, and to probe at a small niggling in his mind. It protruded like the tail of a buried memory, but all his heaving couldn't haul the rest of it into view. He gave it up as impossible. "I dunno, they just heard about it somewhere. The thing is, there's a bootleg factory—"

"Where?"

"I don't know, but wait. You grab the factory, and let us take a couple dozen crates—"

"Are you out of your mind?"

"No, sir. Just listen. If they're dummies, mock-ups you can't tell from the real thing except by results, we could fool them for a while. I mean, you can't remember what your target was, right? What I was thinking, you rig these copies with homing beacons, raid the factory just before we get there, and swap dummies for Tissers. Your people impersonate the rads and give us the mock-ups with the beacons. I bring them back, pass them out to the crazies. Right after I signal that they've been distributed, you sweep in with receivers and triangulators, and pick up everybody who's got one. You can jail them all, if only for receiving stolen property. And the proof of the crime is in each guy's possession, right? It's like you're separating the underground out into the crazies and the sane, but you don't have to do the deep background checks. You let them do it for you." Panting slightly, he waited, apprehensive, for the answer.

"What do you think they'll be using them on?"

"Uh ... the New England offices of the FBI?"

Thorn chuckled. "I'd like to see another district besides us make do without a central office." Then he stayed silent for a long time. Through the phone scratched a lead pencil—more doodles. "All right," he said at last. "How are you going to make it look real? You can't simply bring them home on the train."

"No problem," he said impatiently, revolving again and ducking under the phone cord. "I've already told them there's this family friend, served under Dad in Vietnam. He's in charge of van permits for the ICC, and he'll break some rules for me."

"What's his name?" asked Thorn with sudden interest.

Singleton scowled at the receiver. "He's fictitious, sir. He's you, you know? What I said was, I'd ask him to issue me a temporary permit to drive a van from New Haven to DC, and back. We can get the van; you just provide the permit—and the mock-ups. What do you think?"

Thorn sighed. "I think you're one helluvan undercover agent, is what I think. I'll set it up."

"Great. I have to go. I'll call you as soon as I know where the factory is and give you our time of arrival. You mail the permit to the PO box. All right?"

"Fine. Good night, Doug. My best to your family." He hung up.

Three days later, Singleton was walking down the second-floor corridor of McDermot's house when Willie Willams's door opened. "Douglas, my man!" Willams leaned into the hallway. He wore jeans and a red T-shirt. "If I might take just a moment of your time—?"

"Sure, Willie." He turned around and went back. "What's up?"

Willams had beer on his breath. "I have done the deal with our friends in DC; the time has come for you to get us that permit. Plan on moving out Thursday, real early, and on getting back late. Make sure the permit shows those times."

He took out his pocket computer and keyed the memo pad. "That's Thursday the—" He called up the computer's calendar. "—the 25th. And the address?"

"Of what?"

"Of where we're going."

"I know the way," said Willams, narrowing his dark eyes.

"Yes, but for the permit—"

"Make one up."

"Sure, but if they stop us and we're not near there, we're in trouble."

The rebel's voice was cold. "We going to take that chance."

Singleton sighed. "C'mon, Willie, give me a break, huh? I've got to do all this over the phone tomorrow morning, and if it sounds fishy, Dad's friend's going to hold up on it. Just give me the street, I'll make up a number."

Willams pursed his lips and stared at Singleton for a long while, as if weighing him on an unsteady scale. "K Street," he said at last.

"Thanks. Our permit'll be in Wednesday's mail."

"It better be."

"It will be," he said, annoyed despite himself.

"Douglas, I don't know if you are dumb, or if you really do have some fine connections—"

Singleton stood motionless, not liking at all the emphasis Willams had placed on "connections." *Jesus, does he suspect?*

"—but it seems to me you are trusting a crat, and that's a dumb-ass thing to do. I ever tell you about my Daddy?"

It was all he could do to shake his head.

"He's a pharmacist, owned a little drug store down in South Carolina. Now there are forms which you have got to fill out when you dispense certain drugs, but it so happened that he ran out of one of them. Lady came in, old widow lady had dinner with the family once a month as long as I can remember. She needed her medicine then, couldn't wait no two weeks for the next shipment of forms to come in. Well, Daddy's store was the only one in town; he couldn't see telling her take the bus to the city. So he called up the man in charge of processing those forms at the district office—and he said, 'Charlie, it be okay if I fill the prescription now and do the form later?' Charlie says, 'Why sure, TM, you just do that.' So Daddy did. And good ol' Charlie, he changed his mind, hauled Daddy up before the Board, and had his license lifted. So what I say is, don't ever put your faith in no bureaucrat—'cause you are bound to get burned."

"Is that why you're in the movement?" asked Singleton cautiously.

Willams yawned. His teeth flashed white and even. "That's just one of the reasons, Dougie—just one of the reasons. Catch you later." He closed his door firmly.

Singleton went to find a phone.

When the ICC permit arrived, Singleton stuffed it in his pocket and headed for McDermot. At her door he hesitated, suddenly daunted by the chipped wood. Pushing it open would mean assuming a different, more difficult role. Outside he could be reserved, enigmatic, deceitful—whatever persona the scheme demanded—but within ... within, he had to love. And though that was easy, because Sheila McDermot could cage his soul like a bird with his thanks, it was also dangerous. Even now, insulated from her voice, her glance, he ached to make them warm with approval by revealing the trap he'd laid for her crazies. When he was next to her, touching her ... he shook his head. He hoped for control, but he was afraid. If he let slip clues that her brilliant mind could piece together, she would never believe he'd been anything but a liar ... and that would hurt. His inevitable execution would be agony, but the real pain would spread from her conviction that he hadn't ever cared.

Jesus, he thought. If they pull off my agent provocateur mask, they'll tear away my real face with it ... Christ, I need her. He knocked.

"Come!" She stood near the left wall, facing a large map of New Haven. Colored pins bristled her lips. With a nod, she jabbed a red marker into a downtown intersection, and spat the rest into her palm. "Hi."

"Hi." He took her into his arms and hugged her, feeling her breasts against his chest. "Hold me."

"I already am," she said, stroking his back. "What's the matter?"

"The truth is, I'm afraid."

"The revolution?"

"Yeah." Stooping, he nuzzled his face into the clean smell of her blonde hair. "I mean ... we're talking about death here, destruction—probably famine and plague, too—and I ... I don't know, it terrifies me."

"Poor Doug," she whispered, while she pressed her warmth into him. "It used to terrify me, too. Willie says it's natural."

"I know it's natural, I don't need a crazy to tell me that."

"Doug, he's not crazy—although I will admit I once thought he was, too—but he's not. He's almost eerily sane."

"He wants to kill people!"

"No." She lifted her chin and focused her blue eyes on his. "He wants the revolution to succeed, that's all. If a few people have to die—"

"You never used to think that way."

Calm-faced, steady-voiced, she nodded. "Maybe I've grown up."

"Willie's a bad influence on you."

"Funny—" Strain showed in her smile, but she hugged him tighter. "—he thinks the same about you. But it'll be all right. We're trying your idea with the Tissers, and they don't kill. We'll bring back the targets afterwards. As long as they work, it'll be all right. Don't worry."

Lost in her scent, he groped, eyes closed, for her lips. Soft and moist, they parted under his; their tongues touched, and tarried. "Let me lock the door," he said hoarsely.

"Not a chance," she breathed. "Not during working hours. Tonight—no, I have a meeting tonight. Tomorrow."

He released her. "Can't make it."

"Why not?"

"I'm going down to Washington to pick up the Tissers." He pulled the manila envelope from his back pocket. "The permit came."

"Doug!" Whooping, she threw her arms around his neck and

squeezed hard enough to hurt. "Fantastic! Oh, I knew we could count on you."

"Look, uh—" He stepped back a pace, and finger-combed his hair. "Don't take one, huh?"

She cocked her head as though trying to drain water from her ear. Her face said she couldn't have heard right: puzzlement compressed the corners of her eyes and quirked the middles of her brows. "Don't take one? Why not?"

"Things I've heard." He shrugged. "This is the first generation, you know? Haven't got all the bugs out ... I hear they explode once in a while, and ..." He tightroped a truth that paralleled the line of his lies. "And I'd feel really shitty if a weapon I brought you injured you."

"Hey, this is revolution, Doug—any weapon I use could hurt me." She ran distracted hands down her pink blouse, smoothing out its wrinkles. "A grenade fuse could be short, a rifle could jam —hell, I could swallow a map pin and choke to death!" Earnestly, she studied his expression. "Not funny, huh?"

"Uh-uh."

"I've got no choice," she insisted. "I'm in charge here; I can't hang back. I can't avoid doing something I'm asking others to do."

Desperate, he gave it one last try. "But—"

"No."

"All right." Awkwardly, he made for the door. "I'll, uh ... see you when I get back, okay?"

This time she really smiled. "Better believe you will."

Singleton was driving; Willams dozed on the seat beside him. The Maryland morning was clear but muggy. He'd cranked down his window for the breeze, yet still felt stale and sticky.

Three jeeps growled by on his left, radio antennas whipping

and helmeted soldiers bouncing up and down. His hands tightened on the wheel.

This is never going to work, he thought. *Mr. Thorn'll put agents in there who won't fool Willams for a minute. He'll see right through them. And afterwards, on the way home, he'll ...* Singleton didn't even want to think about what Willams would do to him.

Reluctantly, he reached over and touched his companion's shoulder. "Hey, Willie," he said, shouting to make himself heard over the wind. "We're coming up to the Beltway."

Willams stirred, shook himself, and groaned. Then he rubbed his eyes. "Oh, God—daytime already?"

"You said to wake you when we got to the Beltway."

"Yeah. Pull over."

"The sign—"

"You know, Dougie, that's what I never did like about you—you're chickenshit. 'Don't break any laws,'" he said in a mincing falsetto, "'don't break any heads, don't break any hearts' ... fuck the sign and pull over, will you? I don't know why I'm letting no goddam namby-pamby pacifist come along'th me, anyway. A revolution ain't no Boy Scout picnic."

Slowing, he bumped onto the shoulder. At a thumb jerk from Willams, he got out and walked around the front of the van while the other slid over. His knees wobbled; he stopped and stretched muscles cramped by nearly six hours of worry. The ligaments felt better, but not the nerves—his hands still shook.

As he climbed into the passenger's seat, Willams lifted the CB mike. "Wild Bill is on the air and looking to hear from Annie Oakley." He broadcast in a voice more rural, more gravelly than his own. "Annie Oakley, Wild Bill has come to town, six-gun loaded, and he be looking for action. Whatchew doing tonight, babe?"

Static crackled. Somebody down in Alexandria said something undistinguishable. Singleton froze, realizing too late that Willams had set up a code with the locals so that he could learn, in advance, if it were safe to approach—or if he should stay away to avoid arrest. Jesus, Singleton thought, no way Thorn can handle this one. I'm dead. Absolutely dead.

"Annie Oakley," said Willams again, his voice just as gratingly jovial but his eyes now searching out Singleton. His dark hand gripped the mike so tightly that its tendons stood up. "This here be Wild Bill, Annie Oakley, and I am in town now, ready to stomp. You read me, Annie Oakley?" Then he turned to face Singleton squarely. Nostrils flared, eyes slitted, he said nothing.

"All—" Singleton began.

"Wild Bill," said a liquid female voice, "Belle Starr here, you read me?"

"I surely do, Belle Starr—what happened to Annie?"

"She had some guests, asked me to be your hostess this time through. Why don't you swing on by? You know where I live." She added a girlish giggle that would have sounded convincing to anybody listening in. "See you real soon now, you hear?"

"Cain't be soon enough for me, Belle Starr. I be there right quick." Not even glancing at Singleton, he slipped the mike onto its hook, put the van in gear, and jolted back onto the Beltway.

All he said to his sweating passenger the whole way to D Street was, "They didn't have two bootleg factories here, Dougie, you be dead by now."

"What the hell's that supposed to mean?" said Singleton, trying to hide the ice in his gut with a hot-tempered veneer.

Willams's only reply was a grunt.

When they got to the place on D Street, and had parked in a small, metal-doored garage that needed repainting, Willams strode up to the man in charge. He was a tall young white with thick glasses and a lab coat. "Mike?"

"Yes," said the other, pushing his glasses back up his nose. "You're Willie, I presume?"

Afraid not to, Singleton had tagged along, so he heard Willams say, "The K Street place got taken?"

"At six-eighteen this morning."

"I think this dude might be the dude what talked." He pointed to Singleton.

His heart almost stopped, and he felt his cheeks pale, but he had only one chance: to bluff it out. "Christ sakes, Willie, what is this shit?"

Mike dusted the sleeve of his lab coat. "Willie, I don't wish to be involved in whatever dispute there is between you two, but I have to say that this man didn't do it. It was one of our own people, a bit of a show-off."

"You shit me." Willams sounded disappointed.

"Not in the least. He told his 'girlfriend' what we were doing, and where we were doing it. Would you care to guess who led the raid this morning? Precisely ... he's being disciplined, now." His deceptively mild blue eyes lifted to study Singleton. "Should you have discipline problems in New Haven, Willie, do try to handle them yourself. We have too much to do here. Josh will help you load; please leave as quickly as possible. We're in the process of relocating." With a rustle of starched linen, he turned and walked away.

Singleton needed to sit down and breathe for a while, to regain his composure, but he didn't dare, not yet. Instead, he stalked up to Willams and put all the anger he could muster into: "What the fuck is wrong with you? If that guy had believed you, I'd be dead now." He caught a flicker on his companion's face and leaned in closer, pressing harder. "Why, dammit? Is it Sheila? You jealous?"

Willams held up both hands. "Hey, easy man, easy. I jumped, you know? I put two and two together to make five. Got nothing at all to do with Sheila, that I swear on the Bible, all right? I'm sorry, Doug." He shook his head. "A man gets paranoid in this profession ..."

Let it lie, Doug, don't push it any further. "All right, Willie. I can see what happened. I guess in your shoes, I'd have done the same thing." He held out his hand. "Okay?"

Willams took it. "I owe you more, man. I got to explain.

Three years ago, I was teaching school at Hillhouse High——PE, track team, some sex ed classes. I was sick and tired of all the damn forms they made us fill out, so one night I snuck into the supply room, took 'em out to the football field, and burned 'em. I made the mistake of telling somebody—a clean-cut Yalie like you. Thought he was my friend. The sucker turned me in ... I guess—"

"It's okay, Willie. I understand. You want to load up?"

"Yeah, buddy—let's do it."

Singleton felt like a first-class shit. Willie, he thought, you just have to stop trusting us clean-cut Yalies ... and the whole time he loaded cardboard cartons of T-SS units, he gave a silent prayer of thanks to Whomever had convinced Oscar Thorn to double-cover his double-agent ...

Six hours later, a clatter of taillights reddened I-95. Singleton had to slow down. "What's going on?"

"Looks like a roadblock," answered Willams, who leaned, arms folded, against the passenger-side door.

"Think it's for us?"

"Hard to say. Hey, man, you unTiss somebody, they're really paralyzed? You can disarm them, and they don't know it?"

"Really." He shivered.

The van's headlights sparkled off the chrome butt of a '92 Fiat. Here and there impatient horns beeped, calling to each other across the concrete river like highway loons. Singleton drummed his fingers on the steering wheel. "Think it'll pass?"

"Don't see why not."

The van advanced ten meters at a time, stopping and starting, and when they got to within fifteen meters of the flashlight-waving patrolman, Willams flicked on the stereo. "Local color," he explained, snapping his fingers.

"Good idea." Nervous, Singleton rubbed his palms together.

"Joint?" He proffered a pack.

"I'm driving."

"Then here." He rustled in a paper bag on the seat between them and brought out a thick ham sandwich. "Eat something."

"Thanks, but I'm too shaky."

"Shit." After three quick bites, he handed it over. "Hold it," he mumbled through his full mouth, "pretend it's yours. Be cool but pissed. Dig?"

"Huh." He nodded, thinking about it. "Thanks."

A beam of light dazzled Singleton's eyes. He half held up his hand, and rolled down the window, squinting into the shadowed face of the trooper. "What's this all about, huh?"

"Please shut off your engine and open it up, sir."

"Jesus!" His mouth was so dry that he bit into the sandwich to justify his hoarseness. The music snapped silent as he pulled out the key. "Christ sakes, this rate we won't make New Haven till dawn." He pushed open his door and swung out onto the road.

"Visiting Connecticut, sir?" said the patrolman courteously, leaning inside.

"I live there. Had to deliver a painting to the Corcoran, special exhibit, cocktail reception tonight—you think they'd invite us? Hah!" The engine cover squealed rustily as Willams and the cop hoisted it up. "What are you looking for, escaped convicts?"

"Just making sure your governor's in place, sir," said the trooper as he probed the engine with his flashlight. He tugged on a wire and nodded.

"Do we pass?" Singleton forced himself to ask.

The cop backed out of the van, booted feet first. "Yeah, go ahead. Enjoy the New Haven winter."

But Singleton went around to the passenger side and asked Willams to drive. His hands trembled too badly to steer.

"Shit man," said Willams, as they pulled away. "We get any

more of these damn red tape traps, my heart's gonna give out for sure."

"A governor check," he whispered in disbelief. "A goddam governor check."

"Come the revolution ..."

"Uh-huh." He breathed easily for the first time in half an hour. "And it can't come soon enough."

They reached the house before midnight, stretched and yawned as they dismounted, then thudded up the front steps to get some help unloading. They quickened their pace on the porch, for the splintered door, kicked off its hinges, leaned against the siding. The paneling in the vestibule had been torn from the walls. Glass from the shattered inner door crunched beneath their feet. "What the hell?" hissed Singleton.

A shape materialized before them: McDermot. "Hi," she said. Fury radiated from her taut, jittery body. "Doug, I'm glad you're back—I need you."

"What happened?"

"Cops." She stepped towards the living room, into the light that spread out of it. A square of taped gauze bandaged her right temple. "Looking for guns—they said." She passed under the archway; they followed.

The living room was a shambles: plaster pickaxed off the lathing, sofas slashed, floorboards pried up, and light fixtures ripped loose. A bare bulb in a porcelain socket dangled from the middle of the ceiling. It glowed on two dozen faces: angry faces.

Willams whistled, then said, "Jee-zus!"

McDermot glowered at the wreckage. "We're planning a new operation," she rasped. "The cops got our names, pictures, and prints, and dropped a lot of hints about how they'd be coming back for us."

Singleton asked, "They arrest anybody?"

"No," she said, "no grounds for it."

"Your head?" He extended his hand as if to touch it but stroked her soft cheek instead. "Night stick?"

"Believe it or not," she said with an ironic smile, "it was a pure accident. I was getting dressed when they knocked—took a second or two too long. Just as I grabbed the doorknob, they kicked it in." She shrugged. "They apologized."

He wanted to apologize, too, but she'd never understand. "Bastards," he said, to stay in character. "So what's this new operation?"

"Tonight we send most of those Tissers up to Boston for distribution around the country. Then tomorrow," she said calmly, "we're going to Tiss out every cop in New Haven County."

"What?"

Her eyes sparkled. "Sit down. We'll tell you all about it."

The sky was very clear. In the west, stars still shimmered; they'd force the sun itself to blot them out. before they yielded pre-eminence. In the east they'd already faded.

He lay on the bare floor of a strange house. They'd seized it ten minutes earlier and thrown the owners into the street. The window overlooked the back yard, which, neglected, had gone wild. Meter-tall weeds wavered in the pre-dawn shadows. An unpruned rambler rose bulged along the northern fence like a swollen hedge, and cat-fearing sparrows relaxed in its protection. He touched his rifle. "When?"

Willams cocked his ear to the oncoming sirens. "Thirty seconds."

"I'm worried about Sheila."

"She be okay, man."

"Is this really going to work?"

"Yeah." He flicked his safety off, then tugged his gas mask over his mouth and nose. "A siege'll draw 'em like shit does flies."

Singleton emulated his companion, wishing, as he snapped the mask straps behind his head, that he'd been able to find some way to shake the group for ... hell, five minutes, that's all he'd have needed. Five minutes and this wouldn't be happening. Five minutes and ...

He'd either get his ass shot to hell, or he'd witness the successful start to the most devastating revolution the world had ever seen.

He didn't know which he hoped for more fervently.

Dammit!

The phone signaled them with its ring.

Willams stuck his gun out the window and fired into the ground. Instantly, eighteen other weapons—shotguns, 9 mm. machine pistols, even a .38 automatic—burst into angry chatter. A moment later, Singleton's chimed in.

Birds burst from the roses in a frantic cloud. Out front, brakes screeched. Car doors slammed. A brassy voice bullhorned, "You are surrounded, come out with your hands up."

Sirens wailed unabated.

"Be steady, Doug," said Willams.

His stomach knotted; he massaged it with his trigger hand. He wished he'd gone to the john. A gentle breeze came through the window, and he shivered.

Below and to the right, bushes shook violently. A patch of blue flashed here, and there, then farther down the yard. "Cops moving up on the right side," said Singleton.

"You take 'em, man—I got some on the left."

He rested his M-19 on the windowsill. A helmet popped up behind the far fence, then dropped back down. He checked the safety. It was off. He couldn't seem to keep the barrel steady. The helmet surfaced again. He tried to draw a bead on it but couldn't. The barrel kept wandering away. He was glad his father couldn't see him—the colonel would be furious.

The helmet rose higher. A faceplate made the cop a robot. The cop aimed a riot gun. Its over-and-under barrels filled the M-19's sights completely.

He squeezed the trigger. A branch fell from ten meters high in the tree.

The cop behind the fence looked to his right, then to his left. He nodded. On either side of him, a SWAT-squadder stood up and gripped the fence top, preparatory to vaulting it. He fired both barrels.

For Singleton, time went crazy. Smoke and flame bulged from the riot gun. The SWAT-men bunched their muscles and kicked up into the air. The charge spread out, heading for him like an angry swarm of bees. He held his breath. He eased back the trigger. Shattered glass drifted down to his head and shoulders, powdering them like snow. The cop on the left, suspended in mid-air, jerked, and a red dot appeared on his thigh. The shotgun's roar rumbled into the room like a very slow train. Singleton swung the M-19. And caught his breath. And sighted on the second SWAT-man, just about to touch ground. His finger slid back. The cop's knee spouted blood and collapsed beneath him. The riot gun barked again. But there was no glass left to break.

"Nice shooting," said Willams, leaning over to slap him on the back.

He wanted to puke.

From then on, it progressed like a dream. Sirens and screams; blue backs bobbing beyond the fence. Yellowish-gray tendrils of gas reaching like squid arms across the floor. Shiny brass cartridges spurting endlessly from the rifle, ticking into the wall and falling into the gas. The rifle heating up in his hands. More uniforms out there, dozens of them, behind the trees, under the bushes, and if there were that many out back—he glanced over to Willams, who was picking up the phone and punching McDermot's number.

"What's up?" said Singleton.

Willams waved him off, slipped down his mask, and coughed.

Then: "How many cruisers?" He coughed again. "That's all but two, then." Gagging, he explained, "Vomit gas. Now? Sure ..."

Singleton thought, *What'll he do to me if it doesn't—*

McDermot stood at the window, dead phone to her ear. In the distance cried a siren, but after a moment it sputtered into quiet confusion. She shook her head and put down the phone. Next to its cradle lay a sheet of paper. Across the paper's top stomped large red letters: READ THIS NOW!

Turning off the Tisser in her hand, she skimmed the page. She couldn't remember why she'd turned the unit on in the first place ... the ghost of the memory survived, but it was too attenuated to capture. "Aah," she said aloud for the note explained it.

"You have," it said, "just Tissed out most of the police of New Haven County. Press the following buttons in the following order: Memory Display, File, 1, and 'add.' This will unTiss the trap. Send your people in to disarm and imprison the cops."

"But why?" she asked the air. She couldn't recall a thing about it, but it seemed to her that the police were already nicely imprisoned.

As if in answer, the instructions went on: "Not only does the revolution need the vehicles, the uniforms, and the weapons, but twenty of its bravest fighters are in the trap as well, and it needs them, too."

"No, it doesn't." She tried to visualize any of the Tissed-out rebels' faces—failed—and shrugged uncaringly. It didn't matter because, deep down, the fanatics all looked alike. The resemblance showed in their hot, loveless eyes, and their jerky talk of guns, bombs, and blood in the streets. "No," she said again, "the revolution doesn't need that kind. It doesn't. Not this time."

The handwriting looked familiar, but she couldn't place the signature: Doug. Doug? Some kind of code name? One of the time-trapped terrorists? "It doesn't matter." She crumpled the note.

The Earth spun in a shell dyed robin's-egg blue. Dry, too, at least for that time of morning. She hoped it wouldn't get muggy. She realized she was exhausted.

Stifling a yawn, she unbuttoned her blouse, and turned to lie on the mattress covering the floor. So tired ... she'd stayed up the whole night plotting the revolution, executing the trap ... not one person killed, either ... so tired ... the sheets were cold.

Six or maybe eight years earlier, she and her brother had planned to embarrass their mother so thoroughly that the old lady would stop barging in on them and demanding to know what they were up to. The day before her mother's birthday, she snuck a bottle of champagne into the house, while her brother ostentatiously toted a coil of rope up to his room.

They taped a birthday card to the bottle, then hung it out the window, bumping it against the siding and giggling as loudly as they could. Sure enough, the old lady stormed in, spotted the rope, and hauled it up, hollering at them as she did so. McDermot shook her head, half-smiling, half-sad. The card that was to have humiliated the old lady had fallen off ....

The mattress was large. She pulled off her blouse and tried to figure out what was missing. Then yawned and gave up the attempt.

Nothing was missing. Everything was just as it had always been.

And she was just as lonely.

[4]
SPLINTER IN A WHIRLPOOL
OCTOBER 1994

Basil Heffing woke up smaller than he'd been the night before. Not physically—he was as tall and as whip-muscled as when he'd rolled under the blankets—but psychically. He felt ... hollowed, like a limestone hill tunneled and caverned by running water. The assurances of identity which one checks subconsciously each morning eluded his touch. He knew his name, and where he lived, but he couldn't recall if he owned a car, or why he had no job, or what high school had granted him a diploma.

Chill gripped the morning air. He propped himself on both elbows and shook his dark head, hoping to jar filler into the holes of his being. It scared him to feel half-there. He was real, solid ... but the fissures in his soul wouldn't heal, and their emptiness appalled him.

"Dammit." He swung his feet to the hardwood floor, dressed hastily, and reached for the phone. His folks had refused to flee with the rest. He'd call them, see how they were making out, see if the rebels were leaving Bellevue Road alone ... and in the process re-affirm his existence, although he couldn't have articulated that concept to himself, much less to them. He was only nineteen.

He'd punched out the entire number before flat silence reminded him that the line was still dead; he slammed the receiver down. "Aw, shit." Fearful worry sickened him; his stomach bobbed like a helium balloon. Why hadn't the company restored service? It had been a week, easy. Now he'd have to walk the three miles home ...

He gave a wry smile as he realized that he still placed "home" at 35 Bellevue Road; *but why not, I grew up there, spent most of my life there* ... not for the first time, he marveled at how tightly his life had intertwined with his family's, how relatively little he had experienced outside the company of at least one of them ... which was why he instinctively reached for them whenever he seemed a shadow of himself, for touching them restored his own tangibility. Then the fear settled in again because he'd have to walk.

Three miles. Through twisted streets, over fences, across back yards ... moving with a meadow mouse's wariness because the abandoned city did swarm with anarchic rebels and disorganized lawmen and madmen who imagined bull's-eyes on every spine ... damn Southern New England Telephone anyway; if it did its job, he wouldn't have to cold-sweat himself into hysteria every time he wanted to hug his mother.

Leaning forward, he flicked on the radio, hoping the batteries still held their charge. The newscaster said, "... plans to parachute troops into New Haven; a spokesman for the National Guard said that they would maintain martial law until such time as order has been restored."

He rose but couldn't yet muster the courage to go outside. Knuckly hands jammed in his pockets, he slouched to the window and drew what heat he could from the bright October sun. Blue skies domed the city; the air, though crisp, tasted clean. Below, the wind whisked leaves down the street and swept them under the car petulantly junked at the dead end. He wondered if the battered yellow Olds hadn't been dumped there on purpose, to barricade the side yard of that house. After all, there were no signs or curbs or anything to tell that the street would end ... could be annoying, to have tires rutting your lawn because people don't know ... the city should have done something about it, but ...

"State Police Lieutenant Ralph J. Marthon," the broadcaster continued, "reached by CB radio earlier in the day, said he could not comment on charges that fully 70% of the state police payroll is fictitious. With power down to the computers, he said, they're unable to retrieve the personnel files of the alleged 'ghost cops.' Asked when he would assign troopers to the New Haven area, the Lieutenant said his men had to have accurate road maps, first. Apparently, every available map is padded with blocks and streets that simply don't exist. Sounds like his bookkeeper's related to the cartographers."

Heffing shook his head. The cop was right: the maps had been drawn with a lot of imagination, and little attention to reality. The one on his dresser claimed the street outside didn't dead end into somebody's yard. Funny he'd never noticed it before the revolution. Crazy city ... no mayor, no board of aldermen, no city hall ... there used to be a mayor—Heffing remembered him. His parents had taken him and Nicky to the 1985 St. Patrick's Day parade, and right at the head, this fat old guy stood up in the back of a convertible and waved. Serge Heffing had pointed him out and said, "That's the mayor, the biggest crook in town." Basil also recalled asking, "Why don't you arrest him, then?" because to him at that age, his father had been the toughest, strongest, Lone Rangerest man in the world, but Serge Heffing had just given his son a sad smile and said, "I can't."

So nine years ago there had been a mayor, but now ... twisting the ends of his mustache as the deceptively strong sun soaked into his leather jacket and made it flexible, Heffing tried to remember what had happened to the incumbent. He couldn't.

The radio rambled, "... the New Haven Water Company official in charge of civil preparedness and asked him where the water is."

A tape came on; this voice was tired, scratchy with suppressed anger, staticky from the poor recording: "We've got no idea what's happening out there except that a civil war's going on. The crews we sent out are reporting that everything's all f—" bleep "—up. The mains aren't where our maps say they're supposed to be—hell, the goddam motherf—" blee-eep "—roads aren't where they're supposed to be. We got no idea what happened. It's like somebody tossed the city up in the air and the pieces didn't come back down in the same places—God, we can't even find all the damn pieces 'cause nobody knows what they look like. Anybody still here ought to get out quick."

A knock on the door spun Heffing around. For a fearing moment he hesitated—the rebs were armed, and weird—but he'd never politicked, and owned nothing of value. "Come in!" He shut off the radio. "It's open."

A short, pudgy man in blue coveralls bustled in. Sunburn lit up his bald head. He smiled. "Basil, hey, I'm so glad I catch you in today."

"Hiya, Mr. Angeloni," he said without enthusiasm, and backed his shoulders into the shaft of sunlight. "How're things?"

"They all go to hell, and she starts with my memory." He tapped the side of his head. "I'm make my rounds, check out my houses—you know me, I'm climb stairs slow, cozza the fracture I get four years ago, she's still no healed yet. So up I go, ka-thump! ka-thump! my rent book in hand, see?" He waved it; the pages rustled. "There's a name, Gherahoulian, Cyrus. It's on the book, it's on the door, it's on the mailbox out front, too. Only thing is, it don't ring no bell with me, you know? An' a name like Gherahoulian, so maybe I'm no pronounce it so good, huh? But I'm remember if I'm ever see before. An' I never have. Never. I think about this, flip-flip-flip through my book, an' that says this guy, he's paid his rent every month. Now, the kind of tenants I got, I remember if they pay. So I let myself in. Nobody. Furniture, yes. Moldy bread in the fridge, yes. Dust everywhere, lotsa it. But no Gherahoulian. An' I check the other tenants, they never heard of him, neither. So what am I do? Huh? Tell me."

"Well ..." He shrugged. Somewhere outside an automatic rifle chattered. Heffing didn't move. A week of diving for cover had taught him how to distinguish between bullets aimed at him and bullets aimed elsewhere. "As long as he's paying his rent—"

"No, that's the thing." With a moody glance at the window, Angeloni shuffled to the couch and sat. The cushions wheezed dust. "I get no money from him this month."

"Maybe he's in the refugee camp up north. Or maybe the Post Office ate his check."

"Hey, Basil, tell me: who's use the mails anymore? Yeah, sure, when the van comes down my street, I'm naturally gonna check if they got something for me, but alla it's junk. You know, it used to be, once upon a time, a mailman would come to your door once a day, six days a week, regular. Now ..." He threw up his hands. "I tell you, Basil, she's so bad now I wish I'm still in Naples. America, hah! She'sa fall apart like a suit the tailor only basted ... while I'm here, you got your rent?"

"For what?"

"For the apartment, huh?" He waved his hand to indicate the four rooms and bath. "Six hundred, today's already the 12th, I gotta throw you out, too?"

Heffing folded his arms. "Mr. Angeloni," he began, "there's no water. No electric. No gas. No heat. I mean, you got an obligation to provide them, right?"

"Not in the middle of no revolution, I don't gotta," said the older man sourly.

"Yeah, well, in the middle of a revolution, I don't have to pay."

"Says who?"

"Says common sense! I asked my father yesterday; he said I don't get what you promised, I don't have to pay. And if you want to throw me out, fine! Most of the houses in town are vacant, I'll just move into one of them, no problem. But in the meantime, this sits empty, nobody taking care of it, nobody chasing the rats and roaches and rebels away, just empty. Somebody puts a rock through your windows, nobody here to fix it, the rain comes in, the ceilings crack … is that what you want?"

Angeloni squirmed, winced, scrubbed his face with his hands. When he spoke, his words rasped hoarse and tired. "Basil, hey, I'm … I'm old, you know? I'm here twenny-eight years—ever' penny I save, I'm put into land, houses, she's my pension, you know? Last year I'm retire from the restaurant, cozza this stainless steel pin in my leg that hurts so much when I gotta run around the kitchen, but I figure, okay, we live on the rents. Now comes this revolution—nothing makes sense no more—and I got no money. Waddo I do, huh? The mortgage gotta be paid—"

Heffing recoiled at the unreality of that. "You're kidding. Your bank's still open for business?" He felt something go away from him, then, like a thought forgotten before he could get it into words. He looked around, but everything seemed the same. Except he was smaller. "Which bank is it?"

"Ah—" Angeloni snapped his fingers, then touched his head. "Sheesh! I don' remember. I go home, lookit my papers, it's in there." Heavily he rose and brushed the dust off his pants. "You send me the check when you got it, okay?"

He grinned but concealed it with a cough. "Yeah, sure."

"And Basil, that nice brotha yours, Nicky? You tell him I gonna need help shoveling the snow this winter." He patted his leg. "No, I'm drive home, I'll stop in and tell 'im myself. You got his address?"

"Sure, it's—" It was his turn to snap his fingers and touch his head. For an instant he registered only annoyance—damn that stuff I'm smoking; really does a job on the ol' memory—but then a gust of icy fear blew that out of his mind. He felt translucent. "I don't know," he said slowly, wonderingly. "I mean … I thought I did, but …" He squeezed his eyes shut and tried to think. He got a picture of his kid brother: pudgy fourteen, with freckles, green eyes, and a lock of brown hair that kept sliding down over his forehead. But where's he live? New Haven, yeah, but where? Unconsciously, he clenched his fists, and dug his fingernails into his palms as if the pain could spur him to recollection. "Damn," he said aloud, "I don't have the faintest idea where he is."

Angeloni looked disappointed, and accusatory. "So how come you no take him to live with you, a little boy like that? He's too small, live all alone."

"I, um ... I don't know, it just ... never occurred to me. I mean, if he needed a place, he could have come, told me, I could have—I mean, he knows where I live and that I got four rooms here, and—" He couldn't stop his tongue. Fear had dropped a barrier between his mind and his body, and every time he tried to shut up, or even to unfist his hands, he ran headlong into that wall, and it kept him from interfering.

A grenade burst down the street; a scream pierced the sunlight. Both men whirled and made for the window, Heffing in two great leaps. Angeloni with a grim hobble. Heffing heaved on the old double-hung sash. He grunted. "Stuck."

"I can't see nothing," said the landlord, stooping under his tenant's elbow and peering through the streaked glass. "Oh, yeah, 'cross the street, fronna that red thorn bush, there. It's a kid, he's so small—you see? Little black kid?"

"I better go help—"

The screams ended.

The two men gazed at each other for a moment but had to look away. Too naked shone the pain, all intermingled with shame, and to see it was to reflect it, to amplify it with one's own. Heffing turned and kicked the wall. A plaster chip flew.

"Hey!"

"Sorry," said the younger man.

"No, it don't matter, I onnerstand."

"I've got to find Nicky," he said suddenly.

"That's a good idea. Where you gonna look first?"

"It's cold out there at night, you know? If he hasn't got a sleeping bag or something ..." Pivoting, he scanned his shabby living room, searching for something he should take, or something that would tell him where to go. "And in the daytime," he mumbled on, more to himself than to his landlord, "it's crazy, guns and grenades and all that ... why didn't he come to me?" Why didn't I go to him?

"Basil, I got a wife who worries, I'm go now. I see your brother, I tell him to come over here, okay?"

"Yeah, great, thanks," he muttered through his distraction. As Angeloni went his stiff-gaited way out the door, Heffing nodded abruptly, then dashed into the kitchen. From the drawer by the sink, he took a carving knife, with a blade 25 mm. long by five wide. A tentative fencer, he thrust at a shadow, and sighed. It ain't much, he thought, but it's better than nothing ...

Below, a car door slammed. He hurried to the hall. "Mr. Angeloni!" he shouted. "Lemme catch a ride!" While he locked his apartment, an engine coughed and sputtered. He clattered down the stairs. "Hey, Mr. Angeloni!" He jumped the last five steps, dropping onto the landing with a heavy thud. The motor raced, then purred. The front door squealed as he threw it open. "Hey—"

A lanky black man in gym shorts stood on the sidewalk. He took his eyes off the pocket computer he was holding and asked, "You want something?"

"I, uh—" Heffing blinked. "Yeah, but I, um ..." He couldn't remember why he'd been in such a hurry. He stepped onto the porch and let the automatic return gizmo pull the door shut behind him. The knife blade, catching the sun, embarrassed him. He tucked it into his belt with a sheepish grin. "Sorry," he said, "I thought I, um, heard my brother."

"Man, that's a real fraternal greeting you had ready for him."

"What, this?" He tapped the knife, now concealed by the skirt of his coat. "No, that was, uh ... look, you seen him around? Nicky, fourteen, maybe 160 centimeters, brown hair green eyes and kinda pudgy?"

"Uh-uh." He slid what looked to be an antenna back into the

computer and stowed the device in his pants pocket. "Why? He run away?"

"I dunno, I just don't know where he is. If you see him—"

"—I'll tell him his brother's looking for him. Nicky?"

"That's his name." For the first time, he became aware that the other had an automatic rifle slung behind his back. "Are you a, uh—" He didn't know how to phrase the question.

"The word you are looking for, man, is revolutionary. And yes, I am one. And yes, my gun is loaded. And yes, I have used it and will use it again if the need happens to arise, although peashooters are not going to win us this war here. Does that satisfy your curiosity?"

Heffing took a breath. "Uh—yeah, it does." Which it didn't, of course—but he didn't feel he could ask this ominous man what was happening, where were the buses, why was he out of work, how had everything gone wild ... instead, he asked, "Are there any stores open around here?"

"Stores?" said the revolutionary.

"Yeah, stores—I mean, I'm running low on food, and—"

"Man, don't you get it? This is street fighting time! The stores are open 'cause their doors are gone, you dig? Just help yourself." He nodded then, and said, "Later." With that he strode to a motorcycle parked further down the street, mounted up, and kicked it into life. As he pulled away, he raised his hand—a farewell? A threat? Heffing waved back anyway.

The motorcycle roar faded. The street grew silent. Wind rattled through mounds of drifted leaves. Around the corner, pigeons clucked and cooed. Somewhere a hungry dog barked. That was all.

Almost randomly picking a direction, he started walking. Finding Nicky obsessed him; it was his only chance for wholeness. He passed the grenade-blasted doorway, but someone had removed the body. Coulda been Nicky, he thought, pausing. Birds swooped in and out of the flaming thorn bush, and for a moment he assumed they were carrying away leaves. Then he saw the chunks of flesh impaled upon the branches. "Aw, Jesus." He moaned aloud, clutching his stomach and hurrying away. I gotta find him, quick.

A fourteen-year-old kid didn't belong in a war-torn city. Shells weren't falling in the streets, nor were fighter-bombers strafing the rooftops, but that wasn't what worried him. It was the lack of authority, of a system—he hadn't seen a cop for weeks, or a fireman, either. What if Nicky were in trouble? Who could he turn to?

Used to be me, he remembered. Come screaming to me, 'Bazzie, my knee fall down and go ouch! Bazzie, take me home, okay?' Of course, in those days, he'd been embarrassed to have a little kid tagging around after him, whining when something went wrong, bawling when he couldn't get his way. The time Nicky'd wet his pants at the ballgame, he'd pretended not to know him. Coming back, he'd made him walk half a block ahead. In those days, Heffing hadn't understood what being a brother was all about.

His shadow, crisp as dead leaves, rotated 90° as he turned the corner. His eyes followed it, so they didn't see the dogs.

A snarl froze him in mid-stride. He swiveled his head.

Eight dogs blocked the sidewalk. A meter from him stood a huge but gaunt German shepherd, tail down, ruff up, lips back. With another snarl, it advanced, stiff-legged. Blood stained its teeth.

"Easy, boy," he murmured, backing up slowly and gliding his hand inside his coat. "Real easy." He'd heard somewhere that if you stared a dog in the eyes it wouldn't attack, so he focused on those glittery pupils and wondered if they reflected sunlight or madness. His fingers curled around the handle of the carving knife. "Real easy, boy, real easy."

A yelp broke from the back of the pack as a beagle bit a miniature poodle. The two flew apart as if the owners who'd abandoned them had heaved oppositely on their missing leashes. Heffing glanced into the space between them. A fang-torn human corpse lay face down on the cement He couldn't tell if it had been male or female.

"Bastards!" He drew the knife with one smooth motion. The blade gleamed as he waved it. The shepherd stopped. It tossed its head from side to side and growled softly. Then it leaped for his wrist.

He jerked his hand back and the yellow teeth snapped on the stainless steel blade. The animal's strength drove the edge of the knife through its tongue and gums well into its lower jaw. Blood spattered the concrete. Whimpering, the dog whipped its muzzle back and forth. Its paws clawed Heffing's stomach and thighs.

He clung to the handle and kicked at a yapping Yorkshire terrier. Then he raised his arm, lifting the struggling shepherd onto its hind legs. With a shout, he chopped his stiffened left hand into its throat. It whined piteously. He chopped again; this time, it went limp. He dropped it. And jumped on its head. The skull cracked under his boots. After twice losing his grip on the slippery wood, he wrenched the blood-smeared knife out of its jaw. Then, panting, he straightened up, and looked at the others. The Yorkie chased its tail through small fluffy circles. The poodle was pissing on the fence. A black-spotted white mongrel barked at him. He stomped his foot. They ran.

"Jesus." Blood dripped from his coat and soaked into his pants. His breath steamed and clouded, only to be shredded by the wind. Overhead arched the sky, clear and innocent and aloof. What's happened to us? he thought. It's all come apart like confetti out a window ... Nicky, where are you?

A motorcycle hummed in the distance. Heffing's instincts pushed him off the sidewalk and squatted him behind a long-neglected rose bush once trained to the fence. Autumn had browned its leaves, but not taken them. It even had flower fragments.

Up the street came the cycle. It passed in front of his hiding place. A woman rode it, a good-looking blonde in a ski coat and jeans. She cruised slowly; her gaze panned from side to side. Grenades dangled from the gas tank, and an assault rifle diagonaled her back. He held his breath until she had disappeared from sight and hearing.

"Fucking city's fucking crazy," he whispered to the roses, which shook their hips at him. "Man-eating dogs, rebels on 'cycles, a kid brother I can't find 'cause I don't even know where to start looking ..." With the thumb and forefinger of his left hand, he pinched the bridge of his nose. The knife tip trailed in the dirt. "It makes no sense—a fourteen-year-old kid oughta be at home, with his parents—" He stopped, and squinted at the sky.

What he'd just said stuck in him like the barbs of a fishhook. He and Nicky didn't have parents. Or a home. They'd never had them, not as far back as he could remember.

Which didn't make sense, either, because he'd only been renting the apartment for a year. Before then, he'd ... dammit, he thought, as a cold panic settled onto him, where did I live last year? I had to've been somewhere.

He tried painstakingly to reconstruct those twelve months. He'd been a high school senior at—Mrs. Jamison had taught English, yes, an ancient biddy with a hooked nose and a thin white mustache. But what school? His phone number was—I must have written or called it a thousand times, how come—865-8932? No, that belonged to Marj Thompson, his girlfriend ... Address, then, was—The Thompsons lived across the street, at 36 Bellevue Road, which means I must have lived at either 35 or 37, but how come I can't remember?

The parent thing, though, really scared him. I must have had them—or foster parents, or guardians. I didn't raise myself, somebody had to have—I mean, Nicky's five years younger'n I am, so they had to've been around in what, '80? Yeah ... what happened to 'em? Why can't I remember them? Gotta find Nicky ...

A distant grenade shattered the quiet and shook him out of

his wonderings. The parent puzzle wouldn't matter if he got himself killed, so he had to do something about that, first. A gun, he thought, and skulked towards the corner, around which was a sporting goods store. Its door hung open, blown off its hinges by someone with similar ideas. The rifle racks had been ripped apart; only a few smaller weapons remained. He chose a .38 automatic that fit his hand nicely, then ransacked drawers and cupboards until he uncovered six boxes of shells.

Outside again, the weapon a cold weight of comfort in his jacket pocket, he studied the streets. Dogs packed a few blocks down, nosing the brown weeds in a vacant lot. Birds whistled overhead. Nothing else moved.

A boxy blue Datsun was parked by the curb. Hot-wiring it would be a snap; driving, he could search more area in less time than he could on foot. He stepped towards it—but stopped. The city was too quiet. As far as he could see and hear, no cars rumbled on the roads. Why? Had the rebs choked off the exodus?

He shivered despite his leather jacket. Convenient though it might be, the car would wait for someone else's touch. He didn't know what kind of risk he'd be taking by starting it up, and wasn't willing to make the attempt.

He didn't want to stand out. Somehow, that struck him as ... dangerous.

So he walked—neck hairs prickled with fear—from doorway to doorway; pause, look, scamper to the next patch of cover where he'd pause, breathe, look, and scamper on. Again, he wasn't sure why, except that owning a .38 heightened his awareness of his own mortality.

By the end of the afternoon, when he turned about and headed for the anonymity, if not safety, of his apartment, he'd found nothing that might lead him to Nicky.

Nothing.

He dreamed that night of houseless homes, and faceless parents, and brothers crying "Bazzie!" in the dark.

"Gonna play some music for you, folks," said the deejay, "because I can't for the life of me see what else to do. Dead air's a no-no. Lemme tell you, with everybody gone, it's quiet. We've got enough fuel to run our emergency generators for another couple days, and then that's it, we go off, too. No statements from the rebels, the army, or the police this morning, which between us is a relief, but stay tuned because they might be coming in later today ... The time at WELI is 8:47 AM, and the weather report, for our listening area calls for ... daytime. More on that later when the engineer comes back inside. So here's Whipple and the Sirens wailing—"

He snapped off the dial and sat up, blankets cascading down his sweat-shirted front. His stomach gurgled. Patting it, he tried to remember if the cupboard held anything but belly-up roaches. Probably not ...

A while later, hair brushed out of his eyes and bladder emptied into the stink of a waterless toilet, he stumbled down the stairs to the street. There had to be a grocery around somewhere, preferably one the looters had missed. He patted the .38 for luck. If anybody there had a bigger gun, fine and dandy, he'd pay whatever he had in his wallet ... but if the store were unattended, well ... their tough luck. He was hungry.

Broken glass crunched under his feet as he walked across the parking lot to the mom-and-pop grocery store. The wind waved its lockless door back and forth, slowly. Even from the street it didn't smell good.

Breathing through his mouth, he went inside. His eyes needed time to adjust to the darkness, but he was afraid to leave the safety of the bright doorway. Gun in hand, he tried not to taste the foulness of the air, and hoped that he wouldn't trip over anything that should have been buried ...

When the interior focused out of obscurity, he saw that the stench arose from the dairy shelves and vegetable bins. Quicker thieves—survivors, he corrected—had cleaned out the meat coolers and the beverage stands. His eyes swept the floor, spotting the footprints and the dog shit and the smashed beer bottles, but not brushing up against any arms or legs or worse. Carefully, he tiptoed to the canned goods section. It had been picked over, but not emptied. Not yet ...

Though it was a small store, it took the rest of the day to transfer all the non-perishable items up to his apartment, even using the cart he'd found out front. Its wobbly wheels made straight-line pushing impossible. He cursed it a thousand times.

Tomorrow, he said as he fell into exhausted sleep. Tomorrow I'll find Nicky, and we can figure out what to do ... maybe he can remember ...

"Got a communique here from the American People's Glory Hallelujah Liberation Army," said the announcer, "and I thought I'd read it to you, as the gentleman pressing the gun to my temple suggested I might like to do. It says, 'Greetings to the long-oppressed American people from the Central Committee Chairman for Life of the American People's Glory Hallelujah Liberation Army. We have taken command of the New England states and our glorious troops of liberation are already marching cheerfully to commence the reconstruction of our war-ravaged cities. Should they encounter any resistance from fascist, revisionist, or pseudo-proletarian—'"

What I need to find Nicky is to get on the air myself and tell him where I am ... he sighed and rolled out of bed. The darkness of a cloudy October day gloomed the room. He had a can of peaches for breakfast and brushed his teeth in their heavy syrup.

On the street an hour later, he found a bullhorn lying by a burnt-out cop car. He hesitated—his instinct was to stay secret, inconspicuous—but we could sneak right past each other and never know how close we came ... He picked it up, and experimentally clicked it on. His throat-clearing echoed through the neighborhood. "NICKY! NICKY HEFFING!"

No one answered. Out of the corner of his eye he saw a face appear at a third-story window, then vanish. He walked towards it. "NICKY!"

A flight of pigeons took wing, and the face materialized at the doorway. Young and grimy, it belonged to a soldier—a bewildered, stubble-cheeked kid in uniform. "Hey, you!" he called.

"Yeah?" said Heffing warily.

"Where's the Green?"

"The what?"

The kid pulled a wrinkled map out of his fatigue jacket. "The New Haven Green—where is it?"

Heffing shrugged. "Never heard of it."

"Well, it's right here on the map." His dirty finger stubbed the paper and tore a hole in it. "Between Church and College Streets, it says. I musta walked all along College, and I never saw any damn Green. Can you take me there?"

He shook his head. "I'm looking for my brother."

The soldier sagged against the doorframe. "Just point me in the right direction, willya?"

He spread his hands helplessly. "There is no Green, I'm telling you. I've lived here all my life, I oughta know. They gave you one of those bad maps."

"But we're supposed to, assemble there ..." His eyes probed into the distance and saw nothing but fear. "You gotta help me."

"I told you, I'm looking for my brother."

"But we're supposed to be imposing martial law." The soldier's tone was pleading. "You got rebels running all over town, we got to clean them out. You got to help me."

Heffing looked at the kid for a long moment. He felt sorry for him—lost in a strange town with a bad map—but it wasn't his problem. Martial law, restored government—they passed through his soul tunnels without touching, where a missing brother would fill them ... once found. "Sorry," he said, and walked on.

Things happened that day on the edge of his perception: wood smoke wisping on the wind, too faint to label its source; a motorcycle engine murmuring blocks away; a flicker of red cloth racing around a corner and vanishing before he could spot it. In sporadic bursts rattled gunfire, distant and abrasive: a shot here, a volley there, and the deep muffled thud of explosives now and then. "NICKY!" he'd shout, "NICKY HEFFING!"

No one replied.

Even the sun hid from him.

His feet were sore, and his fingers cramped from holding the bullhorn. The gun in his pocket, riding his hip, had scraped his skin through his jeans. He was depressed and weary and not a little frightened. Unless he found Nicky soon, he felt, the hollows within him would expand until his riddled being collapsed into dust. Limping, he began to head for home.

"Basil!"

Startled, he jerked up his head. A bullet kicked dust off the concrete and whined into the gathering dust. He froze, feet spread, arms at his side.

"That's my brother!" said the voice.

Another round snapped out of the impromptu pillbox at the end of the alley, fifteen meters away. The ambushers had built it out of garbage cans filled with dirt.

"Nicky!"

"Run!"

The third bullet awoke his reflexes. He dove for the gutter, rolled behind the base of a fire hydrant, and pulled out his gun. Sparks flew and metal rang as a fourth shot barely missed him.

No fucking sense, he thought bitterly. Why the hell're they attacking me? He told 'em I'm his brother ... he took aim at a patch of blue nylon that showed through the spaces between dented cans and tightened his grip on the trigger. But he couldn't shoot: he didn't know what Nicky was wearing. Sweating, he released the trigger. His hand shook.

"Nicky, tell 'em to lay off!"

A captured M-19 cut loose, spitting at him a hundred slugs that spattered on the sidewalk and clanged the hydrant like the clapper of a bell.

Still he held his fire, painfully conscious of his visibility, maddeningly aware that an indiscriminate shot could strike the one person he most needed alive. Scrunched into the smallest shape possible, he lay flat on the chilly dampness of the gutter and waited for the situation to resolve itself.

But one of the ambushers stood to get a better angle with his automatic rifle. Heffing squinted at the unfamiliar face. Holding his breath, he drew a careful bead and emptied the clip. The other lurched forward. His gun clattered onto a garbage can before falling into the shadows before the pillbox.

"Why'd you do that, Basil?"

"Chrissakes, Nicky, he was trying to kill me!"

Whispered voices almost carried across to him but blurred into unintelligibility before they reached him. Frantically reloading, he braced himself to be rushed.

Hasty shoes did scrape concrete, but instead of charging him, they ran away, down the alley, blocked from his view by the garbage cans. He feared that they were circling around to get him from behind ... and that they bore Nicky in their midst.

He jaw-clenched nausea under control, then sprang to his feet. The sky darkened imperceptibly. A scrawny Doberman pinscher loped in front of him toward the corpse.

He ran forward, crouched, zig-zagging, glad that his leather jacket melted into the dusk. The Doberman growled behind the cans. He vaulted them—and stopped.

Nicky, a bandage on his bloody right thigh, sat propped against the brick wall. The dog stood just before him, fangs bared.

Sweat drenched Heffing's shirt. The October wind cooled it, and he shivered. "Git!"

The Doberman snarled at them both, ears flat, eyes mad with hunger and freedom.

He shot it. It died in Nicky's lap.

"Thanks," said the boy, and shut his mouth before sobs could spill out.

He was so glad to find him alive that he couldn't be angry. "You okay?" he asked, kneeling and laying aside the .38.

"Yeah, I—I will be. Just a g-g-graze ..." He turned his head, but not before the rising moon had laid silver tracks on his cheeks. "They wouldn't stop, Basil, they just wouldn't stop ..."

"They rebels?" He slid his arm under his brother and lifted, grunting with the effort.

"Uh-uh, just kids—my baseball team—but somebody shot Manuel yesterday, and—and—" He gulped, tossing his head. "We were afraid that they were gonna kill all of us, so we got the guns, but then they started shooting at everything they saw, and the soldiers came, and we ran, and they chased us, and we hid, but when I wanted to go to your apartment, Ted called me a deserter and shot me, and ..." He buried his wet face in Heffing's open jacket. "Bazzie, take me home ... please?"

"Nicky," he said softly, "you are home." He winced at a patch of slippery footing. "We'll go to my place."

[5]
CHRISTMAS PASSED
DECEMBER 1994

Christmas Eve of 1994 began, as every day that cruel winter had seemed to, with a screech from the defense console. It tore through the large, lonely house like a flight of seagulls frantic for escape. It echoed off the ceilings and buzzed the window latches. Had there still been police, it would have drawn them in wary dozens.

Dave Kenyer groaned. His nest beneath the woolen blankets was warm; the king-sized bed soft; dreams, more tempting than reality.

The noise persisted.

He tested the air with his nose like a swimmer toes unknown water. It was cold. Breath erupting in a white plume, he shuddered, and vowed to scavenge up another truck of fuel oil. What was left in the tank might keep the pipes from freezing, but he could barely function at 2° C ... and true winter had yet to invade New Haven.

The defense alarm rasped at his nerves. While he took his socks from the pillowcase and tugged them on, he reminded himself to wire up a remote terminal for the console. If one were next to his bed, he would not need to plunge into pre-dawn darkness every day. Then he sighed. He would have to find the time—and the materials—first.

Let's get it on! He threw back the blankets; the chill puckered his skin. He sneezed. Happened every morning. He sneezed while he pulled up his pants, as he eased into his boots, even after he had tugged two bulky cable knit sweaters over his head. The spasms would rack him for another half hour, and then subside till the next day.

He chuckled. David E. Kenyer, PhD, was the kind of man who cried when he was happy and laughed when he was miserable. He had never put it into words, but he had a fear of squandering joy, and of welcoming depression. Forty-three years old, with jet-black hair that brushed his shoulders and blue eyes that could glow or freeze, he stood one ninety-three and weighed ninety-five kilos: larger than average but not, on the face of it, large enough to destroy a world.

Yet he had, and at times guilt so oppressed him that only his sense of responsibility, his feeling that he should put back together what he had given others the tools to disassemble, stayed his suicidal hand.

Racing for the defense console like the athlete he had been, he hoped it would not be one of those days.

The desk-sized unit had a flat-screen TV imbedded in its top. His thumb found the button; the alarm choked off. His ears rang with silence. The screen showed nothing, though he had not expected it to. Whatever had triggered his watchdog was gone—in the most real sense.

He stroked its sleek fibermetal absently, studying its dials and meters, thinking of how best to patch in the remote, and listening, through the silence, to the emergency generator chug-chug in the basement. It ran smoothly, which was natural. He had installed it himself, and he got along better with machines than he ever had with people. Machines were predictable, dependable, reliable even when malfunctioning—from the theory came the diagram, from the diagram the device, and any glitches could be traced to an error in one of those three stages. People were different. Sometimes he wondered if that was why he lived alone ... although now, after months of loneliness, he ached to give humanity another chance.

Briefly he debated going out to disarm the threat. He flicked a switch; the floor-to-ceiling drapes behind the console parted to reveal a picture window. Outside, night still ruled. The glass reflected the dim dial lights, and his grease-stained hands splayed between them. The familiar shapes across the street seemed to loom, ominous and distorted by shadows. Yes, he thought, it is too dark—eat breakfast, wait for dawn. Unworried, he turned away. The enemy was immobilized and would not move until he acted. He headed for the kitchen.

The living room was large—some ten meters long and seven wide, with a ceiling a story-and-a-half tall. The dirty shag carpeting muffled his boot heels. The sofa was old, beaten into comfort by years of usage, but well enough cared for that in strong light it still looked presentable. Bookshelves were banked against the right wall. He moved through the darkness with ease, knowing that though he might forget where he was, his feet would remember. He had crossed that room a million times; instinct charted the bends past the tables and chairs. Except for the scuffs of his walk, the large, empty house was still. Around it, the battle waited, and one of its fields was missing.

Dave Kenyer was (had been? He could never be sure which tense to use: the present, too disordered to ensure a future, was either a hiatus or an ending) a physicist, a theoretical mathematician, an n-space topologist, and a weapons designer for the Pentagon. In his spare time, he tinkered, and could have earned an electronics engineer's certificate if he had ever had time to take the tests.

Which was why he was alive when countless millions of his countrymen were—not dead, precisely, but not alive, either.

The irony was that he had done it all because he hated war.

It had not hurt him personally—he had slithered through the

Vietnam mess on a student deferment and then, once he had graduated, a lottery number of 347. At times that bothered him. Southeast Asia had been his generation's crucible, yet its heat had never tested him. Others had measured their courage against the benchmarks of jungle sweeps, long-range patrols, search and destroy missions—they knew, for better or worse, what they were, what they had—but he had not. He did not know. He could only guess.

But war did revolt him. Not because he had heard it or smelled it or cowered under its fury, but because of the pictures, one hundred thirty years' worth, from Matthew Brady on: the mouths open in soundless screams; the dazed maimed children; the exhausted stubbled faces with their after-images of shame; a shadow etched into a Hiroshima wall ...

He despised it because he had an imagination, because he could visualize within the galleries of his mind what the photos taken after The War would show: nothing.

So he had designed weapons that would deter it forever. When the realization came that there were people sick enough, angry enough, afraid enough to use what could not possibly be used, he had sweated to create the one that spilled no blood, rubbled no buildings, cursed no future generations with skewed genes.

He had done most of the work before he had started—his thesis for MIT. Its three hundred single-spaced pages of equations and text proved that matter (or its reciprocal, energy) is a manifestation of a force (time) flowing through a matrix (space). By age thirty-five he could demonstrate, on paper, that while it took great quantities of energy to manipulate matter, and mind-boggling amounts of it to move space or time, all three could be affected simultaneously by the precisely directed output of a penlight battery.

In the words he'd used to explain it to the President, to convince him to budget the funds for the project, "It's a vast simplification, sir, but what you do is create a negative replica of the time-space field, and project it upon reality." Presidential eyes had glazed; he'd hurried on. "This utterly distorts—for a millisecond—both of them; it's like looping time around space, instead of vice-versa, and bending them both sideways. Once it's done, the matrix—well, it tilts a metaphorical hairsbreadth out of alignment, whereupon the coefficient of friction becomes high enough to produce all the energy the rest of the process needs."

The other had planted his leathered elbows on his desk and his chin on his fists. "So?"

"Well, the matter they'd manifested disappears without losing a quantum of energy."

"Where's it go?"

"May I?" He touched the crystal pitcher on the desk.

"Help yourself."

"Thank you." With a spoon from the coffee tray, he scooped some water out of the ewer. "Is there a hole in the water, sir?"

"Of course not. It flows back." He made a collapsing gesture with his hands, then snapped his fingers. "I think I see. Space is the water, not matter."

"Exactly, sir. We see the matter disappear, but only because (1) the space that had contained it no longer is, and (2) the time that had realized it runs in other beds, like ... like a re-channeled river. So this small pocket of creation winks out of being. Poof!"

"I see ... but its borders?"

"They become a point, in the geometric sense—that is, without dimensions. The eastern neighbor of an object thus treated would suddenly be rubbing shoulders with the object's western neighbor."

"And you can bring it back intact?"

"Oh, yes sir, no problem."

"Fine." The President had reclaimed his high-backed chair and nodded to the door simultaneously. "Tell the generals they'll get their money."

———

Kenyer finished breakfast and stacked the dirty dishes in the sink with the rest. Leaving them there irked him, but he could not wash them. Great chunks of the water mains were missing. He had to hoard what he had and, when that ran dry, drive to the reservoir—through a maze of amputated roads—again to fill his collection of jerry cans.

What a lousy Christmas Eve, he thought, as he walked back to the console. Vinyl tiles floored the corridor, and months of unmopped bootmarks concealed the brown and gold speckles that had seemed so cheery in the showroom. He tried not to look, but the filth nagged at him, practically pulled him to his hands and knees to scour it away. His soles stuck with each step.

At the near end of the living room, he paused. It held two mysteries, two inexplicabilities which he should have been able to explain but couldn't. The first was a door, average height and width, varnished wood with a discreet grain. He ran his fingers down its slickness and frowned at the dust that dirtied their tips. Then he opened it.

Just inside the frame rose a white cinder block wall. He shook his head. There was no reason for it. Or the door, one or the other. If the wall were necessary, why had it not been plastered and papered like the rest of the room? Yet if the door had a function, why the hell had anybody bricked it shut? Someday, when he had the time, he would break through it, see what the mute blocks concealed ... and hope it was not a Poe-esque horror. But he did not think it could be. He had a feeling, vague and unplaceable like the memory of a memory, that he knew the answer, that the riddle would not puzzle him if he could only remember ... he shut the door.

Halfway down the room, easeled on the black marble mantel above the false fireplace, waited the second mystery. It was a photograph of a woman, an old-fashioned portrait in a simple yet elegant silver frame. He touched it. Her middle-aged eyes were green; gray highlighted her long brown hair. She smiled as though glad to see him again.

He called her "Lady," though he had no idea who she was. The photo had probably come with the frame. But he liked her dignity. As he set it back on the mantel, and brushed a wisp of cobweb off a corner, he thought, maybe, when everything's come back, I could find her, talk to her ... she'd be a good listener, it's in her smile, the crinkles around her eyes, the tilt of her head ... maybe when it's all come back ... He walked away shaking his head, as if to dislodge, from the inside back of his skull where it had stuck, a hint to her identity that he could bring forward for inspection. But of course he couldn't. He didn't know her. Unless ... he rejected the suspicion.

Opening the drapes, he gazed out at war-rent New Haven. It was not quite dawn. Fog prowled the truncated streets, overrunning the abandoned cars, shredding itself on dead lamp posts. In the distance cracked a rifle; he ignored it. It was too common a sound for worry.

He keyed the console awake. It was his own creation, built shortly after the troubles began. The work of an afternoon—for him, who had fathered its siblings for the Pentagon and knew where to find the components—it had protected him well. It had a billion-byte memory and could perform 4.6 million operations per second. It was his watchdog; he called it Rover.

"Did you zap an intruder?" he asked.

"Yes." It spoke in Kenyer's own voice.

"What kind?"

"One with a T-SS unit."

He winced at a guilt pang. One of his machines had just wiped someone off the face of the earth for carrying another of his devices. Never mind that the other was probably a rebel, that the unit that had triggered Rover was certainly stolen from the U.S. Government, that the obliterated one had surely used it for wanton destruction—never mind all that. The blame for the sequence rested on him, and its weight crushed him. He would have been happier if the intruder had been smuggling a mini-H-bomb. "What sector?"

"Twelve."

He could not remember it: one of the unit's side-effects was a selective amnesia that launched continuous sly assaults on his confidence. A scientist, an intellectual, he based his self-image on the breadth and depth of his mind. He had to see farther, clearer, or he was no one. Memory was essential for this. Insights were correlations, offspring of unwed data that had clutched briefly, passionately, across barriers of unrelatedness. Were the facts kidnapped, though, they could no longer meet by chance and mate by need.

It depressed him to know that his mind had been mined. So much had to be missing that at times he thought of it as a block of Swiss cheese. People, places, things he had touched or seen or made—they were gone, poof! His insights came fewer, now. Things once familiar were strangers. It reduced him to a trembling rage that he did not, could not, know what he lacked.

He sighed. "How do I get to Twelve?"

"Walk southeast on Edgewood to Norton, turn left on Norton, and proceed to its intersection with Maple. Sector Twelve lies between Maple and Elm."

"Thanks."

"You're welcome."

He unlatched Rover's front. His fingers grazed two T-SS units. He unplugged the one jacked into the auxiliary port and replaced it with the second. Holding the first, he shut the panel. "What's the file number?"

"One."

"Right." He unclipped a chrome star from his sweater. "Test this beeper, will you?" It clicked into a similarly shaped slot on the console's surface. "I don't want to get locked out, or worse, zapped out."

"Signal matched to .2 angstrom; battery good for thirteen

hours of uninterrupted service; the transmitter itself is in good shape."

"Right. I'll see you later."

"Right." It hummed. The calendar clock jarred awake a program written months earlier; a tape whirred. "Dave—Merry Christmas."

Pain contorting his face, he just looked at it.

"Dave? Did you hear me? I said—"

He forced himself to say, "I heard you, Rover. Thanks. Same to you."

"You're welcome."

Ten thousand dollars' worth of radar equipment chased its back on the roof. Looking up, cocking his head to catch the almost inaudible whine of its motor, he decided it was working fine. Rover would have diagnosed any systems malfunctions, of course, but ... though embarrassed to admit it, he felt more secure seeing its integrity with his own eyes. Especially after his struggles to jury-rig it into detecting the faint signature fields of T-SS units. It had been like adapting a stethoscope to hear a fetal heartbeat a football field away. His radar's range was half a klick at best, but it worked. It fed Rover the coordinates of any Tisser that passed through the area; Rover juggled the numbers and activated its own T-SS units to obliterate the carrier. Later, Kenyer ventured out to retrieve them.

Brightness lined the southeast. Shivering with cold and with tension, Kenyer jammed his hands into his pockets and watched his breath condense. Still no snow. "I'm drea—ming of a whi—" With a savage kick at the frozen flowerbed, he cut himself off and turned away.

Since Norton and Maple was almost around the corner, he left the car in the garage. Gas was too hard to come by to waste. It was available—service stations dotted the town, and fuel thickened in their tanks—but with the pumps inert because there was no electricity ... Briskly he strode along the sidewalk. Soggy leaves squished under his feet, and tendrils of fog recoiled from his heat. It might turn into a nice day, if no one Tissed out the sun.

His nervous eyes jittered as he walked. The neighborhood was deserted—most residents had fled in August, when they saw that the troubles would not fade overnight—but rebels did cruise it. So did dog packs. He touched his coat pocket, reassuring himself with the weight of his automatic.

Ten feet up every utility pole, a perforated metal golf ball clung to the wood. Rover's remote sensors, each had a metal detector, a microphone, and an infrared receiver. Three times so far had they saved his life, by warning the console that armed individuals were approaching. Thirty-seven M-19's now filled a closet in Kenyer's basement, along with two dozen grenades, an elephant gun, a brace of hunting rifles, and more knives than he could count.

Ahead shimmered the intersection. Maple bulged away while Elm bowed inwards; they united to form six lanes of concrete where there should have been houses, lawns, and trees. Unspoken protest haloed them, as though the roadbeds resented the distortions and their shotgun wedding.

Eyes skimmed his back. He stopped, turned all the way around, yet saw no one. With another shiver, he chewed his lower lip. On the other side of Elm, a flock of unperturbed pigeons scratched among the leaves. He wondered what they had thought when the free lunches had disappeared, when the city had emptied like an overturned gallon jug.

"Let's get it on," he said aloud, and grasped his Unit. Steadying it, he pressed M for memory, then 1 for memory's first file. His neck skin crawled. He took a breath, scanned the area one last time, and touched the "add" button.

The battery spurted current into the unit's womb, where it met an egg of information that it impregnated with its energy. A field was conceived, a miniature replica of the matrix that the unit had earlier killed. Time surged through its veins, incarnating there all of Sector Twelve. Then the forceps of friction ripped it feet first into the world to grow, expand, and re-establish reality. The force flowed through it. Matter was restored.

To Kenyer it seemed instantaneous. He stood at a two-street intersection; Elm ran a hundred meters away, where it belonged. Everything that hadn't been, was again, including a beautiful woman in a bloated blue ski jacket that padded but did not destroy the lines of her body. The wind had reddened her cheeks, and jewels of dew gleamed in her silky blonde hair. She stood like a statue, still paralyzed by the aftereffects of the Tissing. She wouldn't move for an hour or more.

The breeze fluttered a white patch on her coat. He stepped forward. It was a note, safety-pinned to the nylon, addressed to him. His eyes widened. To him.

"Doctor Kenyer," it read, "we're coming for you. Be ready to surrender, (signed) Mort Primo, Commander-in-Chief, New Haven's Liberators."

The air snapped with suspense, and he wanted to scream. He looked everywhere; saw nothing. "Rover," he jabbered to the chrome star, "anybody moves near me, zap em." The console did not answer—the brooch had no speaker.

Then he inspected the woman. He knew her. Sheila Mac-something, -Dougal? -Donald? -Dermot? She was what, twenty-two, a Radcliffe grad in social psych, a volunteer worker in the Y's summer program ... and a rebel. Even now, that saddened him. He could not remember how he knew her, where they had met, who had introduced them—a sure sign that a mutual friend had been Tissed out, and that the borders of their meeting place were now a point, in the geometric sense—but he did recall liking her. She had a warm, quick intelligence, a throaty laugh, a habit of resting her hand on your forearm while she listened ... why had she come to this? A rebel, a skulker through shattered streets, a render of the social order ... he frisked her thoroughly and tried not to feel what his hands explored. His ears, keen for the faintest footstep, heard only the liquid grumbles of the pigeons.

The T-SS unit filled her hip pocket. After zipping up her coat, he shook his head. How had she gotten it? He could haul her home, wait until she had thawed, and interrogate her—clips from old, bad movies flickered in his mind; he frowned—question her, then, friend to friend, where did it come from? Is there a supply of them in town? Who's in charge of this anarchy? but no, friend to friend she would thank him for saving her from frostbite, compliment his coffee, offer to wash the dishes ... and refuse to rat on her comrades. Or were they calling each other something else?

Stepping away from her, he felt naked. He could do this at home, but ... no, he had to do it here, now, while they watched him undo their damage. His fingers danced on the Tisser's keys: M, 1, add; M, 2, add; on and on, Sheila, what did you do, why so much vengeance, what have I unleashed? and as each Tissed-out area returned to reality its image darted through his head like a vagrant memory, the nine acres of the New Haven Green, the stone lions outside Yale's Sterling Memorial Library ... the visions spun behind his eyelids like ballerinas crossing the stage. His quivering, blue-nailed finger poked key after key. At last a jab at M yielded a reading of 0: he had restored every local the unit had zapped.

Still refusing to surrender to fear, he opened the Tisser, balanced it against the curb, and drew his gun. Touching its barrel to the chips, he squeezed the trigger. The ricochet startled the pigeons out of the mounds of autumn debris. He stood and slipped the automatic back into his pocket. Executing Tissers was the one bit of melodrama he allowed himself.

Then he pivoted to scrutinize Sheila and had to fight the temptation to delve into his pocket once more. Why not, he thought, she's a rebel ... but I'm not a killer. No more blood. Ever. And though he wanted to blame her for the devastation, he could not, any more than he could blame a match-holding baby for a fire-gutted house. It was his fault. He had devised it, produced it, and given it to the government to use on its enemies—without realizing that the government had enemies who were with it, in it, and of it. It was his fault. He had to atone. He had to put it back together again.

A bullet tore through his hand before he even heard the rifle. He ran.

Pacing the living room with barely a glance for the door or for Lady, he demanded again, "Can you get them with our T-SS unit?"

"No," said Rover, "they're just out of range. They're calling you."

He favored his bandaged hand as he bent across the console. Clouds had seized the sky, and the point men of the snowstorm sifted down. He could not hear a thing. "What, are you picking them up with the remotes?"

"Yes."

"Well, run it through the speaker, let me hear."

Almost before he had finished, a huge voice filled the room. "—tor, come out with your hands up and surrender. In five minutes, we open fire. You are surrounded, Doctor, come out with your hands up. In five minutes, we fire."

"Lower the volume," he said. "What kind of weapons do they have?"

"I don't know."

"Four minutes."

"Tiss anyone who comes close enough, armed or unarmed." He wandered to the back of the room and lifted the photo of Lady. "Why are they doing this?" he asked her, chuckling to drive away misery, to make light of his plight.

Rover answered instead. "They resent you."

"For what?"

"For thwarting their plans, for imposing order on their anarchy."

"How could you have deduced that? You're just a computer."

"I've been taping them," it said, "and I paraphrased the grievances they recited."

"Oh." He lowered the picture, careful not to scar the marble with its frame. "I'd better get a gun."

"At this distance?"

"You're right." He guffawed. Unconvincingly.

"Screw it," said the rebel's voice, "fire."

"He's got two minutes," protested another. "Let him—"

"He's not gonna come out, now willya fire?"

Kenyer hurried to the window. A gravel-mouthed giant coughed its throat clear and whistled. The house on the corner exploded. Black smoke churned toward the sky while clapboards tumbled through the air like gut-shot ducks. Broken windows stuck out tongues of flame, tongues that waggled briefly then subsided, to lick away the inside before flicking out again. "What the hell was that?"

"A mortar," said Rover, "and they are still too far away to zap."

"Jesus!" The speaker snapped instructions for retargeting. A mortar, my god, it can hit me, but I can't reach—"Rover, what the hell are we gonna do here?" Panic settled into him like ice water into a thermos. It leached the heat out of his body, starting with his stomach and spreading outward, a deadly, paralyzing chill. He knew he should do something to counter it, but the only option seemed to be to run screaming in circles. While his unceasing laughter echoed off the walls, the small part of his mind that was not hysterical vetoed that suggestion. "They're gonna get the range down and—"

The street blew up. Chunks of paving rose into the air, almost in slow motion it seemed, turning as they climbed, exposing their knobby irregularity, asphalt over concrete over pebbles, mounting towards him, spinning like the blades of a mower and his ass was grass. A window shattered upstairs; its assailant thudded onto the bedroom floor. Another rattled off the roof.

He was going to die. The next shell would fly right, would arc across the sky, a rainbow to rendezvous with Rover's radar, to slam the ceiling onto his head with the inexorability of predestination. He knew then, as his shame ran down his legs, that he was indeed a coward. He wanted to desert. Cowards do that. But he could not, because the rebels awaited and they would catch him alive, which terrified him even more. He wanted to flee, but he would rather be buried in the rubble of his house than be a prisoner. He needed to escape, but the house could not go with him and—

An idea impacted; he dropped to his knees. Oblivious to the battle, to the pebbles that still chattered on the roof, to the gruff voices rasping over the speaker, he groped the idea. It felt better than a drink in the desert. His eyes moistened. It was more reassuring than a cavalry bugle. Tears gleamed on his cheeks. It would work—and it was apt.

"Rover, can you pick up the incoming shells and compute their trajectories?"

"To within a centimeter of where they'll land."

"All right." He stood. "Any time one's going to land within a hundred meters of us, Tiss out—or restore—enough space between us and the mortar to make it land further away."

As he finished speaking, a roar exploded a street away. "How was that?"

"How was what?"

"I did what you ordered, and it missed, instead of coming down the chimney."

"Oh. Thank you. Keep it up."

Rover could, he supposed, Tiss out the shells themselves—but once restored, they would have plummeted along their initial paths. Momentum was not eliminated by a Tissing; it was merely suspended for the duration.

Curses scorched the room as Mort Primo chewed out his gunner for apparent sloppiness. "Chrissakes, it's not my fault, you wanna look at the settings, they're exactly where—" "You overshot him, asshole, don't do it again." "Well he ain't going nowhere and we got a ton of this shit and—"

"FIRE!"

The house shook, but the shell had dropped far short. Grinning as he cried, Kenyer slid into the console's chair. "Nice, Rover."

"Thank you."

"You're welcome."

The speaker shrieked, "Thought you were in the artillery, whadja do there, polish up brass? Gedouda there, let somebody else try it." "Hey, Mort, don't talk to me that way." "Yeah? I talk to you any way I wanna talk to you, asshole." "One more word, amo putta fist down your throat."

"Rover, can you zap them?"

"No, they are roughly one hundred seventy-five meters too far away."

Eyes wet with joy, he slapped his knee like a man watching another take a pratfall. "What if you were to Tiss out two hundred intervening meters?"

"That would bring them into range."

"All right!" Standing, wiping away the tears, he pointed to the horizon. "CHARGE!"

Scenery lurched.

The speaker fell silent.

"How's that?" asked the console.

"How's what?" His hand ached, and he wondered where he had hurt himself. A draft curled around his ankles. Outside, winter had chosen its tactics, and its snowy army parachuted down. A crater filled the street out front, and the house on the corner burned like a bonfire. He could not remember why. "Rover, what's going on here?"

Patiently, it told him.

The sun had gone down. He disliked it. He seemed to live in darkness these days, as the whole world did. He longed for light, for shorter nights ... and wondered how many years this particular night would last.

"M, 1, add."

The gun emplacement appeared.

Some of the rebels were already half-buried by the snow. That part of him which hated wanted to leave them there, to let Nature cleanse the world with her life-stealing frost, to have the worms and rats and dogs rid the city of its vermin ... but he could not. Though they had ruined everything, he had shown them how. Their deaths would also be his fault.

An even dozen of them littered the street. Gasping with each throb of his wounded hand, he dragged them up a slippery, sloping lawn and laid them shoulder-to-shoulder in the vestibule of an apartment house. One had to be seventy if she was a day; a couple were barely teens. They were black and white, big and small, ox-necked healthy and hollow-cheeked ill. He pushed them close together and shut the door, thinking, that'll keep 'em from freezing till they wake up, most of them at least, and I can't do more because there's no more I can do.

Then he walked to their pickup truck, collecting rifles and handguns as he went. Water spotted a patch of bare metal on the hood, where the engine's heat had held out to the last calorie. In the open back, half an inch of fluffy whiteness hid half a ton of high explosives. He set the weapons on top. He muscled the mortar up to the tailpipe. Then, after deciding where to run, he pulled the pins on two grenades and flipped them into the arsenal.

He was seventy meters away when God clapped His hands. The noise or the shock wave or the release from sprinting with an unprotected spine knocked him flat on his face. He tobogganed along the icy street, and snow curled up his nose. Around him rose plopping, hissing noises as bits of shrapnel made steam with their fire. He looked over his shoulder. What was left of the pickup was a roost of jeering flames.

He trudged home.

Drink in hand, he was about to select a book from the shelf when Rover said, "You have asked me to remind you every day, at this time, that you wish to check File Thirty-three on Unit Two."

Shrugging, he crossed to the console and extracted the unit. "What's in this file?"

"I'm sorry, but you have also asked me not to tell you."

"I hope it's not outside."

"Oh, no—it's the door at the other end of the living room."

His black eyebrows lifted. So he solved the mystery of the door every day, did he? Funny he had never left it solved. "How long has this been going on?"

"One hundred thirty-four days."

He set his drink on the console. The ice cubes clashed, then swam wary circles around each other. He stared at the door, so innocent beneath its varnish, and visualized the cinder blocks within. "Do I really want to know what's in this file?"

"You ask that every day," said Rover, "and every day I say, 'I'm only a computer. This is one you'll have to decide for yourself.'"

The ten meters seemed like thirty. A nameless dread put its hands on his chest and tried to push him back, away; he lowered his shoulder and plowed through it as he had in high school football. A hinge creaked as the door swung. "M," he pressed. The cinder blocks met his probing stare impassively, holding their secrets in their hollow hearts. "33," he prodded.

His hand trembled. What the hell could it be—"ADD!" he jabbed.

"The TV room?" he asked as his finger lifted. It had once been a porch, but when Emily reached junior high and metamorphosed into a high-volume TV/radio addict, he hired carpenters to put up walls and install vast quantities of soundproofing. A small room, three meters by five, it had evolved into Emily's refuge, and no one entered without her permission.

"Emily?" He groped for the light switch, even as he recalled (1) he'd forgotten all about her, and (2) there was an excellent reason for it.

The overhead fluoresced into brilliance; it spotlit a sleek, raven-haired beauty: Emily, she of the gray eyes, snub nose, and the grin so real, so bonding, that it made mirrors out of the faces it shone upon, like the sun does with puddles of muddy water. Now, there was no smile on her smooth lips. There was alarm. There was surprise in her over-the-shoulder look. Pleading, in her upraised hand.

And one hundred thirty-eight T-SS units at her feet.

Now he remembered. The political arguments over dinner. The late nights waiting for her to return from her meetings, until came the night she refused to return. The questions she asked about his work. Then the troubles, the power that failed, the pipes that puffed air, the madness of a disintegrating world ... and the guilt, constant, overpowering everything but the embryonic suspicion that maybe it was not, after all, completely his fault. That maybe someone else had ... and then, in August, while he lay in his lonely, king-sized bed, a truck had come up the drive. Booted feet cracked gravel on cement. Husky voices grunted with effort. Through the open windows—but not through the soundproofed walls—came the soft thunks of set-down cases. He had waited for the truck to leave, to rumble down the late-night street and purr off into the distance. Bathrobed, full knowing what he would find, he had set his T-SS unit before leaving his bedroom—then moved through the house like the night itself and worked the doorknob with a stealthy hand and saw the evidence and—

"Traitor!" he shouted again, as he had that night. "You thief!"

Then, she had spun and shrieked and almost cried.

Now, she was frozen, a statue of guilt.

He hated her. Himself, as well.

He wanted to beat her, to kill her, to take on her revenge for the world she had destroyed. Yet that was impossible. He was not God. He was not the State. He was one man, betrayed by his daughter. He was Prometheus at an arson. His gut ached; his heart wept. He was alone, and would be forever, even if he let her thaw.

What could he do but the same thing he'd done for one hundred thirty-four days?

"Rover," he said, "remind me to inspect this file tomorrow."

"Yes, Dave."

He reached for the light switch and forced a laugh. It hurt. "Merry Christmas."

He hit the "subtract" button.

Forehead pressed into the cinder block wall, he wondered anew just what it concealed, and why he was holding a T-SS unit.

The house was very quiet, as a house tends to be when it shelters only one tired man and his flawed memories.

He picked up the photograph. Lady was beautiful. A man could spend a long time with her intelligence, comfort, and cheer ... she would leave a large hole in him if she ever left.

He had more than a few holes in him—but their borders were points, in the geometric sense, so he could not tell where they were.

Setting the portrait down, he laughed a little.

And cried a little.

Then took a book off the shelf and hoped that it would be filling.

[6]
LETHEAN LAMENT
APRIL 1995

A s civil wars went, it had been a quiet affair.

Morning sun in his eyes, Colonel Deke Singleton crept up on an eight-room ranch house with gray aluminum siding. Hillocks of spaded soil had replaced its lawn. Overhead whupped the eggbeaters of its windmill. Solar cells sparkled on the tilted roof. He blinked and switched on the scanner; its immediate bee-buzz announced the proximity of a T-SS unit, a functioning one. Ahead, then, lay the enemy. He crawled closer, peering through the yellow blooms of a forsythia. No sentries patrolled the grounds.

In another war he would have called for an air strike or a paratroop assault—but in this one, he was on his own. The fliers were gone, the paratroops exiled. It was a war of individuals, with the rebels shredding the tapestry of America, and a handful of loyalists trying to reweave it.

At times he wondered why. Middle-aged, exhausted, he derived no personal satisfaction from the conflict—even surviving an ambush failed to thrill him as it had thirty years earlier, in the Nam. Logistical support was non-existent. Reinforcements were for daydreams. Still he persisted.

He felt almost a compulsion, a quasi-mystical sense that the

Union, once sundered, had to be reinstated for him to accomplish anything meaningful. He had met too many homeless, too many starving. The economy had had niches for them when it was complex and highly interdependent. When things fell apart, though, when the distribution network collapsed utterly ... he carried in his memory an image of a naked two-year-old crying in the Vermont winter, tears frozen to his swollen belly.

Habit drove him, too: a soldier, he obeyed his commander-in-chief, especially when he had a personal motivation as well. He had lost most of his past in the first phase of war and would not regain it until the rebellion had been put down.

So he fought.

For months he had been sorting through a nightmare abandoned by its survivors. New Haven County was a mad jumble of areas that should not have abutted each other, but did, like a jigsaw puzzle with half the pieces removed and the rest jammed together.

The cause was the T-SS unit. He did not know how to regard it because, in a sense, it had made him obsolete. Before the war, he had put his faith in massed armies, mighty warships, thundering bombers—but what good were they if one person, with a tap of his thumb, could hurl them off this earth and out of this time—yet splash no blood on his hands?

He pulled his own out of his knapsack, opened its first-corner indicator, and drove that into the ground. Estimating sixty-five meters to the front of the tract, and fifty more to the north boundary, he punched those numbers into the unit. Then he hit the subtract button.

He and half the forsythia fell into the street. It could have caused a car crash—did anyone still drive? He rose, and brushed crushed oak leaves off his lumberjack shirt. The knees of his blue jeans were muddy and wet.

"What am I doing here?" he asked. A cloud stole the sun and shivered him with chill.

"You just Tissed out 3250 square meters of prime residential area," said a metal voice from within the pack. "Presumably, you did it because there was a T-SS unit on the premises."

"Oh?" Hugging himself, he shook his head. He had solved the problem of Tisser-caused amnesia by carrying the Memory in his backpack. Its etched electrons let go of nothing. "I did, huh? Well—"

Jacking the Tisser into another of the machines the fallback Pentagon had been thoughtful enough to provide, he said, "Have you got the coordinates of the most recent Tissing, Mapmaker?"

"Yes." The Computerized Cartographic Unit was a taciturn device, with a vocabulary limited mostly to its specialty. "Store?"

"Yes. What file is that?"

"Memory One," said the CCU.

He recalled Memory One on the T-SS Unit and hit the add button.

The forsythia bush, doubled in size, stood sixty-five meters away, on the far side of a freshly spaded vegetable garden. He gathered his gear and headed in, not even bothering to unsnap the holster of his automatic. It would not be necessary. The trip through—across?—time and space would temporarily have paralyzed the occupants of the gray ranch.

He wondered if the frozen ones were aware—and, if they were, if they felt like they had been damned. He had felt that way, once, on the street around the corner, where he had grown up. His poodle, Nancy, had run out into traffic. A word would have stopped her. A quick scamper could have snatched her back. He had been a statue. Anxiety—fright—the imminence of death—something had sealed his lips and pinned his feet to the crabgrass. Hating himself, he had watched the car—a scarlet '52 Chevy, with two men arguing up front—watched it glide toward the inevitable collision. There had come a thud. A yelp. A screech of tires.

He could not move. Hand outstretched, eyes overflowing, he tracked Nancy's flight and saw her bounce, twice, when she hit.

Red seeped through her cropped fur to stain the concrete. Still he was paralyzed.

His father, a truck driver with Marine Corps tattoos on his forearms, had had to carry him home. His tears had watered the faded blue anchors. The old man hadn't said a word, but made it plain that he knew, and that he forgave.

A long time passed before Singleton himself could do the same.

The eaves threw cool shade, and he shivered again before he went in. An orange-and-white ball of bad temper stretched, hissed, and streaked out the open back door. Why do cats recover so quickly? he thought. A paunchy man and a varicose-veined woman were frozen in position at the kitchen table. The man wore a T-shirt and clutched a sweaty stein of beer; the woman peered myopically at a sock she'd been darning. Music blared from the living room.

"Turn it down!" he shouted, then stopped, off balance, and shook his head. Who'm I talking to? Nobody in the house could have reacted, even if someone could have heard. Damn mission's getting to me ...

The scanner buzzed, not beeped, so the T-SS unit still had to be more than two meters away. He tugged the beer out of the frozen man's hand. It was not his brand—in fact, it was probably home-brewed—but it was cold. It tasted very good.

Still rattled by his behavior, he lingered a moment in the kitchen. The couple seemed too prosaic to be rebels—but that was the saddest part of the war. The enemy were not struggling to impose their values on anyone else. For the most part, they were fighting to keep society's standards from being forced on them. They were secessionists, really. Dropouts. They wanted to be left alone to live their own lives—and were not willing to bankrupt themselves to pay for their own coercion.

He could understand. Retirement was close. A couple acres in the country, a snug little house built to his specs and not HUD's, the freedom to pull weeds without having DEP jail him for endangering a species ... He could empathize with their goals. It was just their methods he abhorred.

The stein thunked on the kitchen table. He trotted through the living room—practically tripping over a boy sprawled in front of the screaming record player, chin propped on his hands —killed the music, and thudded up the stairs. The light switch worked just fine. Like most rebel homesteads, the gray ranch was self-sufficient in energy. Which was why they did not mind zapping power lines. It did not hurt them, but it did throw the rest of society into such chaos that nobody had time to end the rebellion.

The scanner beeped outside a bedroom, a place of frilly pink and white. A young woman was slouched deep in a skirted armchair, reading a library book—probably stolen, he thought cynically—on organic vegetable gardening. The T-SS unit lay on her desk.

As he plugged it into the Mapmaker and waited for the CCU to store the coordinates of the areas that had been Tissed, he caught sight of himself in the woman's full-length mirror.

His face was dirty and unshaven, with black fatigue pouches under his brown eyes and wrinkles all through the fifty-year-old skin. In the right cheek a muscle twitched. A good sleep would have cured it, but no place in town felt safe enough for him to let down his guard. He wanted to wake up the next day, not the next year—or century.

At least, he thought, turning sideways, that damn gut's gone. Long-range patrols do some good ... his belt had not had so many spare holes since the Delta in the sixties ... he had slept poorly then, too. But he had found himself in that war and hoped he could do it again in this.

The Mapmaker gave a polite burp. After separating the two units, he tossed both in his knapsack. He would not need them for a while.

As he tried to muster the energy to leave before anyone awoke, his gaze passed over the woman. He hesitated, hand at his belt buckle. She had long legs, high, full breasts, and a silky blonde mane; she wore a blue halter top and tight short-shorts, and he almost touched her. But he turned away. He was not as young or as strong or as selfish as he had used to be—though he told himself that he abstained because it would have smacked too much of necrophilia, and he wanted no more to do with corpses.

Something caught his eye just before he stepped into the hall: a holo-cube. Roughly 10 cm. on a side, it sat on the woman's maple dresser. He picked it up. The figure inside, wearing dress greens, polished insignia, and all the ribbons, was himself. Next to him stood a stranger.

Slowly he sank to the edge of her bed, cube balanced on his palm. How the hell—What was she doing with a holo of him? Looking her up and down, he decided that she would have been impossible to forget unless Tissed totally out. But how had she come by a holo of him?

A tiny itch began to irritate the darkness at the back of his head: a part of him was trying to recall an object, person, or place that had been zapped—but the memories were gone. All that remained was the awareness that he had forgotten ... something. He sensed a connection to the cube.

"Memory." He and the machine were building frameworks of reverberations around those hollow spaces, frameworks from which to deduce the forgotten, like plotting a pebble's splash point from the outermost ripples. "New file, titled, ah, 'Blondie.' Faint recollection: beach, sand, I'm young and self-centered, night and bonfire and beer, lots of it, blanket and a girl in a terrycloth robe. We're alone and she's bombed and ... overlay, much later, stinking jungle mud, I remember remembering that, and thinking that I'd actually screwed myself. That she'd been the prey, but I got trapped."

Then, taking the cube, he frisked the house for guns, and found a pair of M-19's in the cellar—along with thousands of rounds of ammunition in wooden cases stenciled PROPERTY

US ARMY. He carried them out to the car and set them in the trunk, thinking No sense making life more dangerous for the GI's coming in afterwards ... if there are any GI's left by then ...

The teasing April sun soaked into his tired bones. The cat was up in a bare-branched apple tree, slapping unrecovered birds off its limbs. It made no sense that felines recovered so quickly—but then, cats obeyed their own rules. Across the privet hedge, in the next yard, a pack of bony dogs chased each other through an abandoned garden. Eyes wary, he siphoned all the gas out of the rebel's car and put the jerry can in his trunk. If they wanted to get around, they could walk—they and their friends had taken out most of the through roads, anyway. Then, looking over the hedge again, he returned one rifle and four clips of ammunition to the kitchen. Half-wild dogs shouldn't be unleashed on anybody.

"What's closest, Mapmaker?" he asked, when he was back at the car.

"A large lot 9.6 kilometers due south on Whitney Avenue; it appears to be the Hamden City Hall, Police Station, et al. And if you are going to stand in the sun, please expose my solar cells. The battery is weakening."

He did as the CCU had asked, then looked down Whitney. A clean, brisk breeze riffled past. Nine point six klicks would sink him in the middle of Long Island Sound. Somebody—or many somebodies—had Tissed a lot of that area out. "Got an address on that?"

"About 2370 Whitney. And thank you for the sun."

"You're welcome." He got behind the wheel of his '87 Dodge, slamming the door hard because the dent had warped the frame, and set out. He kept a careful eye on the numbers to either side. They ran sequentially, but with huge gaps. 8229, for example, stood between 9813 and 7717.

He drove slowly, into a sun unblurred by smog. Rotting leaves and broken branches covered the pavement. The human garbage, wrapped as it was in nature's winter coat, was invisible.

His skin prickled. He did not like traveling through territories man had given up. The rules did not hold there. Anything could happen—and probably would: to him.

"Memory," he said, "Blondie file. Any idea yet what that lost memory is?"

"You haven't input enough data yet," it complained. "Lacking that, I can only offer an elementary deduction: it concerns a close relative, or an item of high intrinsic value, such as a gold ingot, or a new carburetor."

"A close relative?" Blondie? No ... He would have known if they had ever been related, in any way, shape or form ...

The growl of a motorcycle was all the warning he got. He yanked the wheel hard right; the car screeched into a side street. The cyclist did not try to make the turn. She was too busy aiming and firing the M-19. A bullet chewed through the soft metal of the left rear fender but missed the gas tank. It was the only one that came close. Maybe Blondie was a lousy shot. Or maybe, when she had twisted her unhelmeted head, the wind had whipped her hair into her eyes. Either way, he was grateful to be alive.

As she sped down Whitney, he kicked himself. I'm getting too old for this, he thought. Making too many damn mistakes ... He tallied them on his fingers. Lessee, like a chump I figured nobody'd chase me, that's one, and I took too long, that's two, then I hadda be a good guy and leave 'em the damn gun, that's three, and then I must have blown the search 'cause she didn't build that damn chopper in the last twenty minutes, which is four, and thank You, Lord or Whoever, for watching over slow, stupid, outtapractice me ...

It was rare that one was allowed to survive four major mistakes. Lucky for me Blondie made the last one ... Climbing back into the Dodge, he turned it around and headed down Whitney. He was not pursuing. He was just going to where he had been going in the first place.

Oughta have my brain checked; somebody's gunning for me

and I'm carrying on like nothing happened ... he did not know what else he could do. He had already lost her, but Town Hall was right down the road, waiting to be thawed. That was what he was there for: to put the pieces back on the board so the players—all the players—could get back in the game.

The 1900 block was to the right; he backed up fifty meters to 2406. Town Hall would materialize somewhere between the two, and he would get there more quickly going forward. The car swayed when he braked. Suddenly he screamed, "You don't like the way I drive, you can walk, damn you!"

"Pardon?" said the Memory.

Eyes squeezed shut, he rubbed the bridge of his nose. "Sorry. Not you. I—I don't know what happened there. Just ... maybe I'm going nuts. For a minute it was like somebody else was in charge; using my body to shout his words ... I dunno. This keeps up, maybe I better call for help."

"Please," said the machine, "this might have a bearing on the absences you feel. If you can offer any new insights—"

"Yeah, right." To buy time to calm himself, he tested the radio—still nothing—then, queasily, tried to think. Outside of the sense that he, maybe the region's last capable person, had a duty to return the world to what it had been ... "Wait. It's very strong, that much I know. And it's associated with memories of ... well, I can taste ice cream, chocolate chip, rich, creamy, the chips are sweet but scratchy on the tongue and I'm licking it, must be a cone ... the sky is clear, the air is fresh, breathing is fun for a change, there's a gentle wind but it's soft and warm, all full of spring scents ... I am high, happy, and leaning on a wrought-iron gate, a big one, its top goes up into shadows and I can shake it forever without even rattling it ..." It would fit, he thought, and opened his eyes. "That's all I can come up with."

"Sorry," said the Memory. "No correlations. You'll have to input hard data or become very serendipitous."

"Me?" He snorted. "That'll be the day. Let's thaw this place, all right? Mapmaker," he said, digging Blondie's Tisser out of the knapsack, "what memory file is this place stored in?"

"Eighteen," it said almost instantly.

He punched the buttons. M, 18, Add.

Ten snow-covered acres, dotted with icicled buildings, shoveled pathways, and naked trees, were suddenly there. Just as they had been all along, insisted his personal memory, the one with the synapses subject to bamboozlement by T-SS units. But they had not been. For months they had been—not-there. While they had been not-there, his personal memory, which had grown up nearby and passed those ten acres maybe ten thousand times, had not even noticed their absence.

He pulled the scanner out of the lumberjack shirt's pocket and activated it. Zero. No Tissers functioned anywhere within a kilometer.

As he sat in the littered front seat of the Dodge, listening for the roar of a motorcycle, a puzzled dog ambled out of the fire station. On a patch of bare driveway suitable for flea-scratching, it raised its head and sniffed. Padding over to a mound of gray snow, it tagged it as its own. Then it sniffed again. April air and February scenery confused it. So it settled back to scratching.

He had an itch of his own. "New one, Memory," he said. "Blondie file. I'm in the shower; the phone rings. I answer it—that's all."

"What was said?"

"I ... can't recall. My stomach's uneasy, though. I'm scared. I'm dripping on the rug and the towel's slipping. I have to steady myself."

"Where was this?" Its metal voice was relentless, its integrated appetites, voracious.

"Home." He took a breath. "I think. Someplace familiar, the bathroom was friendly."

"Fort McNair, in the District?"

He had lived there just before the war. He knew nothing about it—it must have been zapped shortly after he had been sent to Connecticut—but the address was on his driver's license. "I don't know," he said. "Maybe. But—"

"Exactly."

The fire station was still somnolent; the neighborhood, deserted. He remembered the Delta's being that way, just before an ambush. He unsnapped the holster flap. He wore no uniform, the car had been commandeered, and he could have passed for a derelict—but the rebels would know that anyone restoring the old order had to be their enemy. And Blondie had spotted the Dodge once. It was time to be moving on. "What's next, Mapmaker?"

"Is Dixwell Avenue here?"

Instinctively he glanced to the right and knew from the reflex that looking was unnecessary. If the street had been gone, the question would have mystified him. "Yes, it is."

"Go down it to Route 15, the Wilbur Cross Parkway. The interchange—"

"I think I'll pass on that." Thawing one freeway clover-leaf— the 95/91 tangle downtown—had taught him that while people took an hour or so to awaken, inertia manifested itself instantly. The fires and the blood still haunted his dreams, sometimes commingling with bomb-flattened villages. "What else have you got?"

"An address on East Rock Road, New Haven. Some five kilometers down Whitney."

"Huh." Two kilometers away was the ocean—and that interchange. He put the car in gear and rolled south, wondering what kind of woman Blondie was, to have taken out a city government center, a section of parkway, a private house ... and to come chasing after him. What kind of cause was hers, that it could so casually eliminate huge chunks of time and space? Didn't it appreciate what the rest of the country had done for it?

Rifles muttered in the distance. His fingers tightened on the wheel. The book said he should investigate. The book can take a flying leap at a paper shredder, is what the book can do ... He was too old. Besides, it was probably internecine warfare in the rebel camp, or somebody fighting off wild dogs. Either way, it was not his problem. His job was to restore the county so somebody else could end the war.

The government had come perilously close to never realizing there was a war. If the T-SS unit had not been a Defense Department invention to begin with, it might never have caught on. Most people still had not figured it out. They did not notice that things had been Tissed out; they did not miss them. What they did notice was the collapse of civilization-as-they-knew-it: power lines that delivered no power, telephones that died without a whimper, pipelines that gushed their contents into thin air ... he himself, rounding a bend the preceding fall, had almost wrecked his car when the road abrupted into a Maryland horse pasture. Deciding the drinks had been too strong, he had gotten out and walked to a phone booth to call—but when he had gotten there, he could not remember whom to call, or what the number was, or even why that unmemorable character could have helped him in the first place. So he returned to the car and drove halfway home, at which point he forgot his destination ...

He slowed to a halt as close to East Rock Road as he could come. Whitney ended three meters in front of him and, apparently, resumed again fifty meters to the west, behind someone's house. Mapmaker provided the file number; he punched the buttons.

Another seventy meters of avenue returned to reality. A snowplow ran over a Toyota, then veered into a mailbox that stood its ground. Impact must have knocked the driver's foot off the pedal. The motor chugged away without the plow's tearing the box out of its foundations.

He hit the scanner, but again it stayed silent.

The M-19 stuttered! Chips of icy pavement flew through the open window. He sailed out the window on the passenger's side, catching his knee on the door and scraping his left palm raw when he landed. "Stop it!"

"Come out with your hands up, crat," she shouted back. Fear and strain harshened what was probably a musical voice.

"Whaddaya think I am, crazy?" He needed the Dodge, so he sprinted from its flank to the shelter of a concrete bus-stop bench. Blondie was a lousy shot—the bullets hit behind him all the way.

Out of breath, he crouched in a snow heap that was starting to melt. He spotted her across the street, lying behind a huge azalea. "Give it up!"

"Fuck you!" The gun reiterated her sentiments, but the bench shrugged them off.

Why's she trying to kill me? he thought. The unit? Or has she got a special hate for me personally? He listened to a jaybird jeer at the both of them while his heart stopped racing. Feet in the street crunched sand and salt. She was coming. He waited—then jack-in-the-boxed up. Her blue, blue eyes popped wide. The gun barrel jabbed towards him. Her trigger finger—

He blew her left knee away.

"Sorry," he muttered through her shrieks, as he ran for the car, "I had to do it."

By the time he returned, she had passed out. Damn, wanted to ask her—Her blood was spurting, pooling, painting the ice. He whipped a tourniquet around her thigh, then zapped her out of existence—with his Tisser, not hers.

Stumbling in a snowy intersection, he had to ask, "What am I doing here, Memory?"

"You Tissed a woman who'd been shooting at you. I believe you wounded her, and Tissed her so she wouldn't die for lack of medical treatment."

"Oh." He scratched his head and attempted to remember her. He could not. But there was a niggling ... "Media," he said bemusedly. "It was a reporter on the phone, wanting to know what a career army officer thought of—of—"

"Go on," said the Memory.

"No, that's all ... wait! Right at the end, she said, uh,

'Colonel?' And I said, 'Yes?' And she said, 'Can you remember why I called you?' And I said, 'No, no, I can't, I thought you—' And she said, 'Uh-uh, g'bye,' and hung up." He massaged the tic on his cheek. It jumped like a hot-wired frog. "It was very strange."

"Was it personal or professional?"

"No. I mean, I don't know. Maybe one, maybe the other, maybe both." His hand shook; he tucked it under his armpit to steady it. "What would she have wanted with a specialist in counterinsurgency?"

"That was shortly after the war began, wasn't it?"

"Who knows?" he said glumly, returning to the car. "It was when we still had police departments—there were sirens in the background."

"Perhaps it was a terrorist situation?"

"Then why call me? I was a nobody, an anonymous expert." His neck hairs felt exposed, observed. The street was empty even of wind and was, in its stillness, as ominous as tomorrow's battlefield. "Mapmaker, what's next?"

"Whitney and Huntington," it said. "The next block."

The car rolled past the patiently purring snowplow and stopped when the street did. Hungry, he hoped that this thawing would turn up a diner, or a grocery. Inexplicably nervous, he squinted through the dirty rear window. Nobody. Nothing. Just spring air aquiver with tension, and the screaming of his own nerves. Scrunched into a ball to make a smaller target, he asked the CCU for the file number. He hit M, 1, Add ...

The front windshield shattered. Powdered glass dusted his thighs. A dozen bullets slammed into the seat, inches from his ribs. Sirens howled like angry banshees.

Reflexes spun him out of the car and into a squat behind the outswung door. The automatic filled his hand, barrel balanced on the windowsill. In front of him, close to a hundred cops stood as they had at the moment of Tissing, guns drawn, heads down, eyes up. The off-balance ones had already toppled and lay with limbs grotesquely rigid.

In front of them, tear gas billowing through its broken windows, gas driven by the same inertia that had revitalized bullets fired but frozen months earlier, in front of them a three-story wooden house flew the rebel flag from its TV antenna. Rifles jutted from windows, but their fury was fossilized, now; the trigger fingers were petrified.

"Memory," he said shakily, standing, leaning on the doorpost, "that reporter's question was, 'What does a career army officer think of a rebel, when that rebel is his son?'"

"Oh," said the machine.

There was a holo-cube on the dashboard. Glass dust drifted off it as he picked it up. Within, his son stood at his side, proud —then—of his uniform, of his being. Juggling it, thinking of the empty bedroom where it had been, he tried to remember what he would have to tell Doug when he woke up. It was something to do with him, something important ... but it was gone. Maybe the Memory had a file on it ... the cube bounced on the front seat.

He stared at the house ahead for a long time. So much was gone, so many bonds had to be reforged. Someone had to shoulder the responsibility....

Then he walked toward the silent guns, his and theirs, to take them all from the numb hands before battle broke out again. Over his shoulder he asked, "Why'd he do it, Memory? Why?"

He did not wait for its reply. Half the answer was in his head anyway, and the man with the other half would be waking up in a few minutes.

He wanted to be there when he did.

[7]
SHEILA'S STORY
JULY 1995

Before Sheila McDermot awoke, she did not exist. She had, once, but then a grizzled gunman shot away her left knee and, with a T-SS unit, removed her from the continuum so she wouldn't bleed to death. Denied time, the youthful contours of her body ceased to occupy shape. She did not exist.

Except to herself.

In the momentless never-never land of the Tissed-out, she endured. She stared, unable to blink, at a cross-section frozen on a slide an instant deep and an eternity in area. It was herself she perceived, all crystalline static, herself shed of matter and energy and time. A soulflake that filled the universe of her exile, she sprawled and glittered and knew without thought the texture of her being. For the first time ever, she understood herself as an intuitive gestalt.

She was not pleased.

Oh, her laser-sharp mind filled her with pride. So did her organizational skills. They could break a problem into snap-finger components which her political nature could sweet-talk exactly the right person into handling. But there was, unfortunately, more ...

A flaw marred each coin of talent. Intelligence spawned intellectual contempt; efficiency heightened impatience with the less competent. Persuasion became manipulation which became a reflex that barred honesty and sincerity with the few she would have liked to admire. Even her capacity to care for the population at large somehow diluted the intensity and sensitivity of her love for one person ....

Lonely and aloof, she'd rebelled. She'd despised the system, sneered at its attempts to rectify its own mistakes. She'd had no faith in the government—"It's half corrupt," she'd cried at rallies, "and half dumb!"—because it hadn't addressed the problems she and her colleagues had so clearly seen. Like a child with a castle built of blocks, she'd chosen to kick it all down, and raise a new one on the rubble of the old.

To some extent, she'd succeeded.

That is, she'd rubbled the old.

Much good it had done.

She was not pleased, but could not change, because in the non-place where she endured, time did not pass. Events did not occur. Shiva Sheila, the misguided missile, could be nothing else until—

Brilliance seared her eyes.

Clamor charred her ears.

The cells of her body burst into flaming pain.

Her universe melted, and she passed out.

She awoke once more subordinate to time, in the emergency room of a hospital so empty that footstep echoes defined its hollows. One clock switched digits on the wall; another ticked in her brain. Returned to life to resume her march toward death, she didn't know whether to weep or be joyful.

Eyelids slipping shut, she inhaled deeply—tabletop hardness flattened her shoulder blades—an insight kited away like a rose petal on a breeze. It explained her, so she reached for it, but it wafted over a wall of fire to hide beyond her grasp. She clenched her fists. She knew it would lie there for years, and that until she forgot the value of its truth, she would grope for it again and again, but her arms would never be long enough....

She wept.

"I know what you mean," said a quiet voice at her elbow.

"D-D-Doug?" she whispered.

"The one and only, down from the mountain."

She turned on her side, away from him, so her back would shield her tears. Her mother had trained her, never cry in front of men. They don't understand. They'll think you're weak.

"Hey." His hand touched her shoulder, then squeezed it gently.

She sniffed and cleared her throat. "I ... I forgot about you." She said it to indict herself but snuck a hand to her cheeks to wipe away the damp. Apology was one thing, vulnerability, quite another. "I left you Tissed out for—how long was it?"

"Six months or so," said Doug Singleton easily. "Don't worry about it. From what I hear, all I missed was chaos and a cold winter. I don't exactly regret sitting that out."

"But how could I forget you?"

"It's a side-effect of the Tisser—a ramification we never really understood. Don't worry about it. It happened to all of us."

"So wh—" Wincing, she rolled onto her back, and took his hand in hers. He was tall, and skinnier than before the revolution, and his eyes had a haunted look, but he'd gotten some sun and let his hair grow out. "So what happened? Did we win?"

With a chuckle, he said, "The general awakes, huh?"

"Don't call me that," she said, more sharply than she'd intended. "I'm not—never again, uh-uh. Just tell me, did we win?"

He shrugged and shook his head. "Nobody won. I mean ..."

He stared at the ceiling without focusing on it. "The government's gone, so we took that round, but the underground's pretty well destroyed, too, and the country ..." He scratched a sideburn that needed trimming. "Things fell apart. A lot of people died—starved, froze, got murdered—a whole lot."

"I know," she said bleakly, remembering. "But why did it all go wrong? It used to drive me crazy, before ah—" Her hand opened and closed, trying to catch a word that just eluded her.

"Before you went in?" Singleton suggested.

"Went in?" She frowned. Voices passed down the hall outside, subdued and tired. "In where?"

"There," he said, and studied her confusion. He explained, "You know, wherever you are when you're, uh, Tissed out."

"Oh, in."

"No," he said, "there."

"Oh." Smelling something stale and wondering if it were herself, she practiced the idiom silently. It satisfied her, so she returned to her point. "I couldn't figure out why. Wiping out the government should have unclogged the system. Everything should have worked better. But it didn't!"

"Of course not." Though his fingers still curled around her palm, he didn't meet her gaze. "Because we Tissed out the economic infrastructure, too. Every time we zapped something we broke a circuit—a utility line, a water main, a road—and that knocked the props out ... so people died. Lots of them," he repeated.

Her vision blurred, then sharpened abruptly. For one instant of full alertness, she perceived how a severed high-tension wire could kill a boy a hundred miles away. For that one instant she saw an interdependent society, members as symbiotic as the organs of a body, die when its arteries were cut.

Understanding hit like a dropped rock, and forced from her the moan, "I see, I see." She would have cried out in horror and in shame—but he was there, and she knew his need for comforting. She lifted her hand and ran a finger along the taut muscles of his jaw. "You're blaming yourself, aren't you?" she asked softly. "You brought us the units, and they tore things apart, and you feel responsible. Right?"

Anguish in his voice, he began, "If only—"

"Don't!" she said. "It's not your fault. Granted that you didn't anticipate the consequences—"

"I should have! Chrissakes, Yalies are supposed to be—"

"Smart? Well, I'm no Ivy Leaguer, but I am damn smart, and I didn't think of it. You got zapped on Day One, too, so you didn't see things start to tumble down." She pushed herself into a sitting position and grunted as a knife twisted in her bandaged knee. "But I did. I was here. And not only did I not make the elementary connection between the units and the chaos, I made the chaos worse!"

In his eyes shone gratitude, and relief, too, as though he'd expected her to drive him away for his part in the disaster. "What kinds of things did you Tiss out?"

"All kinds," she said bitterly, heir now to the guilt he'd carried. "This shop-owner with a gun, shooting at me as I rode by—I took him out, and his neighbors, too ... I didn't stop to think that I was breaking a gas pipe ... just that I had to take him out. I didn't think about shivering kids ..."

"Easy," he said, patting her hand. "Easy."

The clock's numerals twitched to 10:34. "Aren't there any pillows in this dump?"

He stood. "I'll get you one."

She suddenly realized how many times she'd asked just such a question, knowing full well that someone would scurry to provide whatever "the leader" wanted. Often enough, it was Doug. "No," she said, raising a hand, "it can wait." If I'm starting a new life, I might as well cut out a few character flaws.

He sat back down. "All right."

"So what's happening? What month is this?"

"July. Dad and I—that was Dad who shot you, by the way—"

"I remember him from your holo." She wondered if he knew she'd tried to kill Colonel Singleton.

"—well, we're trying to round up all the Tissers, and restore the city to the way the maps say it used to be. We're missing a few places, so some units might have left town." He clicked his tongue. "Poor bastards."

"Who?" A humming light fixture was giving her a headache.

"The ones who're still there." Fright showed in his eyes. It was clear the experience continued to rattle him. "See, the longer you're in—" He caught himself. "That's world time I'm talking about, real time, so uh, the longer you're not here, the more it affects you. It's like it soaks into your personality or something. Even now, I—" He coughed himself short, and tightened his grip on her fingers.

"You're hurting me," she said gently.

"Oh, Jesus, I'm sorry." He dropped her hand as though scalded.

"Don't let go, just don't break my knuckles."

With a fingertip he stroked the juncture of her thumb and palm. "It's the flashbacks that drive you crazy."

"You re-live it?"

"No, no, you ... whatever mindset you had there reasserts itself, you know? This guy I know, he was a cop then, and just before he went in, his partner was shot. He felt this surge of concern, this enormous anxiety, then zap—he was there. Now, when he flashes back, he grabs whoever he's next to and says, 'Are you all right? Medic! Are you ...?'" He turned her hand over and traced the lines on her palm. "We have all these people running around, flashing back and forth. We don't know what to do with them."

"Are there many?"

He shrugged. "A couple thousand, maybe, tops. But what do you do with them? Housing's easy, and for the time being we've got food and emergency generators and all—" He waved at the lights, the digital clock, and the medical equipment banked against the wall. "But all these weird people have nothing to do. There's work, but nothing to pay them with ... we've already had a couple of near-riots. The best thing in the world would be if they'd just get out of town, but you can't chase them out ... I don't know, Sheila, I just don't know."

"Treat them like adults," she said peremptorily, "and let them take care of themselves."

He gave her a look. "First off, half of them are kids. And the other half ..." His eyes saddened. "Sometimes I think the kids are older than they are."

"It doesn't sound promising," she admitted.

"It's not."

Weariness emptied her, and she eased herself back to a supine position. "I'll tell you what. As soon as I'm up and around, I'll give you a hand."

"I was hoping you'd say that. You'll make a real difference—we need a leader. Let me get you that pillow."

She wanted to protest that she'd never lead anything again, not after all the pain she'd caused, but by the time he'd returned, she was asleep.

The next day, she awoke to voices outside the dusty, two-bed room.

"You are not permitted in there!" snapped a high male one.

"I don't take orders." Reflex hostility rumbled in that voice.

"But she is asleep, and—"

"No, she's not," McDermot called, so weakly that no one heard. She had to raise her voice and repeat it. She felt stale and sticky. The painkiller for her knee dulled her brain as well.

The door opened. A tired old man in a white coat stuck his head and shoulders through the gap. "You should be almost comatose from the drugs," he said. Though irritation roughened the edges of his voice, the wrinkly pouches under his eyes blamed it on fatigue and overwork. He lowered his face while he thought. "Since you are conscious, though ... I'll return shortly to change your bandages. Your friends will have to leave then."

She smiled. "Thank you."

He started to retreat, but instead caught himself on the door jamb and swayed back into the room. "We are maddeningly short-handed, so if you need anything that your friends can provide, please enlist their help."

"Sure thing."

Before the mechanism could suck the door shut, a large hand stopped it, and held it wide for trim Emily Kenyer. "Sheila!" she exclaimed. Her black hair brushed the arm she ducked beneath, then she hurried across the tiled floor. Swinging a hip onto the raised bed, she leaned forward to embrace McDermot. "How are you feeling?"

"A little grungy, Em, but otherwise fine." Over Kenyer's shoulder she winked at the big, brown-eyed man who'd strolled in; he threw her a salute and rolled up the sleeves of his work shirt. Seeing them both alive and well after so long boosted her spirits. She pushed herself toward the head of the bed so she could sit yet lean back. "Were you two there all winter?"

"Yeah." Dan Higgins chuckled, and foot-nudged a chair to the wall by the bed. He sat down facing the door and watched it. "Self-inflicted, though—that Fed's probably still looking for me —but the guy who got the Tisser after I disappeared didn't think my note made sense. If Colonel Singleton hadn't found the unit at the town dump ..." Something—resentment?—tightened the corners of his lips. "Never thought I'd have to be grateful to a soldier."

The artificial mood-lift of reunion vanished when her knee began to throb. Her smile sagged and melted away. Up the pale green wall opposite her crawled a cockroach. "I guess we should all be grateful to the colonel," she said listlessly.

"I don't know about that," said Higgins. Shifting position, he put his feet upon the edge of her bed and crossed them at the ankles. Light brown mud clung to the soles of his boots. "If he'd left New Haven alone, I'd feel a lot more secure."

"He's okay, Dan." Kenyer seemed nervous about something. "He's not after you, or anything."

Higgins's eyes narrowed. "He'd better not be, because if he is—"

"Hush! Enough politics for today—Sheila's supposed to be resting."

"But I have!" Sitting up straighter, she wrinkled her nose as motion stirred pain. "That's all I can do; no TV, nothing to read ... let me tell you, Em, I need something to take my mind off this place." She gestured to the featureless room. "Bad enough it's so bleak, but there's birdshit on the floor."

"You should have seen our place!" Kenyer laughed.

"Your dad's place?"

"No, our place." For an instant she seemed angry, then relaxed and blew a kiss at Higgins, who flashed a grin that belonged on a small boy with a fistful of cookies. "We found this cute little six-room house over on Winthrop, an ES-house—it has a windmill and everything, and—"

"Pardon?" She understood the words, of course, but they and their tone belonged so completely to another era that they bewildered her. She must have heard wrong. Maybe hallucinating on the drugs. "You bought a house?"

"Don't be silly," flared Kenyer. Again she looked angry, but again it ebbed out of her features almost at once.

Higgins said, "Nobody buys, these days."

"Well, then—"

"We just moved in." Kenyer shrugged nonchalantly. The fluorescents gleamed in the rich ebony of her hair. "I mean, we didn't break in—we decided against that; it wouldn't be fair—but somebody had already kicked down the door. Really, don't you think the owner would rather have us live there than have it sit open and vacant? But the cleaning!"

"It smelled like about two hundred dogs wintered there," said

Higgins. "I shoveled up this huge bag of dog shit—" He held his hands a meter apart.

Kenyer giggled. "And then as he lugs it through the kitchen, it splits!"

"All over my feet," he groaned. "Just dusty brown turds crumbling into my boots." He caught McDermot's involuntary glance. "No, I've cleaned them since, Sheil'." He made a face. "Sheesh! So anyway, I'm standing there holding this empty garbage bag, and she—" He jerked a thumb at Kenyer. "She's up on a ladder cleaning the ceiling, but she's seen what happened and is laughing so hard she loses her balance—"

"So I flail around, you know?" Kenyer sent frantic semaphore with her arms.

McDermot could just see how dawning alarm must have pushed amusement off her friend's oval face. She laughed with the two of them until Kenyer bounced up and down. The mattress lurched, jostling her knee. She gasped, then blinked rapidly. "Easy on the wound there, huh?"

"Sorry." Not a bit subdued, she went on, "So there I flap like a drunk pelican, and the ladder rocks around, ka-thunk! ka-thunk! I get really scared I'll fall, 'cause this pail of wash water's dragging me over, so I just let go of it—"

Mock morose, Higgins nodded. "Next thing I know, I'm not only standing in a pile of dog shit, I'm drenched, and wearing a bucket for a hat. That was the last straw. I just wanted to scream. So I whip the bucket off, practically breaking my jaw on the handle, and I open my mouth to roar—"

"And he blows this huge soap bubble!" concluded Kenyer, clapping her hands with delight.

Higgins shook his head. "God, what a mess that place was."

It soothed her to hear them talk of such trivialities as broken garbage bags and dirty ceilings, and to see them gaze so fondly upon each other. She looked at Doug that way. "So are you all settled in, now?"

"Yup." Higgins slouched deeper in the chair, eyes flicking

occasionally to the door. "First time in eight years I've lived at a place long enough to learn the address."

Maybe because they'd dispelled grimness for a while, she asked, "What's your phone number?"

Kenyer raised her eyebrows. "The phones don't work, Sheila."

Reality returned with a jar. For a moment she saw half a billion phones plugged stubbornly into a billion klicks of darkened optical fibers. An entire etiquette made meaningless; vast industries destroyed. All those unanswered emergencies ... "I see," she murmured, almost to herself, then winced. "Sorry. I forgot." The pain in her knee, awakening again, raised its head like a watchdog caught licking a burglar's hand: guiltily, and with renewed attention to duty. "What's the address, is what I really meant."

Before Kenyer could reply, Higgins said easily, "It doesn't have one."

She frowned. "But you just said—" Noticing the anxiety with which Kenyer watched her lover, she let it drop. "Ah ... Winthrop's a good stiff walk from here. Are the buses running now?"

"Sheila," Kenyer burst out, "nothing's running."

"But how do you get around?"

Higgins grinned. "There's a siphon in the Fiat's trunk."

"I don't know why he keeps it there," said Kenyer teasingly. "He uses it so often he ought to keep it in his pocket."

"Makes me nervous to drive around half-empty." He delivered the line with a humorous touch, but even lightness couldn't filter out all its truth. "Never know when I won't have time to stop."

Estimates sprang unbidden to her mind: x number of cars times maybe five gallons per tank ... "That's not going to last you very long."

He threw back his head; his lips quirked. "You wouldn't believe how many cars got left behind."

"Yes, but—" She thought back to what Doug Singleton had

said the day before. "There are two thousand people living here, right? If they all—"

"Em's dad and I just rigged a generator so we can run the jumps at gas stations. There's enough to go around. Remember, we've got storage tanks down at the harbor, too."

She nibbled her lower lip. It irked her that Higgins didn't anticipate the problems she saw so clearly. It worried her, too; he was usually more perceptive. "Something ought to be done about that," she said slowly. "We might need that gas later on."

He scowled at her. "When the time comes, we'll figure something out."

"You ought to ride a bicycle," she said, but when his scowl deepened, she turned to Kenyer and asked, "Ah—so your dad's okay?"

"Oh, he's fine." She answered without interest or concern. "Not real happy about what I did to Mom, though."

"You Tissed her out?"

"She deserved it! Then he caught me with that shipment of units, so he zapped me, and kept me there till May." She shuddered. "I didn't like that at all—just being aware for a billion years—that's what Hell is, I've decided." Over her face passed a hollow look, a compound of shock, fear, and outrage. "But there was something else about it—sort of like when you're really powdered out, you know? For the first time ever, the whole universe makes sense—but then you come home and all you remember is that you've forgotten something really important ...." She trailed off as she looked vainly into the past. "Damn."

"Exactly," said McDermot. She felt the same pang of loss.

Higgins took his eyes off the door to snort, "C'mon! The whole thing was over like that." He snapped his fingers.

McDermot opened her mouth to respond, but a flash of pain caught her off guard. She inhaled sharp and ragged.

"Are you okay?" asked Kenyer in alarm.

"Whew ..." She wiped her forehead. "Yes, I'm fine. It just

took me by surprise. I guess the painkiller's starting to wear off, or something."

Higgins rose smoothly to his feet. "I'll get the doctor."

"No, don't." Sweat glistened on her forehead, but she held up her hands. "I'm fine, really, don't bother the poor man."

"No, but if you need him—"

"—he's already here," grunted a voice from the door. Looking even more tired than he had earlier, the doctor shuffled into the room. "Your time is up."

Higgins said, "I don't take—" but his eyes fell to the dried blood on the old man's jacket. He paled. "Okay." He and Kenyer shook McDermot's hand, kissed her cheek, and promised to come back soon. Then they left. He held the door for her and looked both ways before stepping into the hall.

The physician picked up the clipboard. Peering over its top, he said, "I am Doctor O'Shaughnessy. You may call me Doctor."

"Sheila McDermot."

He lifted a bushy eyebrow. "I know." Then he pointed at her knee. "Is it hurting?"

"Yes, it is."

He fumbled a bottle out of his frayed pocket and shook a single orange capsule into the palm of his hand. "Here." He held it out to her.

"Thanks." She raised it to her mouth.

"Don't." He leveled a finger at her. "Hold that in reserve for as long as possible. I will not prescribe you another until tomorrow."

She eyed it curiously. "What are they, addictive?"

"No, scarce. It is necessary to ration them. Two a day."

"Oh." She set the pill in the woolen bowl of her lap. "You can't get more?"

"From where?" Helplessness embittered his tone. He glared at her, then at the window. "No one is out there to send me more. The salesman fails to call these days, and I just can't reach him on the phone."

Again she felt personally responsible. "I'm sorry."

"Hmf. Less so than you'll be after the first pill wears off."

She took the rebuke more humbly than she would have a year earlier. "How long till I'm out of here?"

"The accommodations lack something?"

"Doctor—"

He waved a hand. "Now I apologize." He took a deep breath. "If you have someplace to go, someone who can take care of you, you may leave ..." Scratching his head, he stared at the ceiling. His lips moved. "I ought to be able to spray the cast on, say, the day after tomorrow, so you could leave the following day. But no walking. Not for six or eight weeks, at least. Should you strain that leg, you would have more than just a limp to worry about."

"A limp?" she asked blankly. Vertiginous fear overtook her, like she'd come unexpected to a cliff. "Is there going to be permanent damage?"

For the first time, compassion screened the fire of his eyes. "Yes," he said. "I am sorry. I did the best I could, which is quite competent, but I am a pathologist, not an orthopedic surgeon. A specialist would have had it functioning better than the original —if I could have found one. They must have left town directly from their country clubs ... maybe when this nightmare ends, they will return."

She closed her eyes, overwhelmed by dread and by self-reproach. She was going to be a cripple, and she'd done it to herself. "Dammit," she said softly. She couldn't escape the ironic parallel between her leg and her city. Biting her lip, she fought back instinctive tears. "Dammit to hell."

He rested his blunt fingers on her shoulder. "I must go— more patients to see, and I haven't slept in thirty-six hours. Delay medication as long as possible."

"Yeah," she said. "Sure."

At the door he paused. "I shall look in on you tomorrow."

"Right."

As his footsteps faded, she held up the capsule. Her knee

throbbed mournfully, like a street waif begging for bread. She dropped back her head, clutching her chemical savior yet reluctant to call for the miracle to begin. "Dammit," she whispered to the cracked, uncaring ceiling, "Dammit, dammit, dammit ..."

The pain stayed with her throughout July, rising with the mercury, ravaging with the mugginess. It became so accustomed a burden that when the pills lifted it off, she felt fifty keys lighter. So light that her spirits could spiral up drafts of euphoria. So light that she could soar like a balloon shed of ballast.

Deliberately, she kept herself earth-bound.

She conserved the weekly allotment for the really bad times, for the jagged-edged nights of insomnia when sweaty sheets abraded her body, and it was all she could do to hold the scream-bulge in her throat. Then she'd take one, just one, and sit, jaws clenched, while crickets chirped, and a warm breeze drifted through the room.

She forced herself to conserve. The surplus built up in a brown plastic bottle with a cap that fought back when pain trembled her fingers. Depending on her mood, she called either her denial a penance, or the accumulation her jet ticket out.

There were good moments, too, spaced apart like planks in a suspension bridge. Even from her hospital bed, she'd heard that silences stretched longer than they'd used to, that hours could pass between gunshots. O'Shaughnessy had freed her, and then conjured up a motorized wheelchair. Her parents had taken her home, and for the first time in years, her mother hadn't harassed her. Mrs. McDermot even scavenged through libraries for books her recuperating daughter could read on the sun-dappled patio.

When Doug located a ranch-style ES-house, her father found plywood sheets that her brother nailed over the broken windows—"A housewarming present for you kids," the old man had said with a wink. Both families helped them move in August

15, more for the inspection tour than because their three suit-cases needed twelve hands. Afterwards, they left the two of them alone.

"You picked a good house, Doug."

He kissed her ear from behind. "Thanks."

She laughed and dodged his next nuzzle. "Let's get to work."

The greenhouse of the Energy-Sufficient home had jungled up, and most of the carp had died, but the windmill spun like a gyro and the solar systems worked just fine. The doors and halls gaped wide enough for her chair; Doug had already plugged the spare battery into the recharger. Though she couldn't help with the heavy cleaning, there wasn't much of it. A fire had scorched the kitchen stove and walls, and muddy tracks crisscrossed the living room carpet, but neither the dogs nor the birds had invaded. She scoured the stove from her chair while he ran a liberated shampoo machine across the rug.

"There's coffee on the hotplate," she said later. "The meth system's gone dormant; not enough sewage lately, I guess." He set something on the counter by the sink, then sat across from her at a pink plastic table she'd spent an hour scrubbing. "You look tired."

He massaged his forearms. Dried mud dusted onto the table; he wiped it off. "I'm not looking forward to dredging the algae tank, I'll tell you that."

"The fish have to eat, Doug, or we don't, either."

"Christ, I cleaned out a grocery store for you!" He pointed to the broom closet. "There must be a year's worth of canned vegetables in there."

"Six months, tops, I counted."

"Sure, but then there's all that stuff in the basement—eight cases of canned ham alone."

"Doug." She clinked her cup on its saucer and tried to ignore pain's distractions. "It's all finite, it's all going to run out—we have to be self-sufficient before it does."

"That means the greenhouse, too." He groaned. He let his

body go limp in a parody of exhaustion. "You going to want a chicken coop next?"

She pretended to consider that, saying "Hmm," until alarm widened his eyes. Then she laughed. "No, but we should get late vegetables planted out back—carrots, cabbage, whatever. The greenhouse just isn't big enough for two people; it's really more a salad patch."

"Well, you can do that from your chair, right?"

"No problem. The troughs are right at waist level. Can you find me some seeds, though? I can take root cuttings off the tomatoes and peppers, but I'm not so sure about the other stuff."

"Sure. Nobody would have looted that. I'll check the nursery tomorrow."

She stroked the plastic arms of the wheelchair, reveling in the warmth of accomplishment. Like sun on a cool autumn day, it soaked into her, and melted tension away. She felt secure, now, certain that her plans would insulate them from the vagaries of the future. Then she snapped her fingers. "We should make sure we have spares for the solar gear—I'd hate like hell to have it go out because we're missing a part."

"I think I can handle that," he said.

She tried to subside once more into contentment, but a stiletto of pain straightened her up. She stiffened. Keeping her face a mask so Doug wouldn't worry, she thought again of the chaos—and the refugees. "You know what I wonder," she said slowly, shaving each word clean of suffering's stress, "is where did everybody go? Where are they? What are they doing?"

"The country, I guess," he said negligently. "Where else could they go? And as for what they're doing ... hell, sleeping in barns, working the fields—I dunno." He shrugged.

The pain mounted. Her hand gripped the cast; sweat sparkled between her fingers. Teeth clenched against a moan, she flashed back: she saw the exodus roll inland like a tidal wave, losing impetus with distance. Leaving itself in any pool deep enough, it petered out quickly. Its peak coincided with a trough of collapse. The desperate displaced struggled to substitute for machines idled by the disrupted infrastructure ... accountants and secretaries slogged through muddy fields, growing more calluses than corn ... an entire populace tried not to remember that once it had wielded skills which disaster had made meaningless ... "I see," she whispered, squirming in her chair. She had caused that.

"See what?" asked Doug.

"Not everybody's got a place like this. So what are they going to do? Even the ones in the city, once the stores are picked clean, what do they do? Starve?"

The remark drew a resentful glance from him. "That's their lookout, isn't it? I mean, wasn't your revolution all about people taking care of themselves?"

It hurt her that he'd said "your revolution." "No," she snapped, "I mean, yes, of course, in one sense, but not in this context. Our goal was to wipe out government, not society. Dammit, Doug, you should know that as well as anyone."

He slumped in his seat. One outstretched hand curled loosely around his coffee cup. "Yeah, I ... sorry, honey. I took a cheap shot. Getting this place set up—" He nodded to the smoke-streaked kitchen walls "—has just exhausted me, and ... and I'm not ready to worry about anybody else just yet. Know what I mean?"

"Sure, but—" She stopped as a distant sound pulsed through the screen window. "Oh, Lord, a thunderstorm. I hope the roof's okay."

"What?" He stared straight at her, a puzzled frown on his lips.

"Don't you hear it? Listen. It's going to pour."

"From a clear sky?" He cocked an ear. The color drained from his cheeks. "That's a mob."

She caught her breath. "Are you sure?"

He scrambled up and crossed the kitchen; at the counter, he

grabbed what he'd set down so inconspicuously: a walkie-talkie set. "Come in, Lao One," he said, twisting dials. "Lao Thirty-eight calling Lao One, come in Lao One."

"Lao One," spoke a strong voice, over a background sound like fire crackling on wood. "Go ahead, Thirty-eight."

"Sounds like a riot on Whitney Avenue," Singleton said. "Far away and loud, but getting closer. I'm going out for a visual."

"Stay inside!" said Lao One sharply, extra-official concern raising his voice. "I'm there now; we've got it under control. Stay put until I show up."

Singleton's face opened with wry surprise, as though he were reminding himself that he should have expected something like that. "Whatever you say, Dad."

"And next time keep your damn radio on, will you? I've been trying to get you half an hour, now."

"Right, Dad. Over." He released the transmit button and lowered the volume, then set the small case back on the counter.

McDermot felt like she'd just reached for her sweater and seized a live lamb, instead. "Lao One?" she repeated in bewilderment.

Singleton smiled slightly and shook his head. "One of Dad's little jokes—it stands for 'Law and Order' number one."

"Like a police force?" She couldn't believe what she was hearing. Of course it relieved her that someone dared cage that beast growling down the street, but ... a police force! She remembered a rally, and the line of blue coats, and the slashing electro-stuns knocking protestors out right and left. A police force! "You didn't tell me about that."

He sagged with sudden fatigue. His eyes focused everywhere but on her. "Yeah, well, Dad got a little upset after the last riot, and ... he'll give you all the details when he comes, if you ask. At bottom it's that old Singleton sense of duty."

"And you're a part of this?"

Shifting uncomfortably, he spread his hands. "Not really, no. Dad just gave me the radio so I could get ahold of him if I needed to quickly. But I have to have a call number, so he gave me Lao Thirty-eight."

She folded her arms, unwilling to admit to him that she'd already reconsidered: that, now that she thought about it, there was a need to protect one citizen from another. She couldn't say that out loud, though, not yet, so she said nothing, and merely stared at him.

"Hey, Sheila—" A knock rattled the front door. "I'll bet that's Dad." He seemed glad to leave the kitchen.

"Look through the peephole, first," she called after him.

"It is," he hollered back, jingling the chain as he unfastened it.

Voices murmured in the vestibule. Alone, she let the stoic mask slip, and grimaced as she wrapped her hands around the cast. Nothing before the shooting had ever hurt that way. Pain lived in her knee like a drowsy but surly bear: grumbling constantly, snarling at any disturbance, and bursting into hot anger over the smallest of causes. The brown plastic bottle in her suitcase could have tamed it, but she wouldn't call on it. Not yet. Instead, she sighed heavily, sipped her lukewarm coffee, and recomposed her features as the two men came into the kitchen.

For a moment they stood side by side, and the pose showed what they shared: the eyes, the cheeks, even the jut of jaw. Doug was taller, but more slender; his father had the shoulders of a wrestler. Neither looked the type to be pushed around, but the colonel had the greater impact. After a moment she felt him and sat a little straighter. On a subconscious level of which she was barely aware, she wanted his respect—and knew she had to work for that.

She lifted her cup in greeting. "There's water on the hotplate; mugs and coffee in the cupboard above."

"Thank you," he said.

"I'll get it," said his son.

"Ah, but will you be this nice when I'm old and feeble? Just black, please." He pulled out a chair and dropped into it.

She could smell his sweat all mixed with a deeper, more acrid odor. "Was anybody hurt?"

"Fortunately not." His smooth-shaven face glistened. "Oh, bumps and bruises, but no real casualties. They were irate friendlies, not hostiles. A posse, almost, looking for bandits to lynch. Once we convinced them that we'd handle the raiders, they dispersed." He wiped the side of his jaw, then dried his fingers on his pants. "And I picked up two more recruits, so it worked out well."

Doug slid a full mug onto the table. "You did say black?"

"Yes, I did." He lifted the mug. Eyes shut and mouth wary, he inhaled the steam. "It always smells better right afterwards."

She saw him, then, for maybe the first time, as a human vulnerable to the concerns troubling her. "You don't like it, do you?" she asked softly.

"It's better than I make myself."

"Being a cop, I mean."

He puffed his cheeks and blew on the coffee. "I'm a soldier," he said. "A professional. I've shown the flag, been rattled like a saber, even spearheaded a few surgical strikes. I learned early; you do what has to be done. Even when it stinks. It's part of the job."

"But you weren't sent here for that."

"They didn't have time for precision when they cut my orders."

"I thought the other thing you learned early in the Army was never to volunteer."

"That's certainly true."

"Then why—"

"Somebody's got to do it." Raising his eyes, he waited to see how she'd take the cliché. When her mouth quirked in disappointment, he nodded. "Sorry. But it is, at least, close to the truth."

She settled back expectantly. She loved Doug, so she wanted to like his father, and for a moment, earlier, she'd even identified with his sorrow and fatigue, but ... she had to hear the colonel's explanation, first, and examine it for hypocrisy—or worse.

He acknowledged the test with a smile. "All right. It's really very simple: I don't know what the hell else to do. Now that I'm back in the field, I'm thinking like a company captain again. When you're on your own, you hit the closest, most obvious targets first. And those roving gangs are sort of hard to ignore."

"So you are acting on your own?"

He blinked. "Why? Do you think I should stand down and wait for orders?"

"No, no, I—" Embarrassed, she tried to say what she did think. Yet she didn't want to sound paranoid or insulting, and that hobbled her. "I get squeamish about—cops, government people. They started a dossier on me when I was in junior high— I've been pulled in for questioning so many times that I knew the clerks there by name. See, I do admire you—for taking the initiative, for risking your own neck to make ours safer, but I'm really leery of what else y—a police force might do, if you know what I mean."

"Politically?"

"Exactly."

"Then let me put it like this: I don't give a good goddamn about politics. I'm not here to enforce one ideology and suppress another. I'm here to keep people, Americans, from hurting each other. And that's all."

After a long moment she said, almost to herself, "I think I see."

"Besides, I grew up in New Haven." He drank some more coffee.

"How do you get your recruits?" In her hankered a need to comprehend the new system, to view the interlocking of the few pieces that had survived her revolution.

The middle-aged man's big shoulders moved a little. "However I can." He forced a tired chuckle. "Most of them used to be city police anyway, and haven't really got anything to occupy their time, so—" The shoulders rose again, completing the sentence.

"Is it like a voluntary association, or what?"

"Noooo ..." He shook his head and gazed down into his half-empty mug. "More like a civic-minded burglary ring."

"Huh?"

"Every day I dispatch four armed men and a truck to the nearest unlooted grocery store. They bring food back to the station. I distribute it. Every man in my command is guaranteed 10,000 calories of food a day; he's free to store, share, or sell his surplus. He also gets every other man's promise that we'll all do our best to protect him and his family. In return, he swears to help keep the peace in the city."

"And it works?"

"It appeals to basic self-interest." He shrugged. "It's a stopgap measure at best, but it is something. Maybe it'll be enough until the country—" He brought his spread-fingered hands together like a man packing a well-considered snowball.

"Have you heard anything from—" The name escaped her. Wa- something. Wabash? Wa—She gave up. "—outside?"

"Not a peep," he said bitterly. "My radio operators do nothing but monitor all channels all day long. Dave Kenyer's programmed his computer to do the same thing. But all we get is silence. Or fruitcakes. From the US, at least. Overseas is a different story."

The word jolted her. "Overseas?" It was like walking into a mirror and finding it a doorway. Long-ignored vistas opened to her mind's eye. Europe, she remembered, Japan! She'd forgotten that a world lay outside the rubble, and her parochialism shocked her, yet confused her as well. "You know something eerie?"

Interest rumpled his face. "What?"

"Before I went in, but after things got bad, I used to wonder about OID, where they were, why they weren't helping out—but since I got out of there, the thought hasn't even crossed my mind." She rubbed her right temple with her first two fingers. "Why not?"

Elbows on the table, Doug Singleton answered, "A side-effect, probably. Part of the flashback syndrome. Like I told you before, the mindset you had when you were in keeps coming back. You don't know it's happening because it—it warps your entire frame of reference. Unless part of your mindset there involved being aware of which mindset was in control ..." Hastily, he abandoned that verbal maze. "What I'm trying to say is that unless you were thinking about foreign relations when you went in, you're not likely to be thinking about them just after you come out. You see what I mean?"

"Not really," she said, blinking. "But I'll trust you."

"Thanks." He made a face.

She turned back to his father. "But what about OID?"

"The Organization of Industrial Democracies," he said with sarcasm, "has come to the aid of America by embargoing us. For our own protection, of course. Canada, Mexico, and Cuba started it last fall, I believe, though I wasn't paying attention at the time. In essence, they put a wall around the country. And from what I can tell, nobody has tried to scale it. Our collapse caused too much confusion overseas: economically, diplomatically, militarily ..." Sighing, he scratched the bridge of his nose. "Apparently the Russians have gone adventuring, and most of OID's attention is fixed on ways of slowing them down. They took Yugoslavia, Greece, Turkey ... they're threatening to intercede in the Italian Civil War ... I'll bet OID's infantry hasn't seen a sunset in a year."

"And that's why OID doesn't have time for us?" She felt insulted but wasn't sure why.

"Pure speculation. They could have sent a contingent over to see what's going on and had it Tissed out on them ... think about the implications of that, for a minute."

"But they'd know it was missing."

"The computers would—but who would remember having

sent it? They'd recall talking about dispatching something of the kind, but not that particular mission itself. They wouldn't even remember the last US administration—do you? I don't—oh, they'd have all the names on paper, but not in their minds. So they'd start to get suspicious. Probably they'd have their intelligence agencies look things over, and the agencies would ... oh," he mused, scraping his cleanshaven jaw with a fingertip, "for example, they'd focus spy sats on us—but the photos wouldn't match what they have on file! The Tisser changed the actual face of this country. Everything they learned would contradict something in their records, and that would confuse hell out of them."

"It would frighten them, too, I imagine," said McDermot thoughtfully. She could see the pattern: maybe thirty nations could come to America's aid, but their resources were limited and diversely applied. They could devote themselves to a single purpose only if their national moods were united, as they would be in times of emergency. But to the average citizen, the monster growling in the east would surely seem cause for greater urgency than the maelstrom swirling in the west. Although the leaders might feel differently ... "All of a sudden," she said, "American civilization disintegrates. Poof! a palace turns into dust motes suspended in the air. They don't know why; they have no clues as to what happened. What they do know is they're all patterned, techno-economically at least, on the American model. And Russia's coming closer."

"But that doesn't explain," argued Doug, "why the Russians aren't taking advantage of the situation."

The colonel lifted a weary eyebrow. "I thought I told you, they took—"

"Greece, Turkey, I know." He held up a hand. "But why aren't they here?" His finger dropped to jab the table. "You'd think they'd have invaded by now."

"Well, that's not puzzling," said McDermot. She moved her mug to one side. "They've never wanted to rule America—"

"Oh, really?" The colonel looked like he found that hard to believe.

"Let me finish," she said impatiently. "They've always wanted to de-claw America, make it impossible for us to keep them from doing what they want in Europe and Asia, where their natural interests lie. Our collapse frees them—invading us would tie them down again."

"That's one explanation," said the colonel slowly, "but there is another factor."

She watched him fiddle with the ashtray. He spun it around and around, seemingly fascinated by it. "You've been holding out on us?"

"Sort of ... my men have been hearing one tape repeatedly, for weeks. It's General McCruthers of the Strategic Air Command; he's reading a warning. If it's not a hoax, then part of SAC must have survived intact. It's got to have food, fuel, generators—ammo and men to defend against ground attack—and working missiles. McCruthers claims that if his radars or satellites pick up plane formations or troop movement towards the US, he'll nuke the country that sent them."

She absorbed the notion of a last command in the North Dakota silos, then: "Is it a hoax?"

He shrugged. "What I think isn't important—what counts is what they think. And if I were them, I'd be a bit on the wary side." He looked out the window at the sparrows in the apple tree and sighed. "For a while, at least."

Despite the cast and the pain, she had Doug drive her around town the next day. The car jounced through potholes born of winter and nurtured by neglect. A dark humus of year-old leaves filled the gutters. The wind blew hot and sticky, but fairly clean; here and there wood smoke tanged it.

"What are you looking for?" he asked,

"People." Her eyes switched back and forth across the road, peering up every driveway and through every window. "Slow down some, huh?"

"You're looking for an ambush is what you're looking for," he grumbled. "You got some kind of death wish? A few of the gangs around here would really like to get you back to their clubhouse."

"Stop it." The suggestion left her queasy. "If anything starts to happen, you can speed up, but in the meantime, don't make me any more nervous than I already am, huh?"

"Okay." He drove with one hand on his lap, touching his pistol. "What do you want with people, anyway?"

"Winter's coming," she said tersely.

"It's August!"

"Even so there isn't enough time." Out of a gray, three-story house with red trim emerged a teenager. Standing on the porch to watch them pass, he held an automatic in his big-knuckled hand. She said, "Stop here."

"What? But he—"

"You've got your own, keep him covered." She opened the passenger door. With a grunt for the pain that lanced her, she levered herself onto the street. "Hey, you!" she called over the car roof.

"Yeah?" He slipped half-behind the pillar. His thumb flicked the side of the gun.

"Can I talk to you a minute?"

"What do you want?" he called back.

Shouting frustrated her. Not only did it hoarsen the throat, but it coarsened the message. She'd never learned to be persuasive at full volume; she'd always had a mike available. "You hungry?"

"Yeah." His gun hand lifted a little, as though he had come to associate food with violence. "So what else is new?"

"You want to eat regularly, come on over and talk."

"Hey!" hissed Singleton. "We can't spare—"

"Trust me, Doug," she whispered back. "I know what I'm doing."

The boy on the porch hesitated, squinted at her again, then made up his mind. After a glance that swept the length of the street, he came towards them, sneaker-clad feet moving light and wary. His T-shirt was more gray than white; both knees peeped through holes in his blue jeans. He stopped two meters from the car. Though he didn't raise the automatic, he gave the impression he'd shoot if Doug so much as sneezed. He looked to be about fifteen. "So what's the deal?"

"I'm Sheila McDermot. This is my man Doug Singleton."

"Nick Heffing." He nodded. "You said something about food?"

"We have to rebuild the economy," she said as calmly as she could. His taut skin and measuring gaze bothered her. "There are some things I think should be done—and I'll give food to whoever does them. How's that sound?"

"Whaddo I have to do?" he countered.

"Depends on what you want to do."

"I move around a lot. I like to poke into places."

"Okay," she said thoughtfully. "I'll pay you to find things for me." A pigeon glided over their heads to settle into the knee-high straw of a browned-out lawn. "Hop in and we'll get started."

"Lemme tell my brother—he worries."

She nodded. Her head bobbed low enough to catch Singleton's small, resigned shrug. She knew he'd understand once he got a chance to think it over, but in the meantime, she was grateful for his silent cooperation. Balky subord—allies, she caught herself, could do more to ruin a well-laid plan than any external opposition. "We'll wait," she told Heffing's departing back.

Heat shimmered off the car roof. She kept her hands away from the metal and wished she could duck in and out more easily. Down the street a cat scampered through overgrown privet hedges. Inside, a door banged.

Then the boy stepped out, followed by an older, mustachioed version of himself. When they came close enough, he jerked a thumb over his shoulder. "My brother, Basil."

Basil smiled. "Ms. McDermot," he said, "nice to see you again."

Her eyebrows went up in surprise, then twitched towards a frown as her memory failed to name the face. "Hi," she said, thrusting a hand across the windshield anyway. "I know you, but I can't place you. Basil Heffing?"

Leaning towards her, he took her hand and squeezed it firmly. "I used to tend bar at McClintock's, the cafe—"

"—by the Green," she finished. "Sure, right. Nice to see you again. You making out okay?"

"Is anybody?" He gave a snort, and a gloomy toss of his head. "We're easing by, nothing fancy, but easing by."

"You lost a little weight." She didn't mention that he'd shed his elegance, as well.

He smiled. "No customers to buy me beers these days."

"Has your brother explained about the reconstruction?"

"We work for you, you feed us?" He folded his arms and cocked his head to one side. The skeptical pose couldn't quite outweigh the hope in his eyes.

"Not that feudal," she said. "And I'm not the boss, either; I'm just trying to get the ball rolling. I envision a group of self-employed people trading goods, services, information—and everybody's invited."

Basil Heffing rocked on his heels and thought about it, to the obvious disgust of his younger brother. "Is quitting as easy as joining?"

"Of course!" It startled her that he could think she might resort to compulsion. Not for the first time, she wondered exactly what kind of image she did project. "Even easier, in fact. Just walk away."

"The gang up the street—" He wagged his chin northwest.

"—says so, too, but they lie." Unspoken pulsed the doubt, so why should I believe you?

"Ah—" She closed her mouth and frowned. How can you convince someone you won't do something nasty? Especially when the last thing in the world you want is the power to do so? "What can I say? If you don't trust me, bring the gun."

Nick blushed and studied the automatic while his brother thought it over. "All right," said Basil at last, "but you better believe I'll use the gun if I have to." He hitched up his pants and reached for the car door. "So where do we start?"

"Well—" As they slid into the back, she sat sideways on the front seat and hoisted the awkward cast inside. "First we find you cars and gas. Basil, I'll pay you a thousand calories for every backyard garden you find, and three thou for an Energy-Sufficient house."

"Windmills and solar gear, right?"

"Exactly. Get the addresses. Find out if anybody's tending the gardens or living in the houses—if they are, invite them into the project—but I'm looking especially for vacant ES homes. We'll need them this winter."

From the corner of the back seat, Nick asked, "So what do I do?"

"You, my friend, are going to find me an abandoned farm with a full complement of equipment. Six thousand calories." She looked over her shoulder into his bemusement. "You did say you wanted to eat?"

The September breeze toyed with the lazy windmills at the farm's edge. Wearily contented, McDermot paused in the bean field to lean on her crutches and watch. By the base of the twelfth mill, six owner-builders sprawled on the grass. As long as the project held its momentum, they'd eat well: already they'd installed enough generating capacity to power the huge refrigerators Doug and his crew had lugged back to the old barn, and by winter would probably have doubled it.

She was amazed at how quickly things had progressed. People must have gotten awfully tired of chaos. In the previous six weeks, more than a thousand survivors had affiliated themselves with "the group"; a hundred of them had signed on as partners in the farm. One partnership had raised the windmills, another the water towers, and a third the four huge storage sheds near the old barn. Colonel Singleton's Lao Group had gathered a fleet of trucks and stripped every food warehouse in the area. Basil Herring's ESH Rehabbers had coalesced almost overnight and had already housed nearly five hundred people.

It looked like they'd make it through the winter. As long as the frost holds off till November, she thought, gazing around the three hundred acres planted in late crops. Carefully, she lowered herself into a sitting position, left leg outthrust, and picked a beetle off a dark green leaf. It popped between her fingers. She cleaned them in the warm, loose dirt.

"Sheila!"

"Over here, Nick." Wishing he'd called before she'd sat, she climbed the crutches like a ladder, then stood in the sunlight. Its diminishing warmth almost made up for the sleep she hadn't been getting. When footsteps scuffed on the path behind her, she wheeled slowly around. "What can I do for you?"

The boy had fleshed out in the last month, and liberated some new blue jeans, but his T-shirt was still gray, and his eyes still watched without commitment. "It's that solar gear Dan wants for the apartment house—I can't find any more."

Some of her contentment faded; the weariness pressed down all the heavier. Why's everybody come to me? I'm only a farmer ... "If you can't find it, Nick, I sure couldn't tell you where to look. What's Dan doing with an apartment—branching out?"

"Aw, he's still hauling trash, but he's working with Basil on this place. Baz is doing the interior, and Dan's setting up a burner so they can cogi—cogenerate. How's it work, now." He frowned and scratched the dirt with the toe of his sneaker. "They put in a new boiler and burn the garbage to boil water to make steam to make electricity. The electricity runs the water pumps. The steam goes into the heat trap in the basement, through about a mile of pipes, and let me tell you they were a bitch to clean, and it comes out as drinking water."

The scheme so bewildered her that she laughed. "Trust Dan Higgins to turn refuse disposal into a Rube Goldberg device. And to make a good profit, too, I bet."

"Rube who?"

"Never mind. If Dan's got the garbage heat, though, why are you looking for solar gear? And why come to me, anyway?"

He gave her a sharp look. "'Cause Willie's trying to hire Dan's crew to work on the trucks."

The non sequitur made her blink. "But—"

"Look," he said, through impatience-pursed lips, "Dan says Willie is trying to run him out of business, and he won't put up with it, but to keep his partners from deserting him, he had to find more work—so he went to Baz with this cogeneration thing and all. But we need the collectors because Dan promised to keep the place at 20° all winter, and there won't be enough garbage for that. The problem is, though, there aren't any collectors left. I checked every place in town—on that damn bicycle, too." He kicked a clod of earth and flashed an appealing smile. "Why don't you give me some gas? I could go down to Bridgeport."

"Sorry, Nick." She put a hand on his shoulder and squeezed. "It's not my product. Dr. Kenyer handles that—he'll sell you some."

"Yeah, at a thousand calories a gallon." But he seemed to take the disappointment philosophically, as if the smile had been no more than a gambit. "In that case, Dan says he's going to need like three hundred fifty square meters of glass, double-pane, so he can jury-rig a solar system."

"Aah, now I understand." She looked across the carrot field

to the rising skeleton of her greenhouse. "He wants me to sell, huh?"

"You got it." Stooping, he picked up a pebble and threw it at a crow. "In fact, you got it all—I looked around, and there's no glass left, either. Ten thousand a square meter. What do I tell him?"

"Tell him ..." Mentally, she weighed the alternatives. "It's a good price, but I can't sell. And that's not bargaining, either. Without the greenhouse, we'll run out of food in about May. He could use sheet plastic, though. You'd hire out to find it for him, and then wood for the frames, wouldn't you?"

Hands shoved deep into the jean pockets, he stared at the cloudless sky. He puckered his lips as he thought. "Yeah," he said at last. "I think I know where I can find it. He's not going to be happy, though."

"Surprise, surprise," she said dryly. "You better get moving."

"Yeah, uh ..." He hesitated, and slowly reddened. "Are you coming to the concert tonight?"

"I forgot all about it." She rubbed her temples, behind which tightened the knot of a headache-to-be. "Probably, yes, if I can. Thanks for reminding me."

"You're welcome. Uh—" He backed away, awkward in his youth. "Maybe—maybe I'll see you there."

"Sure." She waved, tactfully ignoring his flush. "Take care."

"Right." He turned and ran towards the bicycle propped against the fence. Self-consciousness stiffened his sprint.

With a sigh, McDermot resumed her walk. Now you got a fifteen-year-old boy with a crush on you, she thought ruefully. Doug's gonna love that ... Even though she and her lover bicycled back to their "own" house every night after dark, he'd begun to complain that she spent too much time on the project and didn't save enough for him.

When he talked that way, she worried. With his eyes glazed and his speech clumsy, he didn't seem to be Doug, the person she knew and loved. He was someone else, then, someone pathetically afraid of being deserted. No matter what she said, she couldn't reassure him. She suspected he was flashing back ...

The night before, they'd had an argument because she'd stopped at Emily Kenyer's place to help compile the clothing inventory. "Let her worry about it," he'd said in exasperation. "That's her company, right? She knows what she's doing, and she's making a nice profit. So why—"

"I am, too," she'd said defensively. "She pays two hundred calories to fractional partners—and at the same time, I get a chance to argue her prices down. She's charging too much, and my farm partners can't afford to get new clothes. Besides that, she's my friend."

"Okay, she's your friend, I understand that. But why the hell do you have to bargain with her? Get one of the other farmers to do it. I need you, too, you know."

A pigeon glided in to land on motionless wings; the sun winked off the flecks of green in its feathers. And I'll bet he gets jealous of Nick....

Raised voices from the windmills caught her attention. She headed towards them, wondering if one of the millers had been caught poaching carrots again. All around, the wind rustled the foliage of their winter security. As long as the frost holds off ...

By the guy wires of the twelfth windmill, Willie Willams and Dave Kenyer gesticulated at each other. Five other men sat a few meters away and watched with interest. "Dammit, Will," Kenyer was saying, "I can't offer more! There have to be some mechanics who'll take thirty-two. Ask them again."

"Look, Doc," said Willams. "I asked them nice as pie the first time. No way I'm going to do it again. You got to raise your offer, that's all. Unless you do, ain't no use my asking them again, just going to get the same damn answers all over."

"Will, there—" He broke off as McDermot entered his field of vision. "Sheila, hi. Come here a minute, maybe you can help—"

"I heard," she said. Quickly, she ducked responsibility. "And

I'm sorry, Dr. Kenyer. I don't know anything about it. Willie's a genius at placement. Trust him."

Defeat settled over the older man's face. "All right. You said thirty-five hundred calories a day? All right. But that means I can only hire, um, thirty-five? Maybe one or two more. And the tech section's swamped with work as it is!"

McDermot patted his arm. "You do the best you can. Maybe you'll have to cancel a contract or two—maybe raise productivity somehow, I don't know—but you'll get by. You're filling a need."

"Hah!" But he did appear mollified. "Without those seven extra, I can guarantee your refrigerators will work tomorrow, but beyond then—" He spread his hands wide.

"One day at a time," she said, pasting a smile over her anxiety. "That's how we have to take it. Okay?"

He nodded, looked at his watch, and headed for the garage that housed the tech section. Once he'd passed out of earshot, a miller called, "Hey, Willie—that a ten-hour day?"

"Kenyer? Uh-huh. Flextime."

"Get me a night shift—the woman's sick and the cupboard's bare." He turned to his partners. "You guys don't mind my moonlighting for a while, do you?" When they shook their heads, he spoke again to Willams. "I'll pay you Friday."

"Got it." He made a note on his clipboard. "I'll get back to you."

McDermot looked at him. "Can I talk to you a minute?" she asked quietly.

"Sure thing."

"Over here." She led him away from the millers. "We're looking for fifteen new partners, to ride the garden trucks."

"Had to throw a few out, did you?" He took his pen and peeled back sheets on his clipboard. Block letters across the top of the first page read: THINGS TO DO TO SURVIVE TODAY.

"Yeah, they were eating off of other people's dirt. Same deal as before, we provide transportation and storage for ten percent of the harvest, everybody helps with everybody else's garden ..." She shook her head, and pointed to the fields, where some little kids were weeding the stand of Chinese cabbage. As instructed, they mulched the rows with their pickings. "If you could get a couple of families, it'd be perfect. The kids don't mind the stooping, and the parents make sure it gets done right."

"I'll see what I can do." He tucked his notes under his arm. "Doug's dad brought some migrants to my office this morning; they'll probably jump at the chance to get three planted acres each. Hey, I'm going over to the barn, you headed in that direction?"

"Yes. I'll walk with you—or hobble, as the case may be."

Their passage startled sparrows out of the rows of vegetables; the whirring upburst eased her onto a tangent. "There any entomologists around? Bug specialists?"

"No professionals," he said, without referring to his notes. He bragged a lot about his memory and enjoyed displaying it. "We've got a couple hobbyists, though. Why?"

"We're getting worms on the cabbages and carrots. Beetles on the beans, too. We were thinking of hiring somebody to bring ladybugs and praying mantises in. Can you find someone? Negotiable pay."

"I'll see what I can do. But in the meantime, there's something you can do for me."

"What's that?" Her head throbbed with the effort to keep everything straight. She was more tired than she'd ever been.

"Mrs. Angeloni, the lady who runs the preserving team? She says they're not getting enough business, and maybe you—"

"She wants fifteen percent of all she cans. Tell her to cut her charge, and maybe more farmers would be interested."

"Lady's gonna scream ... look, what I really want to talk to you about is Dan."

"What now?" she bridled.

"To begin with, the man won't meet his deadlines. We got

trash sitting out two, three days after he's supposed to have picked it up."

"What can I say? If you don't like the service you're getting, don't pay him. Dump your garbage yourself."

"I don't have time for that." He turned to face her. Briefly, his eyes glazed. "I got a plan, see, and everything'll be okay if I follow the plan, but if I don't ..." He licked his lips. "I got a plan ..."

Leaning on her crutches, she squeezed his upper arm. Sleek muscles corded beneath her fingers. "It's okay, Willie. Just a flashback."

He took a breath and blinked. "He's got to pick up the garbage on time."

The sun was dropping toward the clouds that stretched out of the west. Violet tinged their leading edge. "I think he was in too long," she said at last. "He's not the same. He's a lot more hostile to anything that even smells like authority ... I get the feeling he flashes back twice a minute."

"Don't we all?" murmured Willams ruefully.

"That's only the third time I've ever seen you do it." She set off again, rhythm disrupted by the soreness of her armpits. "Look, I'll talk to him, try to encourage him to fulfill his contracts, but no guarantees, all right?"

"Thanks." He looked up. "Uh-oh. O'Shaughnessy. I be seeing you." He strode toward the barn as rapidly as one can without appearing to flee.

"Sheila!" barked the old pathologist. "Have you seen Dave Kenyer?"

"He's down at the garage," she said, "but he's pretty busy. What's up?"

"He agreed to repair my equipment two weeks ago. I have not seen him since. Microscope, centrifuge, autoclave ... and yet fault is found with my mortality record. I want you to assign him to the hospital immediately."

She stiffened and tried to conceal her anger. The stuffy, fussy

O'Shaughnessy tried to thrust responsibility on her every time they met, and it maddened her. "Doctor," she said tightly, "I don't assign people, you know that. If you paid him already—"

"Before the work was finished? What do you take me for?"

"Then you'll just have to wait, just like the rest of us. I was talking to him this morning—he can't get the people he needs. Nobody can, you know that. And you also know he'll get to the hospital as soon as possible."

O'Shaughnessy looked disgusted. "Is that the best you can offer?"

She clenched her teeth while she counted to ten—and beyond. "Yes," she said at last. "Yes, it is. All I can do is talk to him."

"All right." He grunted. "I shall have to subsist on crumbs. How is the knee?"

She gazed down at her walking cast. "It itches," she said after a moment.

"Try a straightened-out coat hanger." He stooped over to inspect the scratched plastic. "It is rewarding to see an ex-patient vertical, for a change." He blinked, suddenly, and touched her hand. "They die so easily, and I feel so little. It frightens me when I notice that. It frightens me more that I notice it so rarely." He turned away quickly and left.

As she watched him walk off, she wanted only to go home and collapse.

But she couldn't.

Too much remained to be done.

The equinox had passed; September wagged its tired tail. The nights lasted longer than the days, now, and the fields lost more heat than they gained. Garden growth slowed around the city. Zucchini that in August had spurted to arm's length now seemed almost to shrink. Tomatoes clung to their vines, threatening always to pinken, but never collecting quite enough energy for the quantum leap into ripeness.

The old farmhouse they'd converted into offices was cool, nearly chilly; it wouldn't warm up until spring. McDermot didn't mind. She wore a sweater and walked around enough to keep the cold at bay.

Two older men approached her desk. Both were short and sun darkened. Slender Cyrus Gherahoulian, who carried a suitcase, had banded his thick white hair into a ponytail; Guido Angeloni was bald. He spoke first. "Hey, Sheila, I'm so glad we catch you here, and not somma the grumps. How much I got in my account?"

"I'll check for you." She punched the keyboard of the terminal next to her, and it consulted the main computer in the bank downtown. Dan Higgins had set up the accounting system for a share in the partnership. He'd thought it a hilarious joke. "That's G-u-i-d-o A-n-g-e-l-o-n-i, right?" The screen blinked into a new configuration.

"You make an old man feel young when you keep his name on you' lips like that," Angeloni said with a grin.

She winked at him. "That's 47,800 calories."

He nodded. "I wanna transfer five thousand to Cy here."

"Sure." While her fingers sought out new keys, she listened to them.

Angeloni was saying, "—counted right this time?"

Gherahoulian patted his companion on the arm and handed over the suitcase. "Five million exactly, no bill larger than a hundred. Open it, count for yourself."

McDermot interrupted. "The transfer's set, Mr. Angeloni; you'll have to come around here and punch in your code."

He stumped around the desk, ordering, "You turn you' head, little girl."

She smiled, and swiveled her chair 90° away, spinning carefully so her sore leg wouldn't bump anything. O'Shaughnessy had removed the cast, but she still walked with the cane. O'Shaughnessy wasn't sure how much longer it would be before the pain went away. If it ever did.

"There," grunted Angeloni contentedly. "She's done, Cy. Can you get me some more?"

"Papering your walls?"

"Do I make jokes about your hair?"

"Okay, okay!" He rolled his eyes upwards. "I'll find you some more." Ponytail bouncing, Gherahoulian set off.

Angeloni turned, obviously intending to speak to her, but even as he lifted his hand in gesture, the door banged open. A tall, slim man with sallow skin and vivid black hair strode up to her. "Are you Cheila?" He mispronounced her name.

"Yes."

"Hokay, I wanna take out what I got in the barn."

Not recognizing him, she had to ask, "Your full name, please?"

"José Obogado Ruiz." His hands fidgeted with the belt of his jeans; his boots gritted back and forth on the polished wood floor.

She glanced at the screen. "I'm sorry, you don't have anything in your account."

"What you mean, I don't got nothing? I been here nine weeks; I chould have a whole chitload of calories. You musta made some kinda mistake."

Once summoned, the activities record stated that no deposits had been made since July 25. "Just a minute, please," she said, a little puzzled. She pressed the intercom's button and spoke into the plastic grille: "Is Willie Willams there?"

"That he is," crackled the familiar voice. "What can I do for you?"

"Willie, we have a problem at the desk. Could you come down, please?"

"On my way."

"This could take a few minutes," she said to Ruiz, while he

glowered at the uncooperative terminal. "Why don't you have a seat?"

"Hokay," he grumbled, moving towards a chair. "But make it quick, huh Cheila? I got things to do."

Willams entered in a while, and right behind him came Doug Singleton, who blew McDermot a kiss and said, "Boy, I hope you're finished—I'm ready to keel over. Let's go home."

"Just a minute, Doug." She introduced Willams to Ruiz and vacated her chair so the placement specialist could sit at her console. Then she stepped away, forefingers working the skin over her temples. "I hate to say this, but I've got another hour here. Maybe more."

"Did you forget what day today is?"

"September 30, right?"

He raised his hands in mock supplication. "Patience, Lord."

"Well, what—"

"It's my birthday!"

She winced. That was something she shouldn't have forgotten—not when she knew how much their celebrating it together meant to him. "Oh, Doug, I'm sorry!"

"I know." Sadness darkened his eyes till his sense of humor rebounded. "That's okay," he said briskly. "I withdrew a bottle of wine and even picked out a present for you to give me."

She broke into a grin. "You always have been thoughtful."

Behind her, Willams lifted his voice in exasperation. "Look, Ruiz, the rules are simple: you get back what you put in, and no more. You didn't work, so you didn't get paid, so—"

"But I did work, man! Jesu, I focking bust my back—"

Singleton's hands gripped her shoulders before she could pivot to join the dispute. "Ignore them," he said. "Let Willie handle it while we go home."

"I suppose I should," she sighed, making a determined effort to block out the angry voices: "So what's this present I'm going to give you?"

"Yourself." He beamed. "From right now until tomorrow

morning. No interruptions, nothing. Just you and me and that bottle of wine."

She gave a weary smile, but half her attention was directed behind her. "That sounds—"

"—you crazy?" barked Willams.

"Doug, I have to." She slipped out of his fingers, and limped around, balancing herself on the point of her cane.

Ruiz had pulled a knife, a long thin serrated blade of the kind used for scaling fish. Holding it underhand, he waved it at Willams, who backed away, arms loose, eyes sharp and wary.

"Hold it!" she snapped.

"For God's sakes!" Singleton whispered in her ear. "Stay out of this, you'll get hurt."

With an impatient headshake, she moved towards the fight. The men circled each other, hissing like snakes. Irritation kept her from fear. "Ruiz!" She rapped her cane on the floor. "Stop it! Put that down."

"This hijo de puta is ripping me off, Cheila. I gonna rip him some, see how he likes it."

The door hinges creaked. Boots stomped; masculine voices called, "What the hell?"

She paid them no mind. All her attention focused on that outreached arm, that glittering blade. "Put it down, Ruiz," she said. "We'll work out the problem, but put it down."

"No!" Cobra-swift, he lunged for Willams.

She whipped her cane through the air. Its metal tip smacked his wrist. He yelped; the knife clanged onto the floor. Before he could recover it, Singleton pounced, and threw an arm-and throat-lock on him.

"Thanks, Doug."

He shot her a dirty look. "Easy, pal," he told Ruiz. "Easy, now."

Dan Higgins marched over from the doorway. "We caught the end of that, but what touched José off?"

She nodded to Higgins, and to young Nick Heffing, who

stood by his side. Her hand went back to her temple. "He wants food, but hasn't worked."

Higgins's eyebrows rose incredulously. "José?"

Willams joined them, holding the knife's grip like a pro. "Yeah, man, hot-tempered José. Sucker tried to gut me. I'm gonna call the colonel, have him take care of this."

"Hold on," said Higgins. He glanced across the room.

Ruiz stood quietly in Singleton's hold, but rage still darkened his cheeks. "José's been working for me all along, ever since he joined up."

Heffing's head jerked slightly at that, but he said nothing.

"He's not on your pay sheets." Willams made the statement a ruling.

"Of course he's not," said Higgins expansively. "You keep stealing my workers, so I just didn't enter him in. Besides, I, ah ... couldn't afford him."

"'Zat so?"

"Yeah, Willams, it is." His voice cooled to hold implicit threat.

"Well, you just did him—" He jabbed his thumb over his shoulder at Ruiz, who, released, was combing his long black hair. "—out of nine weeks' worth of food. 'Cause you got no cals in your account, and we don't pay your bills. Right, Sheila?"

She stared levelly at Higgins, attempting to read him. His hooded eyes and impassive cheeks slipped her gaze like a mask. "Dan," she said softly, "I get the feeling you're trying to put one over on us."

"Shit!" He stamped his foot. His lips thinned. "I'd pay him myself if I could, but I don't have the cals on hand, now. Dammit, Sheila, José's work is keeping thirty families warm this winter. Pay him off, I'll pay you back. He deserves it, doesn't he, Nick?"

"All—yeah, Dan." He turned his body to McDermot, but not his face. "He's, ah, he's been with us all along."

She knew he was playing on her sense of guilt but couldn't

decide what would be right. "If you're ripping off the system, Dan—"

"Sheila—"

"Willie, the farm's showing a profit, isn't it?"

"You can't—"

"Quiet!" She knew her solution was wrong—the decision wasn't hers to make, for one thing—but the situation demanded a resolution, and nobody else seemed capable of offering one. She touched her fingertips to her forehead. "All right, Dan, you can pay us back. We'll credit him three thousand a day—"

"Sheila!" said Willams.

"Quiet, Willie. Three thousand a day," she continued, "and debit him twenty-five hundred a day for the meals he must have had here, even though we've got no record. Is that good enough?"

He spread his arms. "Hey! Fair's fair, right?"

Unwilling to answer except with a look of contempt, she returned to her desk. Willams said, "Ah, fuck! I got a plan, see ..." He moved unsteadily towards the door. "I got a plan, and he ... I got—" He slammed the door as he left.

Mentally she agreed. The whole thing stank. Not only was it a payoff, pure and simple—though it could be argued that Higgins's skills were worth more than the 35,000 calories he'd just extorted—but in choosing the compromise she had, she'd violated one of her own ethical principles. It was her right, her duty even, to take the initiative in solving a problem that confronted her society—but she'd weaseled. She'd made a personal decision and used partnership funds. That was wrong. No way around it, it was wrong. Dammit, she thought, why did I ...

She entered the transaction into the terminal, which then hard copied out a withdrawal order. "Take this to the barn," she told Ruiz, "and they'll give you your stuff. From now on, if you want to eat, you make sure you're on the pay sheets."

He took the paper wordlessly and hurried away.

When she pushed back her chair, Singleton was gone.

It was a cold, gray day in late October. Crows rode the bitter breeze; leaves tumbled dispiritedly down the street. She cycled toward the farm with one eye on the sky, hoping the frost would hold off: her group still had forty acres left to harvest. The rest of her fretted about Singleton.

Moody, he pedaled beside her in silence. Occasionally he'd set his jaw and pump hard, to sprint forward a hundred meters or so, then coast and loop back to her. He didn't explain why, or even comment on it. She got the impression that he was trying to escape but could not achieve the right velocity.

"The greenhouse is perfect," she said, making the statement a peace offering. "Thanks for all the work."

He shrugged. His gears clicked softly to themselves.

"Look," she burst out, "I told you I was sorry! The damn meeting just wouldn't end. I couldn't get them to shut up! Bicker, bicker, bicker, all night long—you think I enjoyed it? You think I wanted to stay so late?"

He shrugged again but didn't lift his eyes from the pavement.

Her temples already throbbed, and it was only 7:00 AM. Her cheeks stung where the wind whipped them. "Doug, I asked you to come. If you had, you would have seen how late it broke up. Honest to God, I'm not—there's nobody else, really."

He squeezed his hand brakes and slowed to a stop. Cocking his head to her side, he said, "I didn't think there was."

"Then why—?"

He gestured down the slope to the farm. "Them. You're up before dawn, flop into bed at midnight. All you've got time for is the project. I need you, too, you know, but morning, noon, and night the project comes first. It was bad enough before, but now that you've taken over—"

"I haven't—"

"Look, dammit, you're making decisions now that used to have to be made by the partners! And they're enforced, too. Willams juggles accounts, the Lao group encourages people to fulfill their contracts ... you're in charge, all right. And the only chance I get to talk to you alone is when we ride in in the morning. Even then half your mind's somewhere else. I mean, what the hell—"

She stretched out her gloved hand and laid it on his wrist. The bikes wobbled first together, then apart. "I'm sorry, Doug, it's just—" She shook her head. "The harvest is almost in, and most of the work is done. We'll have all winter. Really."

Glumly, he nodded. "Yeah, all right. I ... I, Sheila, I'm sorry, too. I love you, you know? And I get jealous of something I shouldn't get jealous of." His lips twitched. "I also get frustrated sleeping next to you, but never with you."

"You bastard! You think I like using rhythm?"

He made a face. "It wasn't meant to hurt, honestly. I was trying to explain, and ..." His sense of humor surfaced with a smile that surprised them both. "I couldn't resist the phrasing."

They swooped down a sloping curve, coasting against the chill wind. Her hair fluttered behind like a tattered gold flag; she rubbed the portions of her cheeks that were starting to go numb. She wished she could ride a motorcycle again—that there was gas, and parts, and ... They came in view of the farm. She sighed, then stiffened, and half-stood up on the pedals. "Doug! What's going on?"

All four storage sheds loomed shuttered and blank. In their midst, around the old barn, surged a chanting crowd. Above them, a dark figure waving its arms filled the hayloft opening. The wind carried voices: hard, hostile, demanding.

"Jesus, it's a riot!" He held out his hand. "Stop here."

"No." As he braked, she shot past. "Get on your walkie-talkie, call your father. We need the Lao Group."

He raced to catch up. "Sheila, wait!"

Her knee hurt. Through gritted teeth she said, "Dammit, call him now!" She panted. Cold air bit at her throat.

"But you can't—"

"Would you stop worrying about me? Worry about famine next spring!"

"But—"

"Now! Call him." She twisted forward and bent over the handlebars.

His brakes screeched; the wail faded as she pulled away. She blinked against the wind that moistened her eyes and tried to ignore the pulsing anger of her leg. All she dared think of was that the commotion below might endanger the food a thousand people needed to survive. She pedaled harder.

Ten minutes of increasing effort brought her to the barnyard. From the open hayloft, Willie Willams conducted a shouting match with Dan Higgins, who stood somewhere in the heart of the crowd.

"It don't work that way," Willams was yelling. "No way you get a percentage."

"We want our share," the anarchist bellowed back. "We worked to build those stores, and now we want our share."

Dismounting, McDermot gasped in both pain and comprehension. She had to clutch the fence for support, then unfasten her cane from the crossbar and lean on it. As her breathing returned to normal, she realized what she had to do, and shivered. Her role terrified her.

"We don't want to get violent," Higgins was roaring, "but if you don't unlock those doors, we'll knock them down."

"You do that, man, and you be staring at two police with shotguns. They got their orders, and their orders is to keep alla you out. Now you break this up before somebody gets hurt."

McDermot blew air through her pursed lips. Limping forward, she parted the crowd's backs with an extended hand and courteous phrases: "'scuze, please," she said. "I have to talk to Dan." Faces turned, "'scuze, please, coming through, please, I have to talk to Dan."

She osmosed through and came out the other side, into a ring of empty yard half-circling the anarchist. The mob supported Higgins but hadn't yet decided to stand close to him. Except for Emily Kenyer and Nick Heffing, who held positions two meters behind and to each side of him. The ground around their feet lay bare, brown, and hard-packed.

"Dan," she said softly.

He took his hands off his hips and looked over his shoulder. Red anger suffused his face. Shouting had scraped his throat raw. "Sheila," he said. "Talk some sense into your man up there."

She hobbled to within half a meter of him, then propped herself on her cane, both hands cupped over its curving head. She was in no hurry to end the conversation. "What's the problem?"

"Willams."

"What is it you want him to do?"

"I got a hundred fifty people here, we're gonna migrate south for the winter. Too damn cold up here in New England ..." He raised his eyes to the cloud-gray sky and chuckled sourly. "I rigged six buses as wood-burners, they'll take us as far as we want —but we need our food."

"Willie won't let you close out your accounts?" she asked innocently.

"Peanuts!" He spat on the ground. "We're fifteen percent of the group; we want fifteen percent of the food. And he—" He jerked his head to the silent man who hung out over them. "—he says no."

The crowd inched forward, exerting silent pressure. Higgins's brown eyes pinned her with their fervor and their heat. She inhaled to steady herself. An irascible chicken clucked.

"Well?" said Higgins.

She shook her head. The crowd released its pent-up breath in a sound of disappointment—resentment—hostility. "Sorry, Dan."

Her voice quavered a bit; she cleared her throat to control it. "We laid down the rules at the beginning. You get what you agreed to work for—your share of the profits—and no more. You're free to leave any time, but all we owe you is your accumulated surplus. No more."

"Listen, damn you, we busted our butts to collect that food for you—"

"For us," she said gently, but he overrode her.

"Damn you, we got a right to our share. We're not asking for all of it, just for what we put in. Fifteen percent. That's only fair."

Eyes on his frustration-mottled face, muscles cued to snap up the cane in thin defense if he pounced, she listened to the distance. Away off, a speeding convoy growled faintly. Nobody else had heard it, yet. The colonel and his men would arrive soon; all she had to do was keep the crowd immobile for a few more minutes.

"You really think that's fair?" she said challengingly.

"Yes." A roar of agreement rose from all around.

"Even though you and everyone here agreed at the beginning that each person would get no more than a partner's share of anything?"

"Well—"

"You really think," she said, casting her voice to the back of the crowd, hoping to drown out the approaching engines for a bit longer, "that it is fair to go back on your word? To break your contract?"

"Now, wait a minute!" The insult darkened his flush. "I'm not going back—"

"You agreed—"

"We want our fair share!" The mob howled an echo. "You give it to us, or else—"

"Or else what?" Something shifted in his eyes, then. She swallowed hard. Her stomach shriveled to a hard knot.

He stepped towards her, raising his hand. "Or else we'll—"

Emily Kenyer scurried to interpose herself. Nick Heffing joined her. "No, Dan," she said. Her tone was so low that even the front row couldn't have heard her. "You don't hit cripples, not while I'm around."

"But she—"

"We've had enough violence, enough people hurt. You want the food, take it—but don't hurt anybody."

Before he could respond, a sudden siren wailed across the barnyard. The crowd muttered as it turned and peered and hastily parted. A sleek police cruiser glided up to McDermot. Six more followed in its wake.

The bumper stopped a centimeter from her knee. She wobbled abruptly. Releasing the breath she hadn't realized she'd been holding, she leaned on the motor-warmed hood. Above her, Willams relaxed and sat down, legs dangling over the edge. She nodded to the colonel as he got out.

He raised a hand in greeting, then shouted, "Party's over! Everybody go home."

Helmeted police spilled from the other cruisers. They wore holstered automatics and hefted insulated clubs: electro-stuns. One jolt from a stun-club could knock a horse unconscious. The Lao-men, tall and broad shouldered, looked ready to swing away.

At a command from their chief, they formed a line and snapped down their faceplates. Then they took a simultaneous, symbolic step forward.

The crowd grumbled—cursed—yet backed away. Here and there resounded angry yelps as someone retreated across someone else's toes.

The cops held their clubs at arm's length and switched them on.

Buzzing like a disrupted hive, the crowd dissolved into individuals, each making his or her own way back to the road and safety. Hostile faces looked back over stiff shoulders. Scattered fists waved.

The Lao-men swung up their faceplates. Some of them looked disappointed.

Higgins still stood near, yet apart from Kenyer, McDermot, and Heffing. He shook with rage. The muscles in his jaw rippled as his teeth clenched and ground. His lips whitened.

McDermot found it hard to look at Kenyer. Though giddy with relief, she felt a vague guilt over having thwarted her friend's lover. Especially after Kenyer had saved her. She readjusted her grip on the cane. "Em—are you really going south?"

"Dan, me, and—" she patted her waist "—baby."

"Oh, Em!" She felt like hell and had to sniff back sudden tears. "Is there anything you need?"

"Food," Higgins bit off.

His intransigence made denial easier. "Outside of that, Dan." She sighed. "I meant like spare parts or axes or medical supplies or—or anything along those lines."

"Food," he said bluntly.

"That's the one thing we can't give you," she said in true sorrow.

Kenyer moved to ease the tension. Putting her hand on McDermot's shoulder, she said, "We understand, Sheila."

"Like hell we do!" Higgins took Kenyer's arm and pulled her away. "Let's get out of here."

McDermot watched her best friend hesitate, decide, and walk off unprotesting. She called, "Dan!"

He stopped. Turning, he hooked his thumbs into the belt loops of his faded jeans. "We'll be back," he said. "Only next time, we won't leave empty handed." Then he spun around again and marched towards the road.

She sat on the cruiser's hood and dropped her face into her palms. Her head beat like drums. A presence stood next to her for a bit, then cleared its throat. She looked up, and gradually focused on the colonel's concerned features. "I forgot to thank you. That was nice timing."

He waved a deprecating hand. "Higgins is serious."

"I know." She shook her head, blinked, and swallowed hard. "Oh, God, do I ever know."

Willams, the two Singletons, Dr. Kenyer, and McDermot met that evening in the farmhouse office. Every face looked worried. Most were lined with fatigue, and a few eyes glazed in involuntary flashback. They pulled up chairs around what used to be a kitchen table. The colonel put their fear into words almost at once. "Sheila," he began heavily, "what are the odds that Higgins cached a working Tisser somewhere?"

She stared beyond him while she thought. The room smelled of coffee and tobacco—idly she wondered what it would smell like the following fall, when they'd depleted their stockpiles. Herbal tea and marijuana? "High," she said at last. "He's the kind ... I can't see how he would have gotten one, since he was in from before the shipment arrived and didn't get out till you unTissed him, but ..." She sighed. "If anyone around here knows where to find a T-SS unit, it'd be Dan Higgins."

"What about guns?" the colonel said.

She caught Doug's eye and the two shared a wry smile. "You tell him," she said.

"Dad, everybody in town has a gun—somewhere. Knowing Dan, he has a whole armory stashed away."

Left hand gripping the edge of the table, the colonel pushed his chair back, and balanced on its rear legs. Pensively he pulled his lower lip. "All right," he said at last. "I've already deployed my men as perimeter guards, but that won't be enough. We'll need more." He paused to watch the eddy patterns of the smoke beneath the ceiling. "A lot more ... Willams, Kenyer, I'm going to need all your help real fast." Then he thumped forward and began to unfold his plan.

McDermot insisted on staying in the barn, even though both the colonel and his son tried to argue her out. "I know it's danger-ous," she said abruptly. "But—" She caught herself. "I'm doing it, and that's that." She couldn't bring herself to explain her motives. They were too nebulous even for her to pin down—and besides, she knew how Doug would react.

But he knew her well, too. "What are you doing, penance?"

"Somebody's got to monitor the scanner," she said stub-bornly, "and that's me. What the hell, Doug, I'm not exactly mobile enough to skulk around the fields, am I?"

He clenched his fists in exasperation. "Chrissakes, Sheila, if they break through—"

"Then I hide in my cubbyhole and pretend I'm a coat hanger. I know what I'm doing."

"I don't think you do."

"Doug—" She took his hand between hers. "Doug, believe me, I do know. I know exactly what I'm doing. Okay? Trust me. Please."

He licked his lips uncertainly and looked to the colonel. "Dad—?"

Singleton shrugged. "She's made up her mind."

"But—"

"She'll do the job better than anybody else—for whatever reason, she cares more. So let's go." He glanced at his watch. "It'll be dark soon."

Reluctantly, Doug stood. "Take care, huh?" He reached out to ruffle her hair. Over his shoulder, his father saluted. "I love you," Doug whispered.

"Me, too," she said hoarsely. She had a lump in her throat and butterflies in her stomach and her fingers trembled so badly that she had to hide them under the card table. "Go on, will you? Please?"

At the door, he blew her a kiss and vanished down the ladder.

A barn owl hooted in the shadows overhead, drawing her involuntary glance. Mice feet scampered through the rafters.

The voices below diminished as they moved towards the twilight fields.

On the table lay the colonel's scanner, jacked into Mapmaker. Next to them hunched a humble walkie-talkie. They'd tested all three earlier that day, but a sudden, irrational fear assailed her: the batteries might have failed since. In the chill October air, she shivered. She visualized Higgins's gang creeping towards her while she waited for three mute instruments to speak ... the radio crackled. She scooped it up. "Spider here, come in."

"Web One here, all strands strung, all clear, out."

"Out," she said, though she wanted to keep on talking. No, she wanted him to keep talking. She wanted his matter-of-fact voice to shelter her from the fear that invaded like frostbite, paralyzing with its touch. She—

Buzz, said the scanner. The loop of wire above it spun through a complete circle, then shuddered and came to a stop. The light from the bulb overhead broke around the loop and cast a curved shadow on the table. Programmed for laconism, Mapmaker said only, "Spotted."

She pressed the walkie-talkie. "Spider calling Web One, come in."

"Web One here, go on, Spider."

She asked the CCU, "Where is it?" and placed the walkie-talkie before its speaker.

"Strand Four, repeat, Four. Range 9-5-0 meters." The loop jerked; the shadow twitched. "The fly moved. Approach lane now between Four and Five, repeat, between Four and Five. Range 9-0-0 meters."

"Thank you, Spider, we are ready and waiting for—" A burst of automatic weapons fire chattered through the radio, harsh and staccato and sounding almost like normal static. Two seconds later its echo rolled into the barn. No, not its echo, itself, arriving behind its radioed replica because sound travels slower than light ... and behind that flew the knife-edged shriek of a wounded, dying man ... she wrapped her arms around herself and shivered in the cold of the ancient barn ... the firefight raged on outside.

She didn't hear it. She sat in the straight-backed wooden chair and rocked, eyes closed, hugging her body to squeeze out the chill. Yet she couldn't dissipate it. She'd taken the initiative—the responsibility—and blown it. Again.

She snuffled as she breathed. But she couldn't not walk to the window.

Tracers arched across the low hills. Yellow-orange flares skyrocketed into pops of brilliance that drifted down beneath reflector chutes. Men scrambled for cover on the bare October soil. Women, too. Even children.

The radio squawked as the colonel moved his pawns. With a curse like a sob, she slapped the window frame and thought once more of the hundred and fifty who would have followed Dan Higgins into ambush: who wouldn't have, if she'd handled things better.

Through the snap of static roared exultation. "Web Four calling Web One, come in."

"Web One, what have you got, Four?"

"We got the unit, repeat, we got the unit!"

"Nice job, nice job. Did you get the bearer?"

"Down but not out, One. Nicky Heffing. Medic's taking him to the barn now, over."

She pushed herself away from the wall. Wiping her eyes, putting one foot before the other with the solemn care of a child or a drunk, she walked down the stairs. The clump of feet on wood rang hollowly through the chill, empty barn. She listened to it, and to herself.

Upstairs, the scanner said, *Buzz.* Its wire loop spun to home in on the second incoming unit.

Mapmaker said, "Spotted."

She didn't hear. She heard instead the guns and the cries. She pushed through the small door into the barn yard, almost bumping into a haggard O'Shaughnessy. He was waving a pair of stretcher bearers into the farmhouse. Blood stained the front of his jacket.

"Sheila!" He took her elbow. "Sheila, you look—"

"Nicky. How bad is he?"

He shrugged, unconcerned. "Flesh wound, upper arm. No one could lose this one. Though why you care—"

She shook loose and walked for the house.

He caught her from behind and spun her around. "No. Nick is not alone in there, and my people are overworked. Don't get in their way."

She hung her head. "Sorry, Doctor. You're right, I—" She squeezed her eyes shut, then opened them slowly. "I just feel so damn responsible, you know?"

Two more stretcher bearers materialized out of the darkness. O'Shaughnessy patted her shoulder distractedly. "Don't," he said, though his eyes followed the pair and their silent burden. "It is not your fault. They brought it on themselves. We all do. Excuse me, I have to go." Without a backward glance he hurried towards the house.

She was standing alone in the empty yard when the second raiding party crept in—on a path 180° away from that of the first.

She heard a rustle of sneakered feet. She began to turn. A rifle barrel nudged her left kidney. "Don't chout, Cheila," hissed a voice from the night. "An' don' move, hokay?"

Two more shapes loomed up before her, one tall and big-shouldered, the other short and trim. "Cover her, Em," said Dan Higgins. "We'll get to work in the barn."

There was an oblong shape in Kenyer's right hand. Moon-light glinted on its opened first-corner antenna. "A Tisser?" said McDermot.

A dozen forms whispered past, heading on cat-quiet feet for the open barn door. Two stopped, rifles at the ready, to take up positions by the path leading to the house.

McDermot could just make out Kenyer's head-bob. "Em—

you can't—if Dan takes the food!—"

"My baby will eat! You should have just given it to us," said Kenyer angrily. "Just split it up fair and square, and then this wouldn't have happened. Dan said so himself."

"But the system—"

"Please, Sheila?" Her voice quivered in the night air. "If you make any noise, I have to Tiss you out—Dan said so—and I don't want to." She shuddered visibly. "I don't want to zap anybody anymore, it's—it's—"

"Okay," she said, too exhausted to argue any longer. Suddenly nothing mattered. Once again, she'd screwed up, and once again masses of people would suffer for her mistake. Shoulders slumped, she stood helpless and alone.

Inside the barn, a motor coughed into life, and the large doors creaked. They filled that truck quick, she thought dully.

The engine revved.

Floodlights flamed on.

An amplified voice from the fringes snarled, "LAY DOWN YOUR WEAPONS AND COME OUT WITH YOUR HANDS UP."

Desperate, her cheeks pale with fear, Kenyer raised the Tisser and pointed it at McDermot. "I got her covered!" she shrieked. "Dan, I got a hostage, don't give—"

From the hedges spat a rifle.

Kenyer's head exploded.

McDermot gasped "Em!" and fell to her knees. Tears streamed down her face. Her fingers brushed her friend's warm, lifeless hand and dislodged the T-SS unit. It lay between them on the spattered ground. "Oh, God, Em," she said.

The motor roared. Three-meter-high doors burst apart in a flurry of splinters and squeals. The truck leaped into the yard, throwing gravel and dust. Higgins floored it; shots rang out. The colonel shouted, "Hold your fire! Sheila's there."

She raised her head in time to see the pickup careen through a patch of low-clipped yews and disappear up the driveway. From the barn, a man said, "I surrender! Hey, I'm unarmed. I give up." Squinting and cringing, he stepped into the glare with his hands above his head.

She didn't move until the troops came into the yard, and even then, she got to her feet only because Doug Singleton stooped over and helped her up. She clung to him, saddened beyond speech. He didn't understand, and kept stroking her back while saying, "It's okay, you're safe now, it's okay, you're safe."

After a while she said, "I have to sit down."

He led her to the fence, and they perched against the railing. Arm around her back, he held her close.

The colonel came over to stand spread-legged before them. He'd slung his rifle across his back and pushed his cap up on his forehead. "What do you want us to do with them?" He waved at the cluster of guarded prisoners.

"What do you mean, what do I want?" she asked bitterly. "I'm not in charge here."

"I beg to differ." Fatigue flattened his tone. "Like it or not, you're boss."

"No, you—"

"Listen." His eyes flicked from her to his son. "Doug, may I talk to your lady in private a minute?"

"Sure." He hopped down from the fence, stretched, and moved away.

"Must have trained him better than I thought," said the colonel, as he lowered his butt onto the rail next to her. He smelled of cigarettes, crushed leaves, and fresh sweat. He grunted as he got comfortable. "You were pretty close to her, weren't you?"

"Yes." She stared at nothing at all.

"And you probably figure that if you'd handled things differently, she'd be alive, and her kid, too."

"Yes," she said hoarsely.

"She was with Higgins all the way, and he would have gotten

her killed sooner or later. You can't blame yourself."

"But I do!"

"So because you feel responsible for her death, you'll give up being responsible for a thousand lives, is that it?"

"What do you—"

"Listen." He laid a hand on her knee. It was strong, warm, and sincere. "I was here four months before you got out of there, and in all that time, all I did was play soldier. You've been out three months, and you've pulled together a community that just might survive. Now you want to quit—because people died because of what you did—but just think of all the people who died because nobody did what you did."

"But—"

"No. Hear me out. You can walk away from this if you want. I'll take over, or Williams will, or somebody. But it is your vision, lady, and nobody is going to bust ass to make it work like you will. Nobody."

He slid off the rail. When he spoke, he sounded even more tired than before. "Action paralyzes you, huh? All right. Have it your way. A professional soldier's now in charge of your utopia." He began to turn.

"Wait." For one instant, she saw it all—the pain, the suffering, the misery—her fault, all of it. And yet—dammit! And yet I'm doing the best I can, and God knows that's pretty good ... Dispassionately, impartially, she reviewed herself, and though she saw the flaws, she saw the strengths, too ... she raised her head. "You called this 'my utopia'?"

"Yes."

"Colonel," she asked softly, responsively, "don't you know there's no such thing?"

He flashed a deep, real smile. "Good. Now. What do you want me to do with them?" He pointed to the prisoners.

She looked across the yard. Higgins's supporters clustered together under the leveled rifles of a dozen guards. "Give them their choice," she said at last. "They can close out their accounts and split, never to bother us again, or they can earn their keep. Their choice."

"That's what it's all about, isn't it?" he murmured thoughtfully. He again started to tum.

"But," she called after him, voice firmer now, "make sure you can identify them if you see them again. And warn them: nobody endangers the project twice. Nobody."

He nodded and strode towards the captives.

She stayed on the rail, watching, thinking, wondering, seeing ...

And mapping out the spring plantings.

The October wind blew cold, but she didn't feel it. Not anymore.

[8]
LOOKING FOR DAN
NOVEMBER 1995

Nick Heffing checked the clip in his .45 automatic one last time. He hated using it—the recoil practically broke his arm; probably ruin him as a baseball player, in the long run—but guerrillas can't afford to be picky. Especially when they're only fifteen years old.

The November wind blew cold under a pale, cloudless sky. The air smelled good. Clean. That was bad, because it meant the rebels still hadn't restored the economy their stupid revolution had unraveled. *Ol' Sheila drops a lot of shit about weaving it together again,* he thought, *but you can't eat talk....* God, I hate short rations. That McDermot talked while people starved was just one of the reasons he wanted to depose her.

But if the ambush ran as 'grammed, he'd eat well soon. He figured he could pick up an M-19 easy. Most cop cars carried at least one, and as leader pro tem until Dan Higgins got back, he'd have first choice of spoils. Then, with that kind of gun, he could lead an assault on the rebels' storehouse, and seize enough food for the winter. Kath'd love him forever if they got some fresh eggs.

He looked around, trying to spot her. He couldn't see any of his people, and that made him feel great. Real pros, even if we are just kids.

Leading someone as good as Kath Washington upped him like no powder ever had. Sixty-three kilos of muscle rippled on her meter sixty-eight frame, and she knew guns like he knew second base. She'd wanted to be a soldier since the day one of her aunts had made major in the Marines. Be a general herself someday, probably. Even at sixteen, she could snap out commands that made Jason Jones, the fattest and laziest of them all, jerk to attention. Nick still couldn't believe she was willing to take orders from him, much less love him.

He squinted closer and picked out shaggy heads strung at ten-meter intervals along the shoulder of the Wilbur Cross Parkway, the New Haven County stretch of the Merritt Parkway. His troops lay belly-down on the line between the underbrush jungle of the right-of-way and the dead grass matted on the embankment. A cop would have to step on them to see them.

God help any cop who trod on short, skinny Tim O'Reas. The seventeen-year-old had wolverine traits: twitchy nose, ferocious temper, and a strength all out of proportion to his size. Before the war he'd planned to go into space: work construction, mine the Moon, anything just to get out there. He could name every star in the sky. But weaklings died quick up there, so he'd channeled his ferocity into exercise and come out stringily inexhaustible. A cop who stepped on him would lose a leg.

For hours only shadows had moved on the highway. It used to carry a car a second, but now traffic had dwindled to Lao Group cruisers on patrol. Ever since the revolution ... Nick had lost his home and his parents to a Tisser. Not that that bothered him—you don't miss what you can't remember having had—but the rebels had completely destroyed the richest country in the world, and he felt cheated. What really infuriated him was that they could put everything back the way it used to be—yet didn't want to.

Dan Higgins had explained it all to him. McDermot had all

the Tissers in Connecticut. All she had to do was press a few buttons, and things would go back to normal—but she didn't want to, because that would mean surrendering her power. So she just pretended to be putting things back together, and nobody knew the difference because nobody could remember how it all used to be.

Except Dan, who had disappeared. Which left Nick in charge.

He hoped Dan would come back soon.

Until he did, though, Ook could provide the ideas. At two meters ten, the seventeen-year-old seemed custom-made for a basketball uniform—but he hated sports and would rather read than toss a ball around. His bush of brown hair made his eighty-two-kilo body look top-heavy, and the girls kept forcing food on him. What he wanted was to be left alone to practice his writing, but the gauntness brought out the mother in every female he met.

A whine rose in the distance: the cop car. Fingers to his lips, Nick gave a low whistle of warning. Then he burrowed deeper into the leaves behind the fallen log and thumbed off the safety of the .45.

No more exploitation. Never again.

The cherry-topped blue car rolled down the hill a hundred meters away. Nick's muscles tightened; sweat trickled down his ribs. He propped the automatic's barrel on the log. He took a long breath, held it, and peered through the cruiser's windshield. A craggy black face swelled as the car drew closer. He squeezed the trigger.

As the roar sounded, his arm leaped up. The windshield starred; a mad spider spun a crazy web around the bullet hole.

Across the highway, big Ook pulled a cord off a pre-cut pine tree. Fifteen meters tall and wearing a skirt of lower branches five meters wide, the tree trembled on the wind. Slowly it leaned forward, toppling like a drunk.

The driver slammed down the accelerator, and the car jerked

forward. Other guns spoke, now: the twenty-two longs of Tim O'Reas and Jase Jones, Kath Washington's police special, the pocket .25 wielded by Nan Young, Ook's Junoesque girlfriend. The cop in the passenger seat returned the fire. Her M-19 sprayed lead all over the embankment.

At the last possible instant, the cruiser whisked under the falling pine. Beyond, it screeched into a bootleg turn. Its doors opened. The cops rolled out, scrambling for cover beneath the needled branches of the roadblock.

"Shit on a stick!" It enraged Heffing that the goons had escaped. Already they'd have radioed for reinforcements, back-up thugs who'd come in quick and wary. And the Front didn't have the firepower to outslug them toe to toe. "Fall back!" he bellowed. "Fall back."

Keeping low, he wriggled away from the road, squeezing off shots every time a patch of blue showed behind the waving green branches. From bush to bush he worked his way up the embankment, snaked along its top to the far slope, and got to his feet. His clothes were damp and muddy. The late November wind howled with malicious chill. "Shit on a stick!" He started loping towards base camp.

He dropped his gun and nearly lost it—for the second time.

Paroled after the uprising had failed, he'd gone to McDermot's office straight from the hospital, expecting nothing but the chance to hassle her. He'd walked right up, answered her greeting with a cold nod, and said, "You gonna give me my gun back?"

She had to figure he was a total incompetent. After all, she knew how angry he was that she'd become a dictator; she knew he'd even fought with Dan's forces. If she hadn't discounted him completely, why else would she have said, "Damn, sorry, knew I forgot something"?

She'd rummaged around in the drawers of her overflowing

desk—her desk, for God's sakes! Not even locked. She must have tossed the .45 in like a teacher confiscating a water pistol. The whole time she made apologetic noises about how it had to be in there somewhere, she distinctly remembered—"Ah," she said, straightening up and beaming. "Here we go." She slapped the butt into his palm, with the barrel aimed up her arm to her heart, its trigger just begging ...

After checking the clip, he'd raised his eyebrows. "You left it loaded?" He couldn't believe that she took him so lightly. Dan Higgins hadn't.

Her cool, level gaze met his. Something in back of it bothered him, like she wanted him to do one thing but was sure he'd do another. "An empty gun's no good if you need it in a hurry. I sorta got out of the habit. What I do is, I treat them all like they're loaded." She glanced at his grip on the automatic, and her lip twisted a little. "You know," she said conversationally, "if you don't point that somewhere else, I'm going to have to show you how."

With a negligent flip of his wrist, he brought it to bear on the valley between her breasts. He almost fired, then. His memory played back a pre-war chant: Six, five, four, three; we say no to tyranny! For a moment he fancied himself in an open car in the canyons of New York, while ticker tape rained from millions of grateful hands ... but her lieutenants would drop him quick and then take over themselves, and though she was bad, they were worse. He gave her what he meant to be a cold smile. "What's the matter, make you nervous?"

She leaned back. Half-swiveling her chair to face him, she steepled her fingers and rested her chin on their nails. "I had this uncle, a real gun-freak," she began slowly, her blue eyes never leaving his. "He told me, don't point a gun at somebody unless you mean to fire—and don't figure a gun pointed at you is gonna do anything but fire." She ran her eyes down the length of his body and seemed unimpressed.

"You had Dan killed, didn't you?" If I could make her confess ...

She yawned. "He split."

"He wouldn't run out on us."

Her chapped hand combed her long blonde hair and scratched the nape of her neck. "It's my fact against your opinion. He split."

"That's what you say." It hurt—no, outraged him that she sat so calmly beneath his threat. Like she thought she was Superwoman or something, so high up that somebody like Nick Heffing couldn't hurt her. It's why she was such a tyrant. He couldn't believe he'd once had a crush on her. "But I know Dan—"

"Look, you're all patched up and we've set you free. There's a partnership open for you if you want it. Do you?"

"Not today." His cheeks got hot; he knew they were red. That angered him even more, because he could see in her eyes that she was laughing at him. She was just so ... so damn contemptuous, without ever saying as much. Nobody but an egomaniac could relax like a cat beneath his gun and gaze. "What I want—"

A scowl savaged her face.

"Hey—"

She struck. Levered up on the arms of her chair, she lashed out with her right foot. The hard edge of her boot caught his wrist. Pain dazzled his arm and raced up his nerves. When it burst behind his eyes, he saw it as a rope of golden light. His arm flew up—the gun stayed behind, dropping into her open hands.

"I told you," she said evenly, "that if you didn't point it somewhere else, I'd have to show you how."

"Jesus, you broke my wrist."

"Serve you right if I did, but I doubt you're that lucky."

"Lucky?" His voice squeaked on that, and he hated her all the more.

"Yeah. Lucky. A broken wrist'd keep you out of trouble."

He clutched his forearm and thinned his lips. She drove him crazy—there he was, twice her damn size, looming over her angry and in pain—and she just tossed his .45 on the desk. Utterly unconcerned, she leaned back again. She'd never taken him seriously. Never.

"Now," she said, the lord dismissing the peasant, "I've got work to do, even if you don't. Any time you want to start eating again, talk to Willie Willams. He's got partnerships open."

He'd started to move away, then, cursing to himself.

"Hey, Nick," she'd cried. "Nick!"

He'd forced out "What?"

"You forgot your gun."

Snow swirled lazy through the bare trunks; the wind had died an hour earlier. Four white inches already camouflaged the base camp, so Nick felt fairly secure—if cold. He peeked through the flaps of the puptent. The flakes fell fat, heavy, and wet. It looked like the guerrillas were about to lose their mobility.

He tied the flap strings to the pole and lay back next to Kath Washington. "I don't know what you heard, but I couldn't see anything." He ran a gentle hand up the bulge of her belly. "And as I was saying before I was so rudely interrupted, I don't care who else's kid it is. I'm gonna love it 'cause it's yours, too. That's all that matters."

"You sure, now?" Sometimes she made him very aware that he was the younger. But she had doe-soft eyes and coffee skin that felt better than anything his fingers had ever touched. "A lot of guys—"

"Hey, I'm not a lot of guys." Moving carefully because the sleeping bag constrained his legs, he rolled on top of her, and brushed his lips against the softness of her neck.

"Well, you sure got appetites like you were a lot of guys." Hands against his chest, she laughed. "Speaking of appetites, as your official second-in-command, something I want to know: what we going to do about food? There ain't much left."

"Let's not worry about that now." She was so definitely a woman that he felt challenged to act like a man. He fumbled at the buttons of her lumberjack shirt. "Let's—"

"Down, boy." She slapped his wrist. "Mama say no."

"Oh, all right." He eased off to the side and lay on his back, staring into the dimness. The tent pressed in on them; icy air eddied off the canvas onto his cheek. He licked his lips. "I don't know what we're going to do about food," he said after a while. Having to say "I don't know" to Kath made him feel inadequate, like a little kid. "Have to find a store we haven't hit, I guess."

"There any of those left?"

"Not nearby ... we could get a car, though. There're a lot out on the Merritt."

"And let everybody know we're around, huh?"

"Well, we don't have to park it here. We could leave it a couple klicks away, just use it for going up the valley—"

"We could also move camp," she said.

"You mean to like a city?"

"Uh-huh."

He shook his head. Realizing, though, that she might sense the motion without seeing its direction, he said, "I don't think so ... we'd be a lot more, ahm, vulnerable in a city. I mean, remember, McDermot's Lao goons are city cops, and they've had a lot of practice in New Haven this year. I'd rather face 'em out here than in a city ... besides, the bandits go for the cities first. Then you got all the street gangs and ... No, I'd rather stay out in the woods. It's a lot safer."

"Colder, too."

"Well, hell, I can warm you up." He reached for her breasts.

"Uh-uh," she said, fending him off.

"Just a thought." He slid his arm behind her neck and pillowed her head on his shoulder. "You figure he's still Tissed out, huh?"

She didn't need to ask whom he meant. "He's got to be, Nick. I can't remember ever ... doing it, before I met you, but since my belly was already big the first time—with us I mean—I musta done it before. Now that's something a girl's not real likely to forget, you know? Unless the man who ... who loved her, he got himself Tissed out and not brung back."

"You know what scares me?" he said suddenly, as glad of the darkness as he was of their closeness.

"What's that?"

"That somebody will bring him back, and all of a sudden you'll remember him, and you'll tell me to get lost 'cause you love him better."

She said nothing.

The silence hurt. He jerked his arm, jostling, her head. "Well?"

"Well, what?"

"Do you love him better?"

"Nick, how should I know? I can't even remember the dude." Fright shrank her voice to a tinny, tiny quaver. "You know how it is. You told me your own self, you can't remember your momma or poppa. If I ask you, you love them better'n me? What you going to say? You can't say, 'yes, I do' or 'hell no, I don't'—'cause today you don't know one damn thing about them. You can't even be sure they alive—only reason you know they used to be is 'cause you alive, and a body had to have folks at least once. Now, in my case, somebody put this baby in here—" She laid his hand on her belly. "—but I swear this is the only memory of him I got."

He felt chastened, though not confident that her love would endure. He wanted so much for it to last that his very intensity seemed, to him, to stem from his fear that it wouldn't. Silent, he leaned over and kissed her forehead.

Through the tent flaps, muffled by the falling snow, sliced a gasp from Nan: "Oh, God, Ook, you're so good!"

He couldn't help it; the cry broke him up. He tried to bury

his laughter in Kath's hair. "You think," he said, sides shaking, "that they snicker when we make noise?"

"Uh-uh," she said, "'cause they hear us at it so often it ain't funny no more."

"I used to go buzzers when my brother and his woman were making it ..." The memory evoked a sudden image of Basil: cool-voiced, smiling under his brown mustache—and the image brought pain. God, I miss him. I hope he's okay ... He closed the door to that part of his past and set himself firmly in the present. "Think it bothers Jase and O'Reas?"

She chuckled. "Your brother?"

"No." His head bumped the canvas, and ice water seeped into his hair. "You know, I got you, and Ook's got Nan, but who've they got?"

"Each other?" A snicker bubbled behind the words.

"You don't think they—"

"Hey, I don't know. They could just be re-eal tight friends. But don't neither of them look at me or Nan that way."

In the darkness, he propped himself on his elbows, and tried to find her face. He couldn't. "What way?"

"That way—like they waiting for you to leave so they can get close to me, you know?"

"Well, I—" He cut off abruptly. Outside, legs stirred the snow. "Ssh." With one smooth movement, he unzipped his side of the sleeping bag and scooped up the .45. His thumb automatically retracted the safety. He aimed it towards the approaching sounds.

"Uh, Nick?"

He lowered the gun and let out his breath. "Yeah, O'Reas?"

The answer began closer to the ground, as though the visitor had just squatted. "Can I talk to you a minute?"

"Sure, hold on, I'll be right out."

"I could come in." In the offer pealed a wistful note.

"Like hell," Kath said. "Ain't no room in here for two, much less three."

Nick tugged his heavy winter coat off his feet, contorted himself into it, and fastened it. Then he wriggled through the tent flaps and closed them tightly. Brushing snow off his knees, he straightened. "What's the matter, Tim?"

O'Reas rubbed the tip of his long, thin nose. "Jase is gone." A simple statement, almost stark, its echoes hung complex with desolation. "I went for some firewood. When I came back ..." He spread his arms, then let them droop. "His stuff's gone."

The desertion stung Nick's pride. "He never could keep up."

"No! Jase was all right. Except—"

"Now what?"

"He—" O'Reas half-turned and faced the flickering campfire. Flames leaped for snowflakes like outfielders snaring long flies. "He took the food."

Suddenly the night and the cold squeezed Nick so small he had to explode. "He WHAT?"

O'Reas stepped away. "He took the food."

"Shit on a stick! That fat little—"

"Nick," said O'Reas, almost pleading, "he was scared, he thought he was going to die out here."

Canvas snapped behind them. Nick glanced over his shoulder in time to see Kath getting to her feet. "Did you hear?"

She jerked shut the strings of her parka. "Knew I should have ate those potatoes earlier." Though shadows blurred her features, her voice flashed stiletto keen. "Did he leave a trail?"

O'Reas shrugged. "I looked for one, but I'm not Nan."

Nick stared at the sky, where rafts of cloud drifted before the moon. "Dammit. By morning, his tracks will be filled in."

"Then we'll go after him now," said a fourth person.

He looked around. "Hi, Ook. Hi, Nan. You heard?"

"All our food, huh?" He shook that fist with understated vehemence. Though he lacked O'Reas's intensity, he matched him in strength. He had once torn a door off a car just to impress Nan. "When I catch that fat bastard—"

O'Reas stepped in front of the looming guerrilla and lifted

his chin. "He's a scared little kid, that's all. He fell apart, absolutely buzzers. He just sat there watching the supplies run down, and ... and I couldn't up him no matter what I did. He used to go off in the woods and cry. He just couldn't take it anymore."

"A two-ton fool makes off with our food and you want me to feel sorry for him because he cries?" Ook's fist thumped O'Reas's shoulder, but Heffing spread them apart quickly. Over their leader's head, the tall one continued, "I'm supposed to feel bad because he was so worried about going hungry that he made sure all of us will? I can't summon much sympathy for him. Not much at all."

For the first time, Nan spoke up. A tall blonde with a good figure and a bad complexion, she had her arm wrapped around Ook's skinny waist and her cheek resting on his shoulder. "His tracks will fill up," she said, "but not so much that we can't follow them in the morning. Not unless there's a real blizzard tonight, and I don't expect that to happen. It doesn't feel like that kind of weather."

They deferred to her judgment, as they did whenever she spoke about life in the forest. She was the only one who hadn't grown up in the heart of the city. She'd told them, once, around a fire, that she'd always felt more comfortable with trees than people. Trees, she'd said, didn't look at you funny.

"All right," said Nick. "We'll go after him in the morning. He's got to be pretty near here—he's too fat to get very far. We'll start at first light."

Kath said, "Hmph. An hour after somebody wakes up, you mean. I bet we don't get going till noon."

But O'Reas said, "Uh-uh. I'll be up."

Nick couldn't bring himself to ask why.

The sky was paling into brightness. Nan said Jase had made the random unevennesses in the snow. When Ook grunted skeptically, she stooped and brushed away a fluffy top layer. That revealed the rough outline of a boot. "That's got to be his," she said. "Unless somebody else went by here late last night, and one of us would have heard it."

"Nobody went by," O'Reas said quietly. Puffiness slitted his reddened eyes.

Nan touched him on the wrist. "You didn't sleep?"

He shrugged off her pity and turned to the dawn.

Nick's breath misted solid, then vanished. His cheeks stung. Impatiently he stamped his feet. "Let's get a move on."

Nan made a face. "This way." She set off down the slope, bending over occasionally to double-check one of the saucer-shaped depressions, pausing when the bare ground behind a windbreak interrupted the trail. Sparrows fled their coming, and in the distance crashed a deer.

Nick saw its white tail flash as he saw everything that morning: through a cloud of worry. Though he had yet to state it, he thought hunting Jase was a waste of time. If they ever caught up with the little pig, he'd have eaten all their food, and would be glad to come back to camp for dinner.

To Ook, Nan said, "Listen, man, when we get him, let's string him up by his thumbs, huh? Maybe start a slow fire under his bare feet?"

A smile spread across the big guy's face.

"Wait a minute," said Nick. They glanced over to him. "We're just going to take the food back—that's all."

Their gazes hardened. Ook's became ugly. "This isn't a ball game," he said. "The losers don't walk away saying, 'Wait till next year.' Losers die. And if he gets away, we're the losers."

O'Reas's face went red, then white. "Well it isn't a damn spy story, either," he said. "You don't have to kill a double-crosser."

"Ah," said Ook, "but it is a democracy—let's take a vote."

Nick looked quickly at Kath; from the set of her jaw and the glint in her eyes, he guessed she'd probably vote with Nan and Ook. She had too much Marine Corps in her to feel lenient.

"Let's catch him first," he said, before anybody else could speak up. "We'll catch him, and then we'll vote. All right?"

O'Reas nodded, and after a moment, Kath did, too. Ook said, "No!" but Nick was able to say, "Three of us want to wait, and that's a majority."

They moved on in silence—Ook angry, O'Reas sullen, and Kath ... watchful. It worried him.

Shit on a stick, he thought. I'm supposed to be the leader, but I'm following. The best thing to do would be to order them all back to camp and say, All right, guys, enough is enough, let the fat pig go—but he sensed that if he tried it, Ook, Nan, and maybe Kath would ignore him. Mutiny: and if he permitted it even once, he'd lose his authority over them for ever after.

He snorted privately; to keep what he had, he couldn't use it when he needed it the most.

Authority was so damned elusive. One minute you had it tight, and the next it had slithered out of your clenched fist and bounded over to someone else.

In school they'd defined it as the right, granted to a leader by a group, to make decisions for that group. Which sounded real good, on paper. On paper, he exercised authority over the Front because they followed his lead, and he made the decisions.

Usually.

What they'd never explained in school was that real authority was backed up by power. That it wasn't a right, it was an ability. What real authority meant was that people did what you told them to because if they didn't, you could hurt them.

Like Sheila McDermot, who took away your food if you didn't obey.

He decided, as they moved through the snowy forest, that he didn't really have authority. On the one hand, he couldn't hurt anybody in the Front—if he even thought of it, Ook or Nan would pull a gun on him. And on the other hand, he didn't want to hurt anybody—'cept maybe ol' Sheila, and he sure didn't ache to hurt her the way, say, Ook did. She'd given Ook a real bad time, once, and he still bore her a grudge. She'd made him go hungry for like three or four days. He was sicker than a dog and couldn't work, but she'd accused him of malingering, and even got a doctor to back her up with a lie ...

That was the difference between leadership and authority. It was why Dan Higgins had started the Front: to abolish authority and replace it with leadership. It was why Nick and his guerrillas were waging war against McDermot's regime. Uneasily, he wondered if it were wise.

But in the meantime, Nan had nearly topped the next ridge. Silhouetted against the skyline, she froze—wiggled to her knees —and in wild pantomime called for silence. Then she worked her way back down, scrambling quickly yet stealthily. Each footstep jarred loose miniature avalanches.

Nick met her before she reached bottom. "What is it? Did you find Jase?"

"No," she said, panting. Her breath billowed about her head like smoke from a locomotive; she held her ribs as she gasped for more air. "The other side—there's a camp—looks like bandits—"

The others, who'd joined them by then, inhaled sharply and touched their weapons.

Kath said, "What exactly did you see?"

"I don't know. Couple guys—big, beards, knives—mobile home, buncha trash on the ground—I don't know."

"I'll take a look," said Nick. He didn't want to risk himself but felt it might be a way to reassert his leadership. Secretly, he was pleased: an armed camp in their path might convince the rest to halt the futile chase. "You guys stay here and cover me."

"I'll come with you," said Kath at once. "Let's have a diamond formation here—Nan, you stay put, in that bush. Ook —" She raised her arm and pointed to the right. "Take that tree trunk about halfway up, make sure nobody comes on us from the right. O'Reas, you're on the other side, behind that outcropping. Move quiet, stay low, and for God's sakes, if you have to shoot, shoot to kill."

As the others padded off, Nick said, "Ready, General?"

She looked surprised. "Did you mind that?"

He started climbing before he answered, "No. No, it's okay ... you do it well, just ... I don't know, I'm in a bad mood."

She held a finger to her lips; they were nearing the ridge top. He slipped his automatic out of his coat pocket and checked its safety. Their feet sank into six inches of soggy snow. In the still air, voices from the far side rose plainly to their ears. They dropped to their bellies and wriggled forward until they could peer over the edge.

In a clearing below stood two men. Their beards and bulky jackets exaggerated their size, but even discounting that effect, they were large enough to make Nick gulp. One stirred something in a pot over a roaring fire. The other seemed to be complaining.

"Probably that the food's rotten," said Kath. "I can smell it from here."

"So can I, but I'm so hungry it smells good."

The wind revived, then, and picked up the sound of a car motor; it carried it to the men below, as well. The cook dropped his spoon. Both ran to the mobile home, reached inside, and pulled out M-19's. Then the cook took cover behind the wood-pile, while the complainer pressed himself flat against the siding of the trailer.

"I could pick 'em off from here," said Kath, easing out her gun.

"Don't—the car might be the rest of the gang."

Minutes crawled by like hours before a jeep finally bounced into the clearing. The cook and the complainer emerged and called out in greeting. The motor stopped; the doors opened. Two people stepped down. Two more heads stayed in the back seat, but the splattered windshield concealed their faces.

The driver's loud voice carried well. "Picked him up on our way back, maybe a klick and a half from here. He was making for the highway."

The cook said something inaudible.

The dismounted passenger reached into the car and hauled out Jase, bound and gagged. Wetness shone on his cheeks.

"Serves him right," grunted Kath.

"You don't mean that."

"Hey! I ...okay, I don't. But still."

Below, the driver laughed. "Hell, no! I ain't greedy—or dumb." He pushed his seat forward, thrust an arm into the back seat, and dragged out a young girl, also bound and gagged. "I got first dibs, Dirk's second, and then you guys can take a crack at her. Plenty for everybody, huh, sweetie?" Holding her right elbow with his left hand, he reached inside her coat and pawed her. Her knees buckled, but he held her up. The others laughed. "You guys empty the jeep," he said, as he propelled her towards the mobile home. "Give you something to do while you're waiting for your turn."

An elbow dug into Nick's ribs. "We got to do something."

"Like what?" he asked.

"Like rescue her."

"Christ, there's four of them—and four M-19's."

"Come here." She slid back toward the watchful Nan. A few meters below the ridge, she stopped. "Hey, what if it was me?"

"Yeah, but it's not."

"Show some empathy!"

"Like you did for Jase?"

She winced, then, and thunked her fist into the slope. "Okay, I deserved that—but I'm going in. Alone, if I have to."

"You can't!"

"Hey, you gonna stop me?" She glared at him. "No woman should have to—" A scream floated over the ridge. "Come on, Nick. We gotta."

"But—"

"They got food, too, Nick. And guns—real guns."

"Aw, shit on a stick." Her eagerness threatened him. She would go it alone if she had to. Fear caught him in a crossfire. He had to risk losing something: his life or her love. It was his choice. "All right, we'll do it. But if you get your head blown off, don't come bitching to me."

She swiveled her head to wave the others in, but not before he caught the gleam of grateful moistness in her dark eyes.

When the rest had clustered around, he described the situation. "If we move quick, it's five guns to three, but don't forget the guy in the trailer. He'll come out blasting."

"Once he gets his pants up," said Kath. The others laughed nervously.

"We're gonna do it like this." Dropping to one knee, he sketched the plan of attack in the snow, looked from face to face for comprehension, and asked, "All right?"

They nodded. Ook and O'Reas seemed tensely pleased. Nan bit her lip. Kath Washington made sure her police special was loaded.

"All right, move out."

He took the right flank; Ook, the left. He walked some twenty meters along the bottom of the ravine, then looked back to see if the rest were in position. They were, and they watched him. He raised his right arm. They followed suit. Then he brought it down hard, pivoted, and headed up the slope.

Once he'd reached the crest, he waited for the other heads to pop up. Kath appeared to his left, then O'Reas and Nan and Ook, oh, God I'm scared ... He took a huge breath, which he let out very slowly. Trying not to think of what could go wrong, he eased over the edge and began snaking down the far side. He hoped the rest were doing the same. If any of them chickened out ... he didn't want to think about that, either.

Snow melted under his stomach, and glared sunlight into his eyes. He had to keep his automatic raised so it wouldn't clog. He couldn't believe that none of the bandits had spotted them yet. Five teenagers bellying towards three hard-bitten killers ... he expected a bullet to tear through his head any minute.

Fifteen meters away, the cook stood by the woodpile, holding an axe. Kindling lay at his feet. The one called Dirk was sitting on the steps of the trailer, rifle across his lap. The third unloaded cardboard boxes from the back of the jeep. Every time he passed Jase, who leaned against the bumper still bound and gagged, he stepped on the boy's toes.

Nick clenched his jaw to keep his teeth from chattering. His eyes jumped from one bandit to another, convinced that at any moment—Dirk's head jerked up. He started to bring his rifle to his shoulder. His mouth opened, a pink cavern in a tangle of brown underbrush.

O'Reas's .22 long cracked once, cracked sharp. Dirk sagged back against the door. A dot of red, surprisingly bright, appeared on his forehead. His rifle slipped out of his fingers and fell to the ground beside the steps.

The cook reared up, axe raised high. The whites of his eyes showed as he spun. The complainer dropped a box, spilling bright green cans onto the snow.

Cursing, Nick flopped into a sitting position. He tightened all his muscles, held the .45 with both hands extended, and aimed straight at the cook's gut. Just as he squeezed the trigger, Kath's police special roared. Then his own went off, and the recoil threw him onto his back.

"Move it!" yelled Ook.

Dazed, Nick sat up again. For one moment he couldn't move; it was all he could do to shake the noise out of his head. His shoulder ached. But he pushed himself to his feet and stumbled down into the clearing.

The .45 slug had hurled the cook onto the woodpile, where he lay, jaws parted. Red foam seeped into his beard. The complainer had dropped into a pile of canned beans, as though he'd tried to hide behind them and had failed. Dirk had already toppled off the porch, onto his rifle.

They surrounded the trailer at a safe distance and took cover.

Kath motioned the others to silence, then wrapped her

hands around her mouth and bellowed. "Hey, you! We got you! Come out with your hands up."

"I got a hostage!"

Nick gambled. He sprinted to the trailer, and knelt by the door's hinges, out of any of the windows' line of sight. Assuming the police stance, he leveled the .45 at the doorway. Anyone who came out shooting would die quickly: the automatic's heavy slugs could punch right through that thin sheet metal.

Kath, abruptly realizing bullets could rip out of the trailer as well as into it, scrunched down behind a log. "So you got a hostage, huh?"

"Yeah!" Triumph infused the reply.

"Lemme tell you something, muhfuh. We ain't no cops out here. We don't give a shit about your hostage. She dies, ain't nothing at all to us, baby. But lemme tell you something else, man. She dies, you. gonna die, too. Re-al slow. I figure I can stretch you out to three days, maybe four. And 'fore you go, man, you gonna eat your own cock. Now, you wanna tell me some more 'bout that hostage you say you got?"

The doorknob turned. Nick tensed. His finger began to tighten on the trigger. One bare foot touched the landing, then another. The ankles above them looked slim and smooth: the girl.

"I'm setting her loose!" roared the bandit. With the door open, his voice rang startlingly loud. "G'wan, sweetie, get out o' here. She's alive, just like you wanted."

The girl took the steps with excruciating slowness. She sobbed. As she emerged from behind the door, she caught sight of Nick and froze.

He stared back. She was nude from the waist down, and blood stained her pale thighs. Her coat and blouse hung open; her white cotton bra had been pushed above her small breasts. Tears streaked her oval face. Thick rope still tied her hands behind her back. She took a step towards him.

He grabbed her elbow, and started to lead her away, but she

swayed and bumped against him, apparently unable to keep her balance. "Easy now," he said. He swept her into his arms.

She yelped in pain as the position twisted her bound wrists.

"Just a minute, be tough." So conscious of his exposed back that he no longer noticed her exposed front, he ran haltingly to the nearest tree. The snow clutched at his ankles; it seemed to take forever. Hours, maybe days later, he could set her on her feet again.

In the background, the driver roared, "All right, now what?"

"Now you come out with your hands up," said Kath. "Re-al slow, re-al easy, and you better not have no gun."

Nick dug a knife out of his pocket and sawed at the girl's ropes. The sun glinted off its blade. She was crying louder. "Cold," she wailed, "Oh God, oh God, why, it's cold, I didn't I never he just, I'm so cold, it hurts—"

"That's it," said Kath in the distance, "keep 'em high where I can see 'em, keep on coming, keep on—" Her police special barked once.

Nick's head jerked up. "Kath, what the hell'd you do? He surrendered."

She stood over the dead bandit. Hand on her left hip, gun dangling loosely, she looked tired, yet exceedingly dangerous. "Ask her if I did right."

The ropes parted; she immediately closed her coat and shivered. "Your clothes back in the trailer?" he asked.

"What's left of them," she said dully.

"Let's go get them."

"I can't—" She drew away from him, pressed herself against the grooved bark of the tree. "I can't."

"Yeah, okay. I'll get them for you."

He started to turn, but her voice stopped him.

"Sorry," he said, "I didn't hear you."

"I said," she repeated, "she did the right thing."

After they'd stripped the bandit camp of everything they could possibly use, and ferried it all back to their own camp, Ook wiped his hands and said, "It's time for the vote, Nick."

"What vote?" He'd honestly forgotten.

"On whether or not we execute Jase for desertion in the face of the enemy. We can't set a precedent here. We can't let people steal our supplies and get off scot-free. So, all in favor—"

"Uh-uh," said O'Reas. Leveling his captured M-19, he backpedaled until he had them all covered.

"Wait a minute." Holding up his hands, Nick stepped into the line of fire. Ice water eddied in his gut, and he had to remind himself to breathe. "All right, we're all on the same side, here. O'Reas, put it down. Ook, don't go for yours."

Neither looked at him. "Jase is my friend," said O'Reas. "I'm not letting that—that totem pole anywhere near him."

He recognized it as a test of leadership. If he had any authority at all, he had to risk it now, because otherwise there'd be blood on the snow, and it would be their own. "Ook, I don't think a question of life and death should be put to a vote. That sets a precedent, too—and frankly, I don't want my survival to depend on my popularity, you know? Now you're mad at Jase, and you've got cause. But we got the food back, and more, and we wouldn't have gotten any of it if Jase hadn't led us to the bandits. What do you say?"

"I want a vote," said the tall one stubbornly.

O'Reas brought the rifle to his shoulder.

"Put it down, Tim." Without looking to see if he were obeyed, he turned to Ook. "There won't be a vote, Ook. Period. I'm running this show, and I say killing somebody—"

"Executing," said Ook.

"Killing somebody for running off is the kind of thing McDermot'd do. Aren't we trying to do something better?"

Exasperated, Ook tore off his ski cap and threw it at the ground. "Nick, he stole our damn food!"

"We got it back."

"Well, at least let's work him over some, teach him a real lesson."

Triumph surged in him—he'd made Ook back down!—but he kept it off his face. "We already punished him by making him carry back food he's not going to get a chance to eat. Isn't that enough?"

The wind shifted and wrapped a tendril of smoke from the campfire around Ook's head. He jerked away from it and coughed. "I don't like it!"

Persuasively, Nick said, "But you'll agree to it, right?"

"I shouldn't ought to." He glowered across the clearing into the raised barrel of O'Reas's M-19. "But I'm not going to get myself shot for it."

O'Reas nodded and lowered the rifle. "Thanks."

"Don't thank me," snapped Ook. "Thank your buddy, here."

Nick scowled but said nothing. He sensed that he had to let Ook blow off steam in some manner, and that seemed a fairly safe way of doing it. To Jones, though, who was still rubbing his fat wrists even though they'd been untied an hour earlier, he said, "Jase, I don't think most of us want you around here, so ..." He gestured to snow-carpeted woods. "You'd better get going."

O'Reas twitched but made no protest. Biting his lip, he stood still.

Jason Jones, however, didn't seem to realize the delicacy of his position. In a voice high with self-pity, he said, "But it's almost night!"

Jones's whine set Nick's teeth on edge. "Didn't seem to bother you last night," he grunted. "O'Reas, get him out of here."

Gloom on his thin face, O'Reas glanced at every guerrilla in turn, then mumbled, "Right, Nick." He shepherded his friend to the far side of the clearing and spoke to him earnestly for a few minutes.

While he did that, Nick walked over to the girl they'd rescued. Dressed, now, with a bruise on her right cheek and her black hair still disheveled, she stood at Kath's side. Her eyes were as brown as Kath's but watched like a spectator's would. Even her pose projected an aura of non-involvement. "Marie, you said?"

She nodded. "No last name."

"All right, Marie. You want us to take you home?"

Her composure wavered like a mirror tilting out of its frame. He winced in anticipation of the crash, but she sniffed hard. "No."

"Ah—" He wanted to ask why. When he opened his mouth, Kath shot him a look so full of warning that he closed it again immediately. He cleared his throat, instead. "Want to join us?"

Her lips trembled, but her voice rang clear and steady. "Can you use a ballet dancer who wants to kill bandits?"

"Well, ahm—"

Kath interrupted. "Damn straight we can." She winked at Nick. "Now we found out how easy it is to do well by doing good, we're gonna wipe those suckers, aren't we, Nick?" A strange fire shone in her eyes; they glowed like chips of hot obsidian.

"We are going to go bandit-hunting?" Once again he felt authority slipping away from him, only this time, he couldn't see how to hang onto it. By staying silent through the Ook-O'Reas confrontation, Kath had supported him—and now, it seemed, she was asking repayment. "Don't you think that's a little on the, ahm, dangerous side?"

Ook snorted, but Nan said, "He's right, man. We could get wiped."

Kath made a face. "Of course it ain't as safe as roasting weenies—but what the hell, Nick, you been talking about a government in exile. You want the ego-up of running a government, you got to take responsibility, too. And no government anywhere, anytime, ever lasted real long if it let bandits run around loose. So that is your first priority—after making sure your loyal troops get fed, of course."

He felt stampeded. If he dug in his heels, he'd get run over. "But—"

"You just think for a minute. You know how good you going to look to the folks in New Haven? Here they been having bandits shoot down 91 for a year now, 'cause nobody's been willing to come out here to the parks and track 'em down. Now, you tell me, how they gonna feel about the guy who is willing? Huh? You think on it, and you will see what I mean."

He had to admit she was right. The New Haveners would be so grateful if he cleaned out the bandits that they wouldn't resist him when he moved against McDermot—who hadn't kept the people safe. Still, though, it did not sound an inviting prospect. "There are some big gangs out here."

"But they ain't guerrillas," she said confidently. "We just out-mao 'em."

Four days later, fleeing the counter-attack of their intended victims, he turned to her and panted bitterly, "Just out-mao 'em, huh?"

"Hey, am I supposed to know everything?" She ran with one hand on her rifle and the other on her belly. Branches snapped under her feet, and slush splashed up from a half-frozen creek at the bottom of the ravine. "I didn't expect no perimeter guards."

A burst of automatic rifle fire chattered through the trees above their heads; wet twigs and bark chips spattered down. The bandits were gaining on them. Kath's pregnancy slowed her down, and all of them hung back to help her.

The gully split around a man-high boulder, then angled sharply to the right. "Ook," Nick gasped, "quick, up the near bank, we fight here."

The tall kid scrambled to the top of the slippery slope, dislodging rocks that tumbled down to miss the rest by centimeters.

"O'Reas, same side, ten meters farther down."

"Right." With one fast glance at the enemy, now less than a hundred meters away, he rounded the corner and hurried off.

"You three—" he waved to the girls "—up the opposite side, spread out, give us covering fire if we have to retreat."

"What about you?" Concern filled Kath's face, but her voice sounded oddly empty.

"I'll stay here, behind that boulder. They're coming right at me; be like shooting fish in a barrel."

"You're crazy," said Nan, but she turned her back and plunged up the far slope anyway. After a moment, the other two followed her, Marie helping Kath on the steeper stretches.

He squelched across the marshy ground to the jutting boulder. Granite it was, gray, patched with ice and limed by millennia of roosting birds. His boots sank ankle-deep into the muck behind it, but wet socks were the least of his worries. He squatted near the right side. Around it he could both see and arm his M-19. On an icicled tree branch above his head, a sparrow tweeted.

He had a good view of the ravine. It extended like an unroofed tunnel almost back to the enemy camp. Fifty meters down it came four bandits huffing and puffing, their feet spraying up mud and ice.

More figures sprinted along the top of the ridge, to Nick's left. He held his breath. Flitting from tree to bush to stone as they were, they shouldn't be able to see him—but he crouched lower anyway.

Forty meters. Thirty. Twen—

A burst from Ook's rifle drove the sparrow to the air. Four men tumbled over the edge of the gully. Three of them got up again. The fourth lay still, arms and legs splayed awkwardly. The other seven ignored him and continued toward Nick. They moved softly, now; their eyes and their guns stayed raised to their right.

He let them get within ten meters before he popped up, laid

his rifle on the boulder's grooved top, and opened fire. They went down immediately, some hit and bleeding badly, some scrambling for whatever cover they could find.

Guns blazed behind him, whizzing bullets over his head, bullets that smacked into the soggy ravine bottom. Ricochets whined off towards silence.

His rifle stopped bucking. He dropped out of sight, ejecting the clip and slapping in a new one. Then, cautiously, he peered around the edge of the boulder. A hand moved. He fired blindly.

"It's okay, Nick!"

He turned and craned his neck up to where Kath stood, waving her rifle.

"It's all clear," she hollered down.

To get to his feet, he had to clutch at the boulder. His legs shook so much that he slumped against it while he breathed deeply a few times. His breath puffed white and ephemeral before his eyes.

At a sound to his left, he jerked around, rifle leveled and finger on the trigger. Then he stopped himself: it was only Ook, coming down the slope in a half-walk, half-ski.

"Good shooting," said the tall one. "They didn't expect you at all."

Suddenly Nick wanted to vomit.

"Nick!" screamed Nan.

He spun, wishing the day's assault on his nerves would end. No wonder Dan split ... "What is it?"

"Get up here! Kath's down and hurting."

He couldn't remember, later, how he'd reached Nan's side. It seemed, in memory, that he'd been down on the bottom one second and up top the next, though the intervening instant had gloved his hands with mud and blood. He brushed past the tall blonde to hurry to his lover. "Kath?"

She lay on her back, knees drawn up, hands on her swollen belly. Her skin had paled to a dusty gray, and she groaned with every breath. The crotch of her blue jeans was wet.

"Kath, what's the matter?"

"Mis—miscarriage." She gasped. "I—I—"

He grabbed her hand and looked wildly around. "What do we do?"

The others clustered about them, compelled by pain to observe. They seemed abashed by their behavior but helpless to change it, like junkies caught reaching for the needle. Except for Ook, who watched as intently as if he were memorizing the scene so he could use it in a book.

He looked from one to another. "WHAT DO WE DO?"

No one could answer him.

He felt like a kid again, in the worst possible way: young, inexperienced, helpless ... "Dammit, make me a stretcher, get her a doctor, anything!"

They broke apart, then. O'Reas improvised a stretcher, using saplings Ook ripped from the half-frozen ground and the girls zipped-up jackets. They laid it beside the moaning Kath. "Take her feet," Nick told Ook. "I'll get her head." Gently, they lifted her and swung her onto the litter. Nan and Marie stood by, watching and hugging themselves in the cold. At a word from O'Reas they lagged behind and fanned out to form a rear guard.

Five klicks they marched through the lifeless forest, five klicks of mud and naked trunks. At last, they carried her into the camp, eased her under the pup-tent, and warmed her with a reflector fire built so close to the canvas that the flaps charred. But it did no good.

She died two hours later.

Shortly after telling Nick that she did, come to think of it, love him better.

He did not experience the next three months directly, but through a filter ground of grief, shock, and anger. Everything blurred even as it happened. Afterwards, he couldn't recall events: his troops grousing as he rousted them from their bags and drove them onto the trail (but to where? and why?). Partial images, like unblackened sections of vaster murals: blazing guns, screaming bandits, headlong rushes across barren clearings. Snatches of dreams would haunt him through the days he spent counting looted weapons: fires and pyres and severed heads that rolled to a stop in clumps of forsythia.

One scene he recalled out of context but cinematically clear: strong warm sun falling from a sky so blue it wrenched a sob out of his throat, while streamers of black smoke twisted through the forest. Before him knelt a man, big and fat with a greasy brown beard and a black leather jacket. A silver chain held an Iron Cross close to his dirty neck. He knelt and pleaded and groveled in the January snow for mercy.

The M-19 br-r-r ripped apart the illusory calm.

The fat man spasmed his face into the mud.

The grayness returned like a fog.

He came to in a pool of March sunlight, staring vacantly at a patch of purple crocuses. He straightened and shook his head. He wondered where he was, and why he didn't want to dip into memory. He ran a finger along the smoothness of his cheek—and both felt much thinner than they had. No one else was around. He blinked and pondered the white-striped leaves of the flowers before him.

A few minutes later, O'Reas staggered down a trail. His deep-sunk eyes glittered. "There's a farm up ahead. Please, Nick, let's hit it. We gotta eat soon."

"A farm?" He raised his eyebrows.

O'Reas held out hands so gaunt they looked a hundred years old. "Christ sakes, Nick, there're no damn bandits left. I been telling you that for weeks. Please. We gotta find some food, or we're gonna drop."

"But a farm ..." He watched the other's rifle shift; instinct brought up his own. He realized then—and the insight came like a fall into a mountain pool, all ball-shrinking and heart-stopping —that O'Reas and the rest would obey him only so long as he gave them the orders they wanted to hear. He wasn't their leader. It was only that, for a period of time, he'd been the craziest of them all. They respected that, as a pack of wolves respected strength and deep cunning. They'd followed him because they'd been going in that direction anyway, and he'd happened to get a head-start on them. Should he try to stop them, they'd cut him down to clear the path. He met O'Reas's feverish gaze. He gave it one try. "Hitting a farm's banditry, man."

The blade-nosed teenager widened his stance. "There's food on farms. We need food. So ..." He lifted the rifle in a shrug but kept it carefully averted. "Nick, we don't have to hurt them. Just ... hell, call it a tax. For protection, huh?"

The others had assembled behind O'Reas; it bothered Nick that he hadn't noticed their approach. A chill settled in his gut. He could say 'yes,' and keep their approval—as well as his health. Or he could say 'no' ... but he was outgunned. "All right," he said, patting the stock of the M-19 as he glanced from face to emaciated face, "all right—BUT." Lithely, he rose to his feet, and kept them covered without seeming to. "Nobody there gets hurt. Nobody. I mean, we're a government, and like Dan said, a government that hurts its own people isn't worth having. So none of the farmers get hurt, all right?"

"Besides," said big Ook, as the group moved off, "crippled farmers don't have as much on hand the next time you come calling."

They crept through the forest to the edge of the cleared area. The fields lay fallow but, somehow, impatient for the plow, so they could get over the waiting and on with the growing. In their center a handful of buildings nestled around an old stone barn. Across the bareness wafted the lowing of a cow.

"Awful quiet," said Marie. In the intervening three months,

she'd lost one finger off her left hand, and acquired a livid scar on her right cheek. "I think we should wait for night."

Nan had binoculars pressed to her eyes. "I don't see anything, though. Nothing moving anywhere in there."

O'Reas leaned against a birch tree. Silver curls of paper-thin bark broke off and drifted to the ground. "I can't wait till night."

"I can't either," said Ook. He looked down at Nick, amusement tugging the corners of his lips. "Let's do it now."

"Wait a minute," said Nan. "There's some kind of antenna on top of the barn—looks like a wind vane, almost, but it's pointing right at us."

He didn't need to be told that the wind was blowing at right angles to them. "You figure radar?"

"Infrared, maybe?" said Ook. "Nan, do you see anybody?"

"No."

"I say go." And his gaze challenged Nick to act like a leader.

"All right, all right ..." He started across the field, uneasily aware that his back was to them all. But he had to be the first there, because he'd be least likely to meet resistance with gunfire.

Far away a door slammed, and across the open space rasped a sound like bicycle tires on gravel. But that was all. No faces came to the windows, no guns appeared, nothing.

A shiver ran down Nick's spine, but he kept on walking towards the—the—he guessed he was headed for the other side of the small clearing, but he couldn't quite remember.

"Where are we going?" asked O'Reas.

"Uh—" He pointed to a break in the budding bushes across from them. "Over there, I guess. We haven't gone this way before, have we?"

"I don't recognize it."

Nan, light on her booted feet, moved around them and loped ahead. "Look at this, will you?"

He was too tired to hurry. "What is it?"

"A driveway." She stood by it, waiting impatiently, until he came close enough to see for himself. "It just ends here, seems to lead down to the highway." With her rifle she pointed up the stretch of gravel drive to the broken concrete of the main road. "What the hell's it for, though? Runs a good two hundred meters to nothing." She knelt. "And look at this, it's cut off smooth as a knife. It's like an inch lower than what it's touching. A real fresh cut."

Nick scowled as O'Reas lowered himself to the ground with a groan. "I get the feeling that something around here just got Tissed out."

Nan's eyes widened. "Yeah," she said slowly, consideringly, "yeah, man, I'll bet you're right."

"So the question," said Ook as he moved up next to her, "is what the hell got zapped—and why so recently? I thought the Lao goons collected them all."

"There's still a lot floating around," said Nick thoughtfully. "Remember, Dan had two of them."

"And you damn near got wiped for carrying one of them," said Nan. Her eyes darted around; her whole body tensed. "Something's real wrong here, and I don't think I want to find out what it is."

"It's a bit too late for that," said a voice Nick had never heard before. "All of you drop your weapons and freeze. Now!"

Obeying like the rest, he pivoted slowly to his right, to the patch of fat-budded lilacs he'd dismissed without a thought when he'd passed it earlier.

Out of it stepped a very old man in an orange-colored robe that left one shoulder bare. His head was shaven, his feet, sandaled. He held an Uzi in gnarled hands that didn't quiver a millimeter.

Hands in the air, Nick nodded as cordially as he could. "Ahm ... hi."

The old man nodded back. "What's wrong with him?" He jabbed his rifle towards O'Reas.

"Hunger," he said.

"Ah." Keeping his right hand on the Uzi's trigger, he reached inside his robe for a buttoned, black-plastic case that resembled a pocket computer.

Nick stiffened and gaped. A Tisser! Experimentally, he lowered his hands a bit.

"No, keep them up," T-SS unit cradled in the palm of his left hand, he tapped a few of its buttons with his thumb. In the clearing behind him materialized the farm he'd zapped earlier. He exhaled, and squinted at them, then, his faded blue eyes moving from face to face till they'd touched them all. "You're children! How long has it been since you've eaten?"

Marie dropped to her haunches and rocked back onto her butt. "Three days, now. Maybe four, I don't remember too well."

"Kids," their captor said, but with a different emphasis, as though torn between compassion for the young and fear of them. "Where are your parents?"

"Tissed out," said Nick, over Marie's muffled, "Dead."

"You're all orphans?"

Nan shook her head. "No, man, we're guerrillas."

"Ah." His bald head bobbed knowingly. "Fighting against tyranny, eh? And your leader, where is he? Excuse me, or she?"

"That'd be me," said Nick. "At least until Dan gets back. I'm Nick Heffing."

"And I am Brother Puhrsieg," said the monk. His blue eyes seemed to bore into Nick. "Soldiers, eh?"

"Yeah."

"Excellent. Perhaps we can work something out." He lowered the rifle and motioned them to be at ease. "Now that the Russians have landed—"

"Russians?" gasped Nan.

Nick said, "You want us to fight the Red Army?"

"You mean you didn't know? I thought—" He stopped and studied them anew. "When you said guerrillas, I thought ... well, never mind. In answer to your question—Nick, did you say?"

"Yeah, Nick."

"We do not want you to take the field against the Russian Army. You see," he said, "we really do not expect them to advance this far south. However, their presence in Massachusetts will undoubtedly provoke migrations in our direction.

"We would like to hire you to protect us from the, ah, more felonious of those refugees." Again he looked around. "Well?"

Before Nick could speak, O'Reas said, "Old man, if you'll feed us good, we'll keep anybody off your back—including the damn Russians. And if you serve ice cream, we'll even keep the Chinese away."

"I can't believe this place," whispered Marie. "It's so clean! And warm, too ... God, I'd just about forgotten central heating." She did a dance step of joy.

The corridor debouched into another hallway, this one perpendicular to the first. Brother Puhrsieg stopped. "Which would you rather do first: eat, or bathe?" His nose wrinkled slightly.

O'Reas, arm over Nick's right shoulder for support, laughed weakly. "No contest. Food!"

The monk chuckled and turned right. "Our dining hall is down here," he said, leading them along the passageway; "Food is available twenty-four hours a day, so please don't feel constrained to gorge yourselves." He pushed open the swinging doors.

Half a dozen hairless heads turned casually. Gazes sharpened; eyes widened. Six saffron-robed bodies pushed themselves to their feet. For an instant Nick thought they were rushing the guerrillas, and almost let off a burst from his M-19 —but then he saw their concerned looks and outstretched hands.

"Oh, your poor darlings." "Man, you nothing but skin and bones." "Jeez, lady, I hate to be poysonal, but you look like you could eat a shoe."

Nick stood gazing into the bottomless brown eyes of a tall, broad-shouldered man. "Dan," he breathed.

"Nick." A gentle, unfocused smile spread across the face of Dan Higgins. "Gee, Nick, it's good to see you again."

"Dan, what are you doing here? We've been looking for you, waiting for you!"

"Oh ..." Higgins smiled again and shrugged. "Meditating, farming, fixing things that break down ... whatever needs to be done. And you? Have you found the way?" His glance fell to Nick's rifle, and his face clouded. "No, I see you haven't." Then his smile returned, as vapid and empty as it had been before. "But don't give up hope; you'll find it with us."

Too stunned to reply—Dan, this isn't you! What happened? —he let himself be led to a table. A bosomy, middle-aged woman put a glass of milk in his hand and said, "You drink that down while I get you a plate." She squeezed his shoulders and bustled away. He sat there holding the chilled glass and thinking, Shit on a stick! What'd they do to Dan?

Puhrsieg apparently misinterpreted his expression, for he leaned across the table and said, "It's safe; we pasteurize."

"Oh, no, I wasn't—" He tilted the glass and drank deeply, then wiped his lips. He didn't know what to say, so the words just tumbled out. "The guy over there, the tall husky one? That's Dan Higgins."

The monk looked over his shoulder, then shrugged. "Yes, it is. Did you know him before he joined our order?"

"Know him?" He set the glass down with a thunk. "Dan was our leader!"

"Ah." He nodded and settled back in his chair. "And you detect a difference." He made it a statement, not a question.

"He's completely powdered out—what've you got him on?" The bosomy lady slid a plate under his elbow, handed him a knife and fork, and stepped back expectantly to watch. He bent to dig in—then stopped, his eyebrows raised, as a horrible thought hit him. "Is it in here?" He pointed to the mounds of meat and potatoes.

"Oh, no; oh heavens, no. No drugs are involved at all. Please, eat."

He hadn't smelled roast beef for ... too long, he thought, chewing rapidly. The first bite went down so good that he wished he'd taken longer with it, so he could have savored it more. But there was plenty left, and he set to work on it. He speared a piece of medium rare, watched the juice drip out, and gestured to Puhrsieg with the fork. "Then what is it? What made him so—so hollow?"

"Our defense systems," said the monk. "And that is one reason why I wish to hire you people as our guards."

"The Tisser?" He sprinkled some salt onto his potatoes and closed his eyes in bliss as he swallowed.

"Yes. You see, we have used it on the commune whenever intruders approached. By rendering ourselves invisible to their minds as well as to their eyes, we have stayed safe. I restore the grounds when they have passed out of range."

"But—" said Nick.

"Well, there are, of course, several problems with the system. Perhaps most obviously, something could happen to me, or to the T-SS unit, and the commune would stay—" His hands groped for a direction in which to wave. "—there, forever. And the relatives of our members would experience the same turmoil that you do."

"Me? Oh, my parents ... it's not really turmoil." What bothered him was that it didn't bother him; he felt less than human because their loss didn't hurt. He knew he should grieve—Marie still cried over her parents—but no matter how he tried, he couldn't feel a thing. "It's more like, ahm, a feeling that things aren't ... right, I don't know."

"Whatever. That aspect is tangential, anyway. What is directly relevant here is that the brothers and sisters who shuttle between here and there—change. Something in the meditation affects them; I'm not certain of its nature, though I am very certain of its effects. Let me show you." He signaled for Dan Higgins to come over.

"Yes, Brother?" asked the big man.

Puhrsieg half-turned in his chair. Without a word, he drove his fist into Higgins's belly. The ex-rebel doubled over, wheezing in anguish.

"Hey," said Nick, "what—"

Brother Puhrsieg held up a finger. "Wait."

Higgins uncoiled gradually. His eyes watered and he clutched his stomach with both hands. "That hurt," he said mildly.

"You can do it to me if you like," said the old man.

"No!" He backed away. "Cause pain? No, no ... I couldn't." He spun on his heel and walked towards the kitchen.

"I don't believe it," said Nick. His fork rang on an empty plate; it surprised him to discover that he'd finished the meal already. The matronly woman cleared it away with a promise to bring more. "Six months ago, he'd have beat you to a pulp for that."

"I know," said Puhrsieg. He shook his head sadly. "They are all like that, now. Nick, this commune is dedicated to pacificism —and I still espouse it," he said hastily, "but there comes a time when even a pacifist must resort to violence."

Nick lifted one eyebrow.

"Oh, never more than the minimum required, and I'd have serious reservations about hurting someone merely to protect myself, but I would most certainly intervene to save a child or a cripple. These are savage times, which I probably need not tell you, and in savage times, sweetness and light will not keep the innocent from harm. But not one of these people here can raise a finger against a—anybody. Anything. No matter what the provocation."

"Why?" The lady brought back his plate; he picked up his fork.

"I blame it on the Tisser. After every trip there, the list of what the brothers and sisters will not harm lengthens. We've now reached the point at which Zeke won't permit traps in the barn to control rodents—oh, he would not think of stopping me from installing them, but afterwards he springs them—because he feels it is wrong to hurt mice. Needless to say, I had to slaughter the steer you're eating."

"But you can do it; why can't they?"

"Because I have always been outside the unit's sphere of influence—it is I who triggers the device, avoiding its effects, and it is I who restores the commune later."

He was beginning to catch on. "So you want to hire us to protect the place so you don't have to use the Tisser anymore, because if you keep on using it, they'll ..." He stopped, unable to imagine anything more pacifistic than saving rats from traps.

Puhrsieg's shoulders drooped. "Right now," he said, "there's a great deal of debate on the propriety of plowing."

"Huh?" That stopped a fork load halfway to his mouth.

"'After all,'" quoted the old man, "'the worms get hurt.'"

"Ahm ..." He chewed and swallowed and took another swig of milk. "You know something, Brother?"

"What?"

"You got problems here."

They'd barely washed up before they were needed. The lights flashed; a whistle shrieked. While they grabbed their weapons, Puhrsieg hobbled down the corridor. In the dining room, voices raised in a meditative chant. "Eleven bandits are approaching from the northeast," the old monk called. "At present they are approximately two hundred fifty meters away."

A minute later they were flat on their bellies behind the barnyard fence, peering through the slats. Or four of them were: O'Reas was climbing the ladder in the barn. Their best shot, he'd try to pick off the survivors who'd hit the dirt after the opening volley.

"Shit," said Nan, as she lowered the binoculars. "Nick, those aren't plain old bandits—they're soldiers."

"GI's? Christ, hold your fire, guys." Some army units had gone bandit after the collapse, but not many, and he didn't want to make a mistake. Wiping a squad of the real thing could cause them serious trouble. "How do they look?"

"Weird. Real funny uniforms." She tossed the glasses to Ook. "What are they, man?"

He refocused them, then whistled. "Say, Nick?"

"Yeah?"

"I think those are Russian soldiers."

"Aw, shit on a stick." He dropped his face onto the backs of his wrists. "There any more coming?"

"They're alone ... And walking like they're going on a picnic."

"I thought they were staying up north." Sandals scraped as Brother Puhrsieg, bent absurdly double, scurried over to him. "Get down, Bro'. That robe's too damn bright; they'll see you for sure."

"We were just monitoring the radio frequencies, and we heard—"

"That the Russians are moving south, yeah, we know already. You got your Tisser?"

"Well, of course, but—"

"Take 'em out. Quick!"

The monk reached into his robe for it. Its plastic seemed to drink in the late afternoon sun. With a worried glance up the field, he pulled from the unit a folded antenna—then shook his head and pushed it back in.

"Hurry up!" hissed Nick.

"I am, I am." Activating the unit, he looked up, punched a number, made a second visual estimate and tapped in another number, then did it a third time and pressed the subtract button. "As I was saying," he said, "according to the Radio New Haven broadcast, the Russians are advancing in our direction, and will probably be in the area soon." Of no one in particular, he asked, "What am I doing with the Tisser?"

Nick, who was beginning to wonder why he and his people were lined up with their rifles poking through the fence's pickets, frowned at the old man. "I don't know—wait a minute." He thought briefly. "The only thing I can figure is that you just Tissed out some bandits."

The monk sat up. "Where?"

"Out there, I guess." He waved vaguely to the fields beyond.

"Oh ... it's possible, yes. I wonder, though ..." His eyes wandered back to the field. "Are you thinking what I am thinking?"

Nick licked his lips. "Uh-huh. Why don't you bring them out of it, and we'll take a look. They'll be paralyzed for an hour or so anyway."

The monk's fingers scampered over the keypad.

"Damn, will you look at that?" breathed Ook, who'd sidled up next to them.

Eleven infantrymen, stiff as statues, were toppling over in the empty field.

"Shit on a stick!" It was more than he wanted to cope with. First the Lao group, then the bandits, and now the entire Red Army ... for a moment, forgetting himself, he said, "What are we going to do?"

"You're in charge, Nick." Ook laughed softly. "And I don't envy you a bit. Not one bit."

Puhrsieg rose to his feet. The others followed suit. "Radio New Haven ended its broadcast with a call for volunteers—a Colonel Someone-or-Other is attempting to raise an army to defend the city."

"Singleton," said Nan. "That's his style, man. Bet he does it, too."

"And I'll bet he sacrifices his entire force on the first day," said Ook.

"Nick," said Puhrsieg, wiping his muddy hands on his robe, "I fear this means we shall have to terminate your contract."

"Why? With your Tisser and our guns—"

"No." His bald head shook; the setting sun shimmered off his scalp. "We are pacifists, and we cannot take up arms, but we can certainly tend the wounded and feed the hungry. We leave for New Haven in an hour."

———

Night had fallen. The guerrillas sat around the empty barnyard and tried to plan their next move. "We could go back to camp," Ook suggested.

"There's probably a tank parked there already," said Marie.

"Well, what the hell," said O'Reas, "we can slip through their lines and head north, get out of the line of fire. Spring's moving in up there, anyway. I still say we should have frisked those soldiers."

Nick scratched his shoulder blades on the barn's stone wall. They looked to him, waiting for him to decide. No matter what I say, somebody's gonna want to do something else ... let's play it cool. Slowly, he said, "First off, like I told you at the time, we didn't take their guns or anything 'cause we don't want 'em to know we're here. Yet. And second, aren't we supposed to be freedom fighters?"

"Sure, man," said Nan. "But the Russians'll dump McDermot for us; we don't need to fight any more."

"All right, but then we got the Russians in charge," he said. "Which would you rather have?"

"The Russians," said Ook bitterly.

He let it pass. "O'Reas?"

The thin teenager rubbed his nose while he thought, then made a disgusted face. "McDermot. I hate her guts, but I'd rather have her than them."

"Marie?"

"I don't know this McDermot; I joined you guys to kill bandits." She fell silent for a long time. "It seems to me that anybody who breaks into his neighbor's house and takes over is a bandit—so I say, let's go kill some Russians."

"Ook—Nan? We're going to New Haven. Are you coming with us?"

"Dammit!" said the tall one. "I suppose you're right, though. We can always dump McDermot later, after this is all over."

Nan said nothing, but patted Ook on the knee. It looked like a vote.

Dawn would break in an hour or so. They were trudging along the highway, bitching about their feet and wondering if the Russians marched at night. A flame popped in the darkness ahead; a bullet bit the pavement. As they tumbled into the drainage ditch, Nick shouted, "Shit on a stick, you idiot! Cut that out!"

Back sang a voice, delighted and uncertain at the same time, "Nick? Nick Heffing?"

"Yeah," he said, picking grass off his tongue. "Who—Basil?"

"You got it."

Then they were in each other's arms while Basil's patrol looked warily over Nick's band. They pounded each other on the shoulders and in the ribs and called each other obscene, loving names. "Nick, you bastard, I thought you were dead!"

"Yeah, well, I would have been, if your aim hadn't been so rotten. You never were much good with a gun."

"You tote that thing like it's part of you."

He hefted the M-19 absently. "Ahm ... I guess it is, sort of."

Basil drew his brother to one side, out of earshot of the rest. "Nick—why'd you come back?"

"'Cause the Russians are coming."

"They chased you out?"

"Come on." He gave his brother an insulted look. "You guys called for help—here we are."

"When you were here before, you didn't like the system Sheila was setting up. Now you're back to help defend it. Level with me."

"I am."

"You're really here to help?"

He nodded. "At least till the Russians leave. Then—then we'll see."

"She's running things, you know."

"I sorta figured she would be."

"So you can accept the fact that she's in charge?"

The moon crept up over a ridge of hills. A line of birds crossed it, heading north. "Yeah," he said at last, "yeah, I can. I'm not too sure about her system, but fighting the Russians is the right thing to do. I, ahm ... I did some thinking about authority while I was out there." He gestured to the state parks in the distance. "You know what I decided?"

"Tell me."

"I figured authority is the right to use power. People give it to other people because they trust them; they say, 'All right, you can force me to do something I don't want to do because I trust you to force me wisely.' You know, I thought coercion was really wrong, but then I realized that the right or the wrong of it depends on the situation—and on the main goal. So here I am. As long as she's fighting the Russians, I'll acknowledge her authority. I'll give her the right to order me around—because I trust her to do it wisely. Good enough?"

"Good enough. Come on, I'll drive you guys in."

They met in the barnyard where he'd once been shot, outside the office where she'd once humiliated him. Morning sun fell on the hard-packed ground. She said, "You're back."

He nodded.

"Where've you been?"

He waved to the north. "Out there."

"You hit the Lao group a few times early in the winter?"

Again he nodded; his grip tightened on the M-19.

"And then you stopped. Winter slow you down?"

"No ... we decided to get rid of the bandits—first."

She smiled at the implicit challenge. "You did a damn good job of that. Don't think we don't appreciate the quiet nights you gave us. We owe you."

He studied her face for mockery but found none. "Uh-huh."

"So now you're coming over to our side?"

"For the duration."

"That's all we ask—all we have a right to ask." Her eyes swept over him and seemed to respect what they saw. "So how many of you are there?"

"Five. The other four are getting something to eat."

"Five?" She blinked. "Only five?"

"Yeah. Why?"

"'Cause ..." She smiled and shook her head. "We thought there were more of you. A lot more." She laid her hand on his shoulder and squeezed it lightly. "Thanks for coming home, Nick."

In the distance, a howitzer roared.

[9]
WAR OF OMISSION
MARCH 1996

"Man, I don't agree at all! This ain't her war, or their war—
it is everybody's."

The old guy in the radio room with Willie Willams looked
skeptical. "How can you say that we don't even know who's
attacking, huh?"

"We do know, and they Russians." Frustrated, Willams
glanced at his clipboard, and ran his eyes down the checklist
marked THINGS TO DO TO SURVIVE TODAY. The list
was a habit, the glance, a reflex in times of stress. Both had
served him well, once, but he hadn't updated the sheet in a
week. The invasion had distracted him. "You know how I
know?"

"How's that?" said Guido Angeloni.

"I was on the short-wave with this Canadian? And he says his
cousin's in the RCAF, and his cousin saw those troop transports,
and they are definitely Russian."

"Yeah?" said Angeloni. "Well, I'm a hear last night, on the
radio? that it's our own boys, back from Europe. They've come
home to restore law an' order."

"Jesus, man, that's propaganda! They—hold on just one
minute." He leaned forward and flipped a switch on the radio. A

needle swung to the vertical; he pressed the automatic fine tuning to lock it in.

Static popped in the speaker on the shelf above his desk. "New Haven?"

"New Haven here," said Willams, mellowing his voice because he'd be damned if he'd let the world hear how rattled he was. "We read you, go ahead."

"This is Cleveland, New Haven—somebody crashing your party?"

"That's right, Cleveland, the big red bear is dancing in New England."

"The word here was that they're really South Africans."

"Negative, Cleveland, negative." Involuntarily, his eyes lifted to the map tacked onto the corkboard next to the speaker. Red golf tees marked a dozen spots. "These dudes came over the pole by air."

"Canada let them?"

"Canada didn't have no choice." He tried to remember what the man on the short-wave had said. "They flying MiG-31's as escorts. What we hear is, Canada be short one air force soon as it tries to intercept."

"How many you got there?"

"Us or them, Cleveland?" He ignored the old guy's snort.

"Them."

"We count fifty thou in Boston, and the same again in Providence and Springfield. They using those cities as staging areas; be moving to New York City any day now."

"Right over you guys, huh?"

Willams frowned. "No, baby, we gonna stop em." This country be ours, he thought, and ain't nobody going to give it away. Nobody.

"You need any help?"

"Why, you got a couple divisions you don't need?"

"No, but we do have some transport planes, and six battle tanks are sitting out at the Chrysler plant. You want them?"

"Listen here, my man, I'm going to have to transfer you to the colonel. He the man who makes that kind of decision. Just hold on one minute." Cool, Willie, professional. He picked up a telephone and pressed one of the buttons at its base. A throaty buzz sounded in the earpiece.

"Yes?" said a crisp, attentive voice.

"Colonel Singleton? Willams. Man in Cleveland wants to give you six battle tanks; if you'll hold one minute, I'll patch him through to you."

"Six?"

"Yes, sir." His fingers worked the board, jacking lines together. "Yo, Cleveland?"

"Yes, New Haven?"

"Colonel?"

"Got it, Willams. Thanks."

Switching off the mike, Willams leaned back in his swivel chair, exhausted. He felt forty, not thirty-three. Days at the radio controls had sapped him. His mirror that morning had shown him stress lines and bloodshot eyes. He yawned.

"So in your opinion," said the old guy, picking up the argument where they'd dropped it, "these people are Russians, huh?"

"Yeah, that line 'bout they being NATO forces is a bunch of shit. They just trying to put us off guard, you know?"

Angeloni shrugged. "Maybe you' right—an' if you are, maybe I fight. I don't want no Russians here. But hey, you tell me this— you gonna fight our own boys?"

"Damn straight I will," said Willams, meaning it. "If they come here to take us over. If they here as friends, though, that's another story."

"Willie, you crazy!"

"Hell, no—I—"

"We both know they gonna leave tread marks all over our backs, huh?"

"Look, Mr. Angeloni—"

The ex-restaurateur got up from his chair and limped over to the map. His forefinger flicked tee after tee. "Down Interstate 95 they come, down 91, you tell me just a while ago they been spotted on Route 1—half a dozen more roads they could come in on—and you sit there, you tell me it's our duty to die? For what?" He spread his arms, raised his hands, and shook them. "For some flaky girl who'sa start all this? Willie, you tell me, if little Sheila hadn't taken out the old government, would any a' this be happening? For her you wanna fight?" He folded his arms across his chest. "An' I still think they're American!"

Willams sighed. A week ago, he could have debated old Angeloni and wound up convincing the guy to kiss Sheila's boots, but today ... today the lassitude of fatigue lay in his bones like lead marrow. "Listen, man, you best remember I am one of those fiery-eyed rebels who fucked things up, you know?"

"But you did it because you didn't want no government saying, 'You, yeah you, old man, give uppa you money in taxes, and you kid, you give uppa you life in war,' right?" The wrinkles on his face knotted as he peered at Willams.

"No," said Willams sharply. When the old man recoiled from his vehemence, he cursed to himself. Like every survivor of the underground, he was touchy about what they'd done, and why. "Mr. Angeloni, I wasn't no anarchist, I—"

"Then how come before the revolution you people always talking about how it's time to get that big fat government off our backs, huh?"

He shook his head, and wished his mind were clear. "Hey, man, being against one government don't mean you against all governments, dig? You be thinking about Dan Higgins and his crowd, and those dudes are anarchists. They don't want no government no how, but I am not one of them, you hear? I am a patriot, man. I believe in the Constitution and the Bill of Rights and the Declaration of Independence, and freedom. And what we got rid of was a system what didn't respect none of those!" When Angeloni shrank back from him, he realized he'd raised his voice almost to a shout. He took a breath and tried to cool down. He wished it didn't bug him when people misunderstood his motives. "Hey, sorry, man, I didn't mean to get so hot, just ... just I don't like nobody thinking I be one of Dan Higgins's crowd."

The old man's rheumy eyes skipped around the small room, touching on the map, the speaker, the water-spotted ceiling ... at last he said, with forced brightness, "Speakinga Dan, I'ma see him this morning, on the street. He's shaved his head, you know? And he's wearing this funny orange robe like he's some kinda monk."

Willams smiled slightly. "He is some kinda monk—got himself converted when he was hiding out last winter."

"It's hard to onnerstand, somebody like Dan taking the cloth, you know?"

"Aw," said Willams, "that dude always been chasing ideals, and I guess this is just the next in line. Besides, the way I hear it, he got himself Tissed out a whole bunch of times over the winter, and man, even one time do strange things to your head." With a rueful smile, he glanced at his clipboard. That checklist for survival was a direct result of his experience. Being there, in that place out of space and time, had given him a passion for organization, and a reluctance to trust anything that couldn't be outlined on paper. Weird shit, the T-SS unit, but it sure had helped the revolution.

The old man waved his hand dismissingly. "Willie, you talking to somebody who been there, and from my own personal experience I'ma tell you, it don't do anything to you at all."

He raised his eyebrows. "The word around here is that you paid good food for thirty million old US dollars—and you say it didn't change you?"

"Ah," he said, waving his hand again, "I give those to my grandkids. Fifty, sixty years they be worth something to collectors, you know?" But he looked abashed all the same.

"Well—" A moving needle on one of the radio's dials caught his attention. Silencing Angeloni with a finger to his lips, he bent forward to tend to it. Deftly his hands moved across the controls until the carrier wave hummed loud and clear. He nodded, and breathed into his throat mike, "New Haven here, come in."

"New Haven? Supreme Headquarters, Allied Expeditionary Forces." The voice was deep, confident, and very American. "We have a message for whoever's in charge, there."

He looked at the speaker with distaste. "Why you working for the Russians, man? That's treason."

The voice cooled and stiffened. "Maybe you didn't hear me, rad. I said Allied Expeditionary Forces. NATO. That's hardly working for the Russians."

"Flying MiG-31's and Tu-182's? No way, jack."

"Look, are you going to take this message down or not?"

"Yeah, yeah, you hold on just one minute." He peeled back sheets on his clipboard till he found a clean one. His fingers trembled. Anger did that to them. As did fear. And doubt. He rubbed his sore eyes, and said, "Okay, man. You read me that message."

The message gripped her like a hand of ice. For a moment Sheila McDermot was a little girl again, scrunched in a closet during a game of hide-and-seek, so afraid the dark shapes above her would mutate into bogeymen that she had to squeeze her legs together to keep her panties dry. She swallowed hard. "This is the text, verbatim?"

Willie Willams plopped into a chair and laid his clipboard on his lap. "Word for word. I gave a copy to the colonel, too. Seventy-two hours is all we got."

She read it again, surprised as always by Willams's penmanship. The characters looked typewritten. But the content remained the same:

TO THE CITY OF NEW HAVEN:

AT THE REQUEST OF PRESIDENT MCALESTER DONOVAN AND THE CONGRESS OF THE UNITED STATES OF AMERICA, GENERAL WILLIAM C. DODSHIRE, THE SUPREME COMMANDER OF AMERICAN FORCES IN EUROPE, HAS LED A CONTINGENT OF NATO FORCES HOME TO RESTORE ORDER, AND TO RETURN OUR BELOVED COUNTRY TO THE SECURITY OF RULE BY LAW. MARTIAL LAW HAS BEEN IMPOSED ON THE ENTIRE CONTINENTAL US.

THE SUPREME COMMANDER HAS APPOINTED GENERAL G.E. MITCHELL MILITARY GOVERNOR OF THE STATE OF CONNECTICUT; MAJOR CLARENCE HAWKSHEAD HAS BEEN NAMED TO ADMINISTER THE CITY OF NEW HAVEN.
MAJOR HAWKSHEAD WILL ENTER THE CITY IN SEVENTY-TWO HOURS WITH 68,000 TROOPS; SEE THAT A SUITABLE AREA IS AVAILABLE FOR THEIR BIVOUAC.

YOU ARE HEREBY WARNED THAT RESISTANCE WILL BE SEVERELY DEALT WITH.
SUPREME HEADQUARTERS
ALLIED EXPEDITIONARY FORCE.

"Martial law," she said slowly, "that's what gets me the most ... you ever heard of this McAlester Donovan?"

"I checked him out on the Journal-Courier computer," Willams said. "He was a Congressman from South Dakota; was on a 'fact-finding' tour of Paris when the revolution started up. He must have appointed himself president ..." He slapped his thigh with the clipboard. "No, damn it! I don't believe it. This got to be some kind of trick."

She nibbled on her lower lip while she thought it over. "No," she said at last, "no, I don't think so. Oh, I don't think this Donovan character is really commander-in-chief; he's probably just a front man for a military junta ... but I'll bet they are American troops. We had a lot stationed in Europe in '94, and the revolution stranded them. It must have been an incredible headache for everybody involved—our armies, the NATO governments, Russia ... you say the airlift used Russian planes?"

"Yeah, that's why—"

"Listen." She leaned forward. Willie liked things cut and dried, so she tried to sketch as clear a scenario as possible. As she spoke, she massaged her right temple. "Moscow's always wanted our guys out, but now Europe must, too—otherwise Bonn and Paris and the rest would have to pick up our tab. And our commanders would want to come home, too; some of them, to do what they can for the country, and others, to do what they can for themselves." She made a face. "I'll bet they struck one hell of a backroom deal."

Willams narrowed his eyes. "Who?"

"NATO, Moscow, and the US Army. See, the way NATO was set up, the troop planes were based here for an airlift to there if war broke out. To get our army home all at once, you'd need better transport than they had over there. So ... I can see Moscow saying, 'Listen, we'll fly you home and make everybody happy.' And I can see the junta accepting, 'cause they'd really have no other choice."

"Uh-huh." Willams took out a pen and drew a wavy line through an item on his checklist.

"What's that?"

He shrugged. "Guess I don't have to look up the Russian for 'I surrender.'"

She could tell he was trying to cheer her up, so she laughed, but inside, where he couldn't see, she shivered.

"What are we going to do?" he asked.

She lifted her coffee mug, but it was empty. "I don't know ..."

Being Tissed out had changed her. She understood things better than she'd used to.

Outside her office window, March hushed farmland that would burst into green once it had soaked up enough sun and water. Lazy windmills tumbled beyond; the sky arched blue above.

She looked out and saw not that, but war. She saw a defiant New Haven fighting the reimposition of the old order. She heard the guns, smelled the burning buildings and the rotting flesh, felt the rubble beneath her feet as she tried to walk down a ruined street. She shuddered.

Willams fidgeted, apparently impatient for her decision. "Well, we gonna surrender, then?"

"Surrender?" The word dissolved on her tongue; its bitterness evoked images of that-which-might-be, the military commanders "temporarily, of course," who would hang on for years, doffing their uniforms only so the junta could appear in suits; and the discipline, and the bureaucracy, and the orthodoxy ... New England was bleak enough in climate and geography; it couldn't bear that added grimness. "Surrender?" she said again. "No, I don't think so ... let me put it another way, I won't surrender." A shell burst on her desk and outside a tank roared; blood stank, and pain throbbed, and it was almost more than she could stand. "Ah, Willie, it's a hell of a thing, because if we lose ..."

"We won't," he said, sitting straighter. "We got a plan."

"I know, I helped the colonel draw it up." And he told me our chances are one in four, but I'm not going to depress anybody with that fact.

"There you go, then. We got the Tisser, and they don't. And there ain't no way, no how, an army can win against it, even our own, right?"

"That's the theory, at least." She bit her lip again, and rubbed her left temple in smooth, even circles. "As long as the theory's right ..."

"Don't you worry about that. We got Dave Kenyer, too, don't

we? And they tell me he the dude designed the thing in the first place. There any kinks in the theory, he take care of em."

"No, that's not it. What I am worried about—" She cut herself off and cocked her head. Willams's brown eyes looked desperately tired. Though she knew he'd exhausted himself in her cause, she still wondered, Can I trust him? Then she laughed. Because everything she'd ever worked for depended on leaders trusting people. "See, we can cut that army into ribbons, I know we can—if we work together. But that's my question: will our folks fight? Or will they want to surrender"?

If the question troubled him, he didn't show it. "Why give them the choice? Just put 'em on the lines and tell 'em what to do."

"No," she said firmly, "that's not the right way to do it."

"Hey, you're in charge here, just give the orders, you know?"

She recognized the arrogance implicit in his thought: he and she and a few of the others constituted the elite, the small circle whose right it was to make decisions for all. Before the revolution, she'd thought that way, too, though she never would have admitted it. Afterwards she'd changed her mind—at first because she'd grown afraid to decide, since her underground had made such a mess of America, but then because she had finally come to realize that that arrogance was mistaken. "Look, Willie, the people should set policy, and the one in charge should implement it."

He flashed her a look of disgust. "What's the matter, you afraid to show some leadership?"

"No, dammit!" She pushed herself away from her desk and leaned back. Her left knee still hurt from the bullet that had torn through it—how long ago, now? A year? Yes, but she'd been there for a third of it, so it'd be eight months or so ... her head throbbed and her stomach queased. She was afraid. She feared that the politico-economic system she'd ruined the country to institute would die, a casualty of the NATO invasion. "Look. A leader can articulate policy. He can be a focal point, a—" The spread fingers of her hands meshed together. "—a standard around which people can rally. But dammit, if it's going to be worthwhile, they have to be free to choose."

He looked unconvinced. "So what you gonna do?"

"We've got to have a meeting," she said. "Here at the farm, I guess, since most of us live nearby ... tonight, I think." She turned her head to the window and visualized the fertile, waiting fields, plowed by shell and seeded with bone. She winced. "I want everybody here. Everybody in town not only people connected with the project, but everybody else, too. You've got a census directory?"

His nod managed to rebuke her for questioning his efficiency.

"Get the notice out quick, all right?"

Lithely, he uncoiled and rose to his feet. "But what are you going to say?"

She saw it: nighttime, floodlights, rickety stage/podium with the faces upturned and glistening ... just like before the revolution. Could she ask them to die a second time? think ... "I think I'll start by saying ... 'The US Army is on its way! Its generals are seizing power and turning the country into a Korea, an Argentina. They are afraid to let the people rule themselves, so they will subjugate us while they can. If we let them! Well, I won't!'"

Eyes closed, head tilted to one side, Willams murmured "Not bad."

"Then, um ... 'We went through hell to dump the tyrants who hired these generals, but even what we despised was better than government by gun. Friends, I thought I fought hard before, but I'm going to fight harder, now. And I ask you to join me.'"

"Yeah," he breathed, as though he were there, on the scene.

"'But you have to know, all of you ...'"

"—all of you," boomed the speakers her lover Doug had strung for the occasion, "that the Army has given us an ultimatum: surrender within seventy-two hours, or else."

The crowd caught its breath; worry lined the faces in the front row. She waited till the wind had carried off the last echo. Easy, now, sure of herself because these were her people and they trusted her because she trusted them, she let them digest the threat.

"But I'm not worried," she said, feeling it and meaning it. "We can take them. We won the revolution, didn't we? We fought a war with no front, no lines, against an enemy we had once cherished—how can we lose what we've gained? We beat this same military machine when it was the most powerful on Earth—how can we lose to it now?"

She sensed them begin to relax, begin to warm up. Leaning across the podium, stabbing the air with her hand, she shouted, "We can't lose! Do you know why?"

As if on cue, the clouds pulled away from the moon and let its light pour down. "We can't lose because our system is based on freedom, which is why I stand before you tonight. I am here to offer you a choice: fight with us or yield to them. Has the junta given you a choice?"

"No!" hollered somebody from the dark fringes of the crowd.

"Damn straight they haven't!" She slammed her fist onto the podium. "But we do, and that's why we'll win!"

Scattered cheers rose into the brisk night air.

"Now, we also abide by the concept of majority rule, folks, but for this decision, I'm going to amend that slightly. These are lives we're talking here, not zoning laws, so the minority isn't going to do what the majority wants. I'm not going to force anybody to fight if he doesn't want to—nor will anybody force me not to fight!"

A growl of approval rolled up to her, and she let it straighten her. She had them, now, and knew she had them. A flame of triumph danced in her heart.

"Now we're going to vote. The majority keeps New Haven, the minority leaves. I promise you that. If the majority of you want to give up, want to turn this city back to the crats—"

"No!" they yelled. "No!"

"—then I will lead the resistance out of town. But if the majority of you want to fight—"

A chant welled up, "Yes, fight! Yes, fight! Yes—"

She waved them to silence. "If the majority fights, the minority can leave town before the battle starts, no recriminations, no questions asked. Now. Vote with your feet. Imagine a line drawn from me to that flagpole out there—"

She didn't even have to pause. Doug picked up the signal and turned on the special floodlight. The silvery beam washed over something that hadn't flown in New Haven for a long, long time: the thirteen-star American flag, clean and proud and fluttering in the night breeze.

Exultation roared up from the crowd.

"Yeah," she shouted, "yeah! That's what you're fighting for: America! The real America. The one of 1776, not the one the crats warped. Now, vote with your feet. Everybody who wants to live free or die, you come over here, on my right. And everybody who wants to surrender, who prefers life to freedom, you come over here on my left. The majority keeps New Haven, to defend or surrender, however the vote goes. The minority gets out of town quick. Let's go, vote with your feet. America on my right, the junta on my left."

Basil Heffing crossed the line, of course, and stood at McDermot's right. He was nervous—doubtful, even—but how could he do otherwise? Not only did he owe her gratitude for having saved him from certain starvation, but he trusted her in a way that his younger brother didn't. He definitely preferred her to the army. Besides, he had his parents to consider.

They were still Tissed out. He couldn't even remember them. Not their names (though he knew them, now—Serge and Mary —because he'd found an old telephone book and looked through the Heffings until he'd come across an address on Bellevue Road. Though he couldn't recall his own mother, he did remember that quiet side street in its nice residential neighborhood). Not their faces. Not their likes or dislikes or mannerisms. Nothing, in fact.

But because he knew himself, the kind of person he was and the kinds of things he'd been taught to do, and because he could see the same upbringing in Nick, he knew that they must have been good parents, good-hearted at the very least, and probably wise and full of love, as well. He missed them.

Oh, not as people, but as concepts. As nexus in a network of relationships. Nexus that Emily (God rest her soul) Kenyer had had, that Doug Singleton and Sheila McDermot had, that most people, in fact, had, whether their parents were alive or not, because most people could remember.

Him, he felt like he was seining with a torn net.

Ultimately, that feeling drove him across the line, though he knew his choice might cost him his life in the next few days. Yet, as he saw it, he had to resist. The army was deliberately seeking to destroy a strong, healthy family—and to him, no crime could be greater.

He never talked about the way he viewed the world because others could too easily ridicule his visions—but he saw society in familial terms.

He belonged, first, to the Heffing family. Or he had and would again if he ever found the T-SS unit that had zapped Serge and Mary. He had obligations to his family, and it to him, and the obligations balanced out. For example, while he'd had a duty to help Nicky break away from that gang the preceding November, Nicky had also had a duty: to want to split, to make it possible for his older brother to help.

The project was another family, a larger one that included brothers and sisters of different blood. Again, mutual benefits made mutual responsibilities tolerable, like when Sheila McDermot had seen that he'd been fed for rehabilitating houses for the migrants she'd taken in. He liked that family—it shared his life without stealing it.

The nation, America, was a family, too, but the political parents had grown fat, senile, and obsessed with ordering the moments of their children's days.

That's where he drew the line. Parents had the responsibility to let their children go, and when they refused to fulfill it, it was time for the children to disinherit themselves.

As he had just done.

An eeriness slithered through his mind. He was a Catholic, born to high-vaulted churches and candles and air that smelled always of day-old incense. He wondered, then, as he crossed the line with dozens, no hundreds of shoving bodies, if Judgment Day comes while my parents are there, will God remember them? Or will He, too, pass them by, not seeing, not knowing ...

He guarded his ribs from the elbows of a crowd that swelled and swelled until, up at the podium, under the bright lights mounted on the side of the old stone barn, Sheila McDermot wiped her eyes and cleared her throat. In a low, husky voice picked up and hurled out by the microphones, she said, "Thank you all for voting the way you did. I—I feel like you just expressed a lot of trust in me, and I promise that I will do my best to live up to it."

Like everyone else, he looked over to his right, to the side that lay on her left. Only thirty people stood there.

He felt awful damn good about that, because the more defenders there were, the better the chances that his parents would come home safely.

Then he smiled to himself at the phrasing of the thought: wherever his parents were, they had taken their house with them ...

Willie Willams descended to walk through the boisterous crowd, clipboard in hand, organizing work groups. "Anybody who knows explosives, sign up now, the colonel got some bridges to blow," and "People, you real beautiful, and any of you with any kind of medical training or knowledge, I would appreciate it if you would step on up to me and give me your names so I can make certain you on our medic teams."

Hours later—at two AM, in fact—Heffing wound up in a warehouse, counting and checking the resistance's stockpile of T-SS units. Willams had given him the assignment with a wink, a pat on the shoulder, and a whispered, "Search 'em one last time, man, just in case."

A draft blew the length of the high-roofed shed. He compared the serial number on the unit he held with those on the master list and ticked it off when he found it. He removed the batteries and plugged them into the recharger, replacing them with fresh ones from the other recharger. Then, huddled in his blue sweater, he ran through the unit's thirty-two memories to make certain that each and every one of them had been cleared.

A tedious task, Heffing thought. They could have given me something more challenging, I mean, a chimpanzee could do this, but what the hell, there's a war on ... At least he did it thoroughly. It mattered to him, as it might not have to others, whose revulsion for all the units was not outweighed by a need for one of them. So he ran his pen up and down the list of numbers, and pried open the units' backs, and keystroked his way through their long, empty memories.

It was early morning before he'd finished. Eighty-six T-SS units, that was all. Not really enough, but it would have to do.

A man in a yellow robe strode into the dimness of the storehouse; his head was bald and his feet, bare. "Here," he said, setting one more unit down on the card table. "They told me to deliver this to you."

Stifling a yawn, Heffing picked up the master list. Funny, thought I got them all.

"Oh, it's not on there—my commune had it." He stared hard at Heffing's mustachioed face, apparently puzzled by something.

"Commune?" he said absently, while he wrote the number into a blank at the bottom of the page. "Oh, yeah, where my brother Nick was for a while."

The stare dissolved into a smile. "I thought you resembled him. I am Brother Puhrsieg." He held out his hand.

"Nice to meet you." Practiced, now, though weary in every joint, his fingers scampered over the keys, counting down the memories to, "M, 1, Add—"

In the back of his mind, a fishnet re-wove itself.

"My God!" Half rising to his feet, he let the paper flutter down to the bare cement floor. "My parents—you had them on this—they're back!"

"Oh?" said the monk, politely interested but looking as though he had an appointment elsewhere in just a moment. "Were they gone?"

"They were Tissed out all this time ..." He raised his eyes. "Thank you. From the bottom of my heart, thank you." He wanted to hug the old man, and almost did.

But Puhrsieg backed off a pace and waved a hand. "Believe me, it's my pleasure. Now, if you don't mind—" His eyes widened, then narrowed again in a squint. "What's happening to it?" He pointed to the T-SS unit he'd brought in.

Heffing turned. Smoke curled out of the unit's back. Just a wisp, barely acrid, sizzling just this side of silence—but enough to tell him that something was seriously wrong.

"Oh, my God," he said again, but in tones rather different from those he'd used earlier. "This could—I have to get this to Dr. Kenyer right away. You'd better come along; he'll want to talk to you."

Dave Kenyer knew at once that he could not salvage the unit. One glance inside showed too much microcircuitry smudged and, probably, melted. He set it down on his workbench and winced. Then he rested a haunch on the bench's edge. Pinching the bridge of his nose, he said, "I don't know what to say."

The two men next to him kept silent. An incongruous pair, them: one tall and slender with puppy-dog eyes and a friendly brown mustache; the other exotically garbed and shaven, like a Buddha who had taken a wrong turn at the Pacific.

"How many times did you use this?" he asked the monk.

"I really could not say, not with precision." The old man closed his eyes to think and lifted his blank face to the ceiling. "Perhaps a hundred times? One hundred fifty? I really am not certain."

Dismay crushed him: not because of Puhrsieg's inability to be exact, but because of the tangle of wires and integrated circuits at the far end of the bench. "I never expected this," he said, almost to himself though loudly enough for them to hear. "Melting down from overuse ... Jesus, I should have known."

The monk looked puzzled. He half-turned to young Heffing, who said, "Dr. Kenyer invented the Tisser."

"Oh?" The eyebrows, surprisingly dark against the expanse of pale skin, arched into interrogatives. Absurdly enough, the expression reminded Kenyer of the time his wife had found, on their doorstep, a fully-attired clown who had gotten separated from the circus parade and needed directions. Puhrsieg wore the same incredulity as she had, the same polite determination to behave as though nothing extraordinary had occurred. "Really."

"That's me," he grunted. Even after a year and a half, he had yet to shake his guilt over having built the tool that had destroyed his world. Every time he looked around, he felt it, and never more strongly than at that moment. If I hadn't done it, the country'd still be whole, the Army'd still be in Europe ... oh, God, I should have known. Now, though, he bore an extra guilt. "One hundred fifty times, you said?"

"Perhaps." The monk's bare shoulders made his shrug more graceful, more eloquent. "Perhaps even two hundred, though I would be inclined to doubt it."

"Dammit ..." Despite the damaged interior, the unit was clearly identical to the others on which New Haven would base its defense. And he had no idea how many times those others had been used. "Dammit, dammit, dammit ..."

"What troubles you?" said Puhrsieg softly.

"What doesn't?" he said with a snort. "I—" He shook his head.

"Tell me."

He took a breath, then caught himself. "Basil, that's the fifth time in the last three minutes you've looked at your watch. You got a date?"

"My parents," the man said simply. "They were in that unit, but before it went, I got them out, and now they're—"

"And you want to race to their place and make sure they're okay and explain everything that's happened, huh?" He smiled gently. He had gone through a similar emotional fit the preceding year when he had thawed out his wife. "Go. You've told me all you know. Just tell Willams where you'll be, and when you'll be back."

"Right. Thanks!" He spun on his heel and raced out the shop door, already calling, "Willie!"

"We're alone now," said Puhrsieg, making it an invitation.

"All right." He pushed a stool over to the monk and sat on another himself. He tapped the broken unit. "I can't fix this."

Puhrsieg stayed placid. "Then you cannot."

"No, you don't understand! I caused this mess—the revolution, the chaos, the invasion—"

"Surely the NATO gov—"

"No, listen. You have to understand the military mentality. It wasn't NATO, it was our own generals. They want power, they always have, and our system used to give them enough but not too much. Generals ..." He remembered those he'd worked with, and felt like weeping. "They're not dumb. Macho, war-oriented, but not dumb. They knew that though they could seize power, they could never hold it unless they earned at least the tacit consent of at least a sizable minority. But in this country, what could a military government have given the people that a civilian government couldn't?" His guilt hung before him like a bloody dagger. "Now, though, now they can promise order—security—trains that run, to hell with on time ... If there'd been no confusion, they'd never have dared. There'd be no confusion if the revolution had failed. It would have failed without the Tisser!" Clenching his hands, he hung his head. So quietly that even he had to strain to hear himself, he said, "And I built the Tisser."

"This is history," said the monk, "and man cannot change the past."

"No, you still don't understand!" He slid off the stool and began to pace. "I could have recouped—I could have made up for it—because—" He stopped. He licked his lips. Staring without focus at the distance, like one watching a lover drive off with another, he said, "The tactics of modern warfare call for tight integration of ground and air forces. They'll bomb the city before they march in; they'll strafe anything that moves. It's modern warfare. Bombs, bullets, they're easy to build. But people are hard to train. So you strike from a distance, first, to conserve your people."

"Admirable," said Puhrsieg dryly. "But the point?"

"The point is this!" He strode to the end of the bench and hefted the squiggly mass of integrated circuit-chips. "This would have saved us. An anti-aircraft computer. Add radar and radio, let it direct a Tisser mounted on a model airplane. With a 650-meter range, zap! No bombs. No strafing runs. And probably no invasion, because I don't think they'd be too eager to come in after losing their entire air force to mysterious causes." And that would have redeemed me, he did not need to add.

"As a pacifist," said the monk, "I naturally applaud anything that will lessen violence. But tell me, why will this no longer work?"

"That damn design flaw in the Tisser," snapped Kenyer. "I allowed for current flow, but I never stopped to think that restoring ... how can I put this simply enough?"

Puhrsieg cleared his throat. "Doctor, before I joined the order, I had had, for several decades, a degree in theoretical physics."

He felt his cheeks redden. "Sorry." With a rueful smile, he said, "I get so used to being around people who don't understand one word in three that ... well, condescension becomes a habit. In brief, then, this device restores what it has removed by replicating within itself a miniature matrix of the absent space-time configuration. When time flows through that matrix, it creates friction; the friction rips the replica out of the device and establishes it in its original position. Apparently, however, the coefficient of friction is so high that it weakens the key components more quickly than I had expected." He looked down into the blackened circuitry. "They must have given way and allowed the battery to discharge itself all at once. And as I said, it looks like it's a design flaw."

"Which means," said the monk, "that the rest will give out also."

"Sooner or later." He nodded glumly.

"But I still do not see the problem. If you design the system so that the units can be replaced immediately after they have failed, then—"

"Don't you see? We only have eighty-six units! A given Tisser might be good for one shot, or a hundred—and I have no way of knowing. Sure, I've got forty-eight hours, I could come up with an interface that you could just jack the unit into—but every Tisser I keep for replacing those that burn out is one they don't have in the field. So if the ground forces do move in ..." Sorrowfully, he shook his head.

"I see," said the monk. Sympathy informed his tone, and he put a hand on Kenyer's shoulder.

"No," said Kenyer, "no, you still don't see—because I could have avoided this, too! After the revolution, once I figured out what was going on, I started hunting Tissers. When I found one, I emptied its memory—I restored what it had removed—and then I destroyed it." The words rang hollowly in the chilly workshop. He looked down at the veins on the back of his hand. "I must have smashed a hundred of them. At least. And if I hadn't ..."

"Again," said Brother Puhrsieg, "this is all history." He eased himself off the stool and gathered his robes around himself. "You are living in the present, preparing for the future. You must deal with what is, not with what was, or with what might have been. Do you understand?"

The question aggravated him, and he had to bite back an insulting reply. "Of course I understand. But—"

"May I make a suggestion?"

Wearily, he said, "Sure."

"You spoke earlier of the coefficient of friction. When I used this device, I removed ten full acres from reality each time. Perhaps if the target were smaller, the friction itself would be lower. And should that be the case—"

He saw it immediately, and felt reinvigorated, as though his age had been halved and his strength doubled. "Yeah," he said, "yeah! It would take longer to burn out, so ..." He took a deep breath and picked up the unit. "I'm going to run some programs —put this under my microscope—see if there isn't some way to make it all work."

The monk began walking for the door, then stopped, and looked over his shoulder. "Tell me something, Doctor."

"What's that?"

"Are you optimistic?"

"Brother Puhrsieg," he said slowly, "let's just say I'm hopeful."

"Why is that?"

"Because the only alternative is despair."

Field glasses to his eyes, Nick Heffing lay on a ridgetop east of Branford, surveying Interstate 95. The spring sun filtered through his camouflage and warmed him. Into the miniature tape&trans that lay on the soft grass beneath his chin, he said, "Colonel? No question about it. They're close enough to roll in tomorrow." He pressed the red button. The machine rewound the tape and transmitted it as a high-speed burst. It slowed conversation, but hindered homing, jamming, and eavesdropping.

A moment later, the LED on the mini lit up; he pressed the blue button and Singleton's replayed voice said, "How many are there?"

"Even if I take off my socks, I can't count that high." Red button, LED, blue.

"Nick."

"Just trying to lighten the gloom," he said. "I've never had any practice estimating the size of a crowd. A whole bunch. Lots. I count at least fifty big tanks, if that's any help. Hundreds of trucks, a long line of them, got German markings. Troops out on either side of the highway, maybe two hundred meters away from the road, and way the hell ahead of the rest of the convoy are two jeeps. Like a klick out front, and they each have big ol' machine guns. Helicopters, too. I think they're British. Buzzing up and down, skimming along like fifteen meters above ground. They got machine guns, too."

"Have they spotted you?"

"I don't think I'd be here to tell you about it if they had—one of the choppers saw something a little while ago and they poured like a solid rain of bullets into it. A roadside marsh, you know? With the tall salt hay? Looks like a plowed field, now. I'm under a tree, myself."

"Have you heard from any of your people yet?"

A chill passed over him; he turned his head to see if a cloud had cut off the sun. But no, the sky stayed clear and very blue. "You haven't?" He choked on that and had to clear his throat.

"No."

"Damn ... they're supposed to radio you direct if they run into anything. Ook and Nan went down to scout Route One; O'Reas and Marie are up on 80." His stomach refused to unknot. "No word at all?"

"Not yet," said the colonel, and paused. Then his voice came back subtly different in tone. "Nick, as soon as they call in, I'll let you know."

"Yeah, thanks."

"Dave Kenyer wants to know if you're ready."

"Not yet," he said, and abruptly switched the tape&trans off.

Then fixed again the binoculars on the leading edge of the largest armed force he'd ever imagined, much less seen.

He'd thought it would be so different: forest or jungle or some kind of natural terrain where the enemy had to come at you almost singly down the church aisle of the trees, where you could lie behind a rotted log and pick them off with cool, single shots. Oh, he'd expected tanks to churn through the woodlands, knocking down trees and riding up root balls, gun barrels swung toward the sky ... but he hadn't expected this brazen approach down the American highways ... Thieves should come skulking in the night; they shouldn't swagger in at high noon.

It's the air cover, he thought bitterly. They know they've got the only air force, so why shouldn't they take the easy way?

But he just hadn't expected the mass of the invasion. His wildest fantasies hadn't pitted him against a skirmish line far-flanking the column and at least three klicks long ... he hadn't realized how many trucks there would be, nor how crowded they would be with tired, yet alert men whose dark eyes glittered in ways he couldn't understand. They held their rifles tightly, those men, and they looked ready to use them.

Most of all, he hadn't expected to be so afraid.

I could split, he thought. Just sneak along the ridge to the north, get out of their way so they don't see me, let them just keep going because nothing is going to stop those bastards ...

A helicopter roared up the slope, bending the branches below it with the force of its downdraft. It was British.

He tucked the glasses to his chest and buried his face in the sweet grass, hoping the branches woven into his cap would hide him from the flying executioners.

A harsh wind laved his neck with dust, and then was gone.

He breathed again.

I thought I was some kinda hot shit, big guerrilla warrior and all ... Christ, I was dumb. I couldn't lead anybody against something like this. Talk about nightmares ... how the hell can Sheila do it?

The chopper swooped back towards the convoy. As soon as the fury of its engines dwindled, he raised his head. The line was uncomfortably close. The first man couldn't be more than two klicks away.

To his left, the ridge ran north like an invitation.

Straight ahead, some four klicks off, a chopper buzzed a housing development. He brought the field glasses back to his eyes and adjusted the focus. An old man appeared, bald and gray-bearded. He slowly raised a shotgun to the sky.

Darting like a wasp, the helicopter swung about and sped towards the old man. Just before it pulled up, it loosed a rocket that engulfed the house and yard in a ball of smoke-shot flame.

Nick gritted his teeth, and flicked on his tape&trans. "Dr. Kenyer?"

"Yes, Nick, I'm here. What was the trouble?"

He scowled. "You want to waste time, or you want to test your system?"

"Ah ... right." The older man's tone became brisk, business-like. "The microprocessor knows where it is?"

"I did the bit with the reception from the satellite just like you told me." He pulled the shoebox-sized device out of his knapsack. "I thought you're supposed to use two radars with it."

"We'd probably get better accuracy with two, Nick, but do you really want to move five hundred meters and set up the second?"

"Not really." He took the miniature radar from his pack and spiked it into the ground.

"Is the system set up?"

"Yeah, I guess." He looked downhill. The nearest infantryman was still marching forward, though pausing frequently at shouted commands from further down the line.

"Turn the power on."

He pushed a switch up; a red light blinked on. "Power on."

"The plane is moving toward you now; let me know when you see it."

He waited some five minutes, till he heard a tiny drone almost masked by the motors of the convoy. He turned. Towards him flew a small, gas-powered model airplane. "Plane's here," he said.

"Arm the system."

"Wait," said Nick quickly. "It'll search, right?"

"Yes, it will."

"Well, I don't want a chopper to go down nearby—people will come running to investigate, and I don't want them to trip over me."

"Then sight through the back of the radar dish, down the barrel, at a helicopter some distance away. When you've got one pretty much on target, then arm the system. It will zap that one first, before it searches for another."

"Fine." He already knew which chopper he'd take out first. It was still hovering over the housing development. He sighted— tripped the switch—held his breath as a few puzzled soldiers pointed to the metallic speck two hundred meters above their heads—and—

"Nothing's happening," he said.

"Just wait."

The radar told the microprocessor the range, direction, and altitude of the helicopter. The computer translated that information into coordinates which it fed into the T-SS Unit, while it simultaneously directed the plane to 500 meters from that spot. The device hummed once—the chopper disappeared while Nick wondered what he'd pointed the radar at—then, before Nick could re-align the radar, the Tisser hummed again. The helicopter reappeared in its original location. The plane looped around and headed for a second chopper. Nick flicked off the arming switch.

"Dr. Kenyer," he said, keeping his voice down because that damn skirmish line was even closer than it had been, "I guess it Tissed it out, then thawed it back, but nothing happened. It's still flying."

"Give it a minute," said the physicist calmly. "The motor wouldn't have been affected, but the pilot ought to be paralyzed."

He refocused his binoculars. The sound of protesting engines wafted to him. Sun flashed off plexiglass; the chopper began to slip sideways. "I can't see anybody inside," he said. Gathering speed, the machine slid toward the ground, disappearing behind a stand of young pin oaks. Sudden flame seared their branches. Some ten seconds later he heard the explosion. "Dr. Kenyer?"

"Yes, Nick?"

"It works!" He had no time. Switching the tape&trans off, he bundled everything into his pack. That damn point man was less than a klick away. He made a last visual sweep of the area; except for Kenyer's plane, already heading home, all was clear. Cautiously he edged back from the ridgetop. Back towards New Haven.

If Sheila can get us out of this, he thought, she's got my vote for life ...

"Good luck, Nick," said Brother Puhrsieg. He handed the boy the keys to the converted Datsun pickup. Jet engines roared; they both glanced up. Overhead, the setting sun gleamed off the underside of the wings and fuselage of an F-22. It winked out of and back into reality, then arrowed straight for Long Island Sound.

Puhrsieg sighed. He had encouraged Kenyer to finish developing the anti-aircraft system, and that verged on a violation of his principles. He felt vaguely soiled by the pilot's death ... and yet, he thought, had I kept silent, it would have strafed or bombed the city, and people would have died that way, too ... either way I would have contributed to death; either way I would have been stained. He shook his head.

"You don't like it, huh?" said Nick.

It startled him that the boy could read his thoughts so clearly. "I have never liked death," he said.

"You afraid you'll come back as a frog?"

He could not resist a smile. "Something like that."

"Don't think of it as a person," Nick said. "Think of it as a bullet that your shield deflected."

The boy's expression, at once feral and fearful, bothered him. He wanted to change the subject. "You do know about your parents, don't you?"

Nick frowned, cocked his head, and froze. Wonderment crept across his face. "My parents," he whispered, mouthing the word as delicately as if it were a fragile vase that had to be protected. "I remember them." His eyes looked into the distance, then filled with a moistness, a joy that must have embarrassed him, for he turned his head sharply and inhaled. "They're back," he said, and again faced Puhrsieg. For the first time since they had met, Nick lost the mean and hungry look of the guerrilla he tried to be. For one moment somehow insulated from the conflict around them, he grinned and relaxed and looked like a teenaged boy who had found his way back from being lost. "My parents ... goddam, that's great! Talk about extra incentive to fight!"

Some deflections work better than others, thought Puhrsieg ruefully. A child dedicated to war will always return to it, no matter how one tries to side-track him. "Perhaps you should visit them before—before."

"I will," said the boy. He vaulted into the open door of the pickup and started the engine. "Thanks. You don't know how much I thank you." With a wave and another wonderful, exuberant grin, he threw the truck into reverse and backed out of the lot.

Puhrsieg did not know what to think. Handing them the keys is too symbolic, he decided. In this culture, it is too similar to blessing their actions. I am a pacifist. Food. Medicine. Shelter for the homeless. Those should be my functions; I should limit myself to that which is proper for one of my persuasion ...

A saffron-robed figure materialized out of the dusk; its features did not resolve until the newcomer almost trod on Puhrsieg. "Ah, Dan," he said. "Is the hospital prepared?"

Another jeep rolled out of the lot. Before he spoke, Higgins watched it, his eyes lingering on the machine gun bolted to its frame. Then he shook himself. Confusion played about his face. "The hospital?" he said faintly. "Oh, yes, the hospital ... everything's under control there. I've got some of the, um, elderly noncombatants painting a big red cross on the roof. We're low on medicines, and O'Shaughnessy is screaming about that, but there are plenty of bandages and the ambulances are ready to roll. I stationed them at nine locations around the city—near where the roads the troops are using come into the city. Does that sound okay?"

"Yes, Dan, it sounds excellent." He looked into the face of his disciple and saw not the accustomed placidity, but a liveliness that the ex-rebel had lost over a winter of Tissings-out. "Thank you."

"Let me help you with the jeeps."

"But you are in charge of—"

Impatiently, Higgins said, "I set them up so they're self-running; they don't need any supervision till the battle starts. And I do know motor vehicles."

"Well ..." He thought about it. *Now I must decide for another. To jeopardize my own soul is one thing, but to risk the karma of a disciple becomes a moral question of a higher magnitude ... can I truly call this pacifism?* He looked about the yard. Half a dozen mechanics tuned engines, reinforced chassis, and tore the roofs off sedans. Two of them bolted machine guns onto truck beds.

A woman stepped out of the gathering darkness and tugged gently at the sleeve of his robe. He returned to awareness with a start. "Oh, I am sorry, my dear, I hadn't noticed your approach."

A commune member, she was a middle-aged lady with a large bosom and a pleasant smile. "Forgive me for disturbing your meditation, Brother Puhrsieg, but I came to report that all food supplies have been removed to shelters. We estimate that we can provide hot meals to approximately thirty-five hundred people at a time. I don't guarantee their quality, but they will be hot and nourishing."

"Wonderful, my dear," he said absently. He looked around again, then asked the two standing with him, "Are we making a mistake here? Is it right for us to help them make war?"

The woman seemed taken aback. Puhrsieg immediately regretted letting her hear his doubts. *The torch of faith lights the way through darkness, and the one who raises the flame must never let it waver.*

But Dan Higgins stroked his chin, and his earlier vacuity fell away. "It is," he said after a moment. "We're not trying to force our way of life on anyone, but the generals are. We're ..." Then he trailed off and blinked in confusion.

With that much of a nudge, though, Puhrsieg could follow the logic path on his own: *It transcends the individual; the clash is between systems, not people. Ours is far from perfect, but* what they desire ... would it be melodramatic to call it evil? His gaze traveled across the rows of passenger cars converted into war machines. Yes. Mistaken, even, to call it malicious. It is what they believe in, what they feel will work best. The true flaw, that which most closely approximates evil, is not in the system's workings but in its premise: that it is their duty to force their dogma on others. Their discipline is as mystical as mine, but it enshrines violence as policy, and that I cannot, will not, accept. If we resist it, we do so hoping to lessen the ultimate sum of violence ... And yet, and yet, if I equip a car so that it can cause death, do I not abet murder? Even if by causing one death I prevent two? Perhaps I must sin no matter what ... If that be so, let it be my duty to commit the lesser offense. Aloud, he said, "Ah, Dan, I wish you were your old self again. You, of all people, could convince me of the righteousness of our path."

The tall man's lips moved soundlessly. His face twisted from keen intelligence to emptiness and back again. "I—sometimes I am, sometimes. It comes like a flash in the night, and I know ... I know ..." His head drooped and he shuffled his feet.

At least the violence I wreaked upon him in the forest is wearing off, thought Puhrsieg. And though I failed to understand how violent my actions were, and though comprehension is an essential prerequisite to sin, still I feel expiated.

A train whistle blew across the sky, and they all swung around. The ground shook. Down the building-walled streets rolled a tremendous roar.

"My God!" said the woman. "What is it?"

"Artillery," said Higgins, eyes bright again.

Another salvo landed, farther off, and through the twilight came the scream of a dying man. Or woman. In moments of extreme pain, Puhrsieg thought with a detachment contrived to stem the tears, voices lose sexual identity.

Higgins said, "I have to take care of that."

The woman grabbed his arm and swung him around so that

they both faced Puhrsieg. "Wait," she said. "Brother, tell us. Before we do more."

"Tell you what, my dear?"

"Is it moral?"

The screams tore open the sky—and his heart. He took a breath and let it out slowly. "Yes," he said, "yes, my dear, it is. It must be."

He picked up the wrench and went to mount another machine gun.

Artillery shells dropped through the clouds and fell with the rain, but Doug Singleton ignored them. They were meant to maim the city proper, not him. He had his own enemies, and they marched closer to hand.

Singleton lay on the roof of the Clinton Avenue School, some four hundred meters from the point where Interstate 91 swooped over the Quinnipiac River. He was waiting for the lead tank to reach the middle of the short bridge. As soon as it rumbled onto the center, smack dab between two of the squat supports, he could Tiss it and one of the pillars out. The warping of space would bring the remaining segments of the bridge together in a line so closely joined as to appear seamless—but when the next tank crawled across, its weight should collapse that half-supported section, and slow the entire column to a halt. Then he could restore the missing part. Not only would it drop, and with its burden smash the tank that had already fallen, but it would leave a greater span of river unbridged.

Once the convoy backed up and began to mill around, he could start to zap out chunks of it—eight or ten acres at a time; the largest area the Tisser would handle—and he'd keep it up until the memories were full. Or until the unit burnt out, whichever came first, "Then," his father had said to the point men that morning, "you do whatever seems best at the time."

At least he was safe from aerial detection. Dave Kenyer's model planes had ripped NATO out of the sky; in fact, one of the gun choppers still smoldered in the playground below. The rain hissed on the hot metal and vaporized in the flames. Under other circumstances, he might have empathized with the crew, but he could no longer view them as people. They'd had their chance to establish their individuality—to desert or to mutiny or, quite simply, to refuse to take arms against their own people—and they had spurned it. He felt for them what he felt for the downed helicopter: nothing.

He wondered when the high-altitude bombers would strike. Surely some were on the way, though they'd have to fly from Europe to do so. I hope to hell some sympathetic Canadians pick 'em up, he thought. Even if they can only give us five minutes warning, it will help ....

But maybe the generals wouldn't do it. If they were going to bomb, they'd have to do it soon or else risk destroying their own forces—and the enemy on the far side of the river didn't look like it was waiting for the bombers to finish up before it came on in. Besides, his father had said he didn't expect them.

It should have relieved him, but it didn't—because he hadn't counted on the skirmish line.

Dammit, he thought, Nick told us about it, why didn't I take it into account? And why didn't Dad tell me how to deal with it?

The lead jeeps had already purred past him and were moving down the highway to the exit ramp. Less than three hundred meters away, the nearest infantryman threw a leg over the guardrail, tested his rope, and slid down to the ground ten meters below. His entire company followed; the skirmish line would spread out again.

Come on, dammit, come on!

He could have taken them out, but he didn't want to refocus the unit. The prime target was so far away that it would be difficult to return to the original coordinates quickly yet accurately enough to destroy the bridge.

But the soldiers below had regrouped, fanned out, and commenced a building-to-building search. Sooner or later, they'd spot him, and then ...

Come on, you damn tank, come on!

Even at the time, he'd realized how cornball it was, but that morning he'd left a note for Sheila on the bed he shared with her. Sheila, of course, hadn't slept in it the night before—God, I don't know how she does it, every time there's an emergency she stays awake for days—but he, not trusting his stamina, had lain down for a few hours' rest. Sleep had startled him by pouncing like a falcon.

So in the pre-dawn darkness one of the colonel's men had shaken his shoulder, rousting him, and while he sat groggy on the john (visualizing an entire army readying itself for battle by taking one last crap, in formation and cadence), he laid a notepad across his knees and scrawled a few words:

Dear Sheila, he'd written, if you read this it means you've definitely survived and probably won ... and I haven't, because, if I make it out of this mess, the first thing I do will be to rip this off the pillow and tear it up. Forgive me for sounding asinine and maudlin, but it's 4:30 in the morning and I'm scared out of my mind. In half an hour I have to take up a position where I will single-handedly tell 7,500 homesick soldiers that they may not cross a narrow, shallow river ...

Dear Sheila, if you're reading this, it means I haven't made it, and I just wanted you to know that I've loved you since I met you and I wish I could have known you forever.

Down below a door slammed, and boots marched through the stone hallways. Across the way, the lead tank was barely five meters from the middle of the bridge. Singleton gritted his teeth. The Tisser was set, so all he had to do was press one button and—

The boots clattered up the metal stairs to the roof.

He pressed the button.

—and he had to wait for the tank to trundle onto the bridge.

In the meantime, a short, stocky private popped through the doorway that opened onto the roof. Singleton rolled onto his back and leveled his M-19. The GI, shouting, tried to bring up his own automatic rifle, then changed his mind and tried to duck back inside the door.

Singleton put a full clip into the other American's chest. In the distance, the bridge collapsed.

He risked a glance over the parapet. From every point of the compass converged the infantrymen, bobbing in and out of doorways, covering each other with fierce concentration. On the elevated highway, a jeep skidded about, and sped back towards the school. He zapped it out almost casually.

Grenade poised for flipping down the stairwell, he stopped. Instead he crawled onto the roof of the shed that housed the staircase, set the Tisser for maximum area, and aimed its first-corner indicator straight down. Then he crossed his fingers and pressed the button.

He knelt on the ground. Above him loomed the elevated highway. A bullet bit the pavement. The ricochet whined up—and tore into his shoulder. With a gasp and a cry, he fell backwards. A dozen GI's sprinted for him.

He had to push himself up with his left arm. Teeth gritted, he ran, rifle swinging. Blood dotted the concrete. He ducked around a corner, brought the T-SS unit to his face, and thumbed in, awkwardly, M, 1, Add.

A bridge column, twenty meters of roadway, and a tank appeared above the Quinnipiac River. They creaked and collapsed with a roar.

"Dammit!" Sweat trickled down his face—or was it rain?—or tears? He hit M, 2, Add.

The highway healed itself. That jeep that had re-materialized kept going—into the guardrail, and over the edge. It exploded when it hit ground.

Boots clicked on cement. Vertigo carouseled him. He tapped, M, 3, Add.

Ten urban acres surrounding a dirty red brick school came back to reality. The GI's hunted on one side, over by the highway. He slumped against a brick wall on the other side, panting, shaking ... .

And wondering how much longer he could last.

Thought came slowly to Dan Higgins. It drifted to his awareness like a bubble ascending from the muck of a deep pond, but when it reached his conscious mind, it burst in a silvery flash.

He walked, medic pack on his back. Shells thudded into the business district around him, bursting in black fury, shattering whatever glass had survived the revolution and its aftermath. Broken-winged pigeons lay all about. Here and there fires raged out of control; the occasional pile of rubble slumped into the street, exposing torn girders to the misty rain.

He walked, listening for the cries of those who would need him, not now imaginative enough to fear danger to himself. The wind whipped him with his own saffron robe. Grit popped and crackled beneath his sandals.

Five hundred meters to the southeast, M-1 battle tanks surged up the Oak Street Connector that bisected the city. Both I-95 and I-91 fed into it, and it in turn ran north to Route 34. If the enemy could take and hold it, with its dozens of turn-offs into every part of New Haven, the city would be lost.

He walked down the middle of Church Street, while model planes danced through the air like dragonflies. Men screamed and grenades burst and small arms fire rattled everywhere. A cloud of smoke welled up to envelop him. Eyes tearing, he coughed and hurried out of it.

This isn't right, he thought dully. Something is wrong ...

He felt, at that moment, like two people melted together: one a quicksilver shadow, and the other a gross, ungainly weight. Smothered within himself, he wanted to scream.

But he didn't know how to anymore.

He remembered—there, like a rocket, zipping past to disappear almost before being sighted—an Oregon home owner, impoverished by taxes, fettered by law, gagged by politics—and here, wavy-diffuse, like moonlight through haze, an image of a rebel, proud and tall and risking all on a tongue which could charm and inspire—and there, a squirrel flicking around to the far side of the tree trunk, a rebellious rebel, paranoid and distrustful to the point of anarchy. Then fog descended: the robe and the order and the endless eons in otherwhere ...

Five meters ahead, a body bloodied the sidewalk. Not changing his pace, he strode up to it—to her. A woman, young, barely into her twenties. Shrapnel had severed her head from her shoulders, but not marred her snub-nosed face. He searched her body gently, quickly, for identification. He found it in her hip pocket. In his own notebook he laboriously entered, "Tenyo Mitsuke, age 21, 383 Elm Street." Then, as an afterthought, he added, "Found Church & Crown, 7:45 AM." Still on his knees, he moved her head next to her ruined torso.

I should cover her from the rain, he thought as he rose. But I have nothing with which to do it ... Bowing his head, he loomed over the corpse and said a short, mild prayer for her soul.

A shell hit thirty meters away. The street blew up.

That quicksilver shadow acted first. It hurled him down, across the woman's body, and he shielded it from further mutilation. Chunks of cement whizzed past; gravel pattered on his back. Warily, he lifted his head and came again to his feet.

Danny, you got yourself in deep this time. He moved lightly, a spring in his step. Quicksilver ruled; the dim-witted Buddha sat on the side. The robot makers are moving against freedom, and you got caught right in the middle. Again. Not that he minded it, really. He wanted a chance to stop them. And that means staying alive, buddy. 'Cause robots make shitty guests.

At the next intersection idled a jeep. The white-faced driver clutched his upper right arm, and blood trickled between his fingers. The gunner was dead but not down; his jacket had snagged on the machine gun's tripod and his corpse hung suspended, one arm flung over the barrel. Higgins hopped into the passenger seat. "Let me patch you up, Nick."

"Dan," said Nick Heffing, "they keep coming!"

"They do, huh?" His hands directed themselves—antibiotic powder, gauze bandage, tape to hold it all in place. His mind reviewed the situation and looked for a way out. "You hit anywhere else?"

"No, but I got to get back to CRC quick."

"CRC?" He repacked his bag and went around to the back, to detach the gunner and ease him down to the bed of the pickup.

"Connector Roadblock Command, over in the Police Station. We got to stop them, Dan, but they keep coming, there's so many!"

"Let me drive."

Nick sagged forward. "I can drive, that's not the problem."

"So what is?"

"The problem is, I gotta get over there—" With his left hand, he pointed to the far side of the Oak Street Connector, beyond the two burning tanks that marked the jackhammer tip of the NATO force. "—and I don't have enough gas or time to go the long way around."

"Oh." He pulled at his lower lip while he calculated. His mouth was dry, and for a moment he fantasized the goodness of a beer. A tall, cold one. "You do have a problem, don't you?"

"Say that again."

"So why's time a problem? Doesn't matter when you get there, the Army will still be here."

"Dan—" Anguish lit up the boy's eyes. "Dan, I got the CRC's Tisser, and I don't care how good they are, they can't hold out long if I don't get it back to them. The colonel said so himself, it's the only way his plan will work."

"You have a Tisser?" So many ideas came to mind that he felt like weeping for joy.

"Yeah, but I tried that. If I Tiss 'em out, the rear just moves up to the front, and maybe they're confused for a second, but there's a whole lot of them, and one of the non-coms always catches on real quick."

"No, that's not what I meant. Gimme." He took the device from Nick's belt and glanced up Church Street. It ran ruler-straight across an overpass to the far side of the Connector, where it took the mildest of left turns. "Now, my young friend," he said, as he settled himself firmly into the seat, "I want you to start this sucker rolling forward at about five miles an hour. Got that?"

"Dan, we can't run the bridge, they all got their guns on it."

"Hush, and trust your uncle Dan." He turned the T-SS unit and spread its first-corner indicator. Then he shook his head. "This won't work."

"I told you so," muttered Nick.

"No, it's because I'm inside. Stop a minute."

Obedient but bewildered, the kid obeyed.

"Great." Higgins got out, hurried to the front, and hopped up onto the hood. Then he crossed his legs and tucked his robe under his knees so it wouldn't flap too much in the wind. "Okay, go—but don't hit too many bumps too fast."

"Dan, you're crazy!"

"Nick, you've never known me saner." He looked over his shoulder and intercepted a dubious stare. "Honest to God, Nick. The whole time you knew me before, I was flippo from flash-backs. Right now, I'm okay. So trust your uncle Dan and do what he tells you."

Nick bit his lip, but he put the jeep in gear and let it roll forward.

The wind caressed Higgins's shaved head, and blew gritty smoke into his eyes, but he concentrated on the Tisser. He heard a shell burst behind him, and up ahead a manhole cover flipped through the air like an oversized tiddlywink, but all he allowed himself to think of was the necessity of tapping in: "5" meters for height, and "5" meters for width, and "100" for depth, and "subtract."

Immediately in front of the converted Datsun, a section of road five meters wide by five high by one hundred long disappeared; the vehicle rolled over the point that marked their borders. Frowning, Higgins punched in, "M, 1, Add," and that same section returned to reality—but to their rear.

In effect, they traveled seven or eight meters very slowly, jumped one hundred meters instantaneously, then crawled again. The gunners who had tracked them with ease found themselves wildly off-target and had to re-aim. But by then Higgins had bounced them again—and again—and again—until he and Nick were safely out of range.

They stopped in the shelter of a broken-windowed apartment tower, and Higgins swiveled around on the jeep's hood, "Told you to trust me," he said with a grin. "When it comes to figuring a way out of a tight spot, I'm your man."

Nick shook his head in disbelief, then said, "Come on, Dan, get in. I think the folks at CRC are gonna want to talk to you."

The command post on East Rock overlooked six of NATO's nine approach roads. Clouds hung low and heavy; a constant drizzle made footing uncertain. A tape&trans battery linked Colonel Singleton to the field commanders of his ragtag army. Several of them were squawking, and Willie Willams was trying to handle them. Singleton himself was on another line to Sheila McDermot, in the West Rock command post.

"The I-91 bridges are gone, so the troops coming in on Route 80 and Route 17 are bottlenecked, too. Doug and his boys are doing a real fine job there, and if their Tissers hold out, that battle's been won. What about your end?"

"Far as I can see," came the woman's cool distant voice, "they're still holding the parkway at the interchange with Route

10, way up in Hamden. Until the junta breaks through there, they can't really come south. What about I-95, Route 1, and the Connector Roadblock Command?"

"That's the danger spot," he admitted. His field glasses hung around his neck; he lifted them with his right hand and held them to his eyes. "They got about fifteen thousand men across the bridge before somebody finally took it out. The rest of their forces are still on the other side, and somebody, probably from the CRC, is over there zapping them out chunk by chunk. On this side, though, they're right on the edge of downtown."

"Well, can't you take them out?"

He could rein in his temper only because he believed civilians should run the army, and not the other way around. "Sure—but that whole area only has eight Tissers, and we don't know when they'll fail. To use them on individuals is to waste them."

"Are you aware that they are through the block on Route 5, and are coming south fast?"

He spun, and brought his binoculars up, but a flank of the ridge blocked his view. "No," he said, "the part of Five I can see is clear."

"It won't be for long," she said.

A smile rose to his lips. This was what he had trained for all his life: to meet the enemy on a battlefield and beat him. He would get only one chance, but that was all he needed. He knew his opposite numbers; he had gone to school with them. Hawkshead had always been sloppy, so desperate to win that he would take enormous gambles. This time he had rolled once too often. Any commander who could lose his air cover to unknown causes and still attack deserved defeat. "We'll take 'em, Sheila, don't you worry."

"Right."

He set the tape&trans down and turned to Willams. "Willie, get me Dave Kenyer, then the people at the airport."

Still talking into one of the microphones, Willams handed back a mini, then made a note on his clipboard.

"Dave?" He touched the red button and waited.

"Yes," crackled the voice. "Singleton?"

"Yes. Can you shut down the air defense system? I want to get our Cessnas up."

"Sure, flip of a switch." Silence came over the tiny speaker, then: "Done. What are the Cessnas using for bombs?"

He made a face and was glad that no one else could see it. "Two of them are loaded with high-explosive shells that the bombardier's going to throw out the door as they overfly the tanks. The other two ... would you believe a load of bricks?"

"At 250 kph, even bricks'll do some damage."

"That's what we're hoping."

"Will it be enough, though?"

He licked his lips. "All we're trying to do is slow them down so the Tissers can get in and do their work."

"Lots of luck."

"Yeah. Over." To Willams he said, "Get me Tweed Airport."

Willams looked over his shoulder. Sweat beaded his upper lip. "I can't raise 'em."

That hit like a hammer. He had the binoculars up, pressing into his eye sockets, almost at once; his forefinger and thumb twiddled the focus knob futilely. "Dammit. I can't see the airport from here."

"They must have taken it." Willams stamped his foot on the bare rock. "Shit, man, what we going to do now?"

"Get me the command post on—" He swiveled, bent over the map, and picked out the name with his finger. "—what is that; Mill Rock?"

"Done." Willams passed the appropriate tape&trans over immediately.

He snatched it up. Then remembered something and said, "Get back to Kenyer, tell him to put his planes back on duty— explain about ours."

"Right." Willams turned away to pass on the message.

"Mill Rock?" Singleton barked into the mike. "Come in, Mill Rock."

"Yeah, Mill Rock here, Colonel." Small arms crackled in the background like a forest fire. "Little busy here, so let's make it quick, huh?"

"Can you hold them?"

"No, sir. No way. My guess is they got about two thousand men coming at us, and there are only four of us left."

"Do you still have your Tissers?"

"We got two left."

He gritted his teeth. That was incredibly bad news. "Did the rest burn out?"

"Hell, no. Just filled up, that's all." Through the radio came a huge roar and a muted shriek. "Ah, Jesus, Colonel! Mickey's down, now, too."

"Damn ... but you still have two Tissers left?"

"Yeah, but they're not helping! We Tiss out the front no problem, but then the old back is the new front and in the meantime they're another ten meters closer. Chrissakes, we Tissed out at least two klicks of road by now. And they're still coming."

"All right, listen." He glanced again at the map, trying to pick out a place for them to fall back to, a place they could hold until reinforcements reached them. But there were none. It was all residential area in there, with little ground high enough to be significant. The rain ran down his neck and puddled at his feet. He shook his head angrily. A fine spray flew off his helmet. "We're going to get some reinforcements up to you—"

"Colonel, sir, with all due respect and all that goddam bull-shit, they can't get here soon enough to do us any good! I figure five minutes, maybe ten."

"Oh, God." He stared into the underbellies of the clouds, trying to find there some sort of pattern, some sort of answer ... this was his job, to lead men; it was his duty, to defend the country ... why could he not think of something—"Wait. I've got it.

Restore what you took out before. Empty all those memories, quick. That ought to put a buffer between their front line and their rear echelon. Then take out the front lines and bring 'em right on back. You'll have two klicks of frozen-stiff GIs between you and the ones who're still ready to fight. You got that?"

"Yes, sir. We're doing it now."

Singleton held the tape&trans close to his mouth, listening to the sounds of warfare diminish. "Willams."

"Yeah?"

"Get the reserve force up Route Five as fast as possible—"

"The whole thing?"

He inhaled, thought about it, exhaled. "No. Half of it. Split that into two groups. One up Mill Rock to reinforce the people there; the other ..." He tried to visualize the scene and smiled again.

"Yes, sir? The other half?"

"The other group goes for the tanks. If they can't operate them, they can at least blow them up to block the road." He checked his map again; yes, Route Five ran between a lake and a ridge. "But if they can operate them, they should just spin the guns around and do their best to take out the rest of the convoy."

By the time he finished speaking, Willams had already begun to relay the instructions. Singleton said, "Lemme talk to the CRC."

Willams passed back the mini without comment.

"CRC? Singleton here. Listen. I've got a new tactic want you guys to try out down there ... I think it ought to work just fine."

———

The battle raged for another day and a half. Under cover of night, the colonel sent thirty men in three boats across New Haven harbor; each boat carried a T-SS unit. Rather than landing in Morris Cove, they Tissed out enough of the beach to float right up to the borders of Tweed New Haven airport—which they also zapped and restored immediately. Tim O'Reas found the NATO radio and sat before it, sweating coldly while unknown voices crackled through the static. He hoped no one would call. He wasn't at all familiar with their code designations.

In the meantime, the others stripped the invaders naked, laid them out in a hangar, and waited for them to awaken. When they began to stir, big Ook Tissed out, then brought back, the entire hangar. It bought them another hour of silence, an hour during which their own pilots woke up.

"Look," O'Reas told them, "we've got the locations of the artillery marked on these maps. We want you guys to take them out."

"They'll knock us out of the air," said one pilot.

O'Reas smiled. "Not on your first pass; they won't know you're there."

"Yeah, but there's no way—"

"Wait." He held up a hand. "On your first pass, you Tiss them out—and bring them back. Then you overfly them again, and the second time you make with the bombs. Got it?"

They shrugged and took to the air.

Half an hour later, the shelling ceased.

"How many prisoners do we have?" asked Sheila McDermot.

Colonel Singleton squinted into memory. "We've brought back about thirty thousand; you have to figure there are thirty or forty thousand more still there."

She turned and looked down the slope to the ten acres that had just been thawed. Several hundred infantrymen stood about or lay sprawled from lost balance. They were paralyzed and would be for fifteen or twenty minutes more. Among them moved perhaps a hundred elderly men and women who stripped them down to their dog tags. The sun glimmered on pale, frozen flesh; some of it was already beginning to pinken.

An arm moved. "Nick!" she called. "Over there." She pointed to the northeast corner of the section. "One's waking up."

He threw her a mock salute with his good hand and sent Marie over to be there when the GI thawed out completely.

In a moment, the soldier sat up. He blinked in the afternoon sunlight. Above him stood a teenaged girl, M-19 leveled. The POW raised his arms—then gawked at their bareness. Ignoring the rifle, he dropped his hands and covered his groin.

"Nick!" shouted McDermot. "Get 'em on the trucks."

Again flashed the good-humored salute. "Load 'em up, Marie!" he said.

"Let's go, soldier," she said. "But slowly, huh?"

"Shee-yit," was all he said. Blushing, he got to his feet and headed towards the pickup truck. He walked so stiffly and self-consciously that his dog tags jangled. He kept his head down all the way.

"Willie," said McDermot, "are the guards in place at Yale Bowl?"

"They been there for hours, now, Sheila." He glanced at his clipboard. "Last I counted, they already had ten thousand bare-ass GI's in there."

"Will all the POW's fit?"

"Place seats 70,000," he said. "Course those ain't nothing but wooden benches, and I bet they pretty splintery, now they ain't been painted in a couple years, but hell, they wanna seize control, they gotta take the accommodations they get, huh?"

She laughed ... and realized it was the first time she felt good in over a month. "You want to take care of the rest of it?"

"Sheila," he said, "I would be delighted to take care of the rest of it."

Behind them a building collapsed. She winced, anticipating the screams of rubble-trapped victims. When they came, she turned to Dan Higgins—but he was already racing to the scene.

The sun was setting; along the eastern horizon, stars glimmered into life. Dave Kenyer approached. He looked uncharacteristically grim. "Sheila, Colonel—"

She set her jaw and unconsciously leaned towards the colonel. "About Doug?"

He nodded. Sympathy shone in his eyes.

She turned to her lover's father, who stood braced and tight-lipped. The colonel said, hoarsely, "Is he dead?"

Kenyer rested his hands on McDermot's shoulders. "No."

She spun. "No? Then—"

"But he's badly wounded." At her expression he said "Easy! O'Shaughnessy says he'll make it—he just needs time and TLC."

She covered a sob with a shaky laugh and sniffed hard. Her vision blurred and she blamed it on the dusk, because now more than ever she needed to control her emotions. "I—" She looked over her shoulder and reached back her hand to the colonel. "We'll make sure he gets them, huh?"

The wink he shot her was moist. "You bet." He squeezed her fingers just hard enough to be reassuring.

"So he's at the hospital?"

"He's on his way," said Kenyer, shifting uncomfortably "I called a jeep for you; it should be here in a minute."

"Thanks." She slid her free hand into her pocket, where she stroked again the carefully folded note she'd found on her pillow. The road ran into the gloom without a single headlight, so she turned her gaze to the sky. And to the stars. So high and aloof ... TLC and time ... "Colonel?"

"Yes?"

She wanted to support herself on his West Point straightness —but a leader has to stand on her own. "How much time do we have until they attack again?"

"A lot." He slipped his arm around her shoulders. "Doug'll be on his feet before they come back—if there are enough left to come back."

"Is there—" She was almost afraid to speak the thought, lest

NATO HQ overhear. "—is there any chance they'll nuke us?" She held her breath.

Singleton cleared his throat. "No. Not from Europe—NATO will want to save those missiles, just in case ..."

In the distance flared the beams of a jeep. She couldn't wait for it in silence. "What the hell do we do with 70,000 POWs? We can't even feed them."

"Send them home," said Kenyer.

The colonel snorted.

McDermot's first reaction was to say, "On foot?" but the jeep lights swept across them, blinding her—and inspiring her. So instead she said, "That's not a bad idea ... Dave, Dan's trick with the jeeps—could you program a computer and a, a bus or a truck, so you could—"

"Yes." Beside her, Singleton inhaled as he understood.

"No problem," the scientist said.

"And a plane? Could you do it with a plane?"

"Even easier, actually."

"Good." She let out her breath with a sigh. "Good. Because I don't ever want to have to go through this—" She waved a hand at the night-shrouded battlefield. "—again. War gets too much in the way."

The men looked at her. Shadows obscured their expressions, but she sensed their confusion. Singleton spoke for both. "What exactly do you mean?"

"What I mean is, you Dave, modify the trucks and buses, and we'll hire Willie to find people to drive the troops back to wherever they call home. And fix up—hell, fix up the junkiest little plane at Tweed with a Tisser/computer combo. Really junky, now. I want it to be a symbol of how much we can do with nothing much at all—when we try. Colonel, do you know where NATO Headquarters are?"

"I think so," he said with a chuckle.

"Fine. You bundle up those generals and get one of the pilots to fly you to NATO HQ—fast and low, under their radar. Just set the junta down on an airfield with a letter pinned to their ropes saying, 'You keep 'em, we don't want 'em—their kind isn't welcome here anymore.'"

Then she snapped her fingers. "Oh, and while you're at it—swing past Moscow and drop them a note, something to the effect of, oh ... 'You mind your business, and we'll mind ours.' All right?"

"All right," said Singleton. "But what, exactly, is our business?"

She spread her hands in disbelief. "We've got a project here! There's houses to be built, and schools ... and it's getting on time for the spring planting."

"It sounds bucolic," said the colonel.

Fondly, she nudged him. "I prefer 'peaceful,' myself."

ABOUT THE AUTHOR

As the author of ten published novels and over seventy published short stories and articles, Kevin O'Donnell, Jr. had a devoted following of readers. One of his most popular and beloved works is  the McGill Feighan series, a fast-paced and fun science fiction romp.

Kevin was an active contributor to the Science Fiction and Fantasy Writers Association. He chaired SFWA's Nebula Award Committee, ran SFWA's *Bulletin*, and served as Chairman of SFWA's Grievance Committee, where he fought unceasingly for the rights of authors in an era of growing Internet piracy and corporate disregard of personal copyrights. As a result of these activities, he received the Service to SFWA Award.

Kevin spent much of his teen years in South Korea, where his father was Country Director for the Peace Corps. His interest in Asia and language skills led him to take his degree at Yale in Chinese Studies, where he met his wife Kim, with whom he was happily married until his passing in 2012. An avid gardener, O'Donnell delighted in raising bonsai, vegetables, and assorted plants.

WordFire Press is pleased to bring the works of Kevin O'Donnell, Jr. back into print for a new audience.

IF YOU LIKED …

IF YOU LIKED *WAR OF OMISSION*, YOU MIGHT ALSO ENJOY:

Caverns
by Kevin O'Donnell

The Humans in the Walls and Other Stories
by Eric James Stone

Alternitech
by Kevin J. Anderson

OTHER WORDFIRE PRESS TITLES BY KEVIN O'DONNELL

The Journeys of McGill Geighan:
Caverns
Reefs
Lava
Cliffs

Bander Snatch

Mayflies

Our list of other WordFire Press authors and titles is always growing. To find out more and to shop our selection of titles, visit us at:

wordfirepress.com

facebook.com/WordfireIncWordfirePress

twitter.com/WordFirePress

instagram.com/WordFirePress

bookbub.com/profile/4109784512

CPSIA information can be obtained
at www.ICGtesting.com
Printed in the USA
LVHW051330100921
697437LV00010B/644